'*Hekla's Children* is a brilliant novel full of great twists, beautifully drawn characters, exceptional writing, and some really startling ideas. It will leave you questioning the truths of myth and history, and that fine knife-edge between personal perception and reality.'

Tim Lebbon, *New York Times* bestselling author

'*Hekla's Children* marks the emergence on to a vibrant horror scene of an exciting new talent. James Brogden offers us a compulsive and unpredictable page-turner in which the ancient and modern world clash with devastating effect. Engaging characters, mind-bending concepts and enthralling set pieces propel the reader through a story in which the stakes are high and nothing can be taken for granted. Terrific stuff!'

Mark Morris, British Fantasy Award winner

'Brogdan's words have a way of getting under your skin. From the brilliantly creepy first line to the haunting last *Hekla's Children* had me in its thrall. There's some dark, sinister magic going on in these pages. Brogdan's strength is that he knows there is beauty in that darkness, and that makes him one of the most compelling new voices out there.'

Steven Savile, bestselling author of *Silver*

'*Hekla's Children* is at once a very modern dark fantasy, which also harks back to the classics of the genre. Like an irresistible mix of Masterton, Simmons and Gaiman, this novel marks Brogden out as a new rising star. This one's definitely a winner!'

Paul Kane, bestselling author of *Hooded Man*

'Places James Brogden in the company of Neil Gaiman, Tim Lebbon and Joe Hill... for me there was also a strong and pleasing likeness to the magical dream-states of Robert Holdstock. Brogden has a penchant for the darker side of ancient myth and his knowledge of folklore woven into the fabric of *Hekla's Children* makes for a riveting read.'

Jan Edwards, British Fantasy Award winner

'I thoroughly enjoyed it. It's deliciously dark and twisty and filled with toothy menace. A real pleasure to read.'

Ren Waron, author of *Escapology*

Also available from James Brogden and Titan Books

The Hollow Tree (March 2018)

HEKLA'S CHILDREN

JAMES BROGDEN

TITAN BOOKS

Hekla's Children
Print edition ISBN: 9781785654381
E-book edition ISBN: 9781785654398

Published by Titan Books
A division of Titan Publishing Group Ltd
144 Southwark Street, London SE1 0UP

First edition: March 2017
1 2 3 4 5 6 7 8 9 10

A CIP catalogue record for this title is available from the British Library.

Printed and bound in the United States

FOR STUART, SALLY,
SAM AND LILY

'THE TEPID TWILIGHT OF A
PRESENT WITHOUT A PAST.'

JOAN LINDSAY,
The Secret of Hanging Rock

PROLOGUE

It was a sound with which the villagers were all too familiar: the screaming of a mother for her stolen baby.

Across the hill fort they awoke. The women reached for their children in the dark and held them close, thankful that this time it wasn't them, while the men found their bronze-bladed hunting spears and lurched out into the night, drunk with sleep. The embers of cooking fires were blown up to kindle torches, and the men met at the centre of the village in a huddle of wide eyes and whitened knuckles.

Drizzle sifted through the flames, and the light scored the lines of ribcages with shadow; these men were starving. Their families were starving. They had all been starving since their own childhoods when, on an island of rock and ice so far across the northern ocean that it existed only as a rumour on the edge of traders' tales, a mountain of fire exploded, and its anger darkened the skies. Exactly what their forefathers had done to anger the goddess so profoundly was a mystery, but black rain had flooded the land and forest had become fen, driving the animals far away in search of light and warmth. Those who had chosen not to follow – who remained in the Four Valleys hoping for better times amongst the burial mounds of their ancestors – had found nothing but gnawing famine in their absence.

Muttering darkly amongst themselves, the men split into groups of three to search the village and its surroundings, already knowing what they would find.

The *afaugh*.

There were many empty roundhouses to be searched. Once proud homes, the thatch and timber of their steep conical roofs had long since been taken to repair the meagre dwellings of those who remained, leaving only the circular walls open to the elements, pooled with stagnant water and rotting from the inside. Torches and spears held in nervous hands swept from one to another, finding nothing.

And all the while the mother's keening echoed across the hilltop.

They found the *afaugh* outside what remained of the palisade wall, halfway down the slope of the hill, as if it hadn't felt the need to escape, or couldn't wait to enjoy its prize.

It was a man called Nima, once a farmer, whose farmstead had been one of the last to be swallowed up by the encroaching fen. His family had long since perished and he had taken to sheltering in the broken ruins of the old houses, living on vermin and stealing scraps from his neighbours. They knew, and pitied him, seeing in themselves a gaunt shadow of their own futures. What the spearmen saw now, however, was an abomination. The infant hung from his blood-slicked hands, its viscera looped and slithering between his fingers. His face was red and his jaws still chewing when the light found him.

'The *afaugh*,' whispered the men to each other. 'The *afaugh* has him.'

Some said it was the bloodlust of neighbour for neighbour in these dark times that had drawn it out of Un, the spirit world, down through the rivers and streams and into the black peat bogs that saturated the plains. Some said it was a curse upon them by the goddess herself, like the black sky. Regardless, the *afaugh* was a nightmare of terrible appetites, which inhabited the bodies of those too famished to resist, and through them took what little the people had left, including the lives of their children. They would have fled it long ago, had there been anywhere to flee that was not already guarded by jealous spears.

It leered at them from behind the man's face, and licked its tongue across sharpened, cannibal teeth.

They beat it out of Nima with the hafts of their spears. It was a pale thing, thin-necked and swollen-bellied with pitiless hunger, and it fled screeching from their shining metal blades back into the forests of Un where they could not follow.

Enough, they told each other. Enough.

A TRUCE WAS CALLED, AND YOUNG WARRIORS CAME FROM all over the Four Valleys in the depths of that bitter, decades-long winter to compete for the honour of becoming the One From Many who would guard and watch over them. For three days and three nights they fought in a great circle of the lime-whitened poles that the spirit-dancers had built, until the ground was churned with mud and blood. In honour of their ancestors who had escaped the First Ice they fought not with bronze but with spearheads of razor-sharp flint, whilst three times the sun rose and fell, and each time fewer warriors remained until one stood victorious and the howl of his triumph echoed across the land. The spirit-dancers robed their new hero in boar skin and led him to the pools of black water which were called the Mother's Tears, followed by a joyful crowd who sang and played music on bone flutes and skin drums.

The *afaugh* heard their celebrations, and knew fear for the first time.

They took their hero to that place where the skin between the world and Un was thin, and there they bound him tightly with many cords and strangled him so that the strength of his spirit would not escape with his breath but remain in his body. He was a mighty man, and though he had fought hard for this honour his spirit would not be tamed, and it took many of them to hold him. This was his first death. Then they pierced his breast with the bronze blade of a mighty spear that had been forged for him, and this was his second death. At last, they slipped him into the icy black water along with a host of treasures for him to take into Un as gifts for the ancestors and weapons to use against the *afaugh*, and this was the third of his threefold deaths.

Later, when the spirits of land and water had shown their favour by making his skin as black as pitch and as hard as leather, he was buried in a high place above the Four Valleys, to watch over his people, and defend them from the *afaugh* for eternity.

And it worked. The *afaugh* was banished from the world. It found its return blocked by the One From Many, and fled from his spear deep into the wild places of Un. But it was content to wait, for it knew that there were always men whose weakness and hunger would give it a way back.

1

BEFORE

IT IS HAPPENING NOW, AS IT WILL GO ON HAPPENING UNTIL the end of time.

In Sutton Park's main Town Gate car park the coach is surrounded by a milling chaos of students, hauling rucksacks out of its luggage bay and squabbling over them like hyenas disembowelling a wildebeest. The teachers stand at a safe distance, watching, and Nathan takes advantage of the noise and confusion to sidle up to Sue. She's been deliberately avoiding him since they got on the coach, even though he is the only other person who knows why she's been 'off sick' for the past two days, and it worries him that she doesn't seem to want to talk about it.

'I don't want to talk about it,' she says, before he can open his mouth. She looks pale and tired.

'I do,' he says. 'I'll walk with you up to your checkpoint.'

'No you bloody won't!' she hisses, still without looking at him. 'The last thing I need is one of those gossip-mongers seeing us together.'

'Which ones – the staff or the kids?'

That produces a wan smile, which he takes as an encouraging sign, even though she turns from him without response and walks away to help two girls disentangle their bags.

The students are sorted out and given the obligatory safety briefing on what not to do to the local wildlife and how not to get killed by strangers, and as they split up with their respective leaders Nathan surveys his own particular party of brave adventurers. He's been given the latecomers and the remnants of other groups that have imploded due to the shifting allegiances of adolescent peer politics. There are four of them shuffling and grumbling under the weight of their packs. Team Leftover.

'Morning, chaps and chapesses!' he grins. 'Right then. Have you got your map and compass?'

'Here, Mr Brookes!' bellows Ryan, snatching both from Catharine 'Scattie' Powell.

'Knob-end!' she yells, and grabs for it but he easily keeps it out of reach and squints at it. Ryan Edwards isn't the shining star of the school football team, but he is definitely part of that constellation, and has clearly decided that he's in charge. He signed up to the hiking and camp-craft programme late, after someone suggested that it might help his application to the army, and he's turned up in fatigues, with a highly illegal lock-knife in a pouch on his belt. Nathan should probably confiscate it, but he really can't face an argument with a teenage jock today, on top of everything with Sue.

'How's the ankle, Ryan?' Nathan asks.

'Fine, sir,' he says, flexing his left foot. 'The pins came out last week.'

'Good to know. Anything twinges or drops off, you let me know, okay?'

Obviously, Ryan's parents have waited until this morning to inform him that their son had surgery on an old football injury days before the expedition; Ryan shouldn't really be here, but if he's sent home it means the other three can't do the hike either because the minimum group size is four and all the other groups are full, which is another reason not to report him for the knife. Obviously, the parents will threaten to sue if Ryan's ankle is injured in any way today. Obviously, Ryan and his parents are selfish pricks, but at least in his defence he's a fifteen-year-old boy – it's his job to be a selfish prick.

'Sir,' he says, 'it says here that there's a swimming pool in the park.'

'Yes, well sorry to disappoint you but it's not there any more. The lido burnt down ages ago. That's an old map.'

'How could someone burn down a pool, sir? It's full of water!' His voice is loud enough to carry to his mates in the other groups, who laugh at this. He is, after all, a noted wit and raconteur of the class. Nathan ignores it.

'Basically, Ryan, if you find yourself standing in anything that's blue and wobbly and around your knees, you're lost. Plus, that pool is in the opposite direction to the way you're going. You're facing the wrong way.'

'Knob-end,' mutters Scattie, and finally succeeds in snatching the map back. She is wearing a neon-pink headscarf covered in black skull-and-crossbones. She'll be good, Nathan thinks; she can handle a compass and will probably take over completely when Ryan gets bored or distracted by something shiny.

Scattie's first mate is Olivia Crawford, a bird-like girl with fine, angular features, no hips and about as much body fat as a piece of Lego, which is not a good thing given that this hike is supposed to be training for a four-day expedition in the Brecon Beacons. The borrowed rucksack she's wearing is the smallest in the school's store, but even though the waist strap has been tightened as far as it will go, it still hangs loose on her. Still, trying to tell girls these days that putting on a bit of weight might be good for them is treated in much the same way as suggesting that they cut off a limb.

The final member of Team Leftover is Brandon. He is kitted out in a checked walking shirt that Nathan's own grandfather might have thought a bit old-fashioned, trousers tucked into red socks, a leather hip-flask (full of lemonade; Nathan has checked), and a walking stick. Not one of those ergonomically designed, collapsible aluminium trekking poles, but an honest-to-goodness hazel walking stick with carved bone handle. And they're only planning to be out for, at most, six hours. Brandon Whitehead is a legend in the school. He is so far off the scale intellectually that the teachers are happy for him not to hand in his homework because it is intimidatingly good, and he is so entirely without arrogance about it that the other kids, amazingly, don't bully him for it. They actually seem quite protective of him, almost as if he's some kind of school mascot. He is calmly updating his travel journal while he waits for the others to sort themselves out.

'No piña coladas by the pool, then, sir?' Ryan continues, pleased with his own wit.

'Ryan, I will make a deal with you. All of you, in fact. Make it around the park and back here by three, with all of the checkpoints correct, and without getting lost, shouted at by a member of the public, or arrested for molesting any ponies, and I will buy everybody an ice cream. That's the best I can offer. Will that do you?'

He may as well have fired a starting pistol.

He accompanies them for a hundred metres or so, watching Ryan hurtle off ahead without so much as a glance back, Scattie with her head in the map, and Brandon and Olivia bringing up the rear, chatting quietly.

He falls in beside Scattie. 'So,' he says, indicating the map. 'You want to show me where we are?'

'Right here, obviously,' she replies, pointing. Their route takes them west along the park's southern boundary, downhill all the way to the car park at Banner's Gate in the extreme south-western corner. Then they turn right, skirting a small lake called Longmoor Pool, and head north for almost a kilometre, up the shallow Longmoor Valley and its brook, which feeds the lake. Turning more easterly, they cross the brook close to a feature called Rowton's Well, then climb the slope of Rowton Bank to their first checkpoint at a monument called the Jamboree Stone. This is just a leg-stretch to warm them up. After that it's all compass work and micro-navigation in amongst the labyrinth of trails that criss-cross the heathland, woods and marshes of the park's two thousand or so acres. Satisfied that they know where they're going, he drops back to Brandon.

'So, Bran,' he says. 'What's today's factoid?' Bran has a fondness for trivia, trotting out facts and anecdotes, seemingly at random. It is a tradition of Nathan's Geography lessons that they start with Brandon's Factoid of the Day, so much so that, on the rare occasions when Bran is away or hasn't thought of anything, the rest of the class become twitchy and impossible to settle. Of all the things that surprise him about kids, the biggest thing remains how much they crave order and predictability.

'Today's, sir?' Bran scratches his head, thinking. 'I don't know. Have you ever heard of Bark Foot, sir?'

'Can't say that I have.'

'Here we go,' sighs Liv.

'Well, sir, about ten years ago there was a series of sightings of a strange old man living rough in the woods. Some saw him in a lean-to shelter, frying sausages over an open fire. Some even chatted with him. The police never found anyone, but everybody who claimed to have seen him said that he was dressed in clothes made out of birch bark. Hence the name Bark Foot.'

'Creepy-ass tramp, if you ask me,' says Liv.

'Yes, well whoever or whatever he is,' Nathan says, 'you keep well away from strange men dressed in bits of tree, got that? Scattie!' he calls ahead. 'You know where we are?'

She turns and curls her lip at him in disdain.

'Right, then. Liv, let's have a look at those straps.'

* * *

THEY'LL BE FINE, HE DECIDES; THERE'S NO NEED TO SHADOW them the whole way. Sutton Park is no manicured city garden for office workers to eat their sandwiches – it's a nature reserve of woodland, heath and marsh grazed by cattle and Exmoor ponies, albeit surrounded by the suburbs of the town of Sutton Coldfield – but unless the kids deliberately throw themselves into a lake there's nothing that can actively harm them. Ahead of them, they have a half-hour stroll in good weather up the broad sweep of Longmoor Valley, where the only danger is that they might go up to their ankles in peat bog, followed by another half-hour to head back up Rowton Bank towards the Jamboree Stone where Sue will be waiting at her checkpoint. Three sides of a nice, safe square.

He slows down and lets them widen the gap. The last thing he sees is the bright pink of Scattie's bandanna winking through the shadows of overhanging branches as they turn a corner and disappear.

Nathan cuts right, taking a shortcut off the path, and uphill through dense brakes of holly, eventually emerging on the path that Sue has taken to get to her checkpoint. Even though she's taking the shortest route due north through the woods to the Jamboree Stone, she's made slower time than he has expected, and he catches up with her quickly. Compared to the path he left the kids on, this is a lot gloomier, hemmed on both sides by the dark-green gloss of towering holly trees. Cooler, too – almost chilly. *Bark Foot,* he thinks with a wry smile. *Clothes made of birch bark. Too right: you wouldn't want to wrap your arse in holly.*

Sue looks up as he approaches, then sighs and carries on trudging upwards. She's only carrying a light daysack, but her back is bowed as if it weighs a ton.

'Are you okay?' he asks, without thinking.

She laughs shortly.

'Sorry, that was a stupid question.'

'Yes. It was.'

A family appears, coming in the opposite direction: father with a toddler in a pushchair, mother holding hands with an older girl who looks about eight or nine. The child is chattering on about what kinds of sandwiches she had at Naomi's birthday party, and can they feed the ducks later, and are all holly berries red? Nathan and Sue nod to the parents, and wait until the family is out of earshot.

'You know those funny little pills that a lot of women take in the mornings?' Sue asks. 'You know, the ones to stop them from having babies?'

'I know what the pill is,' he replies.

'Oh do you? Do you know how it works?'

That, he can't answer.

'It dumps a load of fake hormones into a woman's body to fool it into not ovulating. That's bad enough. The morning-after pill is a whacking great dose of the stuff. Common side-effects include tiredness, nausea, and a lack of wanting anything to do with the wanker who couldn't put his bloody condom on properly.'

'I said I was sorry,' he mutters.

She stops. 'Actually, no. I take it back. You're not a wanker. I wouldn't be in this mess if you'd been happy with a simple wank.' She stomps on. 'And anyway,' she adds, 'why aren't you with your group? What if something happens to them?'

'Nothing's going to happen. They'll be fine.'

'Will you listen to yourself? You have no sense of responsibility at all, do you?'

'Believe it or not, I didn't follow you up here just for the ear-bashing.'

'Well that's what you're getting, so like it or lump it.'

As they walk on, the slope begins to level out and the trees start to thin, replaced by gorse and heather, and soon they have the spreading breadth of the park visible on either side of them in a shimmering haze of green and brown. To the north, it is wide, flat and open for at least half a mile up to a dark line of woodland following a rail line that cuts through the park. To the west it is more tumbled, with Rowton Bank sloping down towards the Longmoor Valley where his group should be around now. The path on which he and Sue are walking meets many others at a square stone monument, which commemorates a huge scouting jamboree from the 1950s, where walkers with their dogs and children are clamouring around an ice-cream van. Before she can stop him, he has bought them a cone each and presented one to her, grinning.

Sue ignores it. 'This is my stop,' she says, and points. 'You want to be heading in that direction.'

He wilts. 'Tell me what I need to do to fix this,' he says. 'Just tell me. Please.'

Her expression seems to soften, but not in any kind of way which reassures him. It is the expression worn by a doctor delivering the very worst kind of news, and it opens a hollow space in the middle of him. 'Nathan,' she says, 'do you believe in signs? You know, warnings? Do you think that we get given warnings about things that we need to do, or not do?'

He shakes his head. 'I believe, I dunno, that stuff happens. Accidents. Happy coincidences. I don't think any of it means anything unless you want it to.'

'Well, in that case I want this to be a warning. To me, that is, at least. Because I just can't do this any more. Steven and I are getting married in two months, and this, whatever it is I'm doing with you, I'm sorry but it has to end.'

The hollow inside him is growing, filling his ribcage so that his heart is beating in a vacuum. He can barely breathe. 'No it doesn't...'

'Yes! It does!' Her fierceness draws curious looks from those nearby, and she drops her voice in volume, but not intensity. '*Yes, it does.* I thought I was *pregnant*, Nathan, do you understand that? I was terrified, and then I thought that maybe it wouldn't be so bad, just...' She breaks off, swallowing hard, determined not to cry.

'Just not by me, right?'

She nods. 'You asked what you could do to make it better. This is it. Don't spoil this for me. Please.'

'You know that I would never do that.' Maybe another man would – someone more vindictive, who would make her squirm for the way she was emptying him like a gourd and cleave her to him with threats and blackmail. But the best he can do is try to stop the void inside him from imploding.

Her thank-you is little more than a whisper.

The first step he takes away from her is the hardest, like setting foot on another world. The second is slightly easier, the third more so, and by the time he has started down the path to meet his group he is walking almost like a fully functioning human being. At least, he tells himself, the rest of the day can't get any worse.

THERE IS A SMALL L-SHAPED COPSE OF HOLLY AND SCOTS pines called King's Coppice at the point where the trail angles down the slope of Rowton Bank into the Longmoor Valley, which is where Nathan decides to sit and wait for his group. It isn't particularly steep or far, but he just doesn't feel like trudging all the way down there only to meet them and trudge all the way back up again. Besides, from his elevated position he'll have a much better view of their approach.

Stretching away on either side of him to north and south, Longmoor Valley is wide and shallow, catching spring-water and run-off streams from the higher and drier banks which surround it and channelling them into the Longmoor Brook, which scribbles its way south through a waterlogged landscape of sedge and reed and eventually to the pool. The path where the kids should be walking by now dips and rises along its near edge below Rowton Bank where he sits, eroded by centuries of countless feet. Further off, the dark line of coppiced woodland marks the remains of a Roman road at the park's western boundary, beyond which are suburbs and high-rises and the white-noise roar of traffic – but here, at this moment and time, all of that is invisible. It is easy to imagine peat-cutters from a century ago toiling down there with their long-bladed spades in the summer heat; before that, medieval serfs harvesting the rushes for mats and lamp wicks; and further still, what? Did Bronze Age villagers herd their sheep on the upper slopes a thousand years even before the Romans? And in all that compressed weight of time, how many young men have sat in a place like this, disconsolate at a love affair dying beyond their control? It is scant comfort, but better than none.

A flash of colour appears around a bend in the path off to the left, and his group is there: Scattie's pink bandanna, Brandon's bright red walking socks, and the lime green of Liv's borrowed rucksack. Ryan is striding ahead, limping slightly because of course he's buggered his ankle already, and the rest are strung out in a line, no doubt sweaty and irritable in the sun. Nathan stands up and waves in wide, sweeping movements of both arms so that they are sure to see him. A moment later he sees Scattie wave back, and he breathes a sigh of relief. Not that there is a reason for him to have been anxious in the first place, he tells himself.

He sits back down and watches them approach, appearing and disappearing as the path dips in and out of watershed gullies. Eventually he is able to hear them: scraps of singing and adolescent banter carried to him on the capricious breeze.

'...can't have drunk it all already!'

'It's hot, man! I'm going to have to suck the stuff out of my blisters!'

'...such a fucking knob-end...'

And they are gone again. With a sigh of resignation, Nathan decides that he should probably go and meet them at least part of the way, gets up, and starts down Rowton Bank towards them.

He catches one more glimpse of them as he rises: their backpacks, half-hidden by high gorse bushes, moving away from him. He frowns. They've turned left off the main path and seem to be angling down towards the brook, something they've been specifically warned against. Not that there is any need for him to worry; the brook is shallow, and in this weather they'll dry out quickly enough if they do fall in. But if Ryan turns his ankle in a rabbit hole or a patch of bog, Nathan is screwed. He cuts right, hoping to catch them before they do so, and their voices drift to him again.

Ryan's voice is high with excitement. 'Whoa! Look at that!'

'Cool,' from Scattie.

'...you think it's clean?' That's Liv.

A brief silence and then Bran's voice coming back: '... spring, feeding... probably drinkable...'

'Hey, who's that...?'

Then there is a loud splash and whoops of laughter. Nathan speeds up, wondering how a sense of mild urgency should have blossomed into actual fear. Unless the air is somehow magnifying their voices they can't have reached the stream, surely. He is moving so quickly that he almost falls into the well.

It is about two metres across, circular and stone-lined, and completely obscured from the path by the hollow of the land and the surrounding undergrowth. He checks his map – it's called Rowton's Well, and they've been told to avoid it because everyone assumed it would be a deep, dangerous hole in the ground, but he sees now that it isn't a well in the conventional sense. It's a spring; the clear water is only about a foot deep, over a pebbly bottom. As he watches, tiny bubbles shiver up from between the stones and *plip* on the surface. It doesn't matter. The kids shouldn't have come anywhere near here. Propped against the side is Ryan's army-surplus rucksack, but of the children themselves there is no sign. The only sound is the barely perceptible hiss of the breeze in rush-grass.

He spins around. There is a strange, clutching sensation high up in his throat that he refuses to acknowledge as panic because what is there to panic about? There is no way that they can have simply disappeared.

'Okay, I get it!' he says loudly. 'Nice one; good joke. You've still got those ice creams waiting for you, remember?'

There is no reply. Besides, why would they be playing hide-and-seek and yet leave one of their bags in plain sight? Why only Ryan, and not the others? Because he'd taken it off when he'd stopped for a drink?

A flash of colour, lower down and further away, in the marshy terrain towards the stream.

'Come on, you lot!' he shouts. 'Stop messing around!'

They are strolling away quite calmly in the opposite direction, half-hidden by the trailing fronds of a few thin birch trees, none of them so much as looking back even though they must have heard him. Their movements are calm, sedate, even, with their arms hanging loosely by their sides. In single file, Ryan, Scattie, Liv and Bran step easily along what looks like a track of roughly hewn timbers laid as a footbridge across the stream and up the other side. The ground there is a lot higher – more of a densely wooded slope than the open marsh it was before.

'Stop!' he yells, and runs after them.

Birch branches whip his face and he stumbles, falling to his knees in squelching black soil. When he picks himself back up the kids have disappeared again, and now he can't see the wooden track or the tree-lined slope. He splashes across the stream and up the other side, tripped by heather and scratched by gorse thorns as he fights his way up to higher ground for a better view, but once he's gained it he can do nothing but stare in shock.

Under a clear sky, and in a wide landscape empty of any hiding place, they have disappeared utterly.

In the shadowless light of Un, it is happening now.

2

ROWTON MAN

Annie Scott loved walking Maggs first thing on a summer morning – although she thought 'walking' overstated her role in proceedings. As soon as her big black Labrador was off the leash it was all Annie could do most days to stop her from rolling around in the most foul-smelling filth she could find. Still, the advantage of Sutton Park was that it was massive, and at six o'clock in the morning there were so few people around that Annie didn't have to worry about Maggs making an embarrassment of herself.

There were copses and woodland on the western side of the park, but that was for winter and fog-shrouded walks bundled in coats and scarves. Summer was for striding along Longmoor Brook through dew-soaked grass when it was still fresh and the pollen hadn't yet had a chance to rise and make everything dusty, while skylarks twittered invisibly high above and the heather and rushes rustled as small creatures ran for cover from her great stupid lolloping idiot of a dog.

This morning the freshness was burning off more quickly

than usual; it had been a ferociously hot summer so far, and today looked like being no exception. It would be sweltering by mid-morning. Caught up in the moment, she didn't notice for some time that Maggs had disappeared.

'Maggs!' she called. 'Maggsy-Maggsy-Maggsy!' She followed it up with a sharp whistle and was answered by an excited bark from her right, where the wettest part of the bog lay. She groaned. On more than one occasion Maggs had gone home caked in mud to her shoulders. 'So help me, I will hose you down in the back garden,' she promised.

The summer heat had parched the stream valley, and it was nowhere near as boggy as she'd been expecting. Around clumps of sedge grass and rushes the skin of the ground had split open in deep cracks revealing the black peaty earth of its underflesh, and it was in one of these fissures that Maggs was digging furiously, flinging clouds of earth in all directions, and pausing occasionally to tug at something.

'Right, that's it,' said Annie, advancing with the leash, when Maggs pulled back suddenly with her prize.

'Brilliant. You've found a stick. Very impressive.'

Maggs dropped the stick at Annie's feet and looked up at her mistress proudly.

'If you think I'm throwing that horrible smelly thing for you, you've gone out of your doggy little mind.'

It wasn't even a particularly good throwing stick. It was short, black, and branched at the end into five twigs which, it was funny, looked quite like...

Annie bent lower to get a better look. Then she began to scream.

* * *

TARA DOUMANI FINISHED HER MORNING RUN, ROUNDING the corner to her road on legs that burned with that welcome sense of everything having been unknotted, if only for a moment, and enjoying the neatness of timing it so that the last track of her iPod's playlist was just finishing, when she saw the handsome young man in the suit lounging outside her front gate.

And it's not even Christmas, she thought. She gave him a polite but wary smile as she approached, hoping for his sake that he wasn't a Jehovah's Witness. That kind of conversation never ended well.

'Miss?' he enquired, which was at least a good start. 'I'm Detective Sergeant Mark Pryce, West Midlands Police.' He was holding up some form of ID in a flip-out wallet. 'Are you Dr Tara Doumani?'

'Why?' she replied. She pulled out her earbuds and hung them around her neck as she moved past him, uncomfortably aware of the large sweat patch on the front of her t-shirt. *Oh piss off,* she told herself. *There's a policeman outside your door and all you're worried about is your feminine mystique?*

'You're a lecturer in os—' He stopped to consult a scrap of paper. 'Oss-teo-archaeology at the University of Birmingham?'

'Yes,' she replied, fitting her key into the lock, and repeated, 'Why?' To his credit he was still standing on the pavement; he hadn't followed onto her property.

'There's been a body found. My inspector's been told we need someone to tell us how old it is before we can do anything with it. He wondered if you'd be kind enough to lend us your expertise.'

Standing in the open doorway, she turned and looked closely at him for signs that he was making fun of her. He was holding out his ID instead. 'You'll be wanting to check this,' he added. 'Call the station at Sutton Coldfield.'

'Thanks,' she said slowly, and retreated inside. She went straight to the phone and satisfied herself that he was who he said he was. Her only parting gift from her mother when she'd left home had been a healthy dose of paranoia about everything and everyone who might take an interest in a young woman living alone, and it was definitely one of those gifts that just kept on giving. She changed out of her running gear, grabbed a quick shower (Detective Sergeant Pryce could jolly well wait a bit longer; there were limits to how stinky she was prepared to be in public), and threw on the first reasonably decent clothes she could find. Into the battered old daysack which she'd lugged all over the world she stuffed in her tool roll along with sample bags, vinyl gloves, and paracetamol for when all that bending over did her back in again.

We need someone to tell us how old it is, he'd said.

What had they found?

More importantly, what the hell was she supposed to do with it? She'd dealt with her fair share of human remains in her career, and even made a bit of a name for herself with the National Trust tourist circuit giving talks to school groups, but she'd never worked with the police before. Why were they even asking her? Unable to answer that question, she focussed on the ones that she could. *Treat it like any other dig,* she decided.

Outside, DS Pryce was waiting quite patiently in his car. He grinned when he saw the bag. 'No bullwhip, then?'

'I'm sorry?' She slid into the passenger seat and buckled up.

'Indiana Jones and all that,' he explained as they pulled away.

'Oh,' she said. 'Right. Never heard that one before.' She hoped it wouldn't take them long to get to wherever this body was. Dead people were so much easier to hold conversations with.

POLICE VEHICLES FILLED THE BANNER'S GATE CAR PARK, which had been closed to the public, and in the flat, open landscape at the bottom of Longmoor Valley, the bright blue-and-white police tape and large white pop-up shelter that had been erected over the site stood out starkly. Several uniformed officers kept the inevitable crowd of gawping passers-by at a respectable distance. Most were the early-morning type – dog-walkers, joggers and cyclists – but there were a few kids, naturally recording everything on their phones.

'This lot got out early, didn't they?' she remarked to Pryce.

He grunted. 'It's Twitter and Snapchat I blame. Still, most of them will get bored and go home if something doesn't explode or a cute kitten doesn't appear in the next two minutes.'

'Now, an exploding kitten – *that* would keep them interested.'

She saw him watching her sidelong, as if seeing her properly for the first time, or waiting for her to grow an extra head. It was a look she was used to from men. She gave an apologetic shrug. 'My research basically involves cutting up ancient corpses to see what they died of,' she explained. 'It breeds a certain sense of humour.'

'Seems like it.'

Oh well, she thought. *Plenty more cute, uniformed fish in the sea. Somewhere. Probably.*

'It might be best if you don't say anything to any of them,' Pryce advised, as they passed through the car park gate and set off along the path. 'Nothing at all. Some of them aren't just rubberneckers. Do you remember a few years ago, the Longmoor Disappearances?'

She shook her head.

'Really? It was in all the papers. National press, for weeks.'

'I'm sorry, Detective Pryce, but if it happened when I was doing my PhD, World War Three could have been declared and I wouldn't have noticed.'

Pryce seemed genuinely surprised. 'Oh. Okay, so, in 2007 a group of four students – two boys and two girls – from a local school disappeared in the park. They'd been doing some map-reading exercises for a hiking expedition; they left one checkpoint, right around here, but didn't show up at the next. There was a massive search but three of the kids never appeared and their bodies were never recovered. Only one of the girls was ever found – a day later, completely traumatised and unable to tell anybody what had happened to her. No one was ever charged. The papers forgot about it after a while, but trust me, the families never have.'

'Of course,' said Tara. 'How could they? God, that's awful. Hang on, wait.' She stopped. 'You mean there's a good chance that what's in there might be a *child*?'

He simply nodded, and she found herself blushing with guilt at her earlier flippancy. 'I'm sorry,' she said. 'What I said earlier; it's just that I'm used to working with remains that are a lot older, not so much like…'

'Actual people?'

'That's not what I meant.'

'I'm sorry too. I don't mean to be a pain. Just – be aware that there are people who will latch onto anything that seems to offer hope, so it's best not to offer them anything.'

'Got it.'

Now that she knew they were there, the grieving families were a lot easier to see: a knot of half a dozen middle-aged adults huddled together, grim-faced and red-eyed. Seeing Pryce, one of the men detached himself from the group and moved to intercept.

'Detective?' he called. 'What's going on? Why's it taking so long?'

'Mr Edwards, please let me reassure you, we're working as fast as we can to determine…' Pryce laid a placatory hand on the man's arm, but he shook it off.

'That's no bloody good to me, is it? How long is it going to take?'

'I'm very sorry…'

As Pryce spoke he led Tara underneath the police tape and

past a uniformed officer who stopped the man following, though his shouts pursued them: 'How much bloody longer has my boy got to lie in the ground? *How long?*'

Tara was ushered into the body tent and introduced to Pryce's boss, Detective Inspector Chris Hodges, who was clearly not having a good time and made no effort to disguise the fact. He was everything she'd expected from the middle-management of any bureaucratic organisation: ten pounds overweight, balding, and perspiring – although to be fair, the heavy smell of sun-baked plastic and peat made the shelter's interior stifling.

She examined how far the police had got with excavating the remains before the coroner had pressed the pause button on their investigation. She could well understand their confusion. They'd been expecting something skeletal – fragments of bone and skull – but what they'd found was a body whose flesh had been naturally mummified by the chemical action of the peat. Skin and muscle had become black leather. The hair, whatever colour it had been in life, had turned bright ginger, further complicating the task of identifying the victim for someone who didn't know what they were looking at. Credit where it was due, though, they'd done a good job of marking the probable grave area out in half-metre squares with pegs and string and had started digging back from where the hand had been found, putting the spoil from each square into its own numbered evidence bag. Presumably that was for their forensics people but if the remains turned out to be archaeological and she had to take over it would still help her with cataloguing any finds. Somebody here knew what they were doing. They had uncovered the remainder of the arm up to the shoulder and the gleaming black corrugation of the body's spine; the body – no, the mummy – was lying on its right side facing away from them, with its damaged arm bent back behind and its face still obscured so that it looked for all the world like somebody burying their face in a pillow to avoid being woken up.

She bent close, fascinated. It was twisted, the sinews and wizened muscles clearly visible under its glossy, tar-black skin.

Hodges didn't waste any time or effort explaining to her how the body had been found – just that as soon as the coroner's assistant had seen the state of the hand he'd ordered everybody to stop digging until its approximate age could be determined. Looking at it, sealed in its plastic evidence bag, she could well understand why.

It was a right hand, shrivelled and black, the skin stretched tightly over the bones like leather, which made it impossible for her to tell whether or not she was looking at the hand of a child. The dismemberment was just past the wrist, torn and ragged from the dog's teeth, but nothing like a bracelet or a watch had been found nearby, and there was no other jewellery. The fingernails were perfectly preserved, but short and unshaped, so if it was one of the missing children it was likely one of the boys. A cluster of warts on the index knuckle seemed unlikely for a modern hand, though hardly conclusive. Despite the macabre possibilities, she was enthralled.

'This is incredible,' she breathed.

'You know that's not people's usual reaction when they see a severed limb,' Hodges remarked.

'I'm afraid I'm not very usual,' she murmured, only half paying attention. 'I was just saying to your sergeant, dead bodies are my job, after all.'

'You and me both. So what can you tell me about this one?'

'Well, at first glance it's probably not one of the missing children.'

'"Probably" doesn't help me very much, I'm afraid.'

'The mummification makes things difficult, I'll admit.'

He snorted. 'Mummification. Seriously.'

She looked at him. 'Seriously.'

'Miss Doumani...'

'It's "Doctor".'

'Fair enough, *Dr* Doumani. I don't want to contradict the expert, but one doesn't tend to see too many sodding pyramids in the greater West Midlands area.'

'Not that kind of mummification. What you're looking at here might be a bog mummy. That's why it's amazing – there have only been a handful of these found in the UK.'

'Assume for a moment that I haven't got a clue what you're on about.'

'Certain types of peat bog are able to preserve human bodies,' she explained. 'It's a combination of cold, lack of oxygen, and sphagnum moss producing the same kinds of acid that are used to tan leather. Some of the bodies that have been found are over five thousand years old...'

'That's just a tiny bit out of my jurisdiction.'

'...but some are much more recent. Bog mummies have been found of soldiers from World War One. Many of the ancient ones seem to be victims of violence – but whether it's by accident, or ritual sacrifice or just outright murder, the remains are generally so distorted that it's hard to say for sure.'

'Now murder – that *is* my jurisdiction.'

'The mummification process doesn't take very long – six months, a year possibly – and judging from the fact that this one still has bones,' she pointed to the ragged stump of wrist, 'I'd say he or she was taken out again fairly soon afterwards because the same acids which preserve the flesh also dissolve calcium.'

'Do you mean to say that someone dug him up again?'

'Most likely. Obviously I haven't had a chance to look at it properly, but I'd put money on this being a reburial, which makes it religious, which makes it *old*.'

'Exactly how old?'

She shrugged. 'Impossible to guess until I actually get in there.'

Hodges crouched by the hole and frowned at the broken ends of bone which peeped out of the soil. 'I'll tell you this for nothing,' he said. 'Murderers move bodies for lots of reasons, and in my experience religion isn't high on that list. You're saying this could be within the last ten years.'

'Ten, or ten hundred.'

'How soon can you find out?'

'That depends on how much of this you want me to disturb. Reasonably quickly if I find anything else buried with it – clothes, jewellery, that sort of thing – but it depends on exactly what, and I don't want to upset your forensics people. On the other hand…' She held up the evidence bag. 'No pun intended. I seem to have been supplied with a conveniently portable sample for carbon dating. That'll get me to within a hundred years or so, but it'll take a few days.'

'*Days*. Fucking hell.' He chewed this over while he stared at the hole in the ground. Tara could well understand his frustration. It wasn't for himself, but for the relatives who were still being tormented by the hope that their loved ones were out there and might come home. The only options available to Tara were to either destroy their world completely by putting a name to the body, or to confirm that it was ancient and allow their torment to continue.

Eventually Hodges straightened up and brushed dirt from his trousers. 'Do your carbon dating, then,' he said, 'but don't touch anything else. And you'd best get cracking, because soon I'm going to have every bloody newspaper and TV reporter in the country whipping up a load of hysteria about what's in this tent.'

'I'll be as quick as I can,' she reassured him, knowing that it would be anything but quick. 'In the meantime you need to cover this back up, because it's already started decomposing.'

There would be a thousand phone calls to make and authorities to be notified; and if the hand's owner was ancient, permits to be applied for, funding to be cajoled from a cash-strapped university, and all before the body was dragged out of the ground. Just like Tollund Man, or Yde Girl, who had no name but that of the place they had been found, he would be poked and prodded and scanned for secrets, before finally being freeze-dried and stuck in a glass case to be gawped at by more people like the ones outside. As ever she felt a fierce protectiveness well up in her at the idea, and a simultaneous shame at her own part in the process. In the meantime, though, there was this moment of quiet before that whole circus began.

'Rowton Man,' she decided. 'That's what we'll call you.' But it would just be their secret for now. 'I'll look after you,' she promised. 'I'll make sure everything's okay.'

THE *AFAUGH* WATCHES FROM UN AND SEES ITS ADVERSARY weakened for the first time in its long, long memory. Weakened, yes, but still strong enough to deny it entry to the world. The way is not yet open; the timber track remains guarded.

Still, there is a gap.

A gap through which it can reach.

3

CALL ME TINKERBELL

NATHAN LOOKED AT THE KID STUCK HALFWAY UP THE ROCK slope and knew, with a sinking feeling in his heart, that if nothing happened in the next minute he was going to have to climb up there himself and sort it out.

'He's bottled it,' said Robbie, grinning.

'No he hasn't,' Nathan replied.

'Five pounds says you can't talk him up to the top.'

'He has not bottled it!'

For the moment the lad's mates were being nicely supportive; the few who had already got to the top were calling down that it was dead easy, while the majority at the bottom who were still waiting for their turn were calling up to say he could do it, yeah, he could do it. But Nathan knew that soon they'd get impatient and start having a go at him, making chicken noises and generally getting all *Lord of the Flies* on his ass. Meanwhile, the kid clung to the rock face like a limpet.

'Fucksake,' he muttered, and clipped onto the instructor's

line. Robbie belayed him up without a word, but the shit-eating grin on his face said it all.

The rock face was, quite literally, kids' stuff. They'd all done fine on the climbing tower back at Bryncaer Mountain Centre, so this should have been no problem; it wasn't particularly high or sheer, and some parts of it were virtually like a flight of stairs. But there was no telling – what felt safe on a nice artificial climbing tower with chunky handholds could feel like the north face of Everest when you were outside and it was windy and there was moss and dirt and bird shit and all kinds of horrible outdoorsy stuff – especially if you were a seventeen-year-old lad from a Bristol housing estate.

Nathan got up level with him. 'Hi,' he said. 'What's your name again?'

'Tyriq,' mumbled the lad. His eyes were tight shut, his fingers hooked into white-knuckled claws where they gripped the rock face, and his breath was coming in harsh little gasps. 'I want to go down.'

'Sure, Terry, sure. We can do that, no problem. Easy as.'

'I said it's Tyriq. Not Terry.'

'Oh, okay, right, sorry. Listen, Ricky…'

The kid opened his eyes and glared at him from under the orange plastic of his climbing helmet. 'Are you fucking deaf? I said my name is Tyriq, and I want to fucking go down!'

Nathan gave him a big grin and stuck out his hand. 'Hi, Tyriq. We met before. I'm Nathan – but you can call me Tinkerbell.'

Suspicion replaced anger in the boy's eyes. He thought Nathan was taking the piss. 'You what?'

'*If* you make it all the way to the top, that is.'

Tyriq shook his head. 'No way. I can't do it. It's all slippery and shit.'

There was a whistle from below. Robbie was waving. 'How's it going up there?' he called. 'Enjoying the view?'

'Just fine, thanks!' he yelled back. 'Me and Tyriq here, we're just taking our time, having a bit of a chat, that's all.' The last thing he wanted was the lad freaking out over how high up he was. Robbie could be a bastard at times.

'I don't want to chat and I don't want to look at the fucking view. I just want to go—'

'Down, yes, I know. Listen, Tyriq, I don't think you appreciate the value of the offer I'm making here. Everybody else in your group has to call me Nathan, or Mr Brookes, or, God help them, "sir" – but you, and only you, will have the privilege of being able to shout across a crowded room "Oi! Tinkerbell!" and have me come running like a fairy in a tutu.'

Tyriq made a snorting noise that might have passed for a laugh.

'Good man. Now, see that chunk of rock about five centimetres above your left hand? The one that looks a bit like... well, a bit like a chunk of rock, I suppose. Put your hand *there*...'

And so, taking it one careful hand- and foot-hold after another, Nathan babied Tyriq up the rock face until he stood on top and received from his mates the kind of rapturous cheering usually given to last-second-of-the-game goal-kickers. Nathan thought that the only thing sweeter than the mile-wide grin on the kid's face was going to be the look on Robbie's when Nathan relieved him of that fiver.

'There you go, mate,' he said, clapping the lad on the shoulder. 'Good job.'

Tyriq turned round, and his face had changed. It wasn't Tyriq any more.

It was Ryan Edwards, which was impossible, because Ryan Edwards was nine years dead – or as good as. The soundtrack of the world muted, and everything fell away like a giant scree slope leaving him standing in a high, white buzzing void with nothing except that impossible face in front of him. Ryan grinned and winked. 'Piña coladas by the pool, then, sir?' he laughed.

Nathan recoiled, his heels slipping backward over the slope that he'd just climbed. His arms pinwheeled for a moment, and the stupefaction at seeing Ryan's impossible face was replaced by simple, gut-twisting panic as he fell. He struck the rock face with hip, shoulder, and a jarring blow on his helmet, which made him see stars. Then the instructor's line caught him by his waist harness, and the leg loops rode up into his groin so hard that it felt like his bollocks had been shoved up into his throat. He dangled, twisting and groaning.

Then Tyriq's face appeared over the edge – not Ryan, just some kid who he'd met yesterday and would instantly forget the day after tomorrow, like a thousand before him. 'You all right, Tinkerbell?' he asked.

* * *

TARA HURRIED THE C14 TESTING AS QUICKLY AS SHE COULD by cutting one or two corners that wouldn't be missed, but even then it was a week of kicking her heels and having to field the increasingly stroppy calls of an impatient detective inspector who couldn't understand why it had to take so long. She occupied herself by reading up as much as she could on the history of the park, and when the results finally came she should have been delighted, but all she could manage was a reluctant sort of regret. DI Hodges picked up her call on the first ring.

'Spare me the full bloody *Time Team* treatment,' he said. 'Just tell me whether I've got a crime scene or not.'

'It's ancient,' she replied. 'A thousand years BC, give or take.'

'Shit.'

'I'm sorry.'

There was a long silence on the other end. She could imagine him glaring at where Rowton Man – she could call him that now with a clear conscience – lay safely in the earth, blaming him for not being someone else but at the same time undoubtedly relieved that he didn't have to tell a parent that it might be their child. But when he next spoke, he just sounded tired.

'I'll try to keep a uniform on it until you can arrange to take over supervision of the site,' he said.

'Thanks. I'd appreciate that.'

He hung up without another word.

She looked at the list of people she was going to have to call before she could touch the dig with so much as a toothpick, took a deep breath, and started to dial.

4

THE COSMIC WIND-UP

'HAVE ANY OF YOU GUYS EVER SEEN A SLATE-WORM?' ASKED Robbie, to an answering chorus of 'no's from the nine kids following him like ducklings. At the back of the line, Nathan smiled as he recognised the start of one his friend's Cosmic Wind-Ups. The shock of last week's climbing session had worn off, even though the ache in his groin hadn't entirely.

'So you know how this slate we're walking on is basically sedimentary rock – all mud and gunk compressed over millions of years?'

A couple of the kids said yes, of course they did. The group ranged in age from fourteen to sixteen and most of them had probably learned just enough science to know this. That was the art of the Cosmic Wind-Up: to work with what little the target knew and add layer after layer of detail which was just plausible enough so that by the time you hit them with the unbelievable pay-off they swallowed it hook, line and sinker.

'And you know worms eat mud?'

Well duh, everybody knew *that*, Robbie.

'Well then, there's a particular species of worm which has evolved to eat the slate, just like normal worms eat mud, except that because slate is quite hard, they've had to grow teeth to do it. They're a lot bigger too, almost the size of snakes. Sometimes if you look closely at the slate, you can see holes where the slate-worms have chewed right through – here, just like this one.' He passed back to the first kid in line a piece of slate which did indeed have a hole through it, almost the same size as a two-pound coin.

Immediately half the kids started arguing with each other to have a closer look while the rest began scanning the rocks under their feet. It was a clear path on an easy tourist route up Mount Snowdon, and there was little chance of them straying into danger. The sky was a brilliant mid-July blue and visibility was perfect, from the pyramidal peak ahead of them sweeping down into the wide bowl-shaped valley of Rhyd Ddu on their right, with its twin lakes encircled by high ridges. It was as perfect a day for taking a school group on a stroll up the mountain as anybody could have wished for. Even after nine years, Nathan still couldn't believe he was getting paid for this.

'That's not real,' said one lad scornfully. 'You drilled that yourself. It's bullshit.'

Robbie just smiled to himself and carried on leading them upward. A few minutes later one of the girls gave a squeal of triumph and pounced on a rock.

'Found one!' she yelled. She flourished a piece of slate, which had a hole clean through it. There were murmurs of astonishment from her friends, while the group sceptic just scowled and muttered to himself.

'The other thing about slate-worms,' added Robbie, 'is that they're fast, but timid. While you're walking along, if you see any sudden movements in the grass at the side of the path, that'll be a slate-worm scared off by your big clomping feet.'

By the time they stopped for a break, Robbie had most of them convinced that slate-worms were real, and a few who even claimed that they'd seen one – just a flickering glimpse of grey skin disappearing into the grass. They sat and ate their sandwiches on a broad, grassy shelf, away from the path and the dozens of other hikers who tramped past. There was no such thing as a secluded hike up Snowdon in the summer. Several of the kids wanted to know if they could stop at the café on the peak and get hot chocolates. Nathan said no but if they came back next year they could go to the McDonald's on Scafell Pike, which made Robbie snort tea out of his nose.

'So when are you going to tell them the truth about the slate-worms?' he asked, once they were out of earshot. He knew as well as Robbie that the holes were really caused by smaller, harder pebbles of granite catching in slight hollows in the surface of the softer slate and being washed around and around by the rain over the years like a natural drill-bit.

'What, that it's all just down to erosion? Maybe never. Most of that lot stopped believing in Father Christmas before they were out of nappies. Let them have a bit of mystery, I say. Besides, erosion's boring. See what I did there? *Boring?*'

'Piss off,' Nathan laughed. He looked at his watch. 'Time for a quick round of Spot the Dick?'

It was a simple game, needing only a pair of binoculars and a high vantage point with good views of the popular walking trails up the mountain. Points were awarded for the most stupidly inappropriate kit seen being worn or carried by hikers: flip-flops, pushchairs, handbag-sized dogs, or anything just generally stupid. There was no hard and fast scoring system – just a subjective rating based on how strongly one felt the urge to slap them for being idiots. In some cases it was so bad it verged on the criminally negligent, like that one time they'd had to stop a guy taking his wife and children up into fog, forty-knot winds and horizontal rain dressed in just t-shirts and plastic ponchos, by threatening to report him to the police. That kind of thing was mercifully rare, though.

'Dick,' said Robbie, peering through the binoculars.

'Where?'

'Rhyd Ddu, coming up.'

'Slap factor?'

Robbie so-so'ed with his hand. 'Five or six. Flip-flops, plus bald but no hat. Doesn't look like he's carrying any water. Heatstroke on legs.'

'Giz a look.'

Nathan took the binoculars. He winced and sucked his teeth. 'That's going to sting tonight,' he said, and began scanning the valley.

A fell-runner plodded uphill past them – a forty-something man in glasses and black-and-yellow running top, lean as a whippet and showing no signs of fatigue. He panted a 'Morning!' at them as he passed.

Nathan waited until he disappeared over the next slope. 'Nutter,' he said.

'Tell you what,' said Robbie. 'When I have kids I'm going to do it properly. I'm getting them up here before they can walk. Shit – I want their first steps to be up *here*.' He chewed his sandwich and gazed around.

'You're never going to have kids,' murmured Nathan, still scanning, trying not to be distracted. It was funny – he could have sworn he'd just seen...

'What makes you so sure?'

'You're nineteen. No nineteen-year-old ever really believes they're going to have kids.'

'The fuck *you* know, old man.'

'Thirty-two isn't old!'

'Yeah, and no thirty-two-year-old ever really believes that.'

'Fair point.' Nathan scanned the valley again more carefully, praying that he wouldn't see what he thought he'd seen.

His breath choked in his throat like a stone.

Three figures were heading down the mountain. They were on the same side as Nathan's group, but on one of the lower paths a good hundred metres below, known as the Rhyd Ddu Path. They were moving away from him so that he couldn't see their faces. What with the distance and the way his hands were suddenly trembling, their image through the binoculars was jumping all over the place, but he was quite certain that the tall blond male was Ryan. The other two looked like a girl wearing a pink bandanna – impossible to tell if it had Scattie's little black skull-and-crossbones on it, though – and a second male bringing up the rear with a walking stick. Did that look like Bran's battered, old-fashioned rucksack on his back? They were simply too far away for him to be sure. It had to be his eyes playing tricks on him – a Cosmic Wind-Up from his own brain – because what other explanation could there be for the fact that he was looking at people he was sure had been dead for nearly a decade? He rubbed his eyes hard, cleaned the lenses of the binoculars and looked again, knowing that the figures would be gone.

They were still there. They'd rounded a corner, and though he still couldn't see their faces, he watched a booted foot dislodge a few small stones, which tumbled in little puffs of dust a few metres further down the path.

'There's a group going down Rhyd Ddu,' he said to Robbie. His voice felt dry and croaky, dead in his mouth. 'I have to go check on them. Cover for me, yeah?'

Robbie blinked at him in astonishment. 'You what? Are they in trouble?'

'No, not as such...'

'Then I repeat: you actually *what*? In case you've forgotten,' he pointed to their group of slate-worm wranglers, 'we have a job to do. Whoever those people are, if they're in trouble they can bloody well call Mountain Rescue like everybody else.'

Nathan had already grabbed his bag and was setting off. 'Sorry, mate, no choice.' He didn't look back, because he knew exactly what the expression on Robbie's face would be like. He heard one kid saying, 'Where's Tinkerbell off to?' and Robbie doing his best to cover, despite being royally pissed off, replying, 'He's off looking for perygils. Did I ever tell you what a perygil is? Funny creature, bit like a dwarf giraffe...'

NATHAN PLUNGED TOWARDS THE RHYD DDU PATH AT A reckless speed, letting his momentum carry him down the slope and only really using his legs to keep from pitching forward uncontrollably. Mini-avalanches of scree went ahead of his feet, and dust kicked up around him, sticking to his skin with the sweat that drenched him in minutes. The group was disappearing around yet another of the path's many zigzag turns, moving easily and slowly, as if they had all the time in the world. *It is happening now,* he thought, *it is always happening*, but had no idea what that meant. His brain was hammering in his skull, red-hot and swollen with heat and the need to concentrate on keeping his balance, so hard that all he could take in were scraps: a swing of arm, the heel of a boot, a glimpse of pink bandanna with little black skulls, the ring of a wooden walking stick on stone.

'Scattie!' he called out, knowing at the same time that it could not possibly be her. 'Brandon!'

But they didn't hear him, or chose to ignore him, or weren't even there in the first place, and they moved out of sight again. He staggered after them, hitting the path hard enough to jar his knees, ran around the bend and clapped his hand on the shoulder of the figure ahead.

The three middle-aged ramblers – who looked absolutely nothing like the figures he'd been chasing – turned in shock and surprise.

''Ere!' protested the man whose shoulder he was clutching. 'What d'you think you're up to?' He shook Nathan off angrily. 'Get your bloody hands off me!'

Nathan fell back, stammering apologies, even as at the same time he was peering past them down the trail, thinking maybe that the kids had got ahead of these adults, but the trail was clear for a good few hundred metres. The angry man's companions were ushering him away from a confrontation, seeming to accept that it was all a strange misunderstanding, and that there was no harm done.

No, thought Nathan, as he began the long trudge back up to Robbie. *No harm done. Not for a very long time.*

ROBBIE DEPOSITED A PINT OF PURPLE MOOSE ALE DECISIVELY on the table in front of Nathan, and sat down opposite.

'Talk,' he ordered.

Nathan looked at the larger picnic table over at the other end of the pub garden where the rest of the centre's staff were laughing, and understood why Robbie had insisted that they sit over here, in one of the quieter spots. This late in the day it was still quite light, and the Bryn Tyrch Inn was busy with walkers who were finishing a long day in the mountains with a well-deserved beer and an outrageously expensive gastro-pub meal (prices were way beyond what an activity instructor could afford, but the beer was excellent), and it was too noisy for Nathan and Robbie's conversation to be overheard.

'Talk about what?' said Nathan.

Robbie reached over, took Nathan's pint, and drank from it.

'Hey!'

'I've just invented a new drinking game,' Robbie replied. 'Every time you try to bullshit me, I take a drink from your pint.'

'Jesus, man, you want to explain the rules to me first?'

'That's rich, that is, coming from you. Twice in two days you've had some kind of mental I-don't-know-what, and left me in the shit or put yourself or the kids in danger. None of which is remotely cool. So, either you talk to me or I talk to Lorna.'

Lorna McCaig was the Bryncaer Mountain Centre's duty manager – as implacable as a geological event and probably just as physically hard. It was rumoured that she had represented Scotland at the 1990 Commonwealth Games throwing the javelin, and that she still had one stashed somewhere on site for dealing with would-be burglars and vandals. She also made it clear that as far as she was concerned there was next to no difference between wrangling a group of barely civilised teenagers and her own staff, and Nathan didn't blame her.

'It's not going to make any sense,' he warned.

Robbie reached for his pint again.

'All right! All right!' Nathan clutched his beer protectively.

He told Robbie a heavily edited version of the truth – no

more or less than he'd told the police, and absolutely nothing personal about him and Sue. That had never been anybody's business but theirs. All he needed to know was that Nathan had been in charge of a group, that the group had disappeared, and that because he hadn't been where he was supposed to have been, his career was irretrievably fucked.

At that, Robbie gave a little laugh, shook his head, and drank.

'What?'

'Nothing.'

'No, come on – what? What's so funny?'

Robbie looked down into his pint. 'Mate, it's not my place to judge you, all right? I wasn't there.'

'But?'

Robbie looked at him now. 'But career? Four kids go missing and what you take from that is the damage to your career?'

'Oh come on, man, that's not what I meant. Besides, it wasn't all four of them. The next day, someone riding a horse through the park found Liv, exactly where the others had disappeared. She was alive, no injuries, but in a bad way all the same: suffering from exposure and in severe shock, exhausted, starving, missing all of her kit. She couldn't tell the police what had happened or where the others were. She couldn't say how she'd got to where she was – there was no way she could have been just lying there the whole time with the search going on, so she'd either walked or been dropped off there, but they never found out the answers to any of it.'

'All of which is very well,' pointed out Robbie. 'But this was years ago, yeah? It still doesn't explain why you've been acting like a twat all this week.'

Nathan drew a deep breath and told him about the hallucinations he'd been having.

To his credit, Robbie didn't laugh it off. He took a thoughtful drink, nodded, and said, 'Must have been the heat. You don't drink enough water, your body temperature rises, brain starts making things up. Like you say, just a hallucination.'

'I know, I know. I must have been imagining it.' In Robbie's position, that was exactly what Nathan would have believed, so he let Robbie have his rational explanation despite knowing that it was crap. He hadn't been dehydrated when Ryan had winked at him from Tyriq's face, and even though he might well have imagined the kids on the mountain today, there definitely had been nowhere for them to hide on the day that they'd disappeared. They'd gone *somewhere*.

'So,' said Robbie, sounding like he was figuring something out, 'you know when you applied for the job here?'

'Yes?'

'And there was that bit of the form where you have to declare whether or not you have any criminal convictions...'

'Okay, listen.' Nathan leaned forward, his voice low and intense. 'I wasn't charged. I wasn't even fucking *arrested*. I answered some questions and provided a witness statement just like about a dozen other people who were there at the same time.'

'So why not just tell them you were with your colleague

when it all happened? I don't get it. You had an alibi, problem solved.'

'Because a couple of months before all this happened she nearly got sacked on account of me.'

'Oh, this just gets better,' said Robbie, propping both elbows on the table and his chin in his hands, and staring at him expectantly. 'Go on.'

Nathan grimaced. 'I'm glad you're enjoying this. So the school had this programme of Saturday clubs, and everybody had to help with a club – Chess Club, Robot Club, Camping Club, you get the idea – with absolutely no exceptions. We were both on Camping Club. Anyway, one Friday some old mates from college arrived in town and we went out for some drinks and fair to say, I got slaughtered. I was so sick the following morning that I couldn't possibly go into work so I asked Sue to cover for me and she said yes.'

'But they found out.'

'Of course they did. We both got hauled in to the headmaster's office like kids and got a roasting for it. It wasn't so bad for me, but Sue was in her probationary year, newly qualified, and needed to make a good impression, which that most definitely wasn't. She just about passed the year and I promised that I would never put her in that kind of situation again. Anyway, after the Sutton Park thing I wasn't sacked. I got a perfectly good reference when I resigned.'

'Oh come on, mate, you know better than that. Schools never actually sack people, do they? They've got their reputations to worry about.'

'Yeah, well, so do I, and I'd like to think that nine years

pretty much speaks for itself, reputation-wise.'

'I don't want you to take this the wrong way, but why are you even still here?'

Nathan frowned. 'Not sure there's a right way to take that...'

'I mean, you've got a degree – you're a qualified teacher, for God's sake – and some of the people you work with haven't even finished high school. Shit, man, you should be doing Lorna's job by now.'

Nathan shrugged, trying not to let Robbie see how much this line of conversation nettled him; talk of the future made him far more uncomfortable than talk of the past. 'I like what I do. I'm good at it. I'm a long way from being the best, but I'm not particularly ambitious either. I suppose at the end of the day it's my time to waste. My round, I think.' He scooped up their empty glasses and went to the bar before Robbie could say anything.

THE PING OF NATHAN'S PHONE WOKE HIM IN THE EARLY hours, and he floundered upward from sleep. Reception was notoriously unpredictable in this part of Snowdonia and it wasn't unusual for messages to come through hours or even days after they'd been sent, or for dead zones to suddenly get full signal for no reason. This wasn't the first time he'd forgotten to switch the bloody thing off and paid the price. The screen lit his room with a cold, undersea glow.

His quarters at Bryncaer was a reconditioned Portakabin furnished with bits of scavenged furniture; what little wall-space he had was cluttered with climbing harnesses, ropes, waterproof clothing, and the overlapping sheets of Ordnance Survey maps. Calling Bryncaer an 'outdoor education centre' was somewhat grandiose given that it was basically a rambling eighteenth-century farmhouse whose outbuildings had been converted into dormitories, classrooms, equipment stores and workshops, and due to the nomadic nature of its employees – primarily young people who were only looking as far ahead as the next season's climbing – accommodation was as basic as the owners could get away with. Nathan, as a long-timer, was accorded the unimaginable luxury of having a whole Portakabin to himself.

He grunted, rolled over, and clawed the phone towards him. A Facebook notification. Jesus, was that all? He looked at the time. It was just past four.

He checked the link anyway. What he saw woke him up like a bucket of cold water: it was a link to a news article.

Human remains found in nature reserve

Police were called to Sutton Park, West Midlands, at about 7:00 GMT on 17 July after the remains were found by a member of the public.

The death of the unidentified person is being treated as unexplained, but it is not yet believed to be suspicious, police said. The local beauty spot is a designated Site of Special Scientific Interest due to its unique wildlife and archaeological remains, and experts are currently working to determine...

But it wasn't the article that made his blood run cold – it was the identity of the person who had sent it to him.

> **Susannah Vickers**
> shared a link on your timeline.

Wide awake now, he stared at it. That was all it said. What it should have said was

> **Susannah Vickers**, who used to be called **Susannah Jones** and once shared a bed and almost a child with you but didn't share your vague and half-arsed dreams for the future, and then finally shared nothing for years except a need to forget that any of it happened at all, has shared a link on your timeline.

There was no message, no comments, no profile picture, and when he tried to follow up her details he found that her privacy controls were so tightly screwed down that he couldn't even find out how many friends she had, never mind who they were or whether they included a husband or children. His finger wavered over the SEND FRIEND REQUEST icon like a metronome ticking off eternities of indecision. In the end, he didn't. She'd made the effort to track him down but only to send that link and nothing else. So, if she didn't want to be friends, then why send it? Was she warning him? Or accusing him? Did she, God forbid, think that it might be nothing more than a matter of passing interest to him, as if it were on the same level as a video of a bloody skateboarding dog?

Underneath the post he commented, *Thanks, I think*. Then he typed, *How are you?* and deleted it and retyped it and deleted it again half a dozen times before deleting the whole thing and dropping his phone to the floor in frustration. Its dead glow continued to fill the room.

Bring on the ghosts, he thought. It was the living he couldn't deal with.

5

THE FLOOD

'So what did Lorna say when you asked her for a day off?' asked Robbie.

'Her exact words were "Get tae fuck, ye lazy gobshite",' Nathan said, getting out of the van. Robbie had given him a lift into Betws-y-Coed, the nearest town with a train station. It was a picture-postcard tourist trap of slate-roofed hotels and gift shops, with narrow streets and humpbacked bridges which would become choked with walkers and sightseers by lunchtime, but the four-hour journey Nathan had ahead of him meant that he needed to catch the earliest train of the day and the only signs of life in town at the moment were delivery trucks and a few hard-core hikers heading out while the hills were still quiet. 'No, not really,' he added. 'She said it was fine. I'm owed time, anyway. I think she was a bit pissed off that it was short notice, but she said it was okay because you'd do my clean-up rota.'

Robbie laughed. 'Fuck off.'

'Love you too, honey. Don't wait up.'

He slammed the van door and went into the station to find out how badly he was going to get screwed for a day return to Sutton Coldfield Station.

HE'D EXPECTED TO CATCH UP ON HIS BROKEN NIGHT'S sleep, but instead found himself hypnotised by the passing landscape. It was something of a shock to realise that in nine years he'd never been back. It wasn't that he'd been living the life of a hermit – he'd odd-jobbed around the country and followed the seasonal winter work to Europe and even led school expedition groups to Africa – but in all that time, either by chance or subconscious choice, he'd shied away from the Midlands.

As the train took him closer, with changes at Llandudno and Crewe, the country became flatter and more populated and gave way to the edgelands of suburbia and semi-wild industrial buffer zones which filled the gaps between not-quite-separate towns, and he realised that he was looking to see what had changed, even though he had no clear recollection of what it had ever been like in the first place. He fixated on buildings, road junctions, signs and places which he told himself could not have existed nine years ago, because otherwise he found himself experiencing the uneasy sensation that while he was moving forward in space he was also moving backward in time.

Then there was the change at Birmingham New Street and a slow crawl on a suburban line, and by mid-morning he found himself standing outside the main gates of Sutton Park.

He tried to tell himself that there was no reason why this business should have had anything to do with his missing kids. The park was huge and ancient; these 'skeletal remains' were more likely to be the victim of some random and tragic crime. And yet the kids had shown themselves to him on the mountain, he was certain of that. Something much deeper and more powerful than his reason told him that they were connected – Sue must have felt it too, otherwise why send him the link in the first place?

He stopped at the small hexagonal visitors' centre and waited while a friendly ranger dealt with the enquiries of a family. Inside there was the predictable range of tourist maps and leaflets, interpretation boards and treasure hunts, but also a large glass case containing stuffed examples of the park's wildlife. A badger stared at him with glassy eyes. He stared back, and lost.

'I heard there's been some excitement,' he said, when it was his turn at the counter. 'Police in the park?'

The ranger was tall, with glasses and a young man's beard, but canny enough to know that Nathan's question wasn't just idle curiosity. 'I couldn't say, I'm afraid. The bottom stretch of Longmoor Valley has been closed to the public. You'll see the signs, but not much more than that.'

'Fair enough.' Nathan smiled, polite and harmless. 'I'll keep out of everybody's way.'

HE RETRACED THE ROUTE HE'D TAKEN WITH RYAN, SCATTIE, Bran and Liv, replaying the details of their banter, leaving the path exactly as he had left it before and striking through the dense holly to find the path up to the Jamboree Stone. He replayed the row with Sue, knowing how he must seem to the people he passed – a lone man having a one-sided argument with himself – but not caring because the colours of his memory were so vivid that the rest of the living world was nothing more than an insubstantial shadow.

There were walkers picnicking up by the memorial stone, just like before, and an ice-cream van, so he bought two cones and then had to eat both once he'd realised what he'd done, walking westward out towards the copse of trees from where he'd watched the group toiling along Rowton Bank towards him in the sun. He'd sat here and tried to imagine the faces of the people who had also sat here for thousands of years – labourers, farmers, lovers – and knew that there was now another: the shade of himself.

Looking south, he saw the distant flutter of blue police tape, and knew that it couldn't be one of the kids that had been found; they had come right up here, crossed the stream by the well, just below him, and continued up the valley on the other side.

Yes, on a timber track of which no evidence was ever found, remember that? He'd brought the police up here several times in the days of frantic searching which had followed, and it was the absence of anything resembling a bridge, compounded by his equal insistence that he had *seen* it, which had hardened their suspicion of him more than anything else. To their minds, if he'd been lying about that he could have been lying about all sorts of things.

He carried on, past Rowton's Well where a man was letting his dogs drink, to the edge of the stream. It was low, fed only by the area's springs in this dry season. It trickled over a bed of rounded pebbles between banks cut low into the black peat, shaded by the branches of birch trees like the long hair of young women thrown forward to dry in the sun. Its sound was a secretive whispering, and he crept forward to listen more closely.

WITH A WHINE OF ELECTRIC MOTORS A WINCH STARTED TO turn, and Rowton Man slowly began to rise from his grave. In the end it had been far simpler and quicker for Tara and her team to remove the mummy along with the surrounding earth in one large block, once the basic excavation had been completed and the finds logged. She couldn't begin to calculate the significance of what they'd uncovered so far.

The cable ran over a trestle framework erected above the excavation. It was attached to a pair of wide cargo straps running under the block, which had been wrapped in layers of protective foam, plastic sheeting, and good old-fashioned bubble wrap. The whole mass was heavy and unwieldy, and Tara held her breath as it inched clear of the surface.

'Steady…' she murmured.

'Hey, Steady is my middle name,' said Simon, the winch operator. He was one of three undergraduate diggers she'd been able to scrounge together to help out with the excavation. It had been mainly heavy spadework, loosening the block from the ground and then wrapping it up so that it could be transported to the Queen Elizabeth Hospital for a proper examination before the warmth of the open air could restart the decomposition process. Still, they'd come willingly enough; it was good for their grades and they'd have something to brag about in the pub to their mates.

'I thought they said your middle name was Shadow,' laughed one of them, Callie, a West Country girl with blue hair. 'On account of that time you spent a day digging the shadow of an electricity pylon because you thought it was a wall line?'

'Hey, I wasn't the wanker who put it on the pre-excavation plan in the first place!'

Tara shushed them fiercely and watched another inch of the block clear the surface. If it started swinging...

'Jesus Christ, is that a fucking spear?'

The thing with begging undergrads to drop everything at no notice in the middle of their summer holidays and help out on a dig unpaid, she thought, was that you couldn't be choosy about who turned up.

'No, Callie,' she said. 'It's a probable bronze artefact until we get a closer look at it.'

'Sorry, Doc.'

But there was definitely something pointed and green with verdigris lying under the figure, and her heart quickened at the sight.

There was a large wheeled trolley nearby, of the sort used to transport landscaping material in garden centres, ready to transport the block out of the work shelter and over to the van which she'd hired (and had to jump through another dozen bureaucratic hoops just to get permission to bring up here), and as soon as the block came free of the ground it would have to be swung over to the trolley, rotated through ninety degrees and lowered gently. She and the students hovered close, ready to guide it with their hands.

The bottom of the block cleared the ground.

Without warning, from around its edges gushed a sudden flood of ice-cold water. It was black, and it stank, and it was too fast for any of them to get out of the way. It poured over their feet in a freezing torrent, saturating their shoes, making them leap away with cries of shock.

The stream's whisper rose to a sudden roar, and Nathan backed away hurriedly as a surge of black water came barrelling down towards him, sluicing over a crude wooden footbridge which hadn't been there before. It passed in a single wave and was gone, as if someone further upstream had opened the gates of a small dam, but Nathan hardly noticed; his attention was fixed on the track.

It was constructed from lengths of timber set end to end, held in place with smaller pegs hammered into the ground, as it zigzagged up the opposite bank. As he gazed at it, he became aware that, without there having been any movement, a human figure was watching him from the trees on the other side. It was like an image of a face emerging from a puzzle mosaic, as if it had always been there and only required a shift in his perception to be seen.

The man was large and dressed in layers of animal furs,

coarsely woven fabric leggings fastened around with birch-bark strips, and a scarf wrapped around his face. Only a pair of glittering eyes and the stub of a nose were visible. He must have been sweltering; whoever he was, he looked like he was dressed for arctic conditions rather than midsummer.

'Who are you supposed to be?' Nathan asked. 'Bark Foot?'

Whether startled by the name or just the simple fact of being seen, Nathan couldn't tell, but the figure abruptly turned and walked away, upstream through the trees.

'No! Hey! Wait!' he called, and pushed through the trailing strands of birch branches on his own side of the stream to reach the timber track – but it was gone. The opposite bank was empty marsh, just as before. No higher ground, and no trees. He splashed across the stream anyway to the other side, but it was no use, just as it had never been any use. The doors to whatever secrets were being withheld from him had slammed shut in his face again and he could do nothing but throw his curses into the bright, empty air.

THE BLOCK, UNCHECKED, SWUNG FREE AND COLLIDED WITH one of the trestle legs, nearly toppling the whole thing.

'Somebody grab that!' yelled Tara.

With much shouting and staggering in the suddenly sodden ground they managed to get the penduluming block under control, and lowered it to the trolley.

They took a breather, grinning at each other, splashed with black mud up to the knees.

'Right,' said Tara, tugging her work gloves up. 'Now for the hard bit.'

'Um, Dr Doumani?' Her third shovel-monkey, Shandeep, whom she had sent out to open up the back of the van, was peering around the shelter's door-flap, looking nervous.

'What is it, Shan?'

'Uh, well, it's the van.'

'What about it?'

'Best if you come see.'

Tara sighed. 'Have you got this?' she asked Callie and Simon. They nodded. 'No playing silly buggers with it while I'm gone, all right?' They shook their heads. She followed Shan out of the shelter to see what the fuss was about, and swore in a most un-academic manner when she saw what had been done to the van she'd hired.

The wheels had been slashed, and huge, scrawling letters had been scratched into the paintwork along one side:

PUT HIM BACK

Seething, she took out her phone and dialled DI Hodges. Her dig had just become a crime scene again.

BARK FOOT IS JUST ONE OF MANY LONG-FORGOTTEN NAMES he has worn in the countless time that is no time in Un. It will serve as well as any.

He retreats to his camp – the clearing in the forest from which he guards the timber track into the world – and listens to his ancient enemy howling and smashing away its frustration amongst the trees, incensed at how close it has come to escaping. The shock of being severed from the earth's embrace had made him lose his grip on the track for a fleeting moment – but no more than that. The world remains safe. He fulfils his purpose.

All the same, he is weakened now, and will only become weaker. He settles down by his fire and fancies that in the *afaugh*'s screams he can hear a new note of triumph.

6

SUE

All Nathan had intended to do was have a look at the site where those 'skeletal remains' were being examined and, if he was lucky, pick someone's brains about what or who it was they'd found. He hadn't meant to stay much longer than a few hours before catching the last train back to Betws. He hadn't planned on having to squelch his way along Sutton Coldfield High Street shopping for dry clothes. He certainly hadn't expected to find himself booking a room for the night at the nearest cheap hotel – he didn't know why, only that he wasn't ready to leave. But the most surprising thing of all was how he found himself standing outside an apartment block in Hall Green staring at the list of names on the buzzer panel, and kicking himself because of course Sue wouldn't be living here any more. She was married; her name was Vickers now. She could be living at the other end of the country for all he knew.

He pressed the button for her apartment anyway.

Nothing happened. He was just about to press it again

when a woman's voice which wasn't hers ventured, 'Hello? Who is it?'

He realised he had no idea what he was going to say. 'Um,' he tried, but more seemed necessary. 'I'm looking for, uh, a Miss Susannah Jones. I don't suppose you've heard of her, have you?'

'Are you a friend of hers?' The voice had a tremulous quality, which suggested age.

Where to begin with *that* one. 'Yes,' he replied helplessly.

'Then you'd better come up, dear.' The door buzzed, and he entered the echoing stairwell.

Sue's apartment was (*had been*, he told himself), number five, on the first floor. The walls were still painted lilac, but he saw pot-plants on the landing which were new, and in his memory she's

FUMBLING HER KEY IN THE LOCK AND GIGGLING, WHILE HE leans against the door frame and watches her breasts shift inside her blouse as she bends over; they're both drunk, but not so much that they won't be fucking each other's brains out in about ten minutes on the other side of that door. He's had a few lovers at college – nothing outrageous, he doesn't consider himself to be a 'player' like some of the lads who would screw anything in a spangly micro-skirt, but enough to know what a rare and incredible turn-on it is to find in Sue someone who is just as open and insistent on what she wants. She is the first woman he's had sex with who keeps her gaze locked firmly on his when she comes, and in that weightless moment – when time itself is caught and suspended in the space between each gasping spasm – he sees something which might be eternity in her eyes, or the closest a mortal soul can come to comprehending it. To not fall in love with her, even knowing that for her this is just a bit of fun, becomes impossible

THE DOOR OPENED, ON THE SECURITY CHAIN, AND A LITTLE old lady peered through the gap. 'I'm terribly sorry, dear,' she said, 'but would you mind telling me how you know her?'

'We used to be colleagues. Teachers. I've been abroad for a few years and wanted to catch up, but I think my address book needs updating.' He smiled sheepishly, trying to look just like another member of the feckless younger generation. It seemed to do the trick; the chain fell away, and the old lady opened the door a little wider. She was holding a bundle of envelopes in one hand.

'Oh, that's lovely,' she cooed. 'You know, if you'd said anything else I wouldn't have believed you. Can't be too careful these days, can you? You'll be the perfect person to give her these when you see her, then.' She handed him the bundle. It was mostly junk mail – circulars, catalogues, union mail-shots – but on each item the old lady had written Sue's new address in neat, miniscule handwriting. 'I usually pop them in the post once a month or so – I suppose I could tell the post office to redirect it for her but it's a reason to get out, isn't it? It's just that the stairs are getting a bit tricky for me these days. Would you like to come in and have a cup of tea?'

Nathan managed to extricate himself with the minimum of polite small talk and retreated downstairs with his prize.

HER NEW ADDRESS WAS A VERY SUBURBAN SEMI-DETACHED house with a neat hedge, a hanging basket by the front door, and a gleaming little sky-blue Ford in the drive. He tried not to feel like some kind of psycho stalker nutjob as he walked slowly past it for the fourth time, even though some of the neighbourhood kids were having bike races up and down the pavement in the afternoon sun, and if he'd been one of their parents he knew exactly what he must have looked like. He was so tightly wound that when he saw Sue's front door start to open he nearly lost his nerve completely and ran.

The reason that he didn't was because she was backing out of the doorway for some reason and that gave him an opportunity to see her without being seen first. Her hair was longer, and she'd stopped dyeing it; it was a much darker blond than he remembered. Then she turned and he saw why – she'd been manoeuvring a pushchair, into which was strapped a pink-faced toddler swatting at a row of plastic dangly toys.

She had a kid.

It shouldn't have come as such a shock. She'd moved – he knew that. Everybody did. She'd married – but then he'd known that was on the cards when they'd started seeing each other. She'd clearly stuck with it, though, which was nice.

But still – she had a child. She was someone's mother.

'Nathan? Jesus Christ – *Nathan?*'

He'd been so frozen with surprise that the option to run was now entirely academic.

'Hi.' It was simply the first sound his mouth made.

She stared at him. Nine years hadn't made that much difference; maybe she was a little fuller-figured (*Childbirth will do that, you know,* he thought, and squashed it), but the incredible lucidity of her grey-green eyes still had the power to paralyse him.

'Hi?' she echoed, incredulous. 'What do you mean, "hi"? What the f—' She stopped, took a deep breath, absent-mindedly stroked the toddler's wispy fair hair and said, with glacial control, 'What are you doing here, Nathan?'

'I don't really know,' he admitted. 'I was thinking maybe we could go for a coffee? Bit of a chat? Catch up on old times?'

'Old times.' She shook her head and moved the pushchair past him, leaving him no option but to hurry after her as she strode away down the pavement so fast that the plastic wheels of the pushchair rattled like castanets.

'You sent me that link,' he said. 'You know, the body in Sutton Park?'

'I know!' she snapped. 'I was sort of expecting that you would go there, not turn up at my front door. My God, Nathan, what if Steven had seen you?'

'What if he had? He doesn't know that you and me had a thing, does he?'

She strode on, face set forward, not looking at him, not replying.

'You didn't tell him, did you?'

'You don't get to know anything about what I talk about

with my husband,' she said fiercely. 'I sent you that link because I know how badly that whole business affected you, and I thought you would want to know. That's all. It wasn't an invitation for you to doorstep your way back into my life.'

'Well you know me,' he laughed, trying to make light of it. 'Never could take no for an answer.'

'No, Nathan, what you never could take was a hint, so let me spell it out for you. Go. Away.'

He threw his hands up, exasperated. 'Fine! I'm gone! Sorry to have troubled your perfect little suburban whatever-this-is. But I never asked you to cover for me, remember that. I kept my promise. They questioned me for three days because I wouldn't tell them I was with you instead of my group, and those three days cost me my job – you remember that when Steve comes back from whatever job he does to pay for the roof over your head. Forgive me for being curious to see what it looks like.' She opened her mouth to retort but he cut her off. 'Oh, I know, you didn't ask me to be your white knight – you made that very clear – and you don't owe me anything, not even gratitude, but at the very least I could really do without you chewing me a new arsehole. Oh, and I brought your post.'

He offered her the bundle of junk mail.

She stared at it, then laughed shortly and pressed the heels of her hands to her eyes. 'I'm sorry,' she sighed, as if deflating.

'Me too,' he muttered.

The kid in the stroller swatted at his row of plastic toys and babbled, happy and oblivious.

'I was going down the High Street to pick up some stuff,' she said. 'Have you got time for a coffee? We could try talking about this like civilised adults instead of yelling in the street.'

'Probably best if I don't,' he replied, after some consideration. He waved around at the neighbouring houses. 'You'll want to be keeping the curtain twitching down to a minimum, I imagine.'

'Oh, fuck the lot of them,' she said. 'But fair enough. I'm sorry I went off at you like that. It was just a bit of a shock, you know, after so long. It was good to see you again, all the same.'

'No it wasn't.'

He left on that and wandered off in search of a bus that would take him back to his hotel. He was halfway there when his phone pinged to tell him that he had a text from an unknown number.

Yes it was.

7

DISSECTIONS

TARA HAD EXPECTED ROWTON MAN TO YIELD UP COUNTLESS revelations about his life and the world he inhabited over decades of examination by experts in every field from all over the world, but he turned all of their expectations inside out within a few hours, and before they'd even started to remove the peat from around his body.

The CT scanner which her department was leasing was one of five at Birmingham's Queen Elizabeth Hospital Imaging Department – a huge, gleaming white donut of an X-ray toroid into which he was being fed slowly, securely cocooned in protective foam and insulated by a layer of peat, which kept his remains in a stable chemical state, the idea being to limit physical intervention as much as possible. The scanner was slicing him digitally a fraction of a millimetre at a time and feeding the data to a scanning tomography computer, which was building up a complete three-dimensional image of his body at a resolution high enough to distinguish individual sweat pores and swirls of his fingertips. Ultimately, physical dissection would be unavoidable, but for a good long while his virtual cadaver would be available online to archaeologists, doctors, dentists, anthropologists, and even high-school students all over the world. He could be examined from the inside out for years without anyone having to see him face to face, a fact which Tara would have found depressing, if she'd had time to think about it. For now, there was simply too much to see.

She shouldered her way into the knot of scientists huddled around the CT workstation's screen. There were plenty of people who would drop everything at twenty-four hours' notice and come running to see Rowton Man in the flesh – as leathery as it was. And every single one of them had an opinion.

'Look at that,' she said, indicating a point on the image of his pelvis. 'The skeletal structure is incredibly intact.' The foetal position in which he'd been buried, with his legs tucked up high against his torso, meant that the scanner was revealing details of his feet and pelvis first.

'Dr Doumani, we all know where you're going with this,' replied one of her colleagues. Professor Alan Reynolds was stubbled and grouchy, having travelled eight hours straight from a University of Pennsylvania dig in Turkey. 'It doesn't provide evidence of a reburial.'

'Oh come on, Alan,' she said, turning back to the screen even as she spoke, reluctant to miss any of Rowton Man's unravelling. 'Look at that tibia cross-section. If he'd been lying in the same place for three thousand years his bones would be like cardboard. You know as well as I do that when we get a sample the level of decalcification is going to be nowhere near that high.'

'I'll take that wager,' he replied. 'Twenty of your English pounds says he's got less calcium in him than a stick of chalk.'

'Are you still using chalk in the States? We have these things called whiteboards now. They're quite good. See if you can pick one up in Duty Free.'

A ripple of laughter ran through the group, Reynolds included. They shook on the bet over her shoulder, as the picture of Rowton Man continued to build.

'Okay,' she said, staring at the mashed ball-and-socket of his hip joint. 'I will admit, that's weird. Does that look like a hole to anyone else?'

Heads craned closer around the screen.

'Where?'

'In the head of his femur.'

'That? I don't know. Possibly.'

'She is right, it is a hole,' put in a round-faced young doctor of anthropology called Amit Rajhkowa who had flown in from Venezuela. 'Zoom that in, right there. Look, there is another one in the socket rim.'

Reynolds wasn't convinced. 'You can't be sure. That could be the result of disease, injury, scavengers, agricultural activity…'

'Look at those scratches around the edges,' said Tara. 'Those are tool marks.'

'So it's a penetrating injury, then,' Dr Rajhkowa suggested. 'We know that subjects who have suffered these are very often the victims of ritual violence.'

At the utterance of the trigger word 'ritual', the room erupted into a babble of argument and counter-argument as each expert weighed in with his or her own particular and incontrovertible piece of evidence for why bog bodies were everything from accident victims to ritually slaughtered tribal chieftains.

'There's no stress fracturing,' Tara pointed out. 'This wasn't punched through with a weapon – I tell you, someone drilled those holes post-mortem.'

'Look at the Chinchorro black mummies,' said Rajhkowa. 'They took the body apart, preserved the pieces and reassembled it with sticks and cords to reinforce it. Maybe that is what we have here: holes to tie the bones together.'

'The Chinchorro were five thousand years earlier and on a different continent,' said Dr Francine Gillespie, lecturer at the University of Sydney, who had been visiting the UK when news of the find had been released.

Rajhkowa shrugged. 'I was just saying.'

'There's a precedent,' said Tara. 'Cranborne Chase, in Dorset. Bournemouth University are currently examining some Middle Bronze Age remains that have holes drilled just like this. Rowton Man wasn't an accident victim or a murdered traveller. They put him in the bog deliberately, just long enough to preserve him – I'd say six months, maybe – and then they took him out again and they strung his bones together so that he wouldn't fall apart. He was probably put on display somewhere. Whoever this was, he was important.'

'Not too important to stick him back in the ground again, though,' pointed out Reynolds. 'No tomb, no mound.'

'If it's even one person in the first place,' put in Gillespie. 'It could be a composite.'

'Oh please...' Tara groaned. There were limits, after all.

'She's right,' said Reynolds, on her side for once. 'Can everybody's pet batshit-crazy theory please take a number and form an orderly queue?'

But Gillespie wasn't letting it go that easily. 'No, seriously. You brought up Cranborne Chase in the first place, and they were composites. Then there are the Cladh Hallan mummies – two skeletons made up of parts from six distinct individuals. They're the same approximate age: late Bronze Age. If you want to suggest some ritual significance for this bloke...'

'Or blokes,' someone added, to a ripple of laughter.

'...there it is. Your society is transitioning to a more settled, agricultural way of life where ties to the land are politically and spiritually important, so you create an idealised ancestor figure out of bits of grandma and grandpa to legitimise your claim to the land.'

'Goddamned "Frankenstein mummies",' muttered Reynolds. 'I hate the media.'

'If you were a newspaper editor and somebody came to you with a story about a preserved body made up of bits of other people, what would you do?'

'If I were a newspaper editor I'd do the world a favour and kill myself.'

Gillespie squinted at the image. 'You know from this angle that left tibia does look quite a bit thicker than the right.'

'Oh that could be anything!' Tara was getting exasperated now; it was starting to sound suspiciously like Gillespie was mocking her. 'Diet, childhood injury, polio, variations in peat acidity from one part of its body to another. I suggest we all just calm down and wait for the DNA tests – I'll even throw in an extra one for that leg too, Frankie, if it will make you happy.'

'It would make me ecstatically happy.' She grinned.

There was nothing Tara would have liked more than for Rowton Man to turn out to be a composite mummy, if only for the opportunity it presented to study the pathology of several individuals rather than just one. But there was something about the scan of that left leg that niggled at her. It wasn't the thickness of the tibia – that was too obvious and had too many rational explanations. It was some tiny detail that had snagged on the corner of her eye as the scan progressed, too subtle for her to be conscious of it, but scratching all the same, like a single wrong note played repeatedly in a symphony – impossible to determine its source, and impossible to ignore. But then there was too much else to demand her attention as Rowton Man slipped deeper into the machine and the scan rose higher.

His lower spine and abdomen appeared, and then the chest and the rest of his tightly folded legs, including the knee joints, which also had putative drill holes. The scientists quibbled and conjectured over the possible contents of his stomach, his probable body weight, and the evidence for his age being anywhere from late adolescence to middle age. There was debate, compromise and often heated argument over which examinations would be conducted and in which order. Tara felt the familiar simultaneous guilt at plundering the dead man's secrets combined with excitement at the prospect of what those secrets might tell her about his life and his world.

All the same, that underlying sense of wrongness persisted through the discussion, and through the delegates' curry and the pub afterwards, making her conversation curt and unsociable. She spent what was left of that night poring over the scans, and when she found what was wrong it was *so* wrong that she assumed that fatigue was making her eyes play stupid tricks and forced herself to crash for a few hours of fretful sleep.

But it was still there when she woke up.

It remained there when she went back into the pathology lab and ordered it closed to all visitors while she ran and re-ran every diagnostic test on the equipment that she could think of, half-afraid and half-hoping that it was just some tattered shred of dream that somehow persisted in the waking world. It was preferable to think that she was losing her mind.

And it was most definitely, stubbornly there twelve hours later when her head of faculty, Professor Anna Hayden, finally tracked her down and demanded to know what the hell was going on.

Hayden's specialty was in Oceanic folklore and mythology, and she had the wiry, sun-toughened frame of someone who spent a lot of time travelling in remote tropical locations, usually by her own leg-power. She'd inherited the headship almost by default after her predecessor had left under a cloud of sexual impropriety, though this was no slur on her leadership skills; she was happy to give her colleagues as much freedom as she could, which was why, when she did step in, it was never trivial.

'There you are,' she said. Tara was surrounded by a litter of printouts and half-empty cups of vending-machine coffee. 'How's it all going down here?' Tara saw her looking around at the steel benches and the machines and the gleaming sterility of it all with her hands thrust deeply into her pockets and knew that this was one of the last places on earth she would choose to visit. Hayden's interests were anthropological, her laboratory the campfires and story-telling spaces of indigenous peoples.

'Um, badly?'

Hayden responded with a thin smile. 'I have an inbox full of angry emails from our international research partners who would very much like to know why their representatives – who they've gone to a lot of trouble and expense to send here for a look at our bog mummy – now can't get anywhere near it.'

'Because it's wrong.'

'Wrong.'

'Yes, wrong.'

Hayden waited for more, but more didn't seem to be forthcoming. 'Wrong as in…?'

'Let me show you.' Tara pulled up a high-resolution image of Rowton Man's left ankle and turned the screen so that Hayden could see it better. 'Dr Gillespie was right – it is a composite mummy. I mean, *most* of the remains are from one person – male, probably early twenties – but the lower jaw, right clavicle, several ribs, the right arm below the elbow and the left leg below the knee are from different individuals. I'm still waiting for DNA results on those. But it's the leg that is the problem. Down there, just above the knobbly bit on the inside of the ankle, do you see those lines running across the bone?'

Hayden peered closely. 'Yes?'

'Those are heal lines. At some point in this person's life they suffered a medial malleolar fracture – it's not uncommon in people with active physical lives, like athletes or Bronze Age hunters, say. You jump and land the wrong way, or you roll your foot in a rabbit hole and snap.'

'Ouch,' Hayden winced.

'Yep. Very painful. Now look just above and below those heal lines. Look really closely. See those wider, shadowy lines?'

'Yes, I think so. What are they?'

'They,' said Tara, glaring at the impossible image, 'are residual screw holes.'

'What do you mean, screw holes?'

'An ankle fracture like that is often pinned because it's such an awkward joint, and you don't want any chance of it healing crooked. When the pins come out the holes heal, but you can still see where they were. Whoever this was, he or she was treated with modern orthopaedic surgery.'

'That can't be. Are you sure?'

'Tell me about it. I've opened it up and looked for myself. I can show you that too, if you like.'

'I'll pass, thanks. But that means... Shit, we're going to have to call the police.'

Tara gave a short, humourless laugh. 'They're going to be sick of the sight of me. They were there right at the start. I told them that they didn't have a murder victim on their hands because the remains were three thousand years old.'

'But you didn't test this specific leg, obviously.'

'Obviously, because I didn't know it was a composite body. I've tested it since, of course, just to be thorough.' Tara's voice was hollow. She felt on the ragged edge of utter exhaustion, or something worse. 'It's three thousand years old too.'

'That's not possible.'

'I know it isn't. But it's there. I've checked and rechecked everything. The carbon doesn't lie. That three-thousand-year-old leg was treated, *when the patient was alive*, by twenty-first-century surgery.'

Hayden shook her head briskly. 'There must be something wrong with the testing process, then. Or your samples. Some kind of contamination. You need to run it again.'

'I've already run everything four times. I don't think a fifth is going to make much difference.'

'Definition of insanity, isn't it? Doing the same thing over and over again and expecting different results?'

'Yes, but what if it's the results that are insane?'

They both stared at the image in silence. Then Hayden reached across the keyboard and very deliberately pressed the escape key, dismissing the image of Rowton Man, and turned to look straight at Tara. Tara thought she saw something in the other woman's face actually *close*, like shutters going down behind her eyes.

'Then we do what we do with the incurably insane,' said her boss. 'We make them go away.'

Tara gestured helplessly at the blank screen, and there was a raw edge to her voice as she protested, 'You can't just make...'

'Yes we can,' Hayden overrode her with quiet authority. 'We have to. For you, for me, the faculty, the university as a whole.'

'We can't just lie...'

'Yes. We. Can. Do you know how much this project is worth to us in grants? You know as well as I do how much everybody's budgets have been cut, year after year. Think of what we can afford with what Rowton Man brings in. Anyway, nobody's asking you to lie. Bring the others back in and let them have access to examine him inside and out, top to bottom. If someone else finds this too, then so be it – let them have the headache of trying to figure it out.'

Tara shoved her chair back from the desk and got up. 'Come here,' she said, grasping Hayden by the arm and leading her to the lab door. 'I want you to see something.' She steered Hayden out of the CT monitor room, through the lab and over towards where Rowton Man lay in his steel tray, on a bed of the same peat in which he'd been buried, black and shining and twisted, as if frozen in a moment of eternal agony. 'Look at him,' she demanded. 'And if they discover that part of this body is from a teenager who went missing nine years ago, not three thousand, and the whole thing is splashed all over the newspapers, we all become a laughing stock. What do I say to the police then? What do I say to the parents?'

Hayden shrugged. 'That you missed it. It's a completely missable thing. The initial test that tells you that it's prehistoric isn't *wrong*, is it?'

'Well, no...'

'Well then, if it's just your reputation you're worried about, how can you be criticised for failing to find something that shouldn't have been there in the first place?'

'Jesus, Anna, it's not my reputation that I'm worried about!'

'Well it bloody should be!' Hayden snapped, her voice low and hard. 'I'm not exaggerating when I say this, Dr Doumani: by keeping your colleagues locked out while you faff around like this you are currently making yourself and this department look extremely unprofessional and endangering millions of pounds in grant money. That's not the sort of career car-crash you walk away from. I understand that this current problem with the mummy's leg is proving to be problematic for you, so I'll do you a favour and make it very simple: get this project back online by the end of the week or I'll find someone who will.'

8

INTRUSIONS

THE CRASH OF BREAKING GLASS SPLINTERED TARA'S SLEEP and she thrashed around in the dark like a deep-sea fish dragged to the surface, choking and turning inside out. One hand connected with her alarm clock. Ten past two.

She blinked at it. *What in God's name?*

Footfalls downstairs, in her living room.

She froze, listening. The sheet – all that covered her due to the night's mugginess in this heatwave – was bunched by her knees, and she pulled it slowly up to her chin. It wasn't much protection, but it was better than nothing. There was only the clock's slow, complacent tick and the hollow hammering of her own heart, and for half a minute, which felt like hours, she was able to tell herself that she'd imagined it. The dim shapes of her bedroom held fast in the light from the street lamp in the alley behind her house; her curtains and window were open also because of the heat. The back gate had been bolted securely, top and bottom. Hadn't it? Maybe it hadn't been – maybe in all the excitement of the dig she'd forgotten it. Maybe, because it was such a habitual part of her routine, she'd only thought she'd done it?

There was a soft, slithering, bumping noise, as if something was being dragged around. Her bedroom was at the back of the house, directly above the living room; whatever was happening, it sounded like it was right under her bed.

What's happening is that you're being burgled, that's what's happening, you stupid idiot, she told herself. *Now do something about it!* She reached for her phone to dial 999.

'Police emergency,' said the operator; female, calm. 'Can I help?'

'Someone's broken into my house,' Tara murmured, as loud as she dared. 'He's still inside.'

'Okay, what's your address, please?'

She followed the operator's instructions, confirming her name and address, that she lived on her own, and answering half a dozen other questions which she suspected had less to do with any information the police needed and more to do with keeping her calm while they were on their way, which was just fine with her.

'Only a few minutes now,' the operator assured her. 'Do you have any way of securing your bedroom door?'

'Not really.'

'How about the bathroom? Is it upstairs too? Does it have a lock on the door? Would you feel able to shut yourself in there?'

'Yes, yes, and probably not, but sod it.'

She crept to the door, mindful of the creaking floorboards, which had never seemed a priority, and tried not to berate herself. It wasn't as if the home security aisle of her local hardware store had a section on floor screws for those all-important moments when you had to sneak around to avoid the burglars.

Her bathroom overlooked the front of the house at the end of a short hallway; to reach it she had to pass the staircase landing, currently home to a tall wicker laundry basket overflowing with washing that she hadn't had time for. The staircase was dark, but not silent.

Another of those strange, slithering bumps, this time accompanied by the jittering glow of a torch from downstairs.

Nope, no way, not doing this. She reverse-tiptoed back to her room – but just before she did so she hooked one toe around a bra strap dangling over the basket's edge, and flicked it inside. No stranger was getting an eyeful of her smalls, burglar or no burglar.

By the time flashing blue lights appeared and policemen were knocking on her front door, the strange sounds from her living room had ceased, and she hung up on the control room operator with heartfelt thanks. The police didn't seem to mind her double-checking their ID, as if the car with the fluorescent harlequin paint job wasn't verification enough. A young single female victim of a home invasion was entitled to a lower threshold for paranoia. Together they inspected the damage.

The intruder had taken one of the large stones from the border of her garden path and lobbed it through the sliding door that gave onto the back patio. It lay in a debris of mud, weeds and broken glass. More mud had been trodden around the room – great clots of it, as if a crew of construction workers had decided to perform a bit of impromptu line dancing on her rug.

'Does that mean anything to you, miss?' asked one of the police constables, pointing to what had been done to the empty expanse of wall above her radiator. The source of the strange thumping-scraping noise had become quickly apparent. Someone had taken great handfuls of black, peaty soil – which she knew, if she analysed it, would be a perfect match for that of the bog from which she had removed Rowton Man – and written in big, sweeping, smeared letters a yard high:

PUT HIM BACK

IT WASN'T A DATE, SUE HAD BEEN VERY CLEAR ABOUT THAT. Repeatedly. In capitals. She always took Matty and Jake to the museum in town for Family Fundays during the holiday, and if Nathan was going to be there too that was entirely up to him. He wasn't going to be buying anybody any ice creams. Oh, and remember how she was actually married now? All the same, her hair was styled and she was wearing more make-up than when he'd seen her last; something made him hope it was his presence that had caused the change.

Nathan thought that the family craft corner of Birmingham Museum was as close to a physical incarnation of hell as he was ever likely to experience. Teenagers he could handle; they could be reasoned with, after a fashion, or at the very least bribed. These knee-height creatures that swarmed around the activity tables dressed in plastic multi-coloured smocks and clutching fistfuls of crayons seemed to obey no known patterns of predictable behaviour. Any one of them was likely to be drawing with rapt concentration one second and screaming around the room being a pterodactyl the next, which was weird because the theme for the week was Anglo-Saxons.

It was all tied in with the latest display of artefacts from the Staffordshire Hoard, which Nathan had been to see while he was waiting for Sue, marvelling along with the rest of the queuing tourists at how so much gold could have been lying just inches from the surface of a field for over a thousand years.

Not a date, that was understood. He bought her a coffee anyway.

She was helping her eldest, Jacob, colour in a picture of an Anglo-Saxon warrior while his little brother, Matthew, occupied himself by whacking passers-by with a foam sword from the vantage point of his stroller.

'They're good kids,' he said. 'You should be proud.'

Sue narrowed her eyes, suspecting sarcasm.

'No, really!'

She relaxed and took the offered cup, leaving Jake to get on with his drawing. 'It's the worst cliché in the world,' she said, 'but they really are my life. Right now, I mean.'

'You have schools lined up for them?'

She smiled into her coffee. 'Do you know how ridiculous small talk sounds, coming out of your mouth?'

'Sorry,' he grimaced. 'I don't know how this is supposed to go.'

She sighed and swirled her coffee. 'I don't think it's supposed to go at all,' she replied.

'Right then,' he said, brisk and decisive. 'Conversational rule number one: real things only.'

'Right then. "The time has come, the Walrus said,"' she recited, '"to talk of many things: of shoes – and ships – and sealing wax – of cabbages – and kings." You're the cabbage, in case you were wondering.'

'This isn't going to make much more sense, I'm afraid,' he replied. 'The thing is, ever since you sent me that link to the article about the bog body, I've been seeing... having visions, I think. Of them.'

'Who?'

'Who do you think?'

She sat back. 'Shit.'

'Yep, that.'

'I don't understand – what do you mean by visions?'

He explained, expecting her to come to the inevitable conclusion that he was a few sandwiches short of a picnic and call security, but she listened carefully, seriously, not mocking, non-judgemental.

'Try not to take this the wrong way,' she said at the end, 'but I think it's pretty evident that you're having some kind of breakdown, isn't it?'

'You know, I'm actually beginning to hope so.'

Jake was trying to get Sue's attention, to show her what he had drawn. He'd left off colouring in the warrior and instead had given him some companions. There were three of them. One had red shoes, one had a knife, and the third had a bright pink cape with a big black skull-and-crossbones on it. Proud of his creation, he ran off to play in the ballpit, oblivious to the looks of horror that passed between his mummy and her strange new friend.

THIS IS A WEAKNESS SUCH AS HE HAS NEVER KNOWN, THIS unearthing.

At the start, the spirit-dancers kept him strong with offerings of flesh; the strongest arms and swiftest legs of each generation, because he was the One From Many, and he had long since forgotten the name of the warrior who had first given himself to the earth.

Memories failed, and just as he once took the strengths of other bodies to make him stronger, the people who lived in this place took other gods to their protection, and he was forgotten. Those were lean times, and he resorted to acts that shamed him, but with his bones in Mother Earth he at least had her embrace to anchor his spirit. This unearthing makes him as any untethered boat adrift at the mercy of current and tide.

But he now has a spirit-dancer again. Of a sort.

She kneels before him on the other side of the timber track and tries to apologise for her failure.

'They won't listen!' she rails. 'Nobody ever does!'

'Then show them,' he says. 'Find the one who keeps me from the earth and bring her to me, so that she may see the consequences of her actions.'

They can both hear the *afaugh* fretting as it flits between the trees, searching for a way past him. It senses his weakness and is closer than it has dared come for a long time.

'What will you do to her?' asks his new shaman.

'I will show her our common enemy,' he replies, 'and I will defend her. I will defend her to her death.'

9

ABDUCTION

IT WAS LATE, AND THE LONG MIDSUMMER TWILIGHT stretched the world into elongated shadows as if trying to smooth three dimensions into two. Tara felt flat and exhausted, and grateful that for once she didn't have to drive. Since her work for the faculty had already made her the victim of two acts of incomprehensible vandalism, they had agreed to put her up in a suite at the Conference Park hotel on campus – at least while her patio door was being fixed, and possibly for as long as it took the police to catch the nutter responsible. On the plus side, the Wi-Fi was better than home and she didn't have to do any washing-up.

She could have caught a shuttle bus from her office to her temporary accommodation but it was only a few hundred metres, illuminated by bollards all the way, and with campus security all over the place. The only drawback was that it was also where the international delegates were staying, which might lead to a few awkward conversations in the bar – not that she had the energy for it tonight.

She'd be lucky if she made it as far as—

'Excuse me, Dr Doumani?'

She turned. She was in the Conference Park's car park; a young woman in a grey hoodie with the University of Birmingham crest had climbed out of a car and was approaching. A student, by the look of her.

'I'm sorry,' Tara began, 'but I'm afraid I'm far too…'

Then she saw the knife gleaming in the woman's hand, and the woman herself, closer to: a starved face with bruised shadows around the eyes and a bloom of cold sores at one corner of her mouth. But by the time she'd registered these details the knife was up against her stomach and the junkie's bony hand had gripped her wrist.

'Get in the fucking car,' she hissed. 'Or I'll fucking cut you. Get me?'

Tara tried to speak, but nothing worked. She swallowed, her throat desert-dry with fear. 'My… my purse is in my bag,' she croaked. 'Let me—'

The knife drove in – not hard enough to pierce, but not far off – while the restraining hand stopped her from recoiling.

'Okay!' she whimpered, revolted at herself for actually crying, but today had been too much already, just too much. 'Please, just don't.' She glanced back at the wide, bright doors to the Conference Park hotel, barely a dozen metres away. People were in there, towing their luggage to the lifts, chatting with the concierge, signing for keys. A man came out and stood just to one side, lighting a cigarette. It was impossible that none of them could see what was happening. Impossible that this *could* be happening.

The junkie gripped her wrist tighter with fingers like talons, and the knife dug in. 'I ain't going to kill you,' she murmured close to Tara's ear, intimate as a lover, though Tara could smell the rot on her breath. 'But I will seriously fuck you up if you make me. Get. In. The. Car.'

Tara let herself be shoved into the driver's seat of a rusty VW Golf whose footwells were buried in layers of trash and junk-food debris. It stank of old pot and rancid sweat. Her abductor sat directly behind, shifting the knife so that it pricked into her left side just below her ribcage. The keys were in the ignition. What kind of mugging was this?

Tara did as she was ordered, and drove.

THE WOMAN DIDN'T SAY WHERE THEY WERE GOING, JUST grunted directions, but it soon became obvious where they were heading. Tara had driven this way enough times in the past week.

'Why are we going to Sutton Park?' she asked, not expecting an answer, but the one she got made no sense anyway.

'If you won't be told, you'll have to be shown, won't you?'

Then it clicked.

'You were in my house!' she said. 'You trashed my van!'

'You wouldn't be told!'

'Told *what*? Shown *what*? Please, for God's sake will you just tell me what it is you want from me?'

The young woman's voice was at her ear again, snarling. 'I wanted you to just fucking put him back! That wasn't so hard, was it? But no, you've got to go poking and prodding and prying and digging, haven't you, and you've got no fucking clue what it is you're digging up.'

Convinced now that she was dealing with someone far more dangerous than a simple mugger – someone with serious mental health issues – Tara tried to keep her voice as reasonable and level as she could. 'Well why don't you simply tell me?' she asked. 'If I know what I'm disturbing I can try to do something about it.'

The woman laughed; a high, broken bray of derision. 'People like you,' she said, and prodded Tara with the knife for emphasis, 'never believe people like me. That's why you've got to be shown. That's why I'm taking you to meet him yourself.'

'Meet *who*?'

'The man you dug up.'

EVERY TIME TARA CHANGED GEAR SHE WAS UNCOMFORTABLY reminded of the knife angling in from behind and under her left arm. She wondered inconclusively if there was any way she could attract the attention of an oncoming driver, or someone next to her at the traffic lights, or even a pedestrian. But what could she do – wind down the window and scream for help? Assuming that anybody who heard her didn't think she was batshit crazy herself, how many of them would so much as come up to ask if she was okay? None of them, it was certain, would approach quickly enough to prevent the young woman from doing something terrible with that knife. The most anybody was likely to do was film her with their camera phones as she was stabbed to death. She watched in dismay and a boiling, impotent rage as a police car passed them serenely. She even saw the officers' faces lit by a soft blue dashboard glow.

'You're an archaeologist, right?' said the woman suddenly, making her jump.

'What?'

'An archaeologist. Did it take long?'

'I don't know – about seven or eight years altogether, not including school. Why?'

'Yeah,' the woman sneered. 'I bet I know what kind of school, too. Paid for by Mummy and Daddy. Ponies and shit like that.'

Tara should have kept quiet and let the woman rant, but this kind of thing always pushed her buttons, even in polite company. 'My parents are Lebanese, actually,' she found herself saying. 'They escaped the civil war in seventy-eight – a few too many massacres for their liking. My dad worked on the railway and my mum cleaned floors in office buildings, so sorry, but no, there wasn't a lot of money for ponies and shit like that.' She tensed, waiting for the blade, but instead there was a thoughtful pause.

'So, are you, like, a Muslim then?'

'No,' she sighed. 'I'm an archaeologist.'

They lapsed into a brooding silence, which felt like a truce. When the young woman next spoke, her voice had lost its ragged edge of hysteria and become thoughtful, almost dreamy.

'How do you stand knowing what you know?' she asked.

'What do you mean?'

'I mean, like, in eighty-one this man in his garden in Erdington digs up a Stone Age hand axe more than two hundred and fifty thousand years old, right?'

Despite herself, Tara was surprised enough to engage. 'How do you know that?'

'I can *read*, you know.' The knife point punctuated her sudden irritation but then relented as the dreamy tone returned. 'My point is, how do you go back to mucking around in your garden with your, your *petunias* and your *water features* and whatever, when you know that two hundred and fifty thousand years of darkness is right under your feet, waiting to swallow you up? How do any of them?' She waved the knife at the window and what was outside: the cars and the streetlights and the aquarium brightness of shop fronts. 'Because it's so thin, you know? *You* know, because you're under it all the time. I know, because...'

Tara waited. 'Because?'

The reply, when it came, was so faint that she almost didn't catch it. 'Because there are holes, and sometimes people fall in.'

'If you ask me, people should pay more attention to the risk assessments.'

As an attempt at humour – to build on whatever twisted interest in archaeology this woman had and develop some kind of camaraderie – it was horribly miscalculated. She stiffened, jabbed the knife hard enough to make Tara cry out, and hissed, 'Well what would you fucking know, anyway? Miss oh-so-clever, make it nice and safe, put it in a glass box with a nice little interpretation card, "tool marks on the bones indicate probable cannibalism, now run along and do the colouring-in sheet, kiddies", wash the dirt from under your nice perfect fingernails and then go home for supper.' She leaned in close. '*You have no fucking idea what's down that hole.*'

The woman lapsed into moody silence and said nothing more than to give directions until they got to the Banner's Gate car park. For Tara, the sense of déjà vu was sickening; how was it possible that less than a week ago she'd been here surrounded by the safety and sanity of her dig? There were a few cars but no people that she could see; no large groups that she could run to for rescue.

'Take your shoes off,' the woman said, grabbing the keys and getting out.

'My shoes? Why?'

'Because they're adorable and I've always wanted a pair exactly like them and I thought we could swap just like sisters,' she answered, her voice as dry and mocking as grave dust. 'Just fucking do it.'

Tara just fucking did it.

She soon discovered that far from having any chance to run away, she was going to be hard put to even walk properly; first it was the gravel of the car park which dug painfully into her soles, then once they got onto the Longmoor Valley path it was the sharp bristles of heather roots which made her hobble and wince. She actually forgot the knife, more worried about what a hidden shard of broken glass would do to her.

She had assumed that they'd be angling off towards the dig site and prepared to go ankle-deep in bog, but was surprised when the woman ignored it completely and continued to lead them up the valley, now following the brook in its deeply carved, peat-black channel.

'Where are we going?'

But her kidnapper said nothing. The only people they passed were lone dog-walkers in the distance – nobody Tara could risk appealing to for help. The last breaths of a lingering midsummer twilight were exhaling shadows towards them from Westwood Coppice, while the height of Rowton Bank caught the last light in shades of sandstone and russet. The sky behind it was gloomy with approaching dusk, making the hill glow even more brightly in contrast as if detached and floating above the surface of the world.

They crossed the brook and arrived at Rowton's Well, by which time Tara was limping badly. Fortunately, this was where the woman had apparently decided that they were to stop, and Tara took advantage of the situation to sit on the well's stone edge and bathe her feet. The woman was becoming increasingly agitated, pacing and muttering to herself, obviously waiting for something that wasn't happening. Tara used the massaging of her soles as cover for palming a fist-sized stone from the water. *I'll give you Stone Age bloody axes,* she thought.

'He's here!' cried the woman suddenly, clapping her hands together in what was either childish glee or pantomime terror – Tara couldn't tell. She was staring towards where the stream ran a few metres away, her eyes wide with a mixture of fear and anticipation.

And the water around Tara's bare feet turned ice-cold, instantaneously.

She pulled them out with a yelp, at the same time as the woman grabbed her by the collar of her jacket and hauled her out. She was still clutching the stone, but the other woman didn't notice – or if she did, she didn't care – dragging Tara after her through a thin screen of birch branches to where the stream ran much wider and louder than it had when they'd crossed it lower down. The bank on the other side was higher too, crowned with straggling trees which *definitely* hadn't been there before, and reached by a zigzagging timber track at the top of which stood a man who...

Tara's breath punched out of her in a single stunned gasp, and for all that the other woman was dragging her by main strength, simply collapsed to the ground like a dead weight, immovable. She tried to say something, anything, even if it was just 'No!' to exercise the rationality of speech and make what she saw disappear, but all she could do was shake her head stupidly.

The man's already large frame was made even bulkier by the weight of the furs he wore, by which alone she would have recognised him; his body, when she had examined it, had been naked, his black-tanned flesh twisted and compacted by three thousand years in the ground. It was the spear he carried that gave him away: planted beside him like a walking staff, its leaf-shaped bronze blade identical to the one that lay green with age in her lab. She knew that if he moved – if he started down the slope towards her – he would be limping slightly on his right leg, the one that didn't belong to him.

'Rowton Man,' she whispered.

'Bark Foot!' her captor crowed, and brandished the knife in Tara's face. 'You wouldn't be told! So you'll have to be shown, won't you?' She grabbed Tara by the front of her collar and tried to drag her forward, towards the stream and the timber track and the man who could not be alive on the other side of it all.

'No.' This time Tara resisted. 'No!' Knife or no knife, she wasn't going an inch nearer that thing. '*Noooo!*'

The madwoman wound her fist in Tara's hair and began to drag her again. Tara shrieked at the pain, and beat at her fingers with the rock.

'Fucking bitch!' The knife reappeared, shining. 'Still, I don't suppose he'll mind if you're cut a bit, just so long as you're not too dead.'

If Rowton Man did mind, he didn't protest, but watched impassively as Tara crawled backwards from the gleaming steel and began to scream.

Then a new voice intervened: deeper, male, an ordinary mortal bellowing a wordless 'Oi!' and someone crashed into her attacker.

ENOUGH WAS ENOUGH, THOUGHT NATHAN. HE'D BEEN here for over a week now, wandering aimlessly around the park, maxing out his credit card and burning up what little savings and leave he had. He'd achieved nothing more than watching people going in and out of a police tent and reopening old wounds with Sue. After they'd met in the museum she had told him to keep whatever this was away from her children, and he'd been only too happy to oblige. He was no closer to getting any answers about his hallucinations, and he didn't suppose he ever would be. He decided to take one last wander around the park, watch the sunset from Rowton Bank, and then call it quits. Enough was enough.

That was before he heard the screaming, and saw two figures struggling in the twilight beside the stream.

He threw himself at the figure holding the knife, and the pair of them crashed to the ground in a grunting tangle of fists and limbs. His opponent was a lot lighter than had first appeared, and he was able to bear them down easily, although they kept their grip on the knife with dumb ferocity despite his attempts to hammer it free against the ground.

Then the hoodie fell back and he saw who he was fighting, and shock stole the strength from him.

'Liv?'

The last time he'd 'seen' her had been through Robbie's binoculars halfway around Snowdon, her sixteen-year-old self smiling and chatting with Ryan and Brandon and Scattie, nearly a decade out of time. The face below him, grimacing with fury, was that of a gaunt, hollow-eyed adult.

'Hi, Mr Brookes,' she replied, and kneed him in the crotch. Molten agony erupted and she shoved him off, took to her heels, and ran.

The pain was so overwhelming that the world faded away for a moment, and it took him a while to realise that the woman he'd just rescued was going through his pockets.

'You're... mugging me?' he croaked. 'That's gratitude.'

'I'm looking for your phone,' said Tara. 'We need to get you to a hospital right now.'

He waved it away. 'Oh God, it was just a tussle. It's not that...'

Then he looked down at his stomach and saw the blood.

'...bad.'

10

BEDSIDE MANNER

It is happening now.

He dreams of a drowned landscape; silent forests of emaciated trees stretching their pale trunks towards a sunless sky like worms, tumorous with bracket fungi; no undergrowth except an endless mufflement of moss, green hummocks which might be the graves of giants, absorbing all sound, even that of the relentless dripping; everything smeared into everything else like a watercolour left out in the rain.

A figure ghosts through the spectral groves, stick-limbed and swollen-bellied with starvation. It wears a necklace of children's hands and feet around a throat too thin to swallow anything, and its wide-gaped mouth is filled with far too many teeth. It roots amongst the moss for worms and beetles, the only life this land will sustain, and the bitter juices of what it chews runs over its chin. This is the land of hungry ghosts. The land of the Man of Ash.

A voice, its owner unseen, whispers in his ear, 'This is Un.'

* * *

NATHAN JERKED AWAKE.

The muted murmur of the sleeping hospital ward closed back over him like a pool of water momentarily disturbed. From the long row of beds either side of him came only the rustle and sighs of sleeping patients, and at the far end a small oasis of light at the nurses' station, with one man in medical whites bent silently over some paperwork. It reminded him of that Hopper painting, *Nighthawks*. Just moving to see this made him aware of the dressings pulling tightly, about six inches above his right hip. The ten stitches they'd put in should probably be hurting like a bastard too, except for the world-class drugs they'd given him. A tube ran from a cannula in the back of his hand to an IV antibiotic drip. It actually took him a little while to realise that there was also a man in a suit sitting in the chair at his bedside.

'Wait – what?' he said. 'How did you get in here?'

'How did I get in?' the man laughed softly. 'Nathan, this is the National Health Service. If you want security you're going to have to go private. Frankly, if I were you, I'd make sure they haven't harvested an organ or two before you check out. Still, one of these always helps.' The man flipped open his police warrant card, but Nathan didn't need to see it to know who he was talking to. It had been nine years but the face and voice were branded on his memory.

'Hello, Detective Constable Hodges,' he said thickly.

'It's actually "Detective Inspector" now.'

'My, haven't we gone up in the world.'

'"We"? I've done a bit of digging about you, Nathan. You've been working in the same pissant little outdoor centre for the best part of a decade. That's hardly a meteoric career progression.'

'Am I under caution?'

'No. Why would you be?'

'Good. In that case kindly fuck off and let me sleep. Either that or stop bullshitting around and tell me why you're here.'

Hodges smiled and leaned in. 'Funny – that's exactly what I was about to ask you. Why are you back here after so long? What's changed?'

Nathan pushed the button to call the nurse. Over at the nurses' station, the man in whites glanced around at whatever alert the button had signalled, looked down the ward to where Nathan was now waving, and then pointedly ignored him.

'Hey!' Nathan called, to no effect. '*Hey!*'

'You're just going to wake everybody up with that,' Hodges commented. 'You're going to piss off a lot of people. But okay, point made. I'll back off. Believe it or not, I really did just want to talk to you about what happened earlier tonight.' He indicated Nathan's dressings. 'It's still my patch, that's all.'

'I got stabbed is what happened. Which part of that is problematic for you?'

'Did you see the face of the person who attacked you?'

'No.'

Hodges rubbed his face with both hands and sighed. 'See,

here is exactly where it does become problematic for me, Brookes. I ask you one perfectly simple, straightforward question and you lie to me.'

'I'm not lying.'

'Yes, you are. While you were in theatre, uniform took a statement about the incident from Dr Doumani, an archaeologist at the university. She's the person you "rescued" – at least that's the word she used. I've also been working with her on the excavation of a body in the park, and it's that sort of coincidence that really makes my arse twitch. She said that just before you were stabbed you called the attacker "Liv". Did you?'

'She's mistaken. What I said was, "Leave her alone," except I didn't finish the sentence because by then I realised I'd been cut. She misheard.'

'Did she mishear the attacker call you "Mr Brookes", too? No, wait, maybe what she really meant was how it had been ages since she'd been to the park and she'd particularly loved that stream as a child and what she was really saying, just before she stabbed you, was how much she "missed the brook". That must be it.' Hodges sighed again, as if even the effort of being sarcastic wasn't worth it. 'You're lying, Nathan. You always have done. The really tragic thing is how spectacularly bad you are at it; you could have guessed we'd talk to Dr Doumani and saved yourself the embarrassment, but I think it's just habitual with you, isn't it? Lying.'

'Maybe it's because you inspire such trust.'

'Of course, once we had your ID and that name we knew it was Olivia Crawford and collared her. She still had Doumani's shoes in her bloody car. So then.' He leaned forward again, rubbing his hands together. 'Let's get down to it. You can go for the hat trick or you can start telling me the truth for once. Why are you protecting her?'

Nathan said nothing.

'How about this?' All trace of humour was gone; Hodges' face was impassive, all lines and planes in the gloom, like stone. 'Nine years ago you groomed her and made her your accomplice in the killing of those other three kids, then dumped her and fucked off. Then Dr Doumani digs up a body and you panic, thinking that they've finally been found, so you get Olivia to kidnap the lecturer and bring her to the park where you can do away with her in the same sick way you did them. Except when Olivia gets back to that place the trauma of it makes her snap, and she stabs you, having finally decided that revenge is a dish best served late rather than never.'

Nathan looked at him. 'And you really believe that?'

Hodges shrugged. 'Not really. As a story it's got more holes than a knitted condom, but it's the most plausible thing I've got to run with unless you give me something better.'

'I'm giving you nothing. Not any more. You've got nothing. Liv's said nothing like that to you – if she had I'd be in cuffs right now, wouldn't I? I lied to you about recognising her because all told I think she's suffered enough, don't you?'

'That's pretty magnanimous given that she's just tried to carve you a new belly button.'

'She panicked. It was an accident. You and I both know that.'

Hodges looked at him closely, and then nodded to himself. 'Well there it is, then.'

'There what is?'

'You still think you're her teacher, don't you? That you have a duty of care. As far as you're concerned she's still a fifteen-year-old girl, not a twenty-four-year-old woman, despite the fact that she's terrorised and abducted another human being at knifepoint. What did you think that was – a cry for help?'

'I think fundamentally, yes, she probably still is a scared teenager underneath it all. Some of us aren't so good at moving on with our lives, *Inspector*.'

'She...' Hodges coughed and looked away, his legs crossing and recrossing.

'She what? She's okay, isn't she? You haven't done anything stupid like shoot her, have you?'

'Don't be an idiot, Brookes, of course it's nothing like that. She has indicated that she will tell us everything that happened – not just what happened tonight, but originally. Back then. Everything.'

That made Nathan sit up sharply enough for his dressings to pull painfully. 'What?'

Hodges nodded as if this revelation made him sick rather than promising the solution to a mystery that had tortured all of them for years. 'She has only one condition, which she's quite annoyingly firm on: that it is you to whom she tells the story. Even more annoyingly, her case worker seems to think that there's no harm in you listening in on the interview – which is all you'll be doing.'

Nathan began to laugh, but quickly stopped at the pain this caused, so he put the full force of it into the mocking grin that he flung at Hodges instead. 'My God, no wonder you're pissed off. You must be so jealous.'

'Understand that you will not say *one single word* to that girl,' Hodges shot back. 'You will be in that room and whatever she says she can say to you, or me, or the sweet baby fucking Jesus for all I care, just so long as she does talk. You'll be there if I have to handcuff you to this bed and wheel you there myself, but you will *not* be asking any questions.'

'What makes you think I wouldn't want to come? Wild horses couldn't stop me. You really do think I have something to hide, don't you?'

'I know you do. That's why I'm giving you this chance now, to tell me first. It's the only way I can protect you from your own lies.' He took out one of his business cards, jotted some notes on the back of it and tossed it onto Nathan's chest before standing. 'Then. There. That's the extension number to call. Discharge yourself once the doctors are happy with you; the last thing I need is you bleeding like a stuck pig all over my police station.' And with that, he left.

'Thanks for your concern,' muttered Nathan.

He lay awake in the murmuring darkness, trying to sort out his jumbled memories of the brawl by the stream. Of one thing he was absolutely sure: Liv's voice crowing *Bark Foot!* just before she attacked Dr Doumani.

Some time later the nurse came over and asked him if he would like a drink of water. Nathan told him exactly what he could do with it.

* * *

When the police arrived, Steven Vickers had the garage door open to the humid evening air and was sanding down one of the wheels on Matthew's new pull-along caterpillar toy. He wasn't much of a carpenter – it was more for the relief of doing something with his hands after a day spent wrangling spreadsheets and invoices. Some men drank, some played *Call of Duty*, he made stuff. It wasn't a big thing, but more than once he'd thought about maybe trying to sell the odd toy or two to friends or neighbours or on that website, Etsy. Money was tight, and the government sure wasn't making it any looser.

There was a knock on the rattling steel of the roll-up door and an *ahem*.

'Excuse me?' said DI Hodges.

'Yes?' Steve looked up.

Hodges saw a man in his early thirties with thinning hair and a frame that had once done a fair bit of sport in his youth but wasn't having any favours done for it by an office job. It was depressingly similar to what he saw in the mirror every morning.

Hodges showed the man his ID. 'I'm looking for Susannah Vickers.'

'I'm her husband. Is she in trouble? Is she okay?'

'Yes, fine, nothing to worry about, sir. It's nothing like that. It appears that a, ah, friend of hers has been involved in an incident.'

Later, as Hodges sipped the obligatory cup of tea and

explained about how the doctors had come to find Sue's number as the only local contact in Nathan's phone, for want of next-of-kin details, it occurred to him that it might have been better if he'd knocked on the front door and spoken to her directly, because this was not going to be a happy little domestic unit when he left. She'd flushed bright pink at the mention of Brookes' name and was darting furtive little glances at her husband while she tried to twist the handle off her own mug. He, on the other hand, followed the conversation with the same kind of expression as a man who's just walked into his home and discovered that all the rooms have been moved around.

'Actually,' Hodges continued, 'I was particularly interested in whether or not you're able to shed any light on the motivations of his attacker.'

'Why the hell would she?' demanded the husband.

'Because it was Olivia Crawford, one of the four children who disappeared from his charge. A student at the school where you both used to work.'

Sue Vickers didn't rise to defend Brookes, just looked more and more bewildered – which told him everything he needed to know. Much as he hated coincidences, it seemed that this was one of them. 'Well,' he said, standing. 'Sorry to have been the bearer of bad news.' Though truth be told the only sympathy he felt was for her husband. 'Thanks for the tea.'

He let himself out and was nearly at his car when the shouting began.

11

COFFEE AND CONFESSIONS

NATHAN DISCHARGED HIMSELF THE FOLLOWING MORNING, and was coming out of the hospital pharmacy having collected his post-op care pack and a prescription for antibiotics and pain meds when he was met by Sue.

'Hello, stranger,' she said, and gave him a strained smile. 'I've had three hours' sleep, no breakfast, and the boys are in playgroup and nursery until ten. It's time for Big Dave's.'

'YOU LOOK LIKE I FEEL,' SHE SAID. A HUGE PLATE OF BACON, eggs, black pudding, sausage, mushrooms and beans took up much of the space in front of him while she was picking at some more modest scrambled eggs on toast. The early shift of builders and truckers had given way to hungover students and hipsters playing cardiovascular Russian roulette. Even though it said Big Dave's over the door, it was known to all as the Titanic Café ever since someone had spray-painted 'Absolutely Unsinkable' down one side after one of Dave's many run-ins with yet another faceless corporation looking to gentrify the canalside; it occupied an old observation office overlooking the Tame Valley Canal in a position with prime development material but unassailable in its legal vagueness, and so endured – a shabby middle finger up in the face of modernisation. It had, in days of yore, also been Nathan and Sue's refuelling stop after illicit nights out on the town.

'Getting stabbed will do that to a person,' he commented, and sipped. He took his fork and began to dissect a piece of black pudding. 'Don't think I'm not glad to see you, but I thought you said you wanted nothing to do with me. Again.'

'I don't seem to have much say in the matter any more. The police came to my house last night.'

A forkful of cardiac doom froze halfway to Nathan's mouth, then slowly resumed its journey. 'And what has the ever-friendly DI Hodges been saying about me, then?'

'Well, that you'd got yourself stabbed, for one thing. How do you think I knew where to find you? He said that it was Olivia Crawford who did it. How can that be true?'

Nathan laughed shortly. 'I bet he loved telling you that. Look, it's not as simple as he's making out. Strictly speaking, she didn't stab me at all – not deliberately, I mean. I'm sure of that. It had to have been an accident.'

'An *accident*? She didn't spill your pint, Nathan. That's an accident. She stuck a bloody knife in you!'

'There are things about it which I can't really go into.' How could he explain about Bark Foot and the archaeologist woman who Liv had been kidnapping without sounding completely crazy?

'Why not?'

'Because it's not safe, that's why not. Speaking of which, does Steven know you're here?'

'Well I didn't run it past him for his permission, if that's what you mean.'

'That's not what I meant.'

'I know. What you meant was, have I told him?'

'Well, have you?'

'Yes,' she said, as simple and emotionless as that, as if it were of no more significance than a discussion about the weather.

'Everything?' he asked, not quite believing it.

'Every last thing.'

'Shit. Why?'

'Because a policeman came to my *home*, Nathan, asking questions about you, and somehow an explanation to my husband seemed appropriate, you know?'

'How did he take it?'

'Who – the policeman or Steve?'

'Oh for God's sake...'

'How Steve took it is none of your business. What happens in my marriage generally is none of your business. But I didn't tell the detective that you lied to protect me that day because that *is* your business. You just need to know that whatever you choose to do now, you're not responsible for protecting my honour like some knight of old.'

'So why are you here, exactly? If it was just to tear another strip off me then consider it torn, finish your eggs and bugger off. If you came to see if I was okay, then that's really nice of you, cheers, finish your eggs and bugger off.

Either way, you could have done it over the phone. You didn't, though. You came here to *see* me.'

'Still so up yourself, aren't you?'

'You used to like that.'

'No,' she sighed, 'I used to be *attracted* to that, once upon a time, when I was younger and less sure of myself and about to get married and, I don't know – scared, I suppose. We were a mistake. There's a world of difference between being attracted to you and liking you, but you never got that. You still don't. You haven't moved on at all, have you? Jesus, you hardly even look any older.'

'The secret is lots of moisturiser and regular self-abuse.'

She laughed in spite of herself, but it didn't last long, as if the effort tired her. She finished the last of her tea and started gathering her things together. 'Okay, well, it's been lovely, but if you've got nothing more than witty repartee to offer I'll just bugger off, like you say.'

He watched her organising the mundane treasures of everyday existence – putting her purse away, neatly stacking the cup on the saucer on the plate and stuffing the paper napkin in the top – and found himself fishing for something that would stop her from leaving.

'It's like *Jurassic Park*,' he blurted. 'You know, those mosquitoes in the amber that they were using to clone the dinosaurs?'

She paused, surprised and suspicious that he was mocking her. 'What are you on about?'

'That's me. That's what it's been like ever since those kids got taken. Permanently frozen, stuck in time. Especially after that thing with you and me and the condom.'

She flushed, embarrassed, but remained in her seat. 'Keep your bloody voice down,' she murmured.

'When it happened,' he continued, not wanting to lose the momentum, 'and this is going to sound stupid, but a whole thing spooled out of it in my head. I imagined you getting pregnant, and keeping it, and leaving Steve, and you and me would settle down and...' He stopped then, painfully self-conscious of the ridiculous adolescent stupidity of it all. 'It'd be different, that's all. Different from this... this stasis.'

'That,' she said, leaning in close, 'was the most terrifying and humiliating experience of my life. The fact that it's some kind of fantasy for you... I just don't know where to begin. Look.' She laid her palms flat on the table and took a deep breath, and when she spoke again it was not with anger but with a terrible kind of patience. 'You're clearly mixed up in something, and if you don't want to tell me what that is, then fine. In fact, good. That would be for the best. I'm glad you're not badly hurt, but whatever it is, keep it to yourself and take it far away from me and my children.'

He was pissed off now. 'What exactly is it that you want from me, Sue? Really. I mean, you complain when I have nothing to offer but "witty repartee" but when I try to tell you something true you tell me to keep it the hell away from you. You could have left well enough alone in the first place, but you didn't. You called me, remember?'

'Yes, well now I'm un-calling you.'

He laughed – a hollow, dry sound. 'I don't think it works that way.'

'You don't think what works what way?'

'There are some things you don't get to chop and change.' The face of the man in the woods on the other side of the timber track emerged out of his imagination's undergrowth, hovering like an unseen shadow across the table between them. He wasn't entirely thinking about Sue when he said, 'You can't go waking up the past and expect it to lie down again when it comes after you.'

'IT WAS BARK FOOT THAT TOOK US,' BEGAN LIV. 'REMEMBER that story Brandon told us, Mr Brookes?'

'Please direct your responses to my colleague,' said DI Hodges. Liv threw a withering, pitying glance, which encompassed him, DS Pryce and her social worker, before continuing as if they weren't in the room.

Nathan sat in the far corner, having been given strict instructions to keep his mouth shut, which hadn't been a problem; this place scared the shit out of him. Just approaching Sutton Coldfield police station's wide front doors had been enough to make his palms sweat. The interview room itself was clean, bright and office-like, with indirect lighting and a single discreet CCTV camera rather than a two-way mirror like in all the cop shows he never watched. But even louvre blinds and catalogue-store furniture could seem like a dungeon of the Spanish Inquisition after hour upon hour of being told *you did it you did it you did it we know you did it you fucking paedo scum how did you do it where did you do it where are the bodies paedo fucker we know you did where are the fucking bodies?* After a while you began to wonder whether or not you could cut your wrists on those nice clean blinds or how easy it might be to peel the birch veneer off that desk with your fingernails and jam the splinters into your own eyeballs, because *they knew it they knew it they knew he'd killed them kids and they'd told his school and they'd told his mum and dad and everybody knew what a sick fucking paedo scumbag he was so he might as well admit it because who else did he have who else who else who else...*

And that was a holiday camp compared to the cells.

Two words could have saved him at any point – two words he would never say, not to these bastards.

With Sue.

And like a hypnotist's willing victim, he was back in the room. Liv was a scarecrow of the teenager he'd known, all angles and knuckled joints. She had old-woman's teeth and self-harm scars laddering her forearms, and he couldn't take his eyes off them. How bad must it have been to be the only one to come back, for her to have done all of this to herself? Had she even gone so far as to try and kill herself?

'Who is Bark Foot?' asked DS Pryce.

Liv persisted in ignoring the two detectives, talking directly to Nathan. 'He's the one that archaeologist lady dug out of the ground.'

'That's not possible,' said Hodges. 'That body is over three thousand years old.'

She favoured him with a small, sly smile. 'Most of him is.' Back to Nathan, she continued, 'You have to convince her to put him back again. He's there for a reason. Every moment he's out of the ground the weaker he gets, and if he doesn't go back something terrible will be let loose!'

'Jesus,' muttered DS Pryce. 'Curse of the fucking Bog Mummy.'

'No,' said Liv. 'You don't understand. He's protecting us from something much worse.'

12

LIV IN UN

It is happening now.

Liv is behind everyone else, toiling up the hill in the hot sun, with an ill-fitting rucksack and boots that are already giving her blisters.

Liv has always been behind everyone else. Last to be picked for teams, if at all. Last to be asked to parties. If at all. Last to be fed in a family where she is the youngest behind one brother who is a junkie and another who is in prison, where Mum drinks away what's left of the grocery budget after this month's 'boyfriend' has stolen his share. Last developmentally since infancy thanks to her foetal alcohol syndrome – it's a special need and gives her extra time in exams, not that this helps much because what's the point of having an extra twelve and a half minutes if you still have fuck-all to write? Everything she's wearing or carrying has been borrowed from the school stores, after the other kids have had their pick. And now she's at the back of the group, where she belongs.

Ahead of her is Brandon, with his walking stick and his trousers tucked into his stupid red socks, and ahead of him is Scattie with the map. She's the one really in charge despite the fact that Ryan is a hundred metres ahead, beasting it up the track in his camouflage trousers like he's on some kind of stupid SAS training exercise.

They've only been walking for half an hour and already there's been an argument about which way to go around Longmoor Pool. Ryan is pissed off with her because she voted against his idea – as if it's her fault when he'd already been outvoted by Scattie and Bran anyway. She doesn't know why she signed up for this stupid expedition in the first place.

That's a lie. She does know. It is because at the end of the day, even though she might have to give back all the kit, and at home she might have everything else stolen from her, nobody is going to be able to take away the fact that she's *done* this.

'Hey, look!' says Brandon. 'You can see Mr Brookes from here.' He's holding something out to her, which looks like a small telescope.

'What's this?' she asks.

'It's a monocular.'

'A mono-what?'

'Like binoculars, except only one half. You know. Bi: two. Mono: one.'

'Yeah, I know.' She grabs the one-ocular more grumpily than she intends. Bran's all right. Weird, but all right. She squints through the lens and fiddles with the focus, slapping Bran away when he tries to show her, but he doesn't seem to mind, and she finally manages to see. Far ahead and further up the valley, where the ground rises on the right to the high slope of Rowton Bank, she can see Mr Brookes sitting in the shade of a copse of trees eating an ice cream.

Bran waves with big sweeps of both arms, and she sees Mr Brookes wave back. He's seen them. *It's okay,* she thinks. *Teacher's here.* She knows this is only a park, not the actual countryside, but the parks and playgrounds she's used to are the kinds of places where you're either dealing or practising your vandalism skills, and as shitty as that is at least it's familiar. This place is just... huge. And wild. She's been walking along looking at her feet most of the time because the lack of buildings is freaking her out. Still. Teacher's here.

'He got up there quickly,' she says.

Scattie turns around. 'He probably hasn't been stopping every ten minutes to argue with himself about which way to go or whether or not to have another rest,' she comments. 'Come on.'

Bran takes his monocular back with a shrug and a smile, and offers her some of his sweets. They start walking again.

They cross the stream by a narrow footbridge and continue on the other side. By the time they get close to where Mr Brookes should be, the lie of the land has hidden him from view, and she's sweating like a pig, her legs are burning, and there is a sharp stinging at the backs of her heels which she knows means blisters. So when she sees the cool gleam of water in Rowton's Well she dumps her pack gratefully, sits on the low circular wall and starts to unlace her boots.

Ryan groans. 'Liv, what the fuck? We can't stop again!' He's been hacking at a stick with his lock-knife and probably fantasising about making jungle booby traps.

'I got blisters, man!' she protests. 'I gotta cool them down.'

'You can't get blisters that quick. We've only been walking, like, ten minutes.'

'More like an hour,' Bran corrects him.

'Oh piss off, hobbit boy.'

Bran just grins at this, taking it as a compliment. That's why everybody loves Bran – his complete immunity to all that alpha male bullshit.

'Give her a break,' says Scattie. 'We'll cool them down, strap them up, and then she'll be good to go. Why don't you take your pointy stick and go spear a fish or something?'

Ryan wanders off and the other two busy themselves with snacks while Liv finishes getting her boots off and soaking her feet. She's too busy inspecting the pale white bubbles on the backs of her heels to pay much attention when Ryan shouts, 'Hey, everybody! Look! It's Bark Foot!' and laughs like a drain.

'Yeah, right,' she mutters, but when she looks up again her heart begins to rattle like a hollow box as she realises that she's alone. There are no walkers in sight, and no sign of Mr Brookes. Ryan's rucksack has been left, propped up against the well. The only things moving are the occasional bubble shivering up between the cool, round stones beneath her feet, and the leaves of a few birch trees which screen the approach to the stream. Even the birds seem to have disappeared. There is just the throaty chuckle of water.

And from the direction of the stream she hears their voices – too far away to make out the words – and her paralysis shatters into shards of bright panic. They're going without her, and this is the worst thing that can ever, *ever* happen to her.

'Hey!' she yells. 'Hey, you guys!' She plunges her feet, sockless and dripping, into her boots, grabs her own rucksack, and clumps off after them through the trees.

There's a steep bank and then the stream – except it's much wider and louder than she remembers from when they crossed it further down, which can't be right, because surely streams get *narrower* the further upstream you go? – and that's where she catches up with the other three, picking their way across by another narrow footbridge. There's something odd about the slow way they're walking, though – something she doesn't notice at the time because she's panicking too much about being left behind. Later, after it's much too late, she recalls that they weren't looking carefully down at their feet, as people walking along a single narrow plank should, but gazing upward and forward at something on the far bank. There the footbridge continues, zigzagging up the boggy bank to more trees where a man stands, watching the children approach.

He is tall and dressed in furs, not bark, from head to toe, and he has a long spear with a bright-bladed head planted next to him. It is he towards whom they are walking, as if something about him compels them.

'Guys? I think this is a bad idea!' She tries to make herself heard but her timid voice is lost in the stream's roar.

Ryan has crossed over completely, and now Scattie, the sedge grass parting and closing around their knees as the timber track creaks beneath their weight, and Bran's left heel parts contact with the soaked timber as Liv reaches for him, because the other two are lost, she feels this instinctively, though lost to *what* she cannot say, but she might be able to convince Bran to come back with her, because he gave her some of his sweets. And then somehow she is on the timber track too, and the four of them are met by the man who is not Bark Foot, but for whom she has no other name, and who she suspects may not be human at all. She looks back, and gasps in disbelief.

The footbridge has gone. The stream is now a river in spate, boiling white and tea-brown. The land on the other side is not the midsummer parkland of home: it is a drab, grey wilderness of fen and marsh, scabbed with copses of starved-looking trees, and pooled with water reflecting a leaden sky of unbroken cloud.

SHE PULLS OUT HER PHONE. HER SCREEN LIGHTS UP, THERE'S power, but no signal. Not a single bar. The phone says 'Emergency Only', so she dials 999, but is answered with silence. Not even a dialling tone. She looks at Scattie, who is putting her own phone away and shaking her head, eyes wide.

'Where are we?' whispers Bran. He too seems to be coming back to his senses.

In answer, something hidden in the surrounding woodland shrieks. It begins as a low moan as of something lonely and full of despair, but rises swiftly in both pitch and volume until it ends in a piercing howl of something like rage.

Ryan whirls in shock. 'What the fuck was that?'

Bark Foot cocks one ear, seeming to judge how far away the owner of the cry is. 'It is not safe here,' he says, and his voice is surprisingly light, almost musical. 'My camp is close.' He sets off through the trees.

Scattie starts after him.

'Oh no,' Ryan protests. 'No fucking way. Are you kidding? We don't know anything about this guy. We don't even know where we are!'

'No we don't,' she agrees. She's obviously scared but keeping a lid on it, and Liv knows right then that she's going wherever Scattie goes. 'But I'm not sticking around to find out what made that noise. He said he has a camp. He might have a working phone.'

As they follow him to his camp, she overhears Scattie murmur to Bran, 'Looks like he's hurt his leg,' after which she notices how badly Bark Foot is limping, and how he uses the butt of his spear as a walking stick for his right leg – not that she knows why she should care one way or the other.

He doesn't have a working phone. In a clearing at the brink of a high bank overlooking the stream he has a primitive lean-to shelter made of branches, a number of rickety wooden racks upon which furs are stretched and drying, and a large domed hut about the same size as an igloo but made out of stitched-together hides with a flap for a door. There is also a campfire with something small and sorry-looking roasting on a stick over the embers. There is nothing here which looks remotely like anything Liv recognises as civilisation.

Still, the fire reminds them of how cold they are in this place, with its drastically altered climate, and they huddle around it gratefully, rummaging in their packs for hoodies and sweatshirts – all except for Ryan, who leaps up in alarm.

'Fuck! My bag!' he cries. 'I left it at the well!'

'You will not see it again,' remarks Bark Foot. He sits on a log, his right leg straight out painfully to one side, chewing on whatever creature was cooking.

'Fuck that, you fucking hipster tramp! It's got all my food in it! And my fags!'

'You will find that the way is shut,' the man replies, monumentally unbothered by the abuse. 'But go if you wish. It matters not.'

Scattie sidles up to Ryan and speaks to him very quietly, very intensely. 'Ryan, listen, I know you're scared by this, whatever it is – we all are—'

'I'm not fucking scared!' he scoffs.

'But do you really think it's a good idea to piss off the guy with the sodding great spear?'

'I'll piss off whoever I fucking want to!'

'Yes,' she sighs. 'Yes, I know you will. And I know you're not scared. But Liv is, and you're not helping. Know what? Go for it. Go find your bag. Have fun with whatever it is out there. At least it'll be quieter around here with you gone.'

As if to contradict her, the unearthly moaning shriek comes again. It sounds like it might be slightly further away, but this is scant comfort; its rawness sends shivers over their scalps just the same.

'Seriously, mate,' pleads Ryan. 'What the fuck is that? And where are we?'

'The place that you are in is no place. It is Un. That which you heard was the *afaugh*, the Man of Ashes, and you have been called here to help me fight it.'

'Mm-hm, uh-huh,' Ryan nods. 'Good, right, fine.' He grabs Liv's rucksack and strides towards the trees.

Liv yells and runs after him, but he easily fends her off and she can do little but follow, swearing at him. Scattie joins her, but he's easily too strong for her also. For a moment Bran hesitates, seemingly torn between going with his friends and staying to hear more, but gives a rueful shrug, takes his own bag and follows. Thus, in a shouting, fighting mob, they crash through the trees, and Bark Foot watches them go.

'You have no idea where you're going, do you?' demands Scattie.

'Look, it's downhill, yeah?' says Ryan. 'That means the stream is this way.' He ploughs on through the trees, snapping branches and stamping on twigs.

'Um, not necessarily,' points out Bran.

'Oh shut the fuck up!' Ryan snarls.

'I mean,' stammers the other boy, 'I'm just thinking, we're at the western edge of the park, so if we use the compass and go in a straight line west we'll hit the boundary eventually and we can get ourselves back on track from there.'

'Great. You do that. Go play with your compass and map like a fucking Boy Scout. I'm going this way.'

Liv drops back and says to Scattie, 'What is Ryan's problem?'

Scattie shakes her head. 'He's terrified, and it's making him act like a bigger dick than usual.'

For the third time, that bowel-clenching shriek rings out from the trees. It is much louder now. Much closer.

'Oh fuck *off*!' screams Ryan. 'We know what you are! Fucking Big Foot Batty Boy making woo-woo noises! You can't fool us!'

Something pale flits between two silver birch trunks.

'Did you see that?' whispers Liv.

'It's… it's a deer,' says Scattie. 'That's what it is. A deer.'

Bran looks at her, and his eyes are wide pools of absolute terror. '*On two legs?*'

And then it is upon them with inhuman speed, its howl mingling with their screams: a starveling face on a neck too thin to support its moon-like head, above a swag-belly distended with unending hunger. Its fingers are claws blackened with the filth of its scavenging, and its teeth – as it launches itself raveningly at Ryan's throat – are filed to points. Ryan can do nothing but fall back, his hands up in futile defiance.

Bark Foot emerges from his hunter's invisibility amongst the trees, there's a flash of bronze, and the head of his spear drives into the *afaugh*'s belly. Black, stinking blood bursts from the wound, and the creature reels away screaming, and disappears in the gloom.

Bark Foot lets them scream and sob and puke and rage and demand and then finally exhaust themselves. He doesn't take them straight back to his camp, but leads them up to a high, bare hillside like a bald patch in the forest and they look out over the place in which they have found themselves, and they are numbed with disbelief.

They can see the Longmoor Brook, now a swollen river, foaming far below, on the other side of which a sere and desolate landscape rises and falls to the horizon, far beyond where the boundaries of Sutton Park should give way to housing estates. Where there should be footpaths cutting through short-turfed parkland there is only bog and pools of black water with the occasional crusting of snow, gleaming like fragments of bone. Where there should be neat coppices of holly and fir there are straggling stands of half-drowned birch and alder. Where there should be people and laughter and dogs barking there is only the rumble of an icy wind knifing their ears.

'The place you are from is no longer there,' says Bark Foot. 'It is futile to search for it. The way is closed.'

They follow him back to his camp, sobbing and supporting each other, too traumatised to even speak, much less notice that his limp is worse than before.

'THE *AFAUGH* SEEKS ENTRY TO THE WORLD SO THAT IT MAY feed, as it has since the beginning,' he explains as they sit at his fire, still numb with shock. He is carving a small bird out of wood, the long shavings of wood curling on the ground between his feet, and he concentrates on it as he talks, not looking at them. 'And I forbid it entry, as I have done since before the time of your forefathers. What you see around you is an echo of the world as it was when I came here.'

'An echo?' says Bran. 'You mean as in ghosts? Is this some kind of spirit realm?'

'Fucksake,' mutters Ryan. He is sitting far apart from the others, trying to hide the damp patch on the front of his trousers where he pissed himself in terror.

Bark Foot frowns. 'I am no shaman. I do not know how to answer such questions. I am a warrior – the strongest in four valleys. I fought for the honour to be chosen as guardian of the valley clans, and won it. That is all I know. The *afaugh* and I have always been too evenly matched to best one another. In that time the strongest would offer themselves gladly for the honour of aiding me with their strength, but the memories of the people falter, and the old ways are lost, and it has been long now indeed since any have come.'

He unwraps the coverings from around his right leg and they gasp at what is revealed. An ugly, suppurating wound runs from mid-thigh to below the knee – swollen with infection, and undoubtedly agony to walk upon.

'I grow weaker by the day, and soon the time will come when I will be unable to stand against the *afaugh*, and all of this will have been for nothing.'

'If we help you,' says Scattie, 'will you show us the way home?'

His response surprises them, both with its starkness and the sorrow of its delivery. 'No,' he says. 'Not all of you. One only may return. To make the way wide enough for all would be to risk the *afaugh* entering the world too. You must decide amongst yourselves who that will be.'

Scattie shakes her head. 'No. Not good enough. If one goes, we all go. That's the condition.'

'There are no conditions. This is not trade. There only is what is.'

'But that's ridiculous! It's no choice at all! How can you possibly expect us to decide who will stay here in this… whatever this place is?'

'Un,' murmurs Bran, prodding the fire with a stick. 'The place that is no place.'

'What*ever*. It's still a big fat fuck-off to Mr Limpy here. I don't care about your precious bloody *afaugh*, or your forefathers, whoever they were or whatever they did. You're getting nothing from us.' Scattie turns to the others. 'Right?'

'Right,' says Bran, feeding twigs into the embers.

Liv nods, her eyes wet with tears.

Ryan merely grunts.

Bark Foot looks from one to the other. 'Then you will all die here,' he says simply. 'There is no life for you in this place. There are no animals for you to hunt; no food for you to eat.'

'You seem to be doing well enough,' she observes, pointing to his roasted critter.

He picks it up and offers it to her. 'I subsist on what the spirit-dancers provided for me. Here. See if you think it will suffice for you, one of the living.'

She takes the skewered haunch and sniffs at it. It smells of roasting flesh and suddenly her mouth is watering.

'That's so gross,' says Ryan. 'You aren't really going to eat that shit.'

She ignores him and cautiously nibbles on a crispy bit at the edge, but then makes a face of disgust and spits it out.

'Told you.'

'What's wrong?' asks Liv, alarmed. 'Is it poisoned?'

'It's – ugh – it's cold! And soggy. And, like, rotten-tasting, like it's been under water for days. It's *vile*.' She looks at Bark Foot with a new and different kind of fear. 'What are you? Really?'

'I am the guardian of the way into the world. Nothing passes from Un but that I permit it, and I have done so for many, many lives of women and men. You may remain here in my camp and I will protect you as well as I can. That too is unconditional – it is what I am. But you will starve soon, and when that happens you will agree to help me, simply so that one of you will survive.'

It's all too much for Liv, and she bursts into tears. 'You bastard!' she sobs. 'How can you do this to us? You've got no right! You've got no *right*!'

'There only is what is,' he repeats.

Bran pulls a stick out of the fire and examines its burning end. 'Let's assume we do decide to help you,' he says. 'What exactly is it that you need us to do?'

In response, Bark Foot stands and begins removing the rest of his attire.

'Hey! Whoa!' shouts Ryan, covering his eyes. 'Put it away, big man! Forest gangbang – never going to happen, mate.'

Bark Foot ignores their embarrassment and disrobes completely, and they see that he is a patchwork – no two limbs match, his skin is of variegated hues, and even the flesh of his jaw does not match that of his neck. 'You ask me who I am,' he says. 'I am the One From Many. I am the best of all who my people have sacrificed to me in order to protect them from the *afaugh*.' He indicates his injured leg. 'One of you will give yourselves to me in order that I may become strong again.'

'Well I'm useless to you, then,' says Ryan cheerfully. 'I buggered my ankle a year ago. Had to have it pinned. Why don't you try Scattie here? She's got better legs than me. Hairier, too.'

'Dickface,' she shoots back.

Bark Foot steps forward. 'Is this your decision, then?' he asks. 'Do you offer me this woman's strength?'

'No!' shouts Bran. 'No we don't! There's no offering here. Right?'

'Right,' says Liv.

Ryan shrugs and rolls his eyes.

'Like fuck there is,' Scattie growls. 'We'd rather die first.'

'So. Do we believe that any of this is real?' asks Scattie. Later, they are huddling as far away as they can get from Bark Foot's strange animal-hide hut and yet still feel the fire.

'I don't think we have much of a choice, do we?' replies Bran. 'Unless we've all gone mental in the same way, which I just can't see happening.'

'Maybe we're tripping,' says Ryan. 'I reckon Liv spiked those sweets.'

Liv says nothing. Her eyes are red-rimmed and she's

shivering, despite wearing all of her extra clothing and her waterproof jacket.

'Look,' he continues. 'If it's all a wind-up, with guys in suits and special effects, then I'm going to beat the living shit out of someone. If it's real, then I don't know what to say, but we're screwed whatever we do. So we need to decide what we *are* going to do.'

This conversation, or a variant thereon, has been circling around for several hours while they repeatedly fail to agree on a course of action. They try their phones a dozen times, from a dozen places, and get no signal. They backtrack to the river, but can find no trace of the timber track. What they discover instead is dozens – possibly hundreds – of carved wooden birds placed in the branches of the silent, half-dead birches. In the absence of any actual living birds, their presence gives the wood the aspect of a graveyard.

It is only after the initial noise and confusion has died down that Liv realises how properly hungry she is. She tries to distract herself by listening to music on her phone, but that only makes her want to text, and then she remembers that there's no signal (and probably nobody left to even send a text to), and then it all comes crashing in on her again. As the afternoon lengthens into dusk, hunger becomes a steady, prowling presence.

Ryan keeps himself busy sharpening a stick with his knife and hardening its tip in the fire. Despite protests from the others, he takes himself off into the trees, promising to bring them back a couple of rabbits. Later he returns empty-handed and morose, picks a pointless argument with Liv in which he accuses her of hiding food, and takes to stripping the bark off nearby trees and stabbing their trunks in impotent fury.

Bran, on the other hand, is hunched down across from Bark Foot, the two of them engaged in quiet conversation while the larger man carves his birds. Liv nudges Scattie and points. 'Looks like Bran's found himself a soulmate. What do you think they're talking about?'

Scattie shrugs. She couldn't care less. 'We need to leave this place,' she says. 'It's too late now, too dark, but first thing tomorrow. We need to get moving. We need to find *something*.'

'But that afarg thing is out there.'

'Bark Foot seems to want to keep us safe from it; maybe he'll come with us. Or follow us, at least.'

'And his leg? He's weak. What if it kills him?'

'What if it does? That could work for us. It wants to kill him so it can escape into the real world, yeah? Well, so do we – maybe we're on the wrong side of this thing altogether. Maybe we can make it work for us – make him follow us, force him to fight it, get killed, and follow it home.' Her tone darkens. 'Maybe we can even do it ourselves. There's four of us, one of him, and like you say, he's weak.'

'That's crazy! We can't *kill* him!'

'Maybe not. But I'm fucked if I'm going to sit around here for much longer waiting for something to change, because I'm sorry, Liv, it looks like it just isn't.'

They have the inner and outer parts of a tent, but no pegs or poles since those were in Ryan's bag, so they string the flysheet between two trunks as a shelter and use the groundsheet to sleep on. Liv thinks that the combination of hard ground and an empty belly is going to make it impossible for her to sleep, but she's underestimated the toll the day has taken, and is asleep in minutes.

SHE'S AWOKEN BY THE WET, ANIMAL SOUND OF VOMITING.

Their startled torchlight picks out Ryan, doubled over, clutching his belly and retching up a thin line of drool.

'What's wrong, mate?' asks Bran, with a hand on his back.

Ryan groans, and retches again. 'Fuckin... mushrooms...' he gasps, wiping his mouth.

Bran's torch finds the pieces of chewed white fungus in a small pool of stomach juices between Ryan's knees. 'Oh you stupid, *stupid* wanker!' he moans.

'Found 'em... hunting...' Ryan continues. 'Wasn't gonna... just so *hungry*...' and he pukes again, even though by now there's nothing much left to come up.

They make him as comfortable as they can and give him the last of the bottled water, which they've been saving for the morning, but he just brings this right back up again. Bark Foot watches all of this impassively. Scattie turns to him.

'Our friend is sick.'

'Yes.'

'Well?' She glares at him. '*Do* something!'

'There is nothing to be done. That which he has eaten will kill him in a few days. If the spirits smile on him, it will be swifter.'

'There must be *something* you can do!'

'I can take his strength to heal myself. It will make his death worthwhile, and in return one of you may go home.'

'That's not what she meant!' yells Liv.

Ryan raises his head and glares at Bark Foot. 'Never,' he rasps, and groans again.

And without warning the *afaugh* comes shrieking out of the darkness and throws itself at him.

The children scream and cower as it grabs Ryan by the ankles and starts to drag him away with its long pale arms while he flails around for a handhold and grabs only leaf mulch; even Bark Foot has been taken by surprise and it takes a moment for him to rally and leap forward with his spear. Still, the *afaugh* is reluctant to lose its advantage and it continues to haul at Ryan with one hand while it fends off Bark Foot with the other – and all the while it is shrieking, its mouth a tooth-filled maw almost as wide as its entire face – and Ryan is screaming, and Bran is screaming and Liv is screaming and it only stops when Scattie seizes a burning branch from the fire and virtually shoves it down the *afaugh*'s throat, and it lets go of Ryan and is gone.

They stare around at each other, panting. Liv is weeping uncontrollably, her face buried in Bran's shoulder.

'It knows that I speak the truth,' says Bark Foot. 'It understands that your friend can do nothing but die, and that you will have no choice but to offer him to me, and it seeks to remove him before that can happen.' He limps back to his fire, and sits down with bone-heavy weariness.

* * *

THIS DESTROYS ANY PLANS THEY MIGHT HAVE FOR LEAVING Bark Foot's camp. All they can do is watch Ryan become weaker, and forage empty-handed in the immediate vicinity, terrified of the *afaugh*. They suck moisture off the leaves of trees, what little there is. Scattie makes a foray to the river and returns with a water bottle of something that looks no more dangerous than iced tea. Desperate, they drink it, and it does exactly what they fear; a day's vomiting and diarrhoea is catastrophic, leaving them even more dehydrated than before.

They never see Bark Foot eat or drink – all he does is sit by his fire and whittle, undisturbed even when they rage and plead at him. The only time he shows any life is when the strangely forlorn cry of the *afaugh* can be heard in the distance. Then he takes his bright-bladed spear and limps off into the trees, returning later to resume his seat without a word.

Bran continues talking to him but Liv can't hear and in any event doesn't really care. She just wants to go home. She tries to cry, but her body has decided that it doesn't even have the water to spare for that.

She pays more attention when Bark Foot starts to tattoo him, however. On the inside of Bran's left forearm, he uses a bone needle and a black paste made from fire ash to painstakingly prick out a three-limbed spiral design. It takes several hours, and afterwards Bran comes back over to her and Scattie, wincing at the red-rawness of it. A mulch of leaves which is evidently meant to be antiseptic has been pasted onto the wound.

'What's that all about then?' asks Scattie, unimpressed.

She's trying to cool Ryan's forehead with a damp rag. 'Joined the big boys' club, have we?'

'Like they say, if you can't beat them…'

'I'm so glad you've made a new friend.'

Bran, as ever, is impervious to sarcasm. 'It's not about friendship. I don't think he's capable of that after all this time, or anything properly human, really. I mean, he looks like a person – he wears the shape of the man who sacrificed himself to be this – but he's really more of a… a function, I think.'

'A function.' Scattie looks at him. 'What the fuck are you talking about?'

'We've been making the mistake of treating this figure as a living human being who is imprisoning us here out of cruelty, but I don't think there's anything actively malicious about what he's doing, or even really conscious. It's like, if you get struck by lightning, you wouldn't think that the lightning was deliberately targeting you to hurt you.'

'You can't tell me not to take this personally,' she says, and points to Ryan, whose skin is as yellow as old teeth.

Ryan slips in and out of delirium. His cries of pain alternate with rambling, one-sided conversations from which the only sense that can be made is the piteous pleading. Inevitably, he loses control of his bodily functions, and the stench of his sickness fills the camp. They have long since passed the point where they can do anything to keep him comfortable, and are just sitting – lethargic with starvation – when Bark Foot limps over to them.

'A third and last time, I ask: will you not offer him to me? His time is near.'

'His time is his own,' snaps Scattie. 'Not yours.'

'Nobody would let even the basest of animals suffer in this way. I can end it for him with honour.'

'If all we can do is die then we'll do it without being part of your sadistic little game.'

'He will be dead by tonight, and you will be dead by the end of three days after that, at most.' He turns to address Liv personally. 'After the boy it will be you. You are weakest. You know this—'

Scattie leaps up in a violent surge which takes them all aback, Bark Foot included, even though the head-rush brought on by nearly two days without food or water makes her stagger. But she plants her feet and stays upright and brandishes Ryan's fire-sharpened stick in his face. 'Don't you *fucking* dare!' she snarls. 'Pick on the weakest, would you? How's that honourable? You don't talk to her! You don't talk to any of us! You send us home or you get *nothing*! Right, Liv?'

Liv nods mutely.

'Right, Bran?'

Bran isn't meeting her eyes. His foot doodles in the dirt, making spiral patterns.

'Bran…'

Still not looking at her, he squares his shoulders and says to Bark Foot, 'I offer you Ryan.'

'*NO!*'

'Well what fucking good is your way doing us?' Bran storms, and this is by far one of the most frightening things Liv has seen because despite all the years of bullying and teasing she's seen him suffer at school, she has never ever seen him lose his temper. 'Getting all stubborn and holier-than-thou? What *good* is it doing? Ryan is *dying*...'

'We're all dying!' she retorts.

'I know that! But at least this way one of us doesn't have to!'

Bark Foot is standing over Ryan. 'Do you all offer him?'

'No!' snaps Scattie.

'Yes,' whispers Liv. 'Scat, I'm sorry, I just couldn't...' she tries, but Scattie shoves her away and collapses with her arms wrapped around her knees, heaving great hollow sobs.

'It is enough,' Bark Foot announces, and gathers Ryan up gently in his arms. Scattie looks up as if she might be thinking of trying to stop him, but just buries her face again, which is the only way she can say *Yes*. Bark Foot takes the limp body to the animal-hide igloo and places him inside. He makes many trips to the river, first bringing water-rounded stones and placing them upon the fire, which he has banked to a blazing height, where they glow cherry red. Then he fills many skin bags with water and takes them and the hot stones into the hut, and soon clouds of steam begin to billow from around the hide door. Bark Foot sings – a low, murmuring, rhythmic chant which falls and rises through the day, pausing periodically to shovel out piles of fire-and-water-shattered stone onto a mound of scorched debris which testifies to many rituals such as this over the endless years.

While they wait, Bran tattoos each of the girls with the same triskelion that Bark Foot gave him. 'I don't know what's going to happen next,' he explains, 'but there's strength in threes. Three of us, three arms on this design. It must mean something. If this is the place of the dead, and we do die, maybe we'll end up together.'

'Whatever,' Scattie mutters, but lets him get on with it. Liv knows it makes no sense but it's as close to a plan as anything.

At last Bark Foot emerges, naked and streaming with sweat, and flexing the gleam of a young, strong leg with no wound – but of Ryan there is no sign, either within the hut or without.

'The way is open,' Bark Foot says, and even to Scattie's ears this sounds like as close to an apology as he can come. He crosses to Liv, who is too weak to even be embarrassed by his nakedness, and helps her to her feet. 'Gather your things. You are going home.'

WITH ONE FOOT ON THE TIMBER TRACK AND THE SUNLIT slope of Rowton Bank ahead of her, Liv turns to look back at Bark Foot, who is flanked by her two friends in the dripping gloom. They can all hear the *afaugh* growling nearby; it senses that the world is close. There is every possibility that despite Bark Foot's new strength it will attempt a reckless dash at the footbridge anyway. This hesitation is dangerous, but when it comes to it, she finds she is reluctant to leave them. For once she is not behind everybody else. She is going ahead, but there's no joy in it, no achievement, because it feels too much like running away.

'Don't,' says Scattie. 'We'll be fine.'

'How can you possibly say that?'

She pushes up her left sleeve and shows Liv the raw red and blue of her fresh tattoo. 'Big boys' club,' she says with a grim smile and a shrug. 'If you can't beat 'em, right?'

The *afaugh* wails, a lot closer, and Liv knows that she must move, now. She treads carefully but quickly along the crudely shaped lengths of timber track, concentrating on her footing, because the wood is shiny and she knows that if she falls now she'll never get up again. The *afaugh*'s disconsolate cries become savage and there's a tremendous crashing in the bushes behind her and Bark Foot is roaring a battle cry and Scattie is shrieking, and Liv almost turns around but Bran yells, 'No! Don't turn back! Go! *Go!*'

She runs, knowing that she's going to fall, and lets her momentum carry her forwards, and by the time it grows too big – like a great rolling boulder pushing her – she is falling, halfway across the revenant bridge, and her final despairing lunge ends with her going face-first into the far bank, legs flailing in the water, hands clawing herself up into the sun and the short springy turf of Sutton Park.

When she has regained breath and courage enough to look back, she sees only bright parkland. The timber track has disappeared, along with the shadows of Un.

Except that's not true. She knows that they're still there, waiting behind the world, and that her friends are there too, fighting to stop a terrible hunger from escaping. So when the rescuers find her she says nothing. In her famished condition it is easy for them to believe that shock has wiped her memory of the last twenty-four hours, so she lets them.

And for a while, it even becomes true.

13

HOME VISIT

THE TABLE OF THE INTERROGATION ROOM WAS A MIDDEN of paper coffee cups and food wrappers. Liv sat on the other side of it, glaring at them, daring them to disbelieve her. 'You can't let it escape,' she finished.

'What?' scoffed DS Pryce. 'Bark Foot the Frankenstein Bog Mummy from Hell?'

'No! Haven't you been listening? The *afaugh*!'

'"Aw-fuck" is right,' he laughed. 'As in this makes fuck-all sense.'

Hodges shushed him, but he was smiling all the same.

'Every day that you have him out of the ground, poking and prodding at him, he gets weaker. Soon he won't be able to stop it from finding the way into our world, and it will do terrible, terrible things! That's why you've got to put him back!'

She shifted her gaze onto Nathan, where it settled like a shadow. 'You have to convince her, Mr Brookes. I know you believe me. I can see it. You have to convince her because when you put him back he will open the way to Un and you can find Scattie and Bran and bring them home.' She pushed up her sleeve and showed him a tattoo. It did look crude and homemade, its outlines smudged with age.

'They're still alive,' she said. 'I would know if they weren't; I'd feel it through this. *They're still alive.*'

A UNIFORMED OFFICER LED LIV AWAY TO THE HOLDING cells, and her social worker went to make a call. Nathan was left in the interview room with the two detectives. He was so anxious to get out of there it felt like his skin was crawling with bugs. 'So are we done?' he asked.

'Oh, we're done,' replied DI Hodges. Beneath the veneer of professionalism he reeked of sour disappointment.

Nathan couldn't resist one last jibe. 'Not what you were expecting to hear, was it? Want to arrest me for dressing up as a monster and running around in the woods scaring kiddies?'

'One more fucking word out of you and I'll have you on obstruction. Get.'

Nathan got.

THEY WERE WAITING FOR HIM OUTSIDE THE POLICE STATION. Whether it had just been the jungle drums of social media which had alerted them to Liv being in custody, or whether Hodges had actually arranged it just to fuck with him, the end result was the same: Nathan barely got to the bottom of the steps before fists were bunched in the front of his shirt and a man's face was snarling into his own.

'Where's my son, you fucking arsehole?'

Ryan's dad: Nigel Edwards, beef-faced and sweating, upon whom it seemed nine years of waiting had accreted physically, making him even more massive than Nathan remembered.

'Well?'

Behind him stood his wife Alicia, glaring through smudged eyeliner, and slightly behind them an older, greyer couple – him in tweed, her in a beige housecoat – not as belligerent but fully prepared to let this happen. Jennifer and Oliver Whitehead. Brandon's parents.

He was shaken by the collar like a dog. 'Well? Who did they dig up? Was it my son? Was it *theirs*?'

Obviously they thought that he was the one who'd been interviewed, and that if the police wanted to know something then he must have something to tell. He opened his mouth to explain, but the impossibility of it choked him more effectively than a pair of hands, and all he could do was shake his head and gasp, 'I'm sorry… I'm sorry…' like an idiot.

'*Sorry*? You fucking…'

Oliver Whitehead came closer. What time had given to Ryan's father it had stolen from Bran's. Brandon had been a late, accidental child in any case and his father had already been in his fifties when he'd disappeared, but nine years of grief had left him looking frail and elderly.

'Please,' said Mr Whitehead. 'We just want to know what happened. Why is Olivia Crawford in there?'

'I'm sorry,' he repeated. 'I can't… I don't have any answers.'

'Has she said what happened? Has she finally remembered?' The naked pleading in his and Jennifer's eyes was almost too much to look at.

Edwards shook him again. 'Did she tell them what you did, eh? Is that it?'

There was nothing he could say about Liv that wouldn't sound like he was mocking them with the most absurd of lies, so he settled on the simplest. 'No. None of it. She's insane.'

'Fucking *liar*,' snarled Edwards.

Then uniforms appeared and pulled them apart, and while the parents turned their helplessness on the police he shuffled away like a criminal.

THE INTERVIEW VIDEO STOPPED AND TARA SAT BACK IN HER chair, feeling like her brain had just been put through a similar forced march to her feet, which still hurt.

'You said you wanted to see it,' said DS Pryce, tucking his iPad away. He'd brought the footage around to her room at the Conference Park hotel as a courtesy, but the fluttery pleasure at having him turn up unannounced had quickly disappeared as she'd watched the footage of Olivia Crawford tell her impossible story. 'I don't know what good it'll do you,' he added. 'That girl's as mad as a box of frogs.'

Yes, she thought. *The maddest thing of all being that it makes perfect sense.* 'Do you think that if two insane things agree with each other then that means they're sane?' she wondered.

'Uhh...' Plainly this wasn't the sort of response he'd been expecting. 'You didn't believe any of that, did you?'

'No, of course not,' she lied. 'Tell me, what are the rules

on reclaiming stolen property? Olivia Crawford stole my laptop when she vandalised my house – I was wondering if I might get it back now you've caught the thief?'

Pryce was on more solid ground here. 'Easy. You gave your local station the details of what was nicked, yes? Colour, size, serial number, et cetera?'

'It was definitely high on my to-do list,' she admitted. 'Things have been a bit busy since.' She waggled her bandaged feet at him.

'So that's what you should do. Then we send some uniforms around to the perpetrator's address with the burglary report and they pick it up. Done.'

'Will that take long?'

He shrugged. 'A couple of days – end of the week, max.'

'Oh.' Tara tried to look as disappointed as possible, which wasn't all that difficult. 'That's a shame. I was really hoping to get it back sooner – today, ideally. Apart from a lot of personal stuff it's also got all my Rowton Man research on it, you see, including some things I was looking at to help your DI.'

It's not an outright lie, she told herself. She didn't feel the need to point out that Hodges had found her information less than valuable. Pryce probably knew that anyway. 'I don't suppose there's any possible way that I might be able to quickly pop into Olivia Crawford's place, grab it and pop out again – obviously accompanied by a reliable detective sergeant to make sure I behave myself? I know it's probably massively against the rules and everything…'

Pryce rubbed the back of his neck and frowned. 'Yeah,' he

said slowly. 'It sort of massively is a bit.' Then he gave her a small, oddly boyish smile. 'About as much as a DS asking a witness in a case he's on out to dinner.'

All of a sudden that fluttery feeling was back.

OLIVIA CRAWFORD'S COUNCIL FLAT WAS IN THE FALCON Lodge Estate on the eastern boundary of Sutton Coldfield, as close as it was possible to get to the countryside without actually escaping the city. It was a labyrinth of cul-de-sacs, alleyways, and wasteland; the lot behind Crawford's building was overgrown with knotgrass, docks, and rosebay willowherb.

'I read a research paper once,' Tara said, as Pryce's car pulled up outside the building, 'which suggested that the types of plants that grown in urban wastelands are the same kinds of species you'd have found colonising the land at the end of the last ice age.'

'Proving what?' he asked and killed the engine.

'I don't know. That we're all just tenants?' She sighed, looking around at the bland uniformity of the brick boxes around them.

Like all the others, Crawford's building was three floors high, with a single entrance reached by a wide slope of concrete lined with rubbish bags awaiting collection. Her one-bed unit was on the top floor, behind an anonymous door, but all pretences to normality stopped at the threshold. The acrid stench that greeted them nearly drove them back outside.

It looked like the post-glacial wilderness had been attempting to colonise the inside of Crawford's home as well. Hanging from the ceiling, the walls, covering the floor and inhabiting much of the space between the furniture were tangles of wood and hand-made cordage – things that looked like they were trying to be nets, baskets, snares, crudely bodged-together stools, tools and bowls, and the scraps and drifts of wood-shavings from their construction formed a mulch underfoot. Animal pelts were strewn across the floor and drying on racks – squirrel and fox, mostly, but also some that looked suspiciously like cat. By the window, which had no glass, the carpet had been cut away to allow for a campfire on some broken slabs of concrete, and smoke and soot had blackened the entire wall and the ceiling above it.

Pryce peered out. 'Top floor, overlooking wasteland,' he commented. 'Nobody to see and call the fire brigade. It's amazing she hasn't burnt the place down yet.' Through the gaping window frame the elements had wreaked havoc with damp, mould and a crust of bird droppings. Feeders hung from the upper frame. But all of that only accounted for part of the smell – the rest came from what they discovered in the bathroom: more pelts soaking in two buckets of dark yellow urine.

'I think she's been trying to tan her own leather,' said Tara. Her eyes were streaming.

Pryce was shaking his head in disbelief. 'Jesus Christ, she really is off the scale, isn't she? Seriously, don't touch anything. You might catch hepatitis. This is a social services job, no mistake. Mental health too, probably.'

'How was this allowed to happen? Was no one looking out for her?'

'There's no father on file. Mother was more harm than good – after the thing in the park Crawford was fostered out but funding for that only lasted until eighteen back then. After that she was on her own.'

'That poor girl,' Tara murmured. Wherever Olivia had gone, part of her had never really left that place.

Un.

'All I can say is, for someone who's been dragged for miles at knifepoint you're more sympathetic than I would be, Doctor. Nobody forced her to do that, and nobody forced her to live like this, either.'

It was in the bedroom that Tara made the most surprising discovery. A jumble of muddy excavation tools were stacked in a corner along with an ancient metal detector, next to a flat-pack bookcase crammed with finds: fragments of bone, stone and ceramics, all neatly bagged and tagged but jumbled together in a way that defied any sense of organisation. There were even a few bits of jewellery. She caught her breath at a cardboard box which rattled with old coins – many of them Roman, all of them invaluable, but casually tossed in together as if of no interest. Books were stacked in tottering towers, all of them in one way or another to do with archaeology, local history, myths and folklore. By the bed – which looked and smelled more like an animal's nest than anything a human had slept in – was what Tara assumed to be her most precious of all treasures: a journal, not much more than a scrapbook, really. It was the kind of cheap glittery stationery that any teenage girl might buy from a high-street newsagent – but stuffed to overflowing with notes and bits of paper and held together with an old Disney hair bobble; Ariel, from *The Little Mermaid*. Tara felt a momentary pang of guilt, quickly crushed, as she slipped the book into her satchel.

'Well, Dr Doumani,' said DS Pryce from the doorway, making her jump. 'If your laptop's here I can't find it. Ten to one she sold it. We'll ask her back at the station. Sorry about that.'

'Oh, not to worry. I have copies of the files back at the lab anyway.' *And my laptop safely on my dining table, but you don't need to worry about that.*

14

SCRAPS

'Riddle me this, Batman,' said Hodges to Pryce. His desk was covered in files from the original disappearances case, and he was holding up two sheets of paper and frowning between them as if he couldn't decide which pissed him off the most. 'Olivia Crawford was found the very next day, right?'

Pryce, who couldn't quite believe that all this hadn't been scanned and shredded years ago, shrugged. 'Right.'

Hodges held one piece of paper higher. 'And yet the doctor who examined her found that the degree of dehydration and starvation were consistent with her having been deprived of food and water for at least three days – possibly as many as ten.'

Pryce looked up from the images of Olivia Crawford's flat on his iPad. 'Where does it say that?'

'Duty doc's report when she was first brought in. He didn't know it was one of the missing kids because he'd been living on fucking Mars or something, and that was his first assessment. He changed it later because of course that couldn't have been the case. He must have made a mistake.'

'Must have.'

'And yet.' Hodges swapped papers, holding the other aloft. 'It says here that she was found only twenty-seven hours later. Hours. Not days.'

'Spooky,' said Pryce. 'Don't tell me you're starting to believe her.'

'No,' Hodges murmured, more to himself. 'Still, I want you to keep tabs on Brookes. I want to know everywhere he goes, everything he does and everyone he speaks to until this mess is sorted out.'

'Roger that.'

* * *

Taken from the Minutes and Accounts of the Warden and Society of Sutton Coldfield, 3 October 1762

...this Account to be sealed herewith and all Memberes of the Societie enjoined on their Honour never to reveal its gruesome Particulars, that the good people of these parishes and wards be neither distressed nor alarmed by matters abhorrent to upstanding and God-fearing folk. The Societie was most astonished to receive upon this day the Testimonie of a Mr Richard Barr, Attendant Keeper of the peat diggings in the Longmoor Slade, who appeared in a state of high agitation, having witnessed, as he himself described it, a scene of the most diabolic and unholy Murder. Upon undertaking his duties in patrolling the extent of the Cuttings, and coming hard by Roweton Bank some houres after sundown, he became aware of a Commotion occurring in the vicinity of Roweton's Well, whereupon, acting with due diligence and bravery as befitting his responsibilities, he ventured forth to confront an assemblie of Drunkards and Ruffians, for so he assumed them to be. On the contrarie, he discovered but three Persons, robed and hooded, in the process of having but lately drowned and mutilated a Fourth. Upon his accosting them, Mr Barr observed with astonishment that they sank directly into the Ground, leaving their unfortunate Victim expired and beyond the help of God or Man. Many grievous wounds had been inflicted upon the Body, the most ghastly of which was the complete dismemberment of one arm, such that in the light of Mr Barr's lanthorn the water in the Well was quite crimson. Subsequent, albeit discreet, attempts to ascertain the nameless Victim's Identity have been to no availe, and it is assumed that he was one of many Tramps and Vagabonds whose numbers have been latterly much increased by the growth of the Town. Moreover, the greatest consternation of all has been occasioned by the inability of any Person investigating the area to retrieve the missing member. Accordingly it is the Societie's decision that...

* * *

Taken from the Diary of Private Arthur Willox, 1st Staffordshire Regiment, 17 August 1915

We have searched under every leaf & bush of this blessed Park and I am so tired that I can hardly write but must get down my thoughts while they are still fresh. It has all been so much like a dream that I am afraid once I wake tomorrow morning I shall have forgot the strangeness of it all and be tempted to make sense of it but it does not make sense and that must be remembered.

I have become great pals with a lad from Tipton called Mickey Grant who is a good laugh and not bad for a Yam Yam. Or should I say he was. We have been billeted in the park for a week, learning how to dig trenches, not full deep ones but practice ones so we know how to do it for proper. Still it has been hot & hard work with Mickey keeping our spirits up with his jokes. Boys, he says, if I had known I would be joining up to dig holes in the ground I would of joined the 1st Gardening Regiment. Men of Hollyhock Company, present arms! And he had us doing parade drills up & down that bank with our shovels over our shoulders like rifles. We did laugh. Of course the SM tore strips off Mickey but he didnt mind about that. So the SM says to him your so clever with that shovel of yours, lets see how good you are at shovelling water. Take it down that stream and use it to fill this bucket and he points to the one we had been using to damp down our trench. Mickey goes to take the bucket too, but the SM puts his foot on it and says oh no, you bring the water up here clever dick. But Mickey doesnt mind, he sees the joke and salutes the SM and off he goes.

The stream wasnt far only a hundred yards or so and we get on with our trench while back and forward Mickey goes like hes in a big old egg & spoon race and the shovel is the spoon, until the bucket is halfway full and you can tell hes getting hot and tired but he doesnt say anything. He was a strong lad was Mickey Grant. He didnt give up on any job once it was started and to this day I do not believe that he was a deserter.

I must have been the only one looking up when it happened because it happened so quick like and I yelled so that the lads asked me what all the fuss was, because they obviously didnt see anything. The ground on the other side of the stream should of been flat and boggy like normal but as God is my witness what I saw was a wooded ridge on top of a steep bank and a zigzag track going up it from the stream, except it wasnt a stream it was a full blown river. And there was Mickey walking up that track as calm as you please towards those trees, like it was no more trouble than stepping out with his best girl.

Then I saw standing under those trees

I will not write down what I think it was I saw standing under those trees. It is enough that soon I will be fighting the enemies of King & Country, I have no wish to go up against the Enemy of Man too. In any event the whole thing, wood and ridge and track, was gone almost as quick as I saw it so I said nothing when they asked me what made me yell.

As I say, we searched the whole of that park, every bush leaf and stone, and never saw a sign of Mickey Grant. The army pegged him as a deserter but thats not what I think happened. To my mind he was conscripted into a worse fight than ever any one of us is going off to face, and I pray that the good Lord has mercy on his soul.

* * *

Taken from A History of Scouting *by Oliver Carswell, 1982*

Even a quarter of a century later, it is still hard to envisage the scale of the 9th World Scout 'Jubilee' Jamboree. Aside from the thousands of scouts camped on sites throughout the West Midlands conurbation, over thirty thousand from eighty-five countries camped in just Sutton Park alone, inhabiting a virtual city of tents which included its own hospital, newspaper and grandstand capable of seating fifteen thousand people. At the time, it boasted the largest cinema screen in the country, and over the twelve days' duration it is estimated that three-quarters of a million day visitors attended the event.

And yet, the great British weather is capable of threatening even such an enterprise as this. After a record-breaking heat-wave, the night of 5 August brought a torrential downpour to the region, with an inch of rain falling in less than an hour which flooded out around a thousand Scouts...

* * *

Taken from the Sutton Register, *7 August 1957*

...concern continues to mount regarding the whereabouts of fifteen-year-old Sean Enright of Workington, Cumberland, following the unprecedented downpour of two days ago. He is believed to have been one of many young men attending the 9th World Scout Jamboree whose tents were inundated when the Longmoor Brook burst its banks. Searches along the length of the stream including the Longmoor Pool have so far proved fruitless, and police are appealing for any witnesses...

Tara shut Liv's scrapbook. She'd read enough.

15

DIFFERENT CELLS

PRYCE WAS NOT AT ALL KEEN ON LETTING TARA TALK TO Olivia Crawford in her cell, but eventually agreed. Tara flattered herself that her agreeing to have dinner with him might have been a factor. However, he point-blank refused to allow her to be alone with someone who had already attacked her once, but was prepared to compromise by hovering like a self-appointed guardian angel just inside the open door.

Crawford sat on the edge of her blue vinyl-covered mattress and stared at her. Ironically, she'd had her shoelaces confiscated.

'I saw your scrapbook,' said Tara.

The stare didn't change.

'Why didn't you show it to me before kidnapping me?'

The stare became a sneer of utter scorn.

'Okay. I get it. Wouldn't be told, had to be shown.'

Crawford leaned forward and extended her right arm, underside up, showing her the tattoo just below her elbow that Tara had seen in the interview video. 'The carbon in the ash in this is three thousand years old,' she said. 'Test it.'

Tara shook her head. 'I'd need a bigger sample. Sorry.'

Crawford sat back again. 'Then why did you come here?'

'Because I thought you might like to see his remains. So you know that he's dead, and has been dead for a very long time. That he can't hurt you any more.'

'What? You mean...' Her eyes flashed to the door.

'Again, no, sorry. Not in person. Photos are going to have to do.' She took out her phone and indicated a space on the mattress next to Crawford. 'May I?'

She shrugged, and Tara sat down. It took the better part of an hour for her to go through all the images and scans of Rowton Man on her phone, minus those of the impossible bone scars. Crawford surprised her, stopping her frequently to ask for clarifications and explanations, many of which Tara didn't have, and by thanking her at the end.

'Don't think I don't know what you're trying to do, though,' Crawford added.

'What do you think I'm trying to do?'

'Convince me that he's dead just because his spirit and his body aren't connected. He's not.'

'You think I'm trying to manipulate you. That's understandable. But I saw your flat and your archaeological finds. You've got a decent collection by anybody's standards. I really just thought you'd be interested, that's all.'

Something flashed up in Liv's eyes. 'Don't you *dare* feel sorry for me!' she snapped.

Pryce looked up sharply. 'Oi, watch yourself.' To Tara he added, 'I think that's about it, don't you?'

'Yes,' sighed Tara, standing and brushing off her knees. 'All done here.'

As she moved away, Crawford halted her with a hand on her sleeve. 'Please,' she whispered, her eyes full of tears. 'I'm sorry; you're a nice person. I went back, you know, afterwards. As soon as I could. To see if I could convince him to let Scattie and Bran go. But they'd left by then, and they were out of his reach. He needed help, he told me, on this side. In the world. Help keeping the *afaugh* from getting in. He taught me things, and I kept his grave safe, but now he's been dug up and I've fucking *failed*. You can see how fragile he is. Put him back, *please*. If it gets loose, you'll die. We'll *all* die.'

'Oi!' warned Pryce, louder. 'I told you. Less of that. You don't make threats, not in here.'

But as the cell door locked behind her, Tara reflected that it had sounded less like a threat and more like a plea.

LATER, NATHAN THOUGHT THAT STEVE VICKERS MUST HAVE been waiting for him at his hotel. Nathan had only popped back to pack. He didn't know if he still had a job to go back to, but at least he wouldn't be here. His room was comfortable enough; clean, corporate, not entirely bland but with so little character that you could lock your door and be anywhere from Aberdeen to San Francisco. As clean as the sterile gauze on his stomach and performing much the same function for his battered brain. He opened his rucksack on the bed and started stuffing his clothes in.

Someone knocked on the door.

Through the peep-hole he saw a man he didn't recognise: thinning on top and red around the eyes, in a grey hoodie and sweatpants as if he'd just stopped by on his way home from the gym. Not a policeman. Probably another of the kids' relatives come to throw their pain in his face. Nathan opened the door, but kept it on the chain; the last few days had given him nothing if not a healthy dose of paranoia.

'Yes?' he asked. 'Can I help you?'

'My name is Steven Vickers,' said the man. 'And before you say anything,' he added quickly, 'I'm not here looking for a fight.'

It was just as well, because Nathan was so taken aback by his turning up out of the blue that Vickers could have knocked him down with a strong sneeze. Seen through the jamb, and without the distortion of the fish-eye lens, Vickers was a lot bigger than he'd first seemed.

'Why are you here?'

'I've come to ask you to leave us alone,' Vickers replied. 'I know that you and Sue... that you have history, but all you're doing by being here is upsetting her. If you have any respect for her, you'll go. Tonight. That's all.' His hands were deep in the front pocket of his hoodie, fidgeting.

Nathan couldn't help a snort of surprised laughter. He wasn't laughing at Vickers but this already bizarre situation had just taken a left turn into the ridiculous. Why was Vickers being so civilised about this? 'That's all?'

Vickers frowned. 'Something funny?'

'No, I—'

'Did I make a joke?'

'Look—'

'You think I find the thought of you fucking my wife *amusing*?'

Vickers was trying to stop working himself up to something – Nathan could see it in the reddening of his face and the way his hands were twisting. He plainly wanted to kick the shit out of Nathan, so what was holding him back? Had Sue made him promise not to get violent? Had she told her husband where to find him or had Vickers forced it out of her? The idea that he might have hurt her made Nathan sick with anger. How dare this fucking hypocrite try to appeal to his better nature?

'Technically she was only your fiancée when I was fucking her,' he pointed out. 'You know, if that makes you feel any better.'

Vickers was through the door with a brutal shove, the chain snapping, his hands reaching out to lock around Nathan's throat. Nathan was borne backwards by the larger man's momentum and the small of his back fetched up painfully against the vanity unit. Things rattled and fell to the floor.

Vickers' face was red and shining, his eyes narrowed, his teeth bared. Sue had once said something about Steve having played rugby for his school, and Nathan could well believe it. Despite being throttled, and the fierce pain that flared from his stab wound, Nathan thought, *Good. Let's at least be honest about what we are.*

'You keep the fuck away from my family, got that?' Vickers snarled.

Nathan nodded as best he could and choked out something that sounded like, 'Goddit.'

'There's nothing here for you, got *that*?'

Nathan was surprised to find that he was becoming more angry than scared – not least by the fact that it seemed like every man and his dog thought they had a right to grab him by the throat these days. 'Did you…' he coughed. 'Hurt her?'

Vickers' eyes widened. 'You what?' His fingers squeezed harder. 'You fucking what?'

'I said…' Nathan drove a fist low and hard into the other man's belly. Vickers loosened his grip, so Nathan hit him again higher up, harder. Winded, Vickers fell away, making choking sounds of his own. 'If you've hurt her…' Nathan coughed again, massaging his throat.

Vickers staggered in retreat to the door, then turned. 'Come near my family again, and I'll fucking kill you.'

'Hurt her, *one* hair—'

But Vickers was gone.

Nathan almost left too. Whatever mysteries were slowly unravelling themselves from around Liv and the timber track, the price of finding out was starting to look like it was too high, and he was halfway packed for his return journey to Wales when his phone rang. He very nearly didn't pick it up. If he'd recognised the number he probably wouldn't have – but it was an unknown contact. He took the call.

'Hello?'

'Mr Brookes?' said a female voice, vaguely familiar. 'My name is Dr Tara Doumani. I'd very much like to show you something.'

16

THE THRICE-DEAD KING

NATHAN LOOKED DOWN AT ROWTON MAN LYING ON HIS bed of peat, and shivered. Climate control in the lab was keeping the temperature as low as possible to help delay decomposition, but that wasn't the only reason.

'Well he's in a bit of a state, isn't he? Jesus, is that a noose?'

'It's a garrotte,' corrected Doumani. 'But yes.'

'You mean he was strangled to death?'

'It's hard to say for certain, but yes, probably.'

'Fuck,' he said quietly; his hand moved to the bruises on his own throat where Sue's husband had choked him.

Now that Nathan had an opportunity to meet Doumani properly, rather than in the darkness of the fight or the fuss afterwards, she surprised him. Her voice on the phone had a depth that had led him to expect someone older and taller, but she was short and pretty with dark hair and skin that suggested Middle Eastern heritage; she was neat, controlled, precise. He wasn't sure whether or not he liked her, but unlike a lot of people he'd met recently she at least gave the impression that she knew what she was talking about.

'A lot of damage is post-mortem and caused by the pressure of the peat over the years,' she continued, 'but if you look here, and here, there are also quite a few stab wounds.'

'They really wanted him dead, didn't they?'

'It's a phenomenon called "sacrificial overkill". It's not enough for the victim to be simply physically dead, he must be symbolically dead too.'

'Symbolically dead?'

'And now we're into the realms of palaeoanthropology, which isn't really my field, but the idea is that if your community is afflicted by a disease or disaster, it's because the gods are displeased with you. You've committed some kind of sin, collectively. The sacrifice takes on the sins of the community and by their death those sins are expiated, and whatever the gods are punishing you with – drought, famine, disease, whatever – will stop.'

'It's a Jesus story.'

'There's nothing new under the sun. Ready for a bit of a lecture?'

'As long as there isn't a test at the end.'

Doumani laughed. 'Generally speaking, across a lot of prehistoric cultures there are considered to be three spheres of human activity: the martial sphere, controlled by warriors and soldiers—'

'And police, I'll bet,' Nathan snorted.

'—the scholarly sphere, controlled by shamans, teachers, wizards, priests; and the domestic sphere, or the hearth, which is all about farms, food and babies. The king or chieftain must be the bravest and most noble warrior, the wisest lawgiver, and the best provider of food and heirs for his people. A healthy society needs all three to be in balance, so when things go wrong, it is deemed to be a fault of the king – he has somehow failed in fulfilling the vows of his sacred marriage to the earth, and the gods are punishing his people. So he – or a representative victim – is killed three times to atone for the sins committed against the three social spheres. As a warrior, he is stabbed. As a shaman, he is strangled. As a father, he is drowned. The gods accept the offering, balance is restored, and everybody lives happily ever after.'

Nathan's hand moved from his bruised throat to the stitches in his side. The whole thing sounded like one of Robbie's pranks, but he didn't find this one funny at all.

'He was found with this,' she continued, leading him to the other side of the lab where the secondary finds were being catalogued, cleaned and preserved in smaller trays – scraps of clothing, shards of pottery and traces of food which the pots had contained, and the prize of the collection: a corroded bronze spearhead. 'The strange thing is its size. It's not ceremonial, but it's much bigger than a standard hunting spear. All of which is neither here nor there, really. It's the X-rays that will give you sleepless nights.'

He watched her hesitate as if unsure of how far she could trust him, despite his having saved her life, but then motioned for him to follow her to a computer monitor. 'These are CT scans of Rowton Man.' She clicked through several images. 'This is his left leg...'

As Doumani explained, Nathan stared at the image, at the

surgical scars. Doumani's voice grew fainter as the rushing in his ears grew louder.

'Mr Brookes? Nathan!'

Nathan felt sick. 'That's Ryan's leg,' he whispered.

'You're sure?'

'Am I...? Are you fucking kidding me?'

'Not even remotely. Now it's your turn. I want you to show me where it happened.'

'YOU BELIEVE LIV, DON'T YOU?' ASKED NATHAN. HE AND Dr Doumani – Tara, as she'd asked him to call her – were walking up the Longmoor Valley in the swelter of another baking afternoon, but somewhat gingerly – she because of her injured feet, he because of his stitches.

'What makes you say that?'

'Because you're here.'

The weather stations were predicting no immediately foreseeable end to the heatwave; the high-pressure system which had clamped itself onto the country like the lid of a Dutch oven stifled any wind and the city air was a white-yellow haze of trapped pollution.

'I believe she went somewhere,' said Tara. 'I'm not prepared to commit to where, exactly. But leaving aside the parts of her story that are obviously delusional, there's enough of what she said that she could only know if she's done some pretty obscure research.'

'Like what?'

'The climate, for a start. And the landscape it made. We

dated Rowton Man, or Bark Foot, or whatever he's called, to about eleven hundred BC, which is a time when the world experienced a period of severe climate change. An Icelandic volcano called Hekla erupted – remember in 2010 when the ash cloud from Eyjafjallajökull grounded air traffic for a week?'

'Yes. And congratulations, by the way.'

'On what?'

'On being able to say eeja-fa-lacky-lokey-whatserface.'

She laughed, and they carried on walking. 'Well, that was a burp in comparison. The Hekla 3 eruption was on a par with Vesuvius and Mount St Helens, big enough to throw seven cubic kilometres of debris into the atmosphere and cool temperatures in the northern hemisphere for nearly twenty years. Some people think it caused famines in ancient Egypt and maybe even the collapse of Bronze Age society in the Near East altogether. What it definitely did do in Britain was turn a reasonably warm and temperate climate that was conducive to agriculture into one that was cold, rainy, dark, and much harder to farm. Olivia Crawford described exactly that in your interview with her: the bogs and scrubby trees, little undergrowth, nothing much able to grow because of the lack of sunlight. That kind of environmental change does drastic things to societies. It's likely most people migrated south to warmer areas or west to drier, more mountainous ones, and those that were left became more tribal, possibly even cannibalistic – it's not surprising that they would have created some kind of protective ancestor figure to defend themselves against what they thought were evil spirits.'

'The *afaugh*.'

'Which is another thing: the hungry ghost. It's in every culture. They call it *preta* in India and the wendigo in North America, and depending on the theological sophistication of the prevailing culture it can represent anything from a simple cannibalism taboo to our unhealthy attachment to worldly pleasures. Stories often describe it exactly as Olivia did: with a belly bloated by greed but a neck too thin to swallow anything, so that it's perpetually starving. She described Rowton Man pretty accurately too, in terms of his height and build, not to mention his spear.'

They had reached Rowton's Well, and watched while two dogs romped around in its shallow water until they were whistled away by their owner. Tara watched them coldly. 'There's a story that the Birmingham Eye Hospital used to have water from this spring delivered every day because of its healing mineral qualities,' she said. 'It's probably not true. Still, using it as a dog bath...' She shook her head.

'You disapprove?'

'I just think people shouldn't necessarily assume that everything exists for their convenience.'

They skirted past the well, through the curtaining fringe of birch leaves and down to the stream. It was even lower than yesterday; the summer had taken its toll, reducing it to a trickle between banks of crumbling black earth. If it weren't for the springs feeding it, Nathan thought that it might have dried up altogether. It certainly wasn't the raging torrent of Liv's story. Nor was there any sign of any kind of bridge, ancient or modern.

'The whole area was dug for peat for centuries,' Tara explained, leading them along the opposite bank. 'In the 1700s, peat diggers found the remains of worked timbers near the well. Some people think they were just bits of earlier workings; some that they were remains of an ancient track. We don't have them to study so it's impossible to say for sure.'

'What do you think?'

'If you'd asked me that yesterday I'd have gone with the first explanation just because it's the simplest. Occam's razor and all that.'

Nathan nodded. Then he shook his head. 'Nope, no clue what you're on about.'

Tara pointed at the ground, and at first he couldn't see anything unusual about it. She bent, brushed aside a thin covering of turf, and picked up an ordinary stone – rounded and river-smooth on one side, but blackened and broken sharply in half on the other. Now he could see that what he had taken to be flat ground was in fact a very wide, very shallow rise, like a blister in the earth. When he shoved the soil with his shoe there were many more such broken and blackened stones just under the surface.

'This is a burnt mound,' she explained. 'It's about three thousand years old. All the stones in it are like this one: they've been heated until they've cracked and then been thrown away.'

'Why would anybody do that?'

'Again, conflicting theories. They almost always occur by water sources, so most people agree that there's some kind of sweat-hut activity involved.'

He looked at her closely. 'Sweat-hut. You are actually taking the piss now, right?'

'Not in the slightest. You make a domed hut out of animal hides or turf. Outside, you heat the rocks until they're red hot, and then you take them inside the hut and you pour water on them so that the hut fills with steam. When the rocks cool, you throw them away on your burnt mound and get some more.'

'Just like Liv described.' He turned a stone over in his hands, as if afraid it might explode. The thought that this might have been one of the stones that Liv had seen Bark Foot working with was unnerving; the being's fingers might have touched this very stone...

He dropped it. 'You think we're standing in the middle of where Bark Foot's camp might have been?'

'I'm still not a hundred per cent sure I'm prepared to believe any of this.'

He tried to picture it as Liv had described, scraping for fragments of his dream: wooded, but with sparse stands of undernourished trees. The stream wider and louder, the bank higher. For a moment he could almost hear it, and he was seized by that same feeling he'd had sitting up on Rowton Bank on the day the kids had disappeared, when he'd had a vision of the landscape layered upon itself eon by eon, and it seemed that the air was only skin-thin. It wouldn't take very much effort – not so much as it would take to burst a soap bubble – to push through it and into that other place: the tepid twilight of a present without a past. *Un.*

'Nathan?' It was Tara's voice, calling faintly, as if from a long distance away. '*Nathan?*'

He snapped back into the moment, and turned to her. 'What?'

She stepped back from him in surprise. 'Where the hell were you just now?' she demanded.

'What do you mean?'

'I turned away for a moment and you were gone. Where did you go?'

He was tempted to say, *I've been right here the whole time*, but suspected that this wasn't entirely true. 'You were telling me about sweat-huts,' he said, trying to divert the conversation back towards something remotely normal. 'What were they used for?'

'Yes,' she said, still eyeing him with suspicion. 'So. Why does anybody take a sauna? Relaxation, hygiene. If you're a sweaty Bronze Age shepherd who's been tending his flock all day, it's probably the closest thing you're going to get to a hot shower. Don't make the mistake of thinking that prehistoric cultures were entirely primitive; in many respects they were as advanced as our own.'

'But that's not what Liv described. Bark Foot didn't use his sweat-hut for a sauna. Somehow he used it to steal what he needed from Ryan.'

'The other theory is that they were for ritual purposes. The tribal shaman would throw not just water on the rocks but maybe something with a psychotropic effect too – magic mushrooms, who knows? – and the intense heat and humidity would combine with it to give visions, hallucinations, out-of-body experiences, that sort of thing.

It's still done these days, except by New Age hippies who think they're undergoing an authentic spiritual journey, *man*. The shaman might have thought he was communicating with ancestor spirits or nature spirits, which is obviously a desirable thing if your crops are failing and your tribe is starving and you want help from the ancestors.'

He wandered around the area, scuffing at the ground with his feet. 'I still don't get how that helps him steal a part of someone's *body*, for heaven's sake.'

'You know what? Neither do I. Nobody knows anything about this, not for certain. We just look at what happens in the world we know today and extrapolate backwards with the least dodgy guesswork. You need to talk to an anthropologist if you want more detailed answers.'

He looked up at her, suddenly joyful at a sudden revelation. 'Oh, but!' he laughed. 'But, but, but! What if there was a way of talking to the right person? Or the right *ancestor*. What if we built our own sweat-hut?'

'Now wait a moment...'

'Listen, I'm already seeing them: the visions – hallucinations – whatever they are. Those kids are *there*. Bark Foot is *there*. You saw him yourself, when Liv kidnapped you. The only way we're going to get answers to any of this is if we make some kind of effort to establish contact.'

'That's insane.'

'Yes. But this is the way it was done, you said – the way Bark Foot's people communicated with the spirit world. Un, that's what Liv called it.'

'Nathan, we're talking obscure palaeoanthropological

theory, here, not… not a *séance*! This is not a thing that people *do*.'

'No, but they *did*, didn't they? They *did*. And who better to show me how they did it than you?'

'Okay then, it's not a thing that *I* do. I don't make a habit of pandering to mystical New Age crap. It's already bad enough that people basically think I'm Lara bloody Croft without me going and adding Psychic Sally into the mix. I'm a scientist – I'm a rational human being.'

'And thankful to still be one, I hope.'

'Meaning?'

'Meaning, to be blunt, and sorry, but you owe me. I don't make a habit of saving people from stabby maniacs, you know. So we're both in unfamiliar territory. Plus, there's Bark Foot's leg – you want answers to that just as badly as I do. Tell me that you're prepared to turn down a chance to talk to him, however insane it sounds.'

He waited for her to make one final, absolute refusal, and when it didn't come knew that he'd won. 'Still,' she said, sounding less strident, 'even if I agreed in principle, it'd be impossible in practice. I wasn't lying when I told you that this isn't what I do. You need someone specialised on the experimental side of things – someone who knows how to build the right kinds of structures out of the right kinds of materials. Me, I have trouble with Lego. And if anybody is available at such short notice, or even willing, this burnt mound is a scheduled ancient monument. The bureaucratic hoops you'd have to jump through… it would take months to get permission, if at all.'

'No hoops,' he grinned, still bouncing with manic energy. 'And don't worry, we don't have to go interfering with any ancient monuments. None of that. I just need your credit card and your car.'

She threw her hands wide at him in stupefaction; he was so far from making sense.

'New Agers,' he explained. 'Hippies. Wales is crawling with them. There's a place that does exactly this kind of thing just down the road from where I work.'

'You want me to go to Wales with you?'

'Unless you want to just give me your credit card...'

'You're not having my credit card. Spend your own money on this madness.'

'I'm tapped out,' he explained gleefully. 'Burnt it all on the hotel. Plus I work in outdoor education. I am what they call a "high risk" borrower.'

'High risk,' she grumbled. 'Never a truer word spoken. No, no, it's fine,' she held up a hand to silence him. The conversation and the heat was making her head throb. 'But I'm driving.'

17

MOONBRIDGE

A FEW MILES DOWN THE ROAD FROM THE BRYNCAER Mountain Centre was the valley of Cwm Trefni, nicknamed the Hippy Valley by Nathan's colleagues. This was due to the fact that a large acreage of woodland deep within the arms of the valley was a private spiritualist retreat owned by an organisation called the Moonbridge Institute. It seemed that in an age when youth and social services were being sacrificed on the altar of austerity there was still a market for places to help those who could afford the luxury of spiritual poverty – not least by lightening them of the terrible burden of their disposable income. It offered everything from straightforward dietary detox programmes and yoga classes up to reiki, fire-walking workshops, and sweat-hut ceremonies. Its services were not cheap. Its calendar was also full, this being the height of tourist season, but when Tara metaphorically waved her credit card down the phone, along with the promise of a possible endorsement from her department about the authenticity of Moonbridge's pseudo-pagan credentials (not that she had any intention of doing so), two spaces were miraculously found. The universe had obviously smiled on them, said Nathan. All praise the Great Spirit.

'That sounds quite cynical for someone who claims to be trying to contact the spirit of a three-thousand-year-old bog mummy,' she observed.

'No, cynical is the fleecing of burnt-out executives,' he replied. 'Not that I care. It's just the screaming hypocrisy I can't stand.'

Even though he'd only been away from this part of the world for a matter of days, there was a strange feeling of déjà vu as Tara drove them along the familiar mountain roads, as if much more time had passed. It was like seeing an old friend on the street but walking past without acknowledging them. He hadn't told Robbie that he was returning; there was no explanation he could possibly give that didn't sound barking mad. Still, he'd been ready to give this business up when Liv had come back into it; if this sweat-hut thing came to nothing he'd go back to Bryncaer and try to do what normal people did: forget the whole thing and move on.

The road dipped down into a densely wooded valley, plunging them from wide, high heathland into a dark green tunnel in moments, and a signposted side road took them between the crumbling pillars of an ancient estate's gateway. The stone walls to either side were furred with moss and ferns, and every so often Nathan caught glimpses of carved totem poles amongst the trees and brightly coloured dream-catchers hanging in the branches.

'Welcome to Rivendell,' Tara said. 'Don't forget your kaftan.'

The driveway ended at a pleasantly old-fashioned-looking building which had evidently been the estate gatekeeper's lodge, and which now served as the Moonbridge Institute's reception. They were met by a cheerfully impersonal young man who took their paperwork and gave them their orientation packs before directing them onwards, deeper into the woodland. They passed turn-offs to other areas of the retreat with names such as 'Yoga Lake' and 'Reiki Dell'.

'It's a maze,' said Nathan. 'We came here once, me and others from the centre, and got completely lost. Some of our kids had got wind of the place and were convinced that it was a commune full of naked hippy-chicks and dope heads, so they came looking to score. The owners called us when the lads were caught trying to buy drugs off a bunch of accountants from Norwich out on a corporate bonding junket. Cunning little sods gave us the slip and we got ourselves lost in here for hours trying to chase them down before our boss called and told us that they'd reappeared back in their dorm, good as gold. Next day we woke them up at five in the morning with a fire drill in the pouring rain.' He laughed. 'Happy days.'

They arrived at a car park and a wide clearing by a stream with tents pitched around its perimeter. In the centre was a large yurt with walls of wicker and a shallow domed roof made from blankets and animal hides. A well-established fire pit stood a little way off, surrounded by simple log seats. The whole clearing was redolent with the smell of wood smoke.

Tara and Nathan were welcomed by a languid middle-aged man with rainbow dreadlocks down to the small of his back and a broad West Country accent who introduced himself as Phoelix and showed them where to pitch their tents.

If Nathan had thought that it was going to be a simple case of jumping straight into the sweat-hut, he was mistaken. After a couple of hours of being allowed to settle in, Phoelix called the inhabitants of all the tents together around the fire pit for the first of the preparation workshops: the inevitable and cringe-inducing getting-to-know-each-other session.

'You have arrived as strangers,' he said, enfolding them in the warmth of his serene smile, 'but you will leave as family. And as family you will get to know each other's hopes and dreams, failings and fears, and through knowing each other come to a greater knowledge of the spirit without, by whatever name you choose to call it – God, Allah, the Buddha, or even the Force' – there were a few nervous chuckles at that – 'and thus begin the process of healing the spirit within yourself.'

When it was his turn to explain his reasons for being there, Nathan made up something about being a burnt-out teacher looking to refresh his commitment to his vocation, which skirted closely enough to the truth to sound believable. The other sweat-hut initiates weren't the crystal-clutching airheads he'd been expecting. There was a predictable number of students, but also a librarian, a bus driver, a website developer and a woman who was on her first respite care break in eleven years from looking after her sick mother. Tara didn't take part but stood off at a distance, the two of them having agreed that one of them ought to keep at least a semi-rational head on their shoulders.

There were ice-breaking games, and a woodland treasure hunt, and a communally prepared vegetarian lunch cooked over the fire, and in the afternoon a drum-making workshop where each participant in that evening's sweat ceremony had to make a simple tabor with which to 'summon the heartbeat of the universal spirit'. Each was to be decorated in whatever style suited the drummer, and Nathan found himself – despite his scepticism – quite concerned to get it right. In the end he settled on a hunter figure in red with a white left foot, executed in a style which he intended to be like a Neolithic cave painting, but in the end looked like a stick man wearing an Ugg boot.

Nathan was collecting firewood when Phoelix took him aside. 'I know that you're thinking this is a load of crap,' he said. 'And that's okay.'

'Hey, no,' Nathan protested. 'It's not that…'

'Yeah it is,' Phoelix laughed, but Nathan found no accusation or offence in his tone.

Nathan relaxed, and returned the man's smile. 'It is a bit full on, you have to admit.'

'Think of it like theatre. You have to let the lights go down and the music come up otherwise you're not *there*, you know? You've got to let your head get in the right place, or there's no story, just a bunch of morons in silly costumes shouting at each other.'

'I suppose so.'

'You don't have to take any of this literally. You don't have to consciously believe that there's a great universal spirit. You just need to give your mind a bit of space and peace and quiet to let it heal itself. That's all this is. Just do me a favour – try not to be too much of a buzz-kill for the others.'

'What if I do take it literally, though?'

'What do you mean?' Phoelix seemed suddenly suspicious that he was taking the piss, and Nathan couldn't blame him.

'What if I'd been talking to someone who'd told me that they'd had... an experience, shall we say, of the other world, and I wanted to know more. What then?'

'Then I'd say this is entirely the wrong place for you. Mental clinics are full of people who literally believe that they've travelled to other planes of existence or been contacted by spirits. Moonbridge is a retreat, not a shrine. What we do here is essentially a form of guided meditation with a bit of added set dressing. If you're looking for calm and healing, then great, but spiritual insight? Go to church and talk to a priest.'

'Fair enough, but the people who come here must believe that they're getting in touch with something, mustn't they?'

'Yes, but we only go as far as to encourage them to get in touch with their inner feelings and the emotional obstructions that are blocking them from true happiness. If they choose to ascribe something religious to their experience here, that's up to them. I can't tell you the "truth" of what the other world is because that truth varies from person to person and culture to culture. If you're a Buddhist it's nirvana, if you're a Catholic it might be heaven or hell, if you're an indigenous Australian it's the Dreamtime. They're all just metaphors to describe the indescribable truth of what lies in our own souls. What did this other person say they had experienced, anyway?'

'It doesn't matter. I want to know what *you* think. You're the closest thing I'm going to find to an expert. What is the other world?'

Phoelix blew out his cheeks. 'Jeez, why don't you ask me a tough one? Okay, try this. The other world is, almost by definition, everything that is not *the* world. The world is definable, predictable – it has time, distance, physical laws which can be discovered and tested by empirical scientific enquiry. The spirit world, however you want to define it, is *not*. It is fluid, indefinable, unpredictable and random. It is a shadow world cast by the light of consciousness; you cannot have the one without the other. It's where creativity comes from and imagination rules. If you like your Jungian theory, it is the collective totality of subconscious human dreams and desires, the diamond that is transformed from the coal of our drab little human lives under the pressure of a hundred thousand years of dreaming. What it is differs from one culture to the next, one individual to another. If you believe in the spirits of nature, gods or demons, that's where you'll find them, but wisdom comes from understanding that they are all just aspects of yourself.'

'The dead, too?'

'There's no such thing as life after death. That's why they call it death. But that's not the same thing as saying there's no such thing as ghosts. The memories of loved ones, and the way they've touched our lives, and the shadows that they cast on our souls – now they *are* real, and when you connect with another place – the Dreamtime, Annwn, Hades; it has lots of names – you unleash very real psychical forces over which you have no control. Some people do say that it is just the gateway to a place that transcends life and death and time itself, but now you're talking about religion and, as I say, that's a line I don't cross.'

AS THE LONG SUMMER EVENING DEEPENED, THE FIRE WAS banked high and large stones deposited in the embers – not river rocks, Nathan learned, but modern sauna-grade peridotite, which would not shatter and need replacing.

'We call these stones the Little Grandmothers and Grandfathers,' said Phoelix. 'Our ancestors, who will speak to the Universal Spirit on our behalf.'

While they were heating up, Nathan found Tara and took her aside to the edge of the firelight. 'Listen,' he said. 'There's something you need to know before we start this.'

'What, more? There's a surprise,' she replied drily.

'You're going to be pissed off.'

'You've just cost me three hundred pounds, Nathan. I'm already there.'

'No, I mean really pissed off. There wasn't any choice, I'm afraid. The thing is, I have no idea what's going to happen when I try to make contact with Bark Foot. Most likely nothing.' He drew a deep breath, thinking of the figures from his dream and Liv's tale of the *afaugh*. 'Maybe something bad. So I decided it might be best to have some kind of insurance policy.' He reached into his daysack and carefully brought out the object he'd stolen from her lab.

Rowton Man's spearhead, though heavily corroded, was still sturdy, and the socket where its shaft had long rotted away made a good handle.

Tara was speechless with outrage.

'Told you you'd be pissed off.'

'Give it here!' she hissed, clearly resisting the urge to snatch it from him.

'I'm sorry, but no. I might need it.'

'Give. It. Here,' she enunciated, 'or I call the police right now.' She took out her phone, daring him. Reluctantly, he handed over the spearhead, then followed her as she stalked back to her car, opened the boot and wrapped it in an old blanket.

'I knew if I tried to explain it to you, you'd have said no—' he started.

'Understatement of the fucking century, right there!'

'—and if nothing happens then you can call the police; Hodges will love that.'

'Except, of course, you knew I wouldn't do that, didn't you? I'd be dropping myself in it for giving you access to Rowton Man in the first place. You bastard! I trusted you!'

'Tara, listen to me. Something terrible is hovering around this business. This is dangerous shit we're messing with. Can't you feel it? Don't tell me you can't.'

Her expression told him that she couldn't.

'I didn't bring you here just for your credit card,' he continued. 'I'm glad you've got my back, but if something… happens, then you might need more than just harsh language to protect us.'

'So you were really thinking of me all along,' she said, rigid with sarcasm. 'How nice. No,' she cut him off before he could reply. 'Just get in that sweat-lodge and do whatever it is you're going to do. I don't want to talk to you right now.' She stalked away to her tent, leaving him to curse himself for telling her about the spearhead. Why hadn't he waited until after the ceremony?

When he looked up from his thoughts, Phoelix was holding the door flap of the yurt open, inviting them in. The ceremony was about to begin.

'Knock knock?'

Tara looked up from where she'd been trying to get her self-inflating mattress to hold up its end of the bargain. Bending low to peer through her tent flap was someone she absolutely had not expected to see.

'Detective Pryce?'

She crawled out of the tent and stood, brushing grass off her backside. 'What are you doing here?'

'Keeping tabs on our boy. Sorry if I alarmed you. I didn't want him to know I was here, but I thought you should.' He glanced over at the yurt; from within came the sound of drumming and chanting. Other than that, and except for a crystal-clutcher type tending the fire, they were alone in the clearing. 'Is everything okay?'

'Everything's fine. Why wouldn't it be?' She hated having to lie to him, and added this to her mental list of things Nathan owed her for.

'Just it seems a little odd, that's all. This.' He gestured around at the clearing. 'Not what I would have expected from either of you, frankly, given everything that's happened.'

'We're not breaking any laws, are we?'

We. As if she and Nathan Brookes were a couple. She felt sick at being forced to defend him in such terms, to Pryce of all people. He'd owe her for that too. She pointed at the tent next to hers, a cheap and flimsy festival pop-up thing that they'd bought en route. 'That's his. You can search it if you like.'

'That's his? Oh. Right. So you're not…'

'No. We're not.'

'Right.'

'Right.' *Why, Detective Pryce,* she thought. *I do believe you're jealous.* Watching him fidget, her alarm gave way to amusement and a kind of pity.

'Well no, I don't think I need to search anything. Don't have a warrant, in any case. I'll let you get on with, uh, whatever. You've got my number, right, if you need anything, or…'

'I have.'

'Right then, Dr Doumani.' He started to leave.

'Tara.'

He turned back. 'Excuse me?'

'It's Tara. My name.' As soon as she said it she mentally cringed. Of course he already knew that. She was making a fool of herself, and to make things worse she was blushing. Just great.

'That's a nice name.' Now he was blushing too. *Christ, we're like a pair of teenagers,* she thought. 'Irish?' he added.

'Lebanese.'

He frowned. 'Really?'

'I think I'd know,' she replied, a little more pointedly than she'd intended. 'It means "star" in Arabic.'

She could see him almost visibly wrestling with the temptation to make some cheesy line out of this, as if she hadn't heard all of them before, and was enormously relieved when he didn't.

'Mark,' he said. 'My name, that is.' And with that as a farewell, he wandered off, making a good show of nonchalantly examining the rest of the campsite until he disappeared in the direction of the car park. She went back to her mattress. It was a good job it was one of the self-inflating kind – she didn't think she'd be able to do it herself what with the fluttery feeling in her stomach.

THE ONLY LIGHT CAME FROM WHAT LITTLE FILTERED between the seams of the yurt's overlapping hides and blankets. It already felt stifling and airless, even without the introduction of steam; Moonbridge's insistence on medical disclaimers made perfect sense to Nathan now. He and the other sweat-hut initiates, all dressed in shorts or sarongs, half-looked at one another in that particular way the British have when faced with semi-naked strangers.

'This may be basically a big sauna,' said Phoelix, 'but we're not Swedes. No naked birch-whipping.' The laughter at that sounded just a little forced as they spread out to find sitting positions around a central shallow pit.

The stones were brought in from the fire on large shovels

and deposited carefully in the pit. The temperature in the hut immediately rose and sweat pricked out on Nathan's flesh. He took a tighter grip on his Bark Foot drum and thought, *Here we go, then.*

In the shadowless gloom of Un, the *afaugh* grinned to itself and mouthed the words:

Here we go, then.

18

THE SWEAT

DURING THE FIRST PART OF THE RITUAL – THE ROUND OF the Earth – there was no steam, just the rocks, and Phoelix led them in chants and supplications to the Earth Mother and Sky Father to help them set aside the burdens which they carried in their spirits. Each initiate was given two handfuls of herbs: sage in the left, mugwort in the right.

'You control your journey,' said Phoelix. 'If you find your breathing becoming difficult, the sage will help to clear your head and lungs. The mugwort is a common hedgerow plant which has been used by shamans and spiritualists for millennia to enhance dreaming and visions. It can be mildly hallucinogenic but is perfectly legal and non-toxic. And you are all, of course, free to leave the sweat-hut at any point if it becomes too much.'

There was a break in which the initiates were invited to go outside for a breath of fresh air. Nathan stayed. He suspected that if he was going to reach Un then he might have to push himself quite hard.

In the second round – the Round of the Sun – more rocks were brought in, and Phoelix introduced a ladleful of water onto them. The heat and humidity escalated, and Nathan had to take several deep breaths to fill his lungs. Around him, limbs and faces were shiny with perspiration. He caught the eye of the woman sitting opposite him – the web designer; Catrin, her name was – who smiled and flapped a hand in front of her face. *Getting hot in here.*

He nodded. *Tell me about it.*

The Round of the Sun progressed, with more drumming and chanting, and in the pulsing monotony of it he lost track of time, because it seemed that only another few minutes had passed before another break was called, even though he knew it must have been at least half an hour. Half of the initiates took advantage of the opportunity for some fresh air, and half of those didn't return when Phoelix announced the third round – the Round of Water.

The remaining seven initiates and Phoelix repositioned themselves equidistantly about the pit. More rocks. More water. More steam – so much so that Nathan found it difficult to see the other side of the yurt clearly. His eyes stung and his head swam. The heavy heat was forcing itself inside him, down into the root-branching fibres of his lungs and up into the spongy, throbbing mass of his brain, and he felt like he was being pushed out of his own clogged skull. He saw – or imagined that he saw – the room from a position somewhere near the ceiling, and the nine human figures sitting cross-legged around the pit of hissing, steaming rocks. It had to be his imagination, because the number was wrong. There should have been only eight of them: himself, Phoelix, Catrin, and five others who had returned.

So who was the ninth? The big man with the heavy beard and patchwork of scars all over his naked body?

Nathan hurtled back into his body and his eyes snapped open to see Bark Foot sitting across the pit from him, glaring through the shifting veils of steam as if daring him to make good on his ridiculous plan of crossing into Un and challenging him for the souls of the children on his own ground.

'Give them back!' Nathan demanded. 'You have no right!'

Then Bark Foot was gone and he was staring into Catrin's shocked face. The chanting had stopped.

He tried to get up, failed as pins and needles crippled his legs, and settled for crawling out of the yurt to lie gasping for breath in the astonishing, cool clarity of the outside air. It was like being doused with ice water. He stared up into the dark shadows of trees towering around him like a circle of disapproving sentinels.

Then Tara's concerned face replaced them. 'Nathan? Jesus, are you okay? You've been in there for nearly two hours!'

'He's there,' Nathan gasped. 'He's so close. *I'm* so close.' He coughed and wiped drool from his chin.

Phoelix appeared on the other side of him. 'I think you should sit the last round out.'

'No. No way. I'm not done.'

Phoelix took his pulse and put an ear to his chest, listening to his breathing. 'Well you're not so badly off in physical terms,' he admitted. 'But, Nathan, the sweat ceremony is supposed to be a healing process. The whole idea is to unburden your soul of the things that are holding it back from true fulfilment and peace, but you seem to be rushing towards some sort of confrontation. This can only cause you great spiritual damage.'

'The damage was done years ago, mate.' Every sentence was an effort, dredged from straining lungs. 'Not just to me. This isn't about peace. It's about setting things right. Let's go back in. Come on.' He struggled up, despite his nerve endings crying out for just a few more seconds lying on this wonderfully soft grass.

Phoelix shook his head. 'I can't let you take the risk.'

'Don't worry. I won't sue you if I fail to be fully spiritually enlightened by the process.' Clutching his handful of mugwort leaves, Nathan shuffled back inside the yurt, ignoring the anxious expressions of the other sweat initiates.

After even just a few minutes outside, the heat and humidity hit him like a truck, and he flopped back into his position, leaning back against the yurt wall, which was warm and slick with condensation, like flesh. *It's a womb,* he realised. Of course it would be.

Phoelix welcomed them to the third and final Round of the Moon. A last load of superheated rocks was heaped into the pit and more water ladled on. Nathan feared this last round was more than he could bear. His chest heaved as his lungs fought to extract what little oxygen they could from the saturated air; his head throbbed like an overinflated football threatening to tear apart at its distended seams. This was crazy. He was going to die. He had to get out.

Instead, he crushed the mugwort in his fist and brought

it up to cup over his face, inhaling deeply. Its thick green stench invaded his skull, expelling his consciousness as before, only with much greater clarity. His spirit divorced itself from his body, and he was in Un.

THE SWEAT-HUT IN WHICH HE FOUND HIMSELF WAS MUCH smaller than the yurt, and more crudely fashioned of willow and raw animal hides. It was empty. It stank of smoke and sweat, and was too low-roofed for him to stand upright. The stones in the central pit were cold. *Bark Foot's shelter*, he thought – the one that Liv had talked about, where Ryan's leg, and presumably his life, had been taken. There was no sign of a body, however.

'Did you feed what was left to the *afaugh*, you bastard?' he asked the empty chamber. 'Is that what you did? Is that the little arrangement that the two of you have?'

There was no reply.

Nathan located the door flap and pushed his way out of the hut.

Bark Foot's camp was exactly as Liv had described, just as the surrounding forest matched that of his dream in the hospital – a dripping grey-green gloom with the pallid fingers of spectral birches rising out of shapeless moss. He wasn't sure if there was such a thing as time in Un, but even if there was, the passage of nine years had left this place untouched. There was the drying rack, the fire pit, even the logs that had been drawn up around it for the children to sit on, but no sign of any of their belongings that had been left behind.

'I know you're out there!' he shouted. 'I know you can hear me!'

'You know nothing,' growled a voice behind him. 'You never did.'

He whirled. A figure stepped out of hiding: bearded, wild, an already muscular frame made more massive by layers of fur and stitched-together birch bark. Yet for all his size, he looked sick; his skin was waxen, and he leaned on his spear as if it were a walking stick. Nathan neither knew nor cared why this might be. 'I've come for my children.'

Bark Foot hobbled forward and peered at him. 'You,' he grunted, and grimaced. 'She should have put me back. All of this might have been avoided. But then possibly it was fated to be so. I am no shaman. I have no wisdom in such matters. I merely serve.' He was talking to himself, in the rambling way of a senile old man nearing his death. For all that Bark Foot was staring straight at him, Nathan might not have been there at all.

'I said—'

'I heard. They are gone, far beyond your reach or my sight. Be content.'

'Be content? What is that supposed to mean? I'm supposed to just forget about them?'

Bark Foot uttered a sigh of weariness that seemed to carry the weight of three thousand years and empty him of the very marrow of his bones. He lowered himself painfully to sit on one of the fireside logs. 'And so there is your choice,' he said. 'I can do no more.' Then it looked at him directly. 'Was it enough, do you think?'

'Was what enough? What the hell are you talking about? Just tell me what you did with Brandon and Scattie.'

'Enough to have served for so long and yet ultimately to have failed?'

Nathan saw now that what he had taken to be a mask of humanity over some ancient and crippled thing was in fact its true face – that beneath the years, this being who was older than his own civilisation, was, in the end, nothing more than a man, nearing the end of his life, and concerned with the same question as anyone: *was it enough?* But far from provoking empathy, its entreaty only filled Nathan with anger. What right had it to ask anything of him, after what it had done?

'No!' he spat. 'It wasn't enough. You stole children! How *could* it be enough? Not while you can still put it right. And anyway, you haven't failed.'

'Yes, I have,' it said, and pointed behind him.

The *afaugh*'s attack was swift and brutal.

It bore Nathan to the ground and straddled him, the sagging weight of its distended belly against his torso, too heavy for him to shove away no matter how much he thrashed. Its flesh was corpse-pallid and as soft as rotting mushrooms, but the claws that clamped his wrists to the ground were like iron. A necklace of rotting hands hung about a throat no thicker than his own wrist: too thin to swallow anything, and far too slender to support the weight of the head which leered above him, spattering drool onto his face from teeth filed to points. A cannibal's mouth.

It paused, its eyes sunken and glittering, and for a fleeting moment something passed between them – something almost like a kind of recognition.

Then it dipped towards him, and Nathan was terrified that it was going to eat him, starting with his face, before he realised that its intention was far worse. It pressed the bulge of its forehead against his teeth, and pushed. He tried to clench his jaws against the invasion, but it prised them apart, wider, and wider still, wider than it was physically possible for his mouth to open. *This is a vision, remember?* his mind babbled. *A dream, nothing but a hallucination, a bad trip from the mugwort; it's not really happening, not really happening.* But it didn't make any difference. The tendons in his jaw popped like the gristle on a chicken leg being pulled apart, and his shrieks were reduced to muffled gagging as it shoved and thrust more of itself deeper down his throat. His fingers clawed at the dirt and his heels drummed.

Impossibly, its whole head was inside him – he could feel the bulge of it working deeper into his gullet – and there was a momentary respite while its narrow neck followed, but then worse torture as it squirmed and shrugged its shoulders into his mouth like someone putting on a tight-fitting pullover. Its feet clambered up his body, digging for purchase with splintered toenails. The moment its claws let go of his wrists, he began beating at it, but its spongy flesh simply absorbed the blows.

Its belly followed, then its scrawny legs, and finally its feet, leaving dirt and leaf litter smeared around his lips like cake crumbs.

There was a moment of stillness, of stasis, when he

was both possessor and possessed. It lasted a fraction of a second, and all eternity, in which he felt the particular shape and texture of every twig and leaf and particle of dirt underneath him. The only other time he'd experienced anything like this had been with Sue, in those rare moments when they'd made each other come simultaneously, and in that shuddering, opalescent haze had forgotten where one finished and the other began. Or when he'd killed, and his victim's death-terror had briefly silenced the glacial howl where his soul used to be.

Then he woke up.

OUTSIDE THE YURT, CHEWING HER NAILS AND WONDERING how long she was prepared to let this insanity go on before she dragged Nathan out, Tara heard the screaming begin: shouts of alarm which escalated quickly into bright, animal shrieks of pain. And something laughing.

The first three initiates came out uninjured, but with the wide eyes of those who'd witnessed something terrible. The next was limping, clutching at the back of one calf where blood ran bright red.

'He bit me!' she was shrieking over and over. 'He bit me!'

Then Nathan appeared, pushing the door flap aside and stretching into a yawn as if having just woken from a refreshing sleep. He looked like he'd been painted red from chin to navel. He saw Tara and grinned, but there was something flat about the shine of his eyes. The red had been painted across his teeth too.

'Tara!' he drawled. 'Hi! Good of you to be keeping an eye on me – making sure nothing bad happens.' He ran his tongue around his teeth experimentally. 'Doing a pretty shit job of it, wouldn't you say?'

'What are you talking about? What's going on? What are you doing, Nathan?' She began to back away slowly. Too slowly. She had no idea what had happened to him inside the yurt, but the deep animal part of her hindbrain recognised a predator and meant to put as much distance as it could between her and it without questioning why. 'Jesus, what have you *done*?' Behind Nathan, a screaming man crawled out of the yurt – awkwardly, because one hand was clutching his belly where grey-purple loops of intestine swung and dragged in the dirt.

His grin vanished. 'Shut up and give me your car keys, bitch.'

She saw it then, the thing behind his face. The *afaugh*.

She ran.

As she fled she dug in her jeans pocket for her keys, and even though the parking lot was only a dozen metres beyond the tents Nathan – no, the *afaugh* – was much faster and would have caught her easily if at that moment Phoelix hadn't emerged from the yurt, bleeding profusely from a bite wound which had torn a chunk of flesh from his shoulder; he was gripping the fire-stone shovel like a battle-axe, and he charged, yelling. The *afaugh* met his attack, taking a ringing blow to the head, which staggered it. It snatched the tool from Phoelix's hands, reversed it, and drove the edge of the shovel's blade deep into the man's belly. Blood fanned out in a lateral spray, and when the *afaugh* pulled the blade out, Phoelix's viscera came with it.

In those scant seconds Tara had fumbled her key fob free and thumbed the remote boot-release button. The hatchback came ajar with a sane little *thunk*, which she heard quite distinctly despite the screaming and wet noises that Phoelix was making. She fetched up against the car with both hands and glanced back. The *afaugh* looked up from the ruin of his victim and winked at her, then came at a run.

Insurance policy, Nathan had said. *Jesus, had he known?*

With trembling fingers she unwrapped the corroded spearhead from the blanket, cursing and pleading as it snagged on folds of material. Her mother had bought her the blanket when she had started university, convinced that halls accommodation would never be warm enough.

As she turned, the *afaugh* barrelled into her, howling. It bore her to the ground, and the impact was hard enough to impale its upper chest on the three-thousand-year-old bronze point, but also to ram the socket end into her own ribcage so badly that she thought she was the one who'd been stabbed. The *afaugh* hung over her for a moment, spitting and growling; its face was Nathan's but there was nothing remotely human about the spirit animating it. Now she saw that his teeth were filed to points, and his hands – not hands, *claws*; when had they become claws without her noticing? – were reaching for her. It twisted, forcing itself deeper onto the blade, which snapped off in its shoulder, and it screeched in agony. She had enough time to think, *Good. I hope it takes you a long time to fucking die,* before it raised its jaws to her throat.

* * *

PRYCE WAS INTERVIEWING THE MOONBRIDGE INSTITUTE'S manager when the screaming began. For a moment they looked at each other, unable to comprehend the sounds as human screams.

Tara.

He ran back towards the sweat-hut clearing, growling, "You fucker, you fucker, you fucker," meaning Brookes because nobody else would be the source of such panic, but also meaning himself because he'd *known*, of course he'd known, that something was dodgy about the whole setup. He should have got Tara out of there straight away, and if anything had happened to her it would all be his fault, because he'd known.

A car slewed past him on the gravel road, spitting dust and pebbles, and he only just about avoided being mown down. Turning, he saw the back of Brookes' head bent low over the wheel. The rear of the car looked like it had been sprayed with tomato ketchup.

Tara's car.

'Shit, no...'

He ran faster.

The clearing was chaos, filled with half-naked people screaming and staggering and clutching at their wounds. He skidded to a halt.

'Tara!' he bellowed, but it was lost in the din.

By her tent: a shape on the ground.

She'd tried to staunch the bleeding with something that

looked like an old blanket, now dark with gore, but shock had robbed her hands of the strength to keep it there and she was lying on her back, staring glassy-eyed at the tree canopy. Her normally dusky skin was ashen. He threw himself on his knees beside her and clamped both hands to the red mess of her throat, moaning, 'Nonononono, don't you do this, don't you dare do this...'

Her eyes swivelled to look at him, wide and terrified, tears running to mix pink with the blood, and her lips moved.

'You're not going to die,' he told her. 'I'm not going to let you die. You stay with me, you hear? Stay with me!' Then he raised his voice to scream for help along with all the others.

19

NEW FLAMES FOR OLD

THREE HOURS AND NEARLY A HUNDRED MILES LATER, IT stood over the mummified remains of its ancient enemy, who lay curled and wizened on his steel tray, to all intents and purposes utterly harmless.

'You're not, though, are you?' it said with soft venom. 'Give you half a chance, get you back in the ground and you'd have me back to that fucking place, wouldn't you? Well, never again. Never again!' With sudden savagery it hooked its fingers into Bark Foot's half-open mouth and tore his lower jaw free with a sound like ripping cardboard, before flinging it away and spitting after it. The *afaugh* was oblivious to the moans and screams of the injured lab technicians through whom he had torn to get here. Gaining access to the laboratory with Doumani's ID had been laughably easy; security had just waved him through without even checking it. Someone was gabbling into a phone, and soon the police would be here, but there was still time enough to tie up this loose end.

The *afaugh* upended the petrol can it had found in Tara's car and filled en route, dousing the bog mummy.

'I like this place too much,' it said. 'I like the noise of it. I like its *heat*.'

It struck a match, tossed it, and stepped back to savour the explosive billow of flame that engulfed its enemy. Fire alarms quickly added to the din, sprinklers went off with a dull hiss, and minutes later the distant wail of sirens could be heard.

The *afaugh* waltzed out through the chaos and lost itself in the mass of people hurrying for the fire exits. It was almost intimidating to be surrounded by so much humanity after so long trapped in the purgatory of Un. It would take time to learn to enjoy its newly won freedom, but for now there was just one last matter to set right.

Susannah Vickers, née Jones, and her charming little family.

New flames for old, it thought, as it watched a ball of fire burst out of a window, and began to laugh.

In her police cell, Liv awoke with a searing pain in the underside of her forearm. Crying out, she pulled up her sleeve and was hit with the scorched-pork stench of her own flesh burning. Bark Foot's tattoo had burned itself out of her skin, as if the ash-and-woad dye which had been pricked into it had ignited like a curling trail of gunpowder.

Finally dead, then.

The *afaugh* would come soon. It would eat her alive and screaming.

Very calmly, she unzipped her hoodie. The police had

taken her shoelaces and her belt, but they had overlooked the drawstrings in its hood and around its hem. When she pulled them out and tied them together, she had about a metre of strong cotton cord. It would have to do. The strip light was behind a long plastic panel set in the ceiling. She took her mattress off the bed, rolled it into a cylinder and stood it on its end, and then stood on that to reach. It took a couple of good hard punches to jar the plastic panel loose, which made her knuckles bleed, but that hardly mattered now. Once the panel was gone, she found that the mounting brackets for the light bulb were nice and solid.

One thing about learning to make your own cordage, she thought, was that it also taught you how to tie good, strong knots.

FOR SUE, WAKING WAS INSTANTANEOUS, LIKE THE FLICKING of a switch – as was the knowledge that there was someone standing by the side of the bed, staring down at her. In the blink-moment before the sluice gates of thought slammed down, atavistic terror filled her, flooding up in a black tide from her dreams, and anything was possible: ghosts, vampires, demons.

And then it was just Jacob in his SpongeBob SquarePants pyjamas, thumb in his mouth, needing Mummy but worried about waking her up.

She glanced over at Steve. He was on his back, snoring lightly, completely oblivious. How did that happen? Was there something hard-wired into only a mother's brain that sensed her child's presence – or was it just the simple fact that when they'd had kids she'd chosen the side of the bed nearest the door precisely so that she could wake up first if they needed anything? Whatever – it could have been a serial killer in the room and he was spark out. *My hero,* she thought.

'Hi, baby,' she murmured. 'What's the matter?'

'Can't sleep.'

'Oh, come here.' She made space and he climbed in. His feet were freezing – God knew how long he'd been standing there. She inhaled his little-boy smell and stroked the feathery softness of his hair. *Don't grow up too soon,* she prayed. *Some day, but not yet. Give me this for a little while.* 'Why can't you sleep?' It would be a bad dream or because he was too hot or because something was bothering him; yesterday's world-ending trauma had been whether or not there would be enough food for the bees after she'd cut some flowers for the kitchen table.

'There's a man outside my window,' he whispered. 'He waved to me.'

Her breath froze. 'What kind of man?' she asked, trying to keep her voice soft and calm.

'A smiling man.'

A smiling man. Please, God, let this just be a bad dream.

'All right then,' she said, still stroking his hair. 'You stay here with Daddy and I'll go see who it is.' Steve grunted and rolled over as she manoeuvred out of bed, but still didn't rouse. She decided not to wake him. His mood had been on a razor's edge ever since the bloody policeman had visited, and she didn't want to piss him off any worse by waking him up for what was almost certainly just a little boy's bad dream.

The boys' bedroom was at the front of the house, overlooking the street. She checked on Matthew in the bottom bunk; he was flat out in standard 'squashed frog' position and had kicked his sheet down to the bottom of the mattress. She pulled it back up. Even for one in the morning it was a muggy, uncomfortable night, but she couldn't leave him uncovered.

Not for the first time, she wondered what they were going to do when the boys were old enough to need their own space. She and Steve could barely afford this house as it was; the idea that they might ever be able to try for a girl was laughable.

The curtains were partly open, allowing a thin band of street light to illuminate the room. Steve could have forgotten to close them properly when he'd tucked the boys in, she supposed.

Holding her breath, she peered sidelong through the gap, down to their driveway, their tiny front lawn, and the road.

It was deserted. She heaved a sigh of relief and pulled the curtains closed.

The front doorbell rang, and its sudden electronic jangle made her scream.

Matty woke up and began to cry. Steve's voice made formless sounds of confusion from their bedroom. She scooped Matty up, went back to their room and dumped him on the bed, where Steve already had his bedside lamp on and was blearing around.

'Whuz goan on?'

'Someone at the door.'

'I'll go...'

'No. You look after these two. I'm already up.'

She took the stairs as quickly as was safe down to the front door, hoping to answer it before whoever it was rang the bell again. Still, she made sure to check that the chain was on before she opened it.

A face grinned at her through the gap and she stared, more in fury than surprise.

'*Nathan?*'

'Hi, honey, I'm home!' he replied, and booted the door. The chain snapped and the door sprang open, catching her on the side of the forehead and throwing her backwards.

He was over the threshold – *in her home* – nodding around with approval as she shook her head to clear it. 'I like what you've done with the place.'

'Steven!' she yelled. 'Call the police!'

'Way ahead of you, my dear,' said Nathan, and waved his phone at her as she backed away on hands and heels to the foot of the stairs. Blood from a gash just below his collarbone stained him all the way down to his knee, and there was something terribly wrong with his teeth.

'What the hell is this?' Steve was at the top of the staircase. Matty was a squirming, squalling weight in his arms while Jacob hid wide-eyed behind his legs.

'Hi, Jakey!' called Nathan, and waved. 'Hey, Matty!'

'Don't you talk to my children!' Sue snapped, getting up. 'Don't you fucking dare!' She checked her forehead. Her fingers came away bloody.

'Oh, but, Susannah,' continued Nathan, 'don't you know by now that they're my children? They're *all* my children. They always should have been. You owe them to me.'

'I owe you this!' she retorted, and slapped his face.

At least, she meant to. Too fast to see, his hand flashed up and caught hers by the wrist. Then, before her disbelieving eyes, he drew it up to his mouth and bit off her little finger. His teeth – she saw clearly now before shock and pain dropped her shrieking to the floor – had been filed to points, like a shark's. He chewed and swallowed, licking his lips.

'I've waited so long for this,' he said. 'Longer than you can possibly imagine.'

Steve gave an inarticulate bellow of rage, plonked his son on the landing, and threw himself down at Nathan, all thought of calling the police forgotten. Nathan caught him by the throat, pivoted with the momentum and slammed him up against the wall, his bare feet a good few inches off the floor. Steve choked and thrashed, his face turning purple. The narrow hallway throbbed with heat, the stink of blood, and the shrieks of terrified children. 'Don't hurt my daddy!' the older one was squealing. The younger just bawled.

'Don't worry, children,' said the *afaugh*. 'He'll be just fine.' Slowly it lowered Steve to the floor and relaxed its grip on his throat; he gasped for breath. 'We'll all be just fine. We'll all be one big happy family.'

Sue squeezed her blood-squirting hand and watched as Nathan leant in close, cocking his head slightly as if to kiss Steve, and then *something*... she couldn't tell what it was exactly – some substance or excrescence which roiled and squirmed with its own obscene life – vomited from Nathan's mouth and into her husband's. It seemed to go on for ever, with Steve gagging and spasming and drool running over his chin, until Nathan staggered away, retching. Sue used the newel post to climb to her feet, light-headed with shock, and edged slowly up the staircase and towards her babies while the two men convulsed.

Steve was the first to recover. When she was halfway up the stairs he straightened and looked around at the chaotic scene as if seeing it for the first time, until his eyes lit on Nathan, who was leaning against the open door frame and wiping away bile.

'One big happy family,' said Steve, and grinned a cannibal's grin. 'All except for you, that is. Me and Sue and the boys are going to be blissfully happy – at least, for a while. Isn't that right, darling?'

'It's too late, you're already fucked,' Nathan said, but it sounded more like a plea than a threat.

The *afaugh* looked down at itself, where a gash had opened just below its collarbone – narrow but evidently quite deep, to judge from the blood which was streaming freely. Its grin disappeared. 'This?' it sneered. 'You think this pathetic splinter following me around is going to do anything more than just make me move to a new body more quickly? Imbecile; all you've done is doomed more souls, not fewer.' It wiped a handful of blood from its chest and flung it contemptuously in Nathan's face. 'Get out of my house. This is *my* house. These are *my* children. I told you, they always have been.'

Sue was crouched with her screaming sons on the landing, staring aghast at her husband, whose blood was speckled across his cheeks. 'Steven?'

He appeared to consider this. 'Sort of,' he conceded, and grinned again.

'What are you?' she moaned. 'Nathan, what's going on?' Everything seemed to be spinning around her head.

Nathan's expression was stricken. 'I'll find a way to fix this, I promise!'

The *afaugh* cocked an ear. 'Why, are those sirens I can hear?'

They were indeed.

'I'm sorry.' Nathan's voice was hoarse. 'Hodges... you know he'll only see...' He stumbled backwards towards the open door.

Sue shook her head. 'See what? Please, Nathan, what was that thing? What's happening?'

'Exactly what the *afaugh* wanted to happen. I did exactly what it wanted.' He turned and ran, ignoring both her pleas and the *afaugh*'s mocking laughter.

She heard the sound of a car tearing away down the street, moments before the wailing of sirens and strobing of police lights filled the darkness outside. There were slamming doors, shouted orders, the crackle of radios. Steven tipped her a wink and then clutched at his shoulder in sudden, mock agony, rolling his eyes and staggering towards the door.

'He's got a knife!' he shouted, and fell to his knees on the threshold. 'He tried... I managed to...'

'No, that isn't...' Sue whispered, as shock and pain

crashed in black waves through her head. 'No.' She clutched her children to her and tried to back away down the hall, to a room with a door that she could lock between her and whatever it was inhabiting her husband's body, but her legs refused to move, and her boys were slipping from her weakening arms. 'No...'

20

HEARTLANDS

In the ambulance, groggy with shock and morphine, hand wadded up to the size of a boxing glove with dressings. Rocking motion and the wail of the siren. Her boys are on the stretcher with her; Matty is curled up asleep, whimpering, while Jacob is wide awake but perfectly still, his eyes large and round. There's an oxygen mask over her face – except it's not oxygen, she knows, it's pumping a fog of entonox into her brain. Just like when she had the boys. Steven held her hand throughout the whole...

A bright flash of adrenalin cut through and she stared around wildly for Steven, but he wasn't in the ambulance. She flopped back. They must have taken him in another one. It was too much to hope for that they would have arrested him. The paramedic saw her movement and bent over her, concerned, checking readouts and monitors. 'Easy now,' he said. 'You're all right. You're safe. Just try to relax.' But the last thing she could afford to be was sleepy so the pain was a small price to pay and she pulled the mask off and croaked at him through a sandpaper-dry throat, 'Husband.'

The paramedic nodded reassuringly. 'Don't worry about him either; my colleagues are taking good care of him too.'

She shook her head. 'No. Husband. *This*.'

The paramedic frowned. 'This? What do you mean "this"?'

Now she wanted to scream at him. Why was he so fucking stupid? Hadn't he ever dealt with the results of domestic violence? Didn't they teach them to think at paramedic school? She licked her lips. They felt like shrivelled orange peel. 'My. Husband. Did. *This*.' And she shoved her bandaged hand in his face.

He got it, and nodded. To his credit, he didn't look shocked, didn't ask any stupid questions, just nodded. 'Okay.' He went forward to talk with the driver.

A FEW MINUTES DOWN THE ROAD, TWO THINGS HIT NATHAN simultaneously: the memory of how he had come by the car, and the weight in his stomach of what the *afaugh* had made him swallow. He pulled over and threw up, and by the time he'd got his breath back he knew what his destination had to be. There was only one place that might conceivably offer answers, or at the very least, escape.

It seemed that the *afaugh* had known too – or guessed – and communicated it to the police via Steven along with a description of the car, because as Nathan neared Sutton Park he saw more and more flashing blue lights. He ditched Tara's car and scurried the last couple of blocks, hunched low into his hoodie – no, not his; he'd stolen it, although he couldn't remember when or where. Right now that was the least of his crimes. Fragments of memory from the last few hours hit him in bursts, making him flinch and stumble as he walked. It didn't matter that the *afaugh* had done those things – his mistake had let it loose, he was ultimately responsible. Those people in the sweat-hut... their screams... Phoelix collapsing to his knees with his guts in his hands...

Nathan was sick again, this time deliberately, jamming two fingers into the back of his throat to force his body to expel as much of the *afaugh*'s filth as it could.

A police helicopter was pounding the air overhead. He had minutes, at best.

Nathan avoided the normal entrances to Sutton Park – which would be locked at this time of night and probably crawling with police – and climbed the boundary fence, tearing his stolen clothes on the barbed wire. Then he ran. After his week of aimless wandering around the park and failing to find anything, he knew its geography well enough by now to be able to navigate it at night without stumbling too much. The thudding in the sky grew louder, and the helicopter's running lights were flashing low overhead; they must have him on their infrared camera by now and were coordinating ground units to surround him.

He missed his footing in the dark and plunged down a steep bank and into cold water. Longmoor Brook, he hoped. He was within metres of the timber track now. He hauled himself up the other side and ran again, panting, feeling a stitch start in his side. Distant shouts echoed across the night, and the barking of dogs.

He passed the round shadow of Rowton's Well, felt birch leaves whip his face and stopped at the stream bank. There was just enough light for him to see the glistening movement of water, and that there was no timber track spanning it.

The track was closed. Of course it was. He'd burned Bark Foot's body, hadn't he? There was nobody left to open it.

'No!' he moaned. 'Not like this. Please, not like this.' Even though he knew there was also nobody to hear his pleading.

Sudden light picked him out from above and behind. 'Drop the knife!' bellowed a voice over the helicopter's snarl.

He turned around. Torchlight blinded him, and more were appearing every moment. 'Drop it! Lie down on the ground and place your hands behind your head!'

Nathan raised his hands in the air and backed away a step, nearly losing his balance; the bank of Longmoor Brook dropped away directly behind his heels. He pinwheeled his arms.

'*Drop the fucking knife!*' the policeman screamed, probably mistaking his movement for a threatening gesture.

'I haven't got...' Nathan started, and felt a sudden stabbing pain in his chest, like a wasp sting. He looked down. Two metal barbs trailing wires had mysteriously appeared, piercing right through the thick material of the hoodie and into his skin. 'Wait...' There was a series of rapid sharp cracks like twigs being broken and he collapsed in a boneless heap, rolling down the bank to land face-first in the water. The first lungful of it made him cough and gag, but it was just reflex; the Taser's charge had destroyed his control of his body. Blind and suffocating, he panicked, twitching, and managed to get his head up slightly, but it flopped into the stream again. It seemed impossible – ridiculous – that he was going to die in such a stupid way, especially since the brook was so shallow. What did they say? That a man could drown in two inches of water?

Drowning: the third of the triple killing of sacrifices, Doumani had said. And he'd already been stabbed and throttled. Could this be coincidence?

Jesus, no, not like this. This isn't funny any more, Robbie. I said I wanted to make things right, but not like this.

As if he was ever going to be given the choice.

His lungs screamed in the blindness of night and the peat-black water, and an even deeper darkness rushed towards him.

Then strong hands were under his armpits and he was being dragged up the opposite bank, dumped on his side, and someone was kneeling on his ribcage. He coughed up a great sour lungful of black water, and his rescuer turned him over onto his back, face bent close to his mouth, checking that he was breathing. In the dark all he had was an impression of scars, furs and a strong animal smell.

Bark Foot, he wanted to say. *You're dead. I burned you.* But his voice, like the rest of his body, refused to obey. He was hoisted over one shoulder like a sack of coal and carried some distance before being dumped, not ungently, onto something softer, a pile of leaves and branches. A calloused hand lingered on his brow for a moment, and then was gone.

Consciousness followed swiftly after it.

* * *

SUE REALLY BEGAN TO PANIC WHEN THEY WERE POKING AND prodding her hand in a curtained-off cubicle at Heartlands Hospital Accident and Emergency department and a woman dressed casually rather than in medical scrubs came in, smiled at her boys and asked their names.

'You're not taking them—!' she started.

'No, I'm not,' replied the woman. She had the tired and harassed look of an overworked office temp, but the smile she turned on Sue was warm, and she held out her ID lanyard. 'My name is Beth Gibbins. I'm with the hospital's Child Protection Support Unit.'

'You can't take them away!'

'I'm not going to. But you need to go into a treatment room for that hand and they can't go in with you, can they? They'll be right here with me until you're done and then I'll bring them to see you. Who can I call to come and take care of them?'

'Don't let him anywhere near them!'

Beth Gibbins clearly didn't need to be told who 'him' was. 'Don't you be concerned about that. He's being treated separately, and the police will be right there. They'll be wanting to interview both of you, and probably your boys too. Now. Who can I call?'

'Nobody. Anyone you call will just be in harm's way too.'

Gibbins nodded. 'I understand,' she said, even though she couldn't possibly. 'I'll call the police at your home and arrange for someone to bring you a bag of clothes, your purse, things like that. Some of the boys' things too. Will that do?'

Sue nodded, only slightly reassured, and allowed herself to be wheeled away to theatre.

* * *

'WHEN CAN I SEE MY WIFE? I NEED TO MAKE SURE THAT she's okay.' In a suture room only a corridor away, the *afaugh* watched with great curiosity as a nurse stitched up the wound in its shoulder. In a little metal tray on a side table, a five-centimetre shard of Bronze Age spearhead lay, greasy with blood. The *afaugh* hadn't been sure that the doctors would even be able to remove it; the weapon and the wound were meant for its own self, not the body it was currently inhabiting. It had followed from Brookes – what would it do now? Was it gone for ever? Would it reappear in a fresh wound if the *afaugh* took a new host? It was almost tempting to try. The *afaugh* sniffed at the nurse bending over him; her aroma of fatigue, stale caffeine and surgical soap was delightful.

There was, of course, the policeman outside the door with his arms crossed, exuding a pungent stench of paranoia detectable even at this distance. He was a complication, as was no doubt the point. They knew something wasn't quite right. Exactly how they knew the *afaugh* didn't care.

'Is she even in this hospital?' it asked.

'I couldn't say, sir,' replied the nurse with a friendly smile, but there was a frostiness at its edges which confirmed his suspicions. 'I'm sure she's being looked after. I'll check with one of the doctors. Things are a bit chaotic at the moment; apparently there was a fire earlier this evening at the Queen Elizabeth, and patients are being shuttled all over the city.'

'A fire?' tutted the *afaugh*. 'What a terrible thing to happen.'

As she was finishing up, the door opened and a man who the *afaugh* recognised from Steven Vickers' memories as DI Christopher Hodges entered, with the same kind of look on his face as the nurse. Hodges waited until the nurse was gone before he spoke.

'Steven William Vickers.'

'That's my name, don't wear it out,' grinned the *afaugh*. There was no point in pretending with this man. Might as well see how much fun could be had in the meantime.

'I wonder if you can help me with a small point of confusion over exactly what happened tonight.'

'I'll give it my very best shot.'

'Well, we went to your home because we received a phone call from Nathan Brookes in which he told us in no uncertain terms that he'd already killed several people and was on his way to do the same to your family. When we got there he had legged it, having stabbed you and bitten your wife. So far, so horrible. Then, in the ambulance over here, your wife says that it was in fact you who attacked her.'

'I can see how that would be confusing. Here, let me explain.'

It showed itself to DI Hodges, and in the stunned moment of disbelief before he could start screaming and alert the uniform outside the door, the *afaugh* took him. When it realised that Hodges didn't know where Sue had been taken, it contemplated taking its frustration out on the shocked Vickers with a pair of scissors from one of the instrument packs, but in the end decided against it. His death would draw attention, and his words would never be believed.

Instead, it popped its head out of the door and asked the uniformed officer to find out where they were keeping the mother and kids. Finally it turned its attention to the wound that had opened afresh in its new body and already soaked through its jacket lapel.

'Shit. What a mess.' It picked up a suture kit and examined it. How hard could this be?

As the police had been unable to find Sue's finger, the best the doctors could do was clean, debride and suture the wound – the irony being that if they *had* possessed it, reattachment would have been much more complicated and taken longer, during which time the thing in her husband (she would not – could not – bring herself to use the word 'demon') would almost certainly have found her. By swallowing it, the bastard thing had actually done her a favour. As it was, the whole process took only an hour under local anaesthetic, and she was able to stay awake throughout, planning what she was going to have to do next.

Heartlands was a busy hospital, even in the early hours of the morning. From the treatment room she saw corridors busy with orderlies, doctors, nurses, consultants, relatives, and managers, as well as patients in wheelchairs, on gurneys, on foot. Easy in the bustle for someone to slip away.

True to her word, Gibbins brought Matthew and Jake to see her, as well as a bag full of clothes – it was one of Steven's large sports holdalls, and for a moment she was afraid to touch it. There was also her handbag and purse.

'I'll leave you with them for a moment,' said Gibbins. 'But then you and I are going to have a conversation about where you're going to stay. I'm thinking home might not feel like the safest of places right now.'

Sue checked Matty; somebody had already changed his nappy. Without knowing she was going to do it, she flung her arms around Beth Gibbin's neck. 'Thank you,' she whispered, suddenly in tears.

Beth patted her on the back and disengaged herself. 'Just for a moment, understand?'

'I understand.' Sue wiped her eyes and blew her nose, in control again. A moment was all she needed.

BETH GIBBINS WAS STILL CHASING UP THE DETAILS ON Susannah Vickers and her children when a police constable approached and enquired after the family. The empty room she led him to came as a surprise, but not as much as it should have. She was three hours over the end of an already long shift. She'd done what she could.

21

AWAKE

A THIN GREY DAWN BROUGHT FORM TO THE WORLD, ALONG with the murmuring of men's voices and the barking of dogs. For a moment Nathan thought the police had found him, but then memories of the previous night prodded him fully awake. Above him slanted a crude lean-to roof of branches lashed together with bark, and a grey sky scratched with leafless trees, while underneath him was a bed of bracken.

He lurched up into a sitting position, and pain immediately set on him from half a dozen directions like a pack of wolves. He examined himself; there were bruises and contusions everywhere, cuts all over his hands, Liv's wound below his ribcage and the much fresher wound below his collarbone, both of which had been plastered with some kind of brown vegetable pulp. The tang of wood smoke drifted from close by. He saw a clearing amongst birches, a fire at its centre around which men in furs were moving. They carried leaf-bladed knives at their belts and hunting spears in their hands. On the other side of the clearing smouldered the burnt remains of a domed shelter, its hide coverings scorched and scattered, its curved supports jutting like blackened and broken ribs.

He was in Bark Foot's camp. But of its owner there was no sign. Nathan winced at the sudden memory of the mummy's tar-black body curling in flames.

His awakening had been noticed. The largest of the men approached with a smile of welcome.

'Bark Foot?' he croaked. 'But you're dead. I burned you.'

'No, Mr Brookes,' laughed the man. 'I'm much less dead than you.' His English was strangely accented, but familiar for all that. 'It's me, Brandon. Can you walk?'

It was no surprise that Nathan hadn't recognised him; beneath a neatly trimmed beard his face had lost the puppy fat of adolescence and become lean, acquiring lines and scars. His voice, too had acquired the timbre of a grown man, but for all that it was unmistakably the boy who had once carried a hip flask of lemonade and tucked his trouser cuffs into his socks.

'*Bran?*' It was almost too much, after everything else. 'I just... give me a second.'

'Fine, but don't take too long. The Oendir don't like it here. They believe these woods are haunted. Between you and me, I can well imagine why.'

They gave him water and a little food – some kind of oatcake baked with hazelnuts and dried fruit – and he experimented with standing up while Bran left him to continue picking through the remains of the camp. Nathan watched him chatting quietly with his companions in a strange language, finding it hard to see the teenager in the shape of the man. Bran's companions – the Oendir, he'd called them – were a little shorter, dark-haired with striking blue eyes. They didn't touch anything and seemed anxious that Bran was.

Suddenly Bran gave a cry of discovery and pulled a long object from the remains of the sweat-hut, which he waved at Nathan, grinning. It was Bark Foot's spear. Not the rotten and corroded remnant from Dr Doumani's lab, but gleaming and obviously lethal, despite the shaft having been snapped in two.

'Gorgeous,' Bran murmured, turning it over in his hands.

One of the Oendir approached and spoke in low, urgent tones. Bran made reassuring noises and the man went away, but he was plainly unhappy.

'Break time's over, old friend,' said Bran. 'They're leaving with or without us.'

Nathan shook his head. 'I can't, I have to get back. The *afaugh* is in Sue's husband – Christ only knows what it's doing.'

Bran looked him up and down critically. 'I hate to sound cold, but whatever it's going to do, it will have done. You're already too late.'

'No! It's not going to kill them straight away! I know, I saw it when it was in me. It wants to make them suffer. That's what it likes. It's going to torture them for days, maybe even *weeks*...'

'Then you've got time to make yourself strong enough to deal with it, haven't you? There will be a feast tonight to celebrate the *afaugh* being gone from our lands, and the arrival of my old friend and teacher.'

'I can't possibly celebrate that, can I? Knowing where it's gone?'

'Nobody's suggesting that. But there will be food. Man eat food. Man get strong. Man kill monster. Stop me when this gets complicated.'

As if in agreement, Nathan's stomach chose that moment to growl, and he slumped in defeat. 'Pair of you, ganging up on me,' he muttered. 'All right, then. Take me to your leader.'

22

BRAN IN UN

BRAN AND SCATTIE WATCH LIV START ACROSS THE TIMBER track into the bright, sunlit lands of the now. Then the pale nightmare of the *afaugh* rushes at them from the trees, desperate to escape into the world. Bark Foot and Scattie stand shoulder to shoulder to fend it away – he with his bronze-bladed spear, she armed with nothing more than a fire-sharpened stick. Bran, guarding the end of the track, sees Liv hesitate and he yells, 'No! Don't turn back! Go! Go!' Then, without any sort of transition, the track is gone, and the sunlit lands are replaced by the desolate landscape of Un once more. The *afaugh* looses a hollow wail of denial, and disappears into the trees.

Without a word, Bark Foot turns and walks in the direction of his camp.

For a while Bran and Scattie stand, she leaning on her stick, regaining breath. A bone-damp chill settles over them like a grey mantle, and Bran's stomach growls.

'We're going to die here,' he says to Scattie. The drowsiness of starvation has lent him a kind of serenity in the face of this fact.

'No, we fucking well are not!' she snaps, and stalks off after Bark Foot.

'YOU WERE HAVING A NICE LITTLE CHAT WITH OUR NEW friend the other day,' Scattie says to him. 'What did he tell you? What have you found out about this place?' She has found Ryan's six-inch lock-knife, and is busy using it to pry apart the casing of her own tiny Swiss Army pocket knife so that she can get the blade free and fix it to the end of her primitive spear. Ryan's is just too useful to mess with. Bark Foot has resumed his inhuman vigil by the fire, carving birds.

Bran shrugs. 'Just stories. I'm as completely in the dark as you are.'

'Bullshit. You're clever. You know all about this kind of stuff. You read all those books about elves and wizards and shit.'

'*Lord of the Rings* isn't exactly a user's manual for people trapped in whatever the fuck this place is, you know.'

'Then guess! Use all that cleverness and give it your best shot!'

'What if I'm wrong?'

'Then we're as dead as we will be if you just sit on your arse moaning about it, aren't we?' There's a desperation in her retorts that comes from simple, understandable fear, and he realises that it doesn't matter what he says, just so long as he says something.

'Fair enough.' He picks up a twig to scratch diagrams in the dirt while he tries to sort it out in his head. 'Bark Foot calls it Un. The place that is not. The land behind the moon. The echo of winter, whatever that means. It's a spirit realm, pretty obviously, probably *the* spirit world. Where the ghosts of our ancestors go. Every culture has one – the Celts called their underworld Annwn, which sounds kind of similar – but it's not just a heaven-and-hell afterlife concept. It's the place where the secret animating forces of nature exist and can be contacted, bargained with, begged for favours.'

'So where are they, then?'

'What do you mean?'

'If nature is full of these spirits, then where are they all? Because I can only see two, and so far they've been bastards. Where are these ghosts of our ancestors? Why is this place so empty?'

'Look, it makes no sense, I get that, but you asked me to guess, so that's what I'm doing, okay?'

She mutters an apology and keeps working on the knife. One side is off, but the rivets on the other side are proving tricky.

'The *afaugh* wants to get into the world and Bark Foot's purpose is to stop him. The timber track is obviously a crossing point between the two places. Realms. States of being. Whatever. It stands to reason that there would be other crossing points.'

She looks up, her eyes gleaming. 'Other ways home?'

'Possibly. Unless this is some kind of weird little pocket universe and it just goes on like this for ever, and there's no way out.'

'I am uncomfortable with this hypothesis,' she replies, doing an uncanny impersonation of their starchy Chemistry teacher Mrs Finlay. 'Please provide another.'

They smile for a moment, sharing the joke.

'Okay then,' he continues. 'Assuming this is part of a bigger world, it doesn't surprise me that this bit of it is deserted, what with those two busting it up for thousands of years.'

'Does not play well with others,' she agrees.

'Which means that if we could get far enough away from them we might be able to find someone, or something, that we can bargain with to help us – we might even be able to find another crossing point and get home.'

'Except,' she points out, 'that was the first thing we tried, remember? That fucking *afaugh* thing is out in the woods somewhere, and it's a lot faster and stronger than us.'

He is silent again, thinking. Listening.

'Stronger,' he says, slowly, a horrible and ingenious idea taking form in his imagination. 'Maybe not necessarily faster.'

'What do you mean?'

'Just listen for a moment – tell me what you hear.'

She listens, then shakes her head. 'Nothing.'

'*Underneath* the nothing.'

'Do not play fucking games with me, Bran,' she warns. 'I'm really not in the mood right now.'

'The river.' His eyes are alight, glittering in the dark

hollows of his starved face. 'It's running high and fast. I bet the *afaugh* couldn't outrun us if we were on that.'

'Are you suggesting that we build a *raft*?'

'Maybe not. I doubt that we have the strength, and anything we make will probably just fall apart anyway. Our backpacks, though – the foam in them. That will float. We could hang on to them, you know, like life preservers.'

'You mean swim?'

'Or just let it carry us.'

'And rocks? And submerged trees? And rapids? And hypo-fucking-thermia?'

Bran chucks his twig down and gets to his feet, swaying slightly. 'Well what's the alternative? Oh, that's right, starving to death! Great, let's do that instead! Look, Scattie, we have rubbish bags – we can put our clothes in them and go in our underwear, since we're going to be soaked anyway.'

'Like you're ever seeing me in my knickers,' she harrumphs.

'And we've got Ryan's lighter, and paper; we double-wrap those to keep them dry so we can light a fire when we get to the end. We've got steel knives – we have technology thousands of years ahead of Bark Foot's time. We'll be fine!'

'If we don't drown first.'

'Sure. And if the *afaugh* doesn't catch up with us.'

She finishes prising the casing off her knife and removes the main blade, seeing how she might lash it to the end of her spear, and gives a few experimental jabs at the belly of an imaginary monster. 'Why not?' she says. 'What could possibly go wrong?'

* * *

THEY ARE AWARE OF BARK FOOT WATCHING THEM AS THEY gather the remains of their kit together, but if he is in the slightest bit curious, he says nothing.

'Do you think he'll just let us go?' Scattie whispers to Bran as she bundles up the tent's outer shell.

'I can't see why he wouldn't. He has no need for us any more. As far as he's concerned we'll be long dead before he needs any more spare parts.'

She grimaces at the idea.

Bark Foot makes no protest or move to stop them as they shoulder their rucksacks. In return, they make no farewell. They simply leave.

'He's not going to protect us this time, is he?' she asks.

'No reason for him to,' says Bran. 'It might even be in his interest for the *afaugh* to have something to chew on for a bit.'

'You have a lovely turn of phrase, you know that?' she growls, and stomps on ahead.

'What?' He stares after her. 'What did I say?' He runs to catch up.

Bran is wearing just his underpants and boots, and is acutely aware of how pale and thin his adolescent body looks. Scattie has stashed her trousers but kept her T-shirt. 'I don't care how cold it gets,' she told him as they were packing. 'Some things you just ain't seeing.' She is gripping her makeshift spear with white knuckles. The modern blade has been fastened with a whipping of nylon cord from the tent's guy ropes, partly melted in the fire to set it like resin, and she's tested it on a couple of trees, but she has no idea how it will stand up in an actual fight.

They walk quickly, without running, as if the sound of that would attract a predator's notice more readily, but they both know that it's only a matter of time. It isn't far to the river and they are close enough to see it churning between the trees when the *afaugh* is after them, shrieking.

'Run!' yells Scattie.

They run. They run stumbling down the bank and keep running even when the ground turns to water and there's nothing left to run on.

The coldness of the water is shocking. It slaps the breath out of their lungs and makes Bran's testicles crawl inwards like burrowing snails. He splutters, floundering in the surging, tea-brown water. He's always hated roller coasters, and this is why. He's dragged under, but somehow claws his way to the surface, choking. A sharp, insistent tugging on his wrist demands attention: the tent rope tethering him to the rucksack, which has been swept ahead, spinning and bobbing. He hauls it towards himself, even though it's like trying to drag an anchor. His arms are so cold the only way he can be sure they are working at all is by watching them, and the river carries him under again and its white-brown roar is inside his skull and all around, until he is able to snag one of the shoulder straps with a frozen claw and hug the rucksack to him. He is so cold he can barely breathe, but he takes advantage of the momentary respite to snatch a few gasps and a quick look around.

Scattie is a dozen metres ahead, on her back, clutching her

rucksack to her stomach and turning slowly in the current. 'You okay?' she calls.

His throat won't work. 'No!' he manages to yell.

'Good!'

It's as much as he can do to hang on, never mind see whether or not the *afaugh* has been able to chase them this far. The river is running so high that if there are any submerged tree limbs he and Scattie are carried right over them, and they don't encounter any rocks that they can't fend away. All the same, it isn't very long before Bran is forced to admit that he can't take much more of this. He keeps losing consciousness, awakening when the water floods over his head. He looks around. There seems to be open ground on both sides. Not that it would make any difference.

'Scattie!' he calls. 'Have to... st-stop! Can't...'

She gives him the thumbs-up, and they do their best to steer for the bank.

Drenched, exhausted, near naked and borderline hypothermic, they crawl out of the water and lie gasping. With fumbling fingers she digs for the cigarette lighter and paper, which are miraculously dry in their plastic bag, and lights a fire, cursing as she has to use both numb thumbs to operate the striking wheel. Just the sight of it lifts his spirits as much as its meagre warmth. They feed the tiny flame with bits of dry grass and twigs from within arm's reach, which is as far as either of them can move. Painfully, they change into their dry clothes and are able to venture further for larger sticks from some nearby bushes – in the process Bran finds a thin trickle of a stream and they briefly debate its drinkability before admitting that at this stage they really have nothing to lose by risking it, so they fill their water bottles. The water goes some way to easing their empty bellies and they watch each other carefully but neither of them is sick, so they refill again. It's once they have a decent fire going that the significance of this strikes him.

'Hey,' he says. 'It's a lot drier here, have you noticed? Not so much of that moss and everything being so damp.'

Scattie hmphs.

'I think we're beyond Bark Foot's range of influence. Hopefully that means it's too far for the *afaugh* to come after us. I think we've made it!'

'So just starvation to worry about, then.'

Unable to put the tent up, they wrap themselves in it to share body warmth. It is the closest Bran has ever been to a girl, and this gets his heart beating as fast as any other terror he has experienced in Un. He can smell her hair and her sweat, and even though neither of them has washed in days, he cannot imagine a more intoxicating perfume. 'Um, sorry about this,' he says, almost inarticulate with embarrassment.

'Sorry about what?' Then she feels his erection in the small of her back. 'Oh. Right. We're swapping positions. Now.' So she ends up spooning him, which is hardly better.

'Still,' she adds with a faint smile. 'That answers one question. You're definitely not gay.'

'People think I'm gay?'

'Not that, you know, it would be a thing. If you were.'

He sighs. 'I can see how people would think that. You know they say that girls mature faster than boys, but trust me, you lot can be just as superficial as lads when it comes to fancying someone.'

'Oh come on. I bet there are tons of girls at school who fancy you.'

'Maybe. But I'm too weird for anybody in our year and none of the sixth formers are going to go out with a kid younger than themselves, are they? But it's fine, though. Couple of years I'm off to uni, and then I'll find my tribe.'

'And all the undergraduate geek pussy you can handle.'

'Are you sure *you're* not gay?'

She laughs. 'In your dreams. Don't worry, when we get home I'll set you up with someone with a thing for geeks. In the meantime, keep Little Bran there to yourself.'

Impossibly, it seems, they sleep.

THEY FORCE THEMSELVES TO MOVE ON EARLY THE NEXT morning, both to put more distance between themselves and the *afaugh*, and because they recognise that while they might have the tools, they certainly don't have the skills to fend for themselves in this landscape. They are going to need to find someone who will help. But the lethargy of starvation is an even more leaden weight than before, and their progress is stumbling, wandering and slow. The woodland through which they travel is nothing like Bark Foot's cold volcanic winter. There are golden-boled ash and green cathedrals of oak, hazel brakes like thickets of silver spears, waist-high swathes of pungent, feather-coiled bracken. But visibility is non-existent, and Bran suggests that they seek higher ground from which to look for human habitation. They are so mentally numb with fatigue and hunger that they don't realise that they've come out in the open and have been walking through well-tended pasture land for nearly a mile before a flock of curly-horned sheep flees from them – followed by a very surprised shepherd, screaming.

23

THE OENDIR

Bran told his story as they set off through the woods at a pace that Nathan was only just able to match.

'When we found the Oendir they were absolutely terrified of us, even though we were so weak we could barely walk. It must have been because we came from there.' He nodded his head behind them, and Nathan turned to see. They'd been climbing steadily since leaving the ruined camp – progressing through normal, sunlit woodland – and through a gap in the trees he saw that what he had known as Longmoor Valley – tame, shallow, open and bright – was here deeply cloven and wreathed with low-lying fog.

Bran saw him looking. 'We call it the Pale Wood,' he explained. 'On account of its appearance and the fact that nothing grows there. It is – was – the area of Bark Foot's influence, guarding the track from our world. The Oendir ordinarily won't go anywhere near it. They say it's full of ghosts.' He chuckled. 'They don't know how right they are.'

'How did you know to come looking for me?'

'I didn't.'

'So who was it that pulled me out of the water, then?'

'Your guess is as good as mine. I can answer your first question, though.' Bran pushed up one sleeve and showed Nathan the underside of his forearm, where there was a new, livid burn. 'Bark Foot's mark. Three nights ago it burned itself out of my skin. I knew that something terrible had happened, so I came to see what it was. Finding you was an accident.'

'Three nights ago? But I... it all happened only just yesterday.'

'The Oendir call it the Pale Wood for good reason. There is only one season there – only one time, or else no time at all. You cannot say with any certainty what will happen when you enter. When Scattie and I stumbled out of it, they must have thought we were spirits like Bark Foot and the *afaugh*. Of course, I might have played up to that, just a little.' He reached into his tunic and pulled out an object on a leather necklace: a cheap plastic cigarette lighter. '"Any sufficiently advanced technology is indistinguishable from magic", right?' He chuckled and put it away. 'By the time that had run out I had demonstrated my use to them, such that they took us in, gave us a home. That's where we're going, incidentally.'

'What about Scattie?' Nathan asked. 'Is she there too?'

'No. She went off to do her own thing a while back.'

'But is she still alive?'

Bran shrugged. 'Couldn't say.' There was a darkness to his tone that made Nathan reluctant to pursue the matter. 'But wait until you see the village!' he added, bright and breezy again. 'You're going to love it!' He clapped Nathan on the shoulder and the muscular force behind it took him aback. 'What happened to you back there anyway? You look like shit!' The ghost of the boy for whom he'd been searching disappeared, and as Nathan walked and told his tale he realised that his audience was a powerful, adult stranger whom he didn't know at all.

As they walked, Bran conversed with his companions but none of them made any move to communicate with Nathan. They would barely look him in the eye. 'What's their problem?' he asked.

'Don't worry about them. They just can't tell whether you're a demon or a slave. Either way it's not good for you; I wouldn't antagonise them.'

'I wasn't planning to,' Nathan muttered.

Bran barked an order and one of the Oendir set off at a brisk trot, soon disappearing ahead.

'And that?'

'Welcoming committee.'

'VILLAGE' HAD BEEN SOMETHING OF AN UNDERSTATEMENT.

By mid-afternoon they came out of what Bran called the Wild Wood into open heathland where forest had been cleared, and large flocks of sheep and goats were herded. This in turn became a landscape of carefully tended fields where livestock grazed and crops grew, irrigated by streams, which had been dammed into pools. Dotted amongst them were clusters of roundhouses with cooking smoke rising in neat lines from their conical thatched roofs, while the ringing of metalwork sang in the air. And everywhere, people: ploughing, digging, weaving, hammering, chopping wood, grinding flour, cutting thatch, clearing ditches, herding cows. It was the landscape Nathan had imagined while sitting on his checkpoint at King's Coppice.

Bran was obviously enjoying his amazed reaction. 'Not what you were expecting?'

'Not from Liv's account, no. This is…' He stopped and waved at the scene.

'A thriving, populous, civilised culture,' Bran finished for him. 'Liv saw only what we all saw at the start: the world that Bark Foot and the *afaugh* had made between them – or that was made for them, possibly.'

'But what is this place? Where are we? Is this…' It sounded stupid, even though it was right in front of his waking eyes. 'Is this the past?'

Bran shrugged as if the question didn't interest him. 'This is Un,' he said. 'This part of it, at least, is mine, and I intend to do something very different with it.'

Dominating the region was a steep-sided hill, which rose out of the undulating folds in the landscape. They approached it along well-maintained roads between the fields, more than once having to step out of the way of farmers driving pigs and sheep. Buildings clustered more thickly at the base of the hill, where Nathan saw smiths, wood-turners and craftspeople working gold and precious stones. Nathan and Bran climbed its slope along a switchback road and reached the summit, where high green walls were topped with a wooden palisade. There was a great gate of bronze-banded timbers set in the wall; it stood open, guarded by sentries with helmets and spears. Beyond the gate were more buildings of the same form as the farmers' roundhouses but grander: larger and made of lime-rendered stone. Children and dogs chased each other in excited clouds of dust while the adults looked at him curiously, though some made odd gestures as if to ward him off. If there was anything outlandish about Nathan's appearance they presumably had become used to that from Bran; both of them were conspicuous in that they stood taller than the majority of the locals. At the highest end of the enclosure stood the largest structure: the biggest roundhouse Nathan had seen yet, fully sixty feet across and the height of a two-storey house, of clean stone, and a roof which was not just one thatched cone but a complex interpolation of six smaller ones surrounding a central seventh, and six doors around its circumference.

'This is my home,' said Bran, and gestured for him to enter. 'One of them, anyway. My office, I suppose you could call it.'

Inside, Nathan found that instead of it being one vast hall, the interior space was divided into smaller rooms by walls like the spokes of a wheel radiating from a central chamber. By 'home' Bran had meant one of these smaller rooms. It was about the same size as Nathan's Portakabin back at Bryncaer, though nowhere near as cluttered. There was a chair and a chest, both ornately carved from dark oak, a straw mattress overlaid with clean linen, earthenware jugs for washing water and night soil, and wooden pegs in the walls for hanging personal belongings. On a low table a large sheet of animal hide had been unrolled; it was covered in diagrams of mechanisms and columns of figures written in what looked like charcoal, and there were half a dozen more of the primitive blueprints lying around. With a jolt, Nathan saw Bran's old canvas rucksack – the one that everybody had given him grief over at school but which he'd taken all the same, bearing its weight and discomfort without complaint because it satisfied whatever weird internal narrative kept him entertained while he walked. Somehow, this made it real.

'Stay there,' Bran ordered. He indicated a smaller curtained doorway in the opposite wall, adding, 'Watch if you like, but don't say anything or draw attention to yourself. At best you're a non-person here. At worst, a demon; they're liable to kill you.'

The doorway led into the wheelhouse's central meeting chamber, lit with torches and a great central fire, its smoke disappearing through the high thatched roof. The walls were lime-rendered and decorated with elaborate, curvilinear patterns, which seemed to twist and knot themselves in the flickering light. On five of six intricately carved logs around the fire sat figures whom Nathan took to be members of some sort of ruling council: two men and three women. They were not particularly old, nor were they bejewelled with much ornamentation, but their collective presence radiated an aura of brooding disapproval, which only deepened as

Bran strode out to confront them. Nathan watched through the tiniest of gaps as Bran threw the broken spear to the floor before them, and its bronze head rang on the stone like a bell. There was a moment of stunned silence, and then everyone started shouting at once. Bran's voice cut through it all in commanding tones, which Nathan understood enough to infer that he was berating the others about something. Eventually Bran snatched up the spearhead, brandished it high above his head and stormed back into his chamber, leaving the others murmuring.

Nathan sat as far back in the corner as he could as Bran poured himself a drinking bowl of something which foamed like beer, drained it, and then threw himself into the chair, glowering.

'What was that all about?' Nathan ventured.

'Politics,' Bran grunted. 'From time to time people just need to be reminded of who's really in charge.' The scowl disappeared, replaced by a sudden grin. 'My God, you come all this way and it's just more bullshit politics!' He began to laugh, and Nathan joined in politely. 'Anyway, you sleep here tonight.'

'What about you?'

'I'm sure there'll be a space for me at Wurun's fire. Her hearth-husband Nupka is with one of his field-wives for a family thing.' He laughed again, seeing Nathan's confusion. 'I'll explain at dinner. You'll like her, and it'll be a great honour for her. In the meantime, make yourself comfortable, feel free to look around. I'll have some clean things sent in.'

Comfortable? As he turned to leave, Nathan stopped him.

'Bran, look, thank you. For all of this. But you know I can't stay, right? I've left Sue in terrible danger – I've got to go back and put it right. Soon. I mean like really quite urgently soon.'

Bran's smile disappeared. 'The *afaugh*?'

'Yes.'

Bran nodded, as if this was unwelcome but not unexpected news. 'We'll talk about that too,' he said. 'But not until you've had a chance to rest.'

'I don't need to rest. I don't need dinner. I need to get back.'

'Yes, you keep saying that.' There was pity in Bran's voice, but ice in his eyes. '*Back*. You actually think there's a *back*? Look, regardless of how long you stay, you're going to need this.' Bran reached into the chest and produced a slender necklace – nothing more than a leather thong and a few beads, but identical to the one that he wore alongside the cigarette lighter.

'What is it?'

'It is your *rhon*; well, technically it's my *rhon*, but since I'm claiming you as a sun-brother it's yours too. It's like a combination of passport and family tree – it indicates your parentage and status, and marks you as one of the Oendir, as opposed to a *shal*, or non-person.'

'Like an untouchable, you mean?'

'Much like. The higher your status, the more wives or husbands you can have. Take Wurun, for example. She's my hearth-wife because she owns a house, and that gives her high status. Erem, who you will also meet, is my field-wife because she works one of the farmsteads. Wurun herself has three spouses, including a spear-husband, Amsu, who both hunts and guards the hill, and so on and so forth.'

'It sounds... complicated.'

'It is, but it's fair. It is desirable to have spouses from across the social spectrum, and a person's *rhon* is how we keep track of who is related to whom. Each bead represents one of your parents and grandparents, and so you can tell someone's kinship and status at a glance. Incidentally, it's also an ingenious way of preventing inbreeding; if a man and a woman's *rhons* are too similar, they will be stopped from having children.'

'Stopped? What happens if they do it anyway? What about gay people?'

Bran smiled. 'For someone who doesn't want to live amongst us you seem keen for a lecture on our legal system. You should be taking notes, Mr Brookes. There'll be a test.'

Nathan laughed, but it was a small, tired attempt. 'Just the CliffsNotes version for now, thanks.' He tied the thong around his neck and examined the beads. Each was different, carved from a variety of materials into intricate shapes and patterns. 'So where did you get yours from? I mean you obviously weren't born here.'

Bran opened the neck of his shirt and showed Nathan the white line of a scar, which curved across his collarbone and in towards the hollow of his throat. 'I spent a long time as a *shal*, let's put it that way,' he said, and closed it up again. 'I've earned my place.'

Nathan was appalled. 'Jesus, man, what did they do?'

Bran shrugged. 'Whatever they wanted. As a non-person,

you have no status. No rights. You barely rank with livestock.'

'And you say this is fair?'

'Please don't get all holier-than-thou about it. You don't have the first clue about how we live. Gay people, you ask? Since they don't bear children there's no need to forbid that kind of relationship, and there's nothing to stop same-sex marriages. We have a few, though they tend to be a minority in combination with straight marriages because children mean status. You could say we are a constitutionally bisexual culture – how many countries back in the world can say that?'

Nathan shook his head. 'I don't care. Slavery is barbaric, whatever the trade-offs. And don't you start getting all "when in Rome" on me, either.'

'How could I?' answered Bran with a straight face. 'Rome hasn't been built yet.'

The two men looked at each other for a moment, then began to laugh.

Bran he was as good as his word, and hot washing water and clean clothes were brought to Nathan. It was only when examining the strange shirt and woollen britches that he realised how badly he stank, and found that all he wanted to do was clean himself. The *afaugh*'s filth was still on and in him. It took a lot of scrubbing before he felt anywhere close to being clean.

On a neighbouring hill to the Oendir fort-village, and close to the edge of the Wild Wood that surrounded their land, was an ancient circle of standing stones, placed in ages past by a people of whom even the Oendir had no memory. There, many cows and pigs were butchered and their meat wrapped in parcels of leaves and cooked in pits with stones heated on great bonfires, while around the flames danced figures in the guise of their ancestors, retelling the tales of who they were and how they had come to be. Their shadows were thrown across the standing stones, but not all of them were human.

Nathan watched from the periphery, not wanting to draw attention to himself, and hoped that what he saw was the product of his overtaxed mind – how else to explain the shapes of tusk and antler that loped and lurched across the fire-red monoliths? The gaping jaws and tossing manes? *This is Un,* he had to remind himself. These people were either not people at all, but spirits, or else so close that there was little difference.

The meat tasted real enough, however. It was tender after hours of pit-roasting but as soon as its juices filled his mouth Tara's face flashed before his eyes without warning – along with a sickeningly visceral memory of how the skin of her throat had resisted when he'd bitten into it, the hot flood of her blood against his teeth, the taut rubbery pull of cartilage and sinew...

It was too much. Frantic to exorcise the memory, he punched a nearby monolith as hard as he could, welcoming the burst of pain. He kept punching until the bright fog of it overloaded his brain and all that remained of his left fist was a swollen, immobile mass and a stain on the stone – his red blood black in the firelight.

24

SIR BOSS

'I don't know what in God's name you thought you were going to accomplish,' Bran growled as they walked through the fields. It was just after dawn, and curls of vapour clung to the hollows of the landscape, rising to thicken in the distance where the Wild Wood's shadow marked the edge of the Oendir's valley. 'There are no hospitals here, and no antibiotics. If that gets infected you're a dead man. There are also no psychologists for whatever cry for help that was, so just bloody get over it.'

Nathan flexed his bandaged hand and grimaced. *Get over it. Right.* Before agreeing to equip him for a return to the Pale Wood, Bran had insisted on giving Nathan a guided tour of the Oendir village and neighbouring farmsteads. It took little persuasion; Nathan was as grateful for something to distract him from brooding as for the chance to gain information on how to leave Un. Under any other circumstances he'd have liked nothing better than to explore Bran's world.

He made interested-sounding noises as he was shown

how the Wild Wood was being cleared to make more room for farmsteads, how the fields' boundary ditches also channelled irrigation water, the grain storage pits where harvest surplus was stored under airtight clay lids, the wells and latrines dug to prevent disease. He nodded politely as Bran showed him different types of grain and explained about crop yields, and the adventures of people he'd sent out to collect them from the wild. Even the flocks of small game birds scratching tamely in the farmyard dust were worthy of comment.

'There are no chickens here, can you believe that?' Bran laughed. 'So we've domesticated partridges instead. You don't happen to know anything about how chickens were introduced to Britain, do you?' Nathan shook his head, finding it increasingly difficult to follow the surreal twists and turns of this conversation. 'Never mind, then. What I wouldn't give for a potato. Might have a bit of a job convincing someone to discover South America, though, I guess. If there even *is* a South America. Okay, come here; this is what I wanted you to see.'

By a small farmstead of three roundhouses a stream had been dammed, forming a large pool, and a scrawny young man – dressed in rags and covered in mud – was hacking at the earth with a crude wooden shovel to widen a channel down one side of an uncharacteristically square-shaped building which itself was only half-constructed. A second man, supervising the work, approached Bran and greetings were exchanged; though Nathan couldn't understand what was being said, he caught his own name.

'This is Arkan,' said Bran, introducing a man who grinned his welcome through a massive moustache. 'He's my field-wife Erem's wood-husband. Don't worry, I know it's confusing. You'll get used to it. Just look at this for a moment.' He went over the construction site with Arkan, both of them peering at joints and rapping timbers, and came back to Nathan. 'Can you guess what it is?'

'I genuinely have no idea.' *And couldn't care less.*

'It's a mill race! We're going to have a watermill right here! It's going to multiply our flour production a hundredfold overnight!' When this failed to elicit any answering excitement, Bran took Nathan by the arm. 'So much of our manpower is expended just feeding ourselves that we don't have the resources to actually build anything like a decent civilisation. With a plentiful food supply we can build some decent infrastructure – schools, make our children literate – be a major trading power with the coastal settlements, find out who the hell has iron in this day and age, maybe even get hold of some potatoes!' He laughed, but as quickly as it appeared he was serious again, declaring, 'Before I die I'll see this place with steam engines. Don't you see what this mill represents? It's the first step from the Bronze Age to the Industrial Revolution in a single generation!'

'You're crazy. It'll never work.' It was said thoughtlessly – his knee-jerk and absolutely honest response while most of his attention was gnawing itself with worry over Sue – and exactly the wrong thing.

Bran's face closed. 'Well, quite. The problem is that I simply don't know enough. I've got twenty-first-century ambitions but my education was stopped before I finished secondary school. Okay, so at sixteen I was a nerd.' He shrugged. 'But what's the use of knowing everything about Weimar Germany and how to factorise simultaneous equations when I don't know what iron-bearing rock looks like or how to extract it? Or how to grow penicillin? Or where chickens come from, for God's sake? Why wasn't I shown anything actually useful? Do you have any idea how fucking frustrating that is?'

'I'm starting to get some idea.'

'That's why your being here is such a stroke of luck for us. You must have – what? – ten, twenty years' more knowledge and experience on me.'

'I haven't got a clue about penicillin either, you know...'

'Forget that! It was just an example. The point is there are *two* of us now!' Bran gripped Nathan's shoulders, fixing him with an intensity that was frightening, and Nathan was uncomfortably aware of just how much more physically powerful Bran was. 'We can bounce ideas off each other and solve those problems *together*!'

And Nathan saw that despite the life he'd built for himself – the wealth, the prestige, the multiple marriages or whatever that was about – Bran was, quite simply, lonely. Away from home for years, of course he wanted to cling to anything or anyone who could provide a connection. 'Who's that guy?' Nathan asked, indicating the man who was digging.

Arkan smiled at Nathan in polite confusion.

'He's *shal*,' explained Bran. 'Introductions are unnecessary.

He doesn't have any name that you need to know.'

'Ah,' nodded Nathan. 'I think I understand.' He approached and shook the young slave vigorously by the hand, saying, 'Nathan Brookes, pleased to meet you,' to the man's evident consternation. A shadow of something unpleasant crossed Bran's face, but when Arkan asked him a question he responded with an easy laugh.

'What was that?' asked Nathan, as they walked away. '"Don't mind my brother-in-law, he's not from around here"?'

'Something like it. I wouldn't do that again if I were you.'

Nathan laughed. 'Is that a threat?'

'Don't be asinine, of course it's not a *threat*. But every social taboo exists for a reason, and if you break enough of them you get stomped on, no matter how many beads are around your neck.'

'Slavery isn't a taboo. It's a crime. I'm surprised that with your obvious clout you haven't done something about that by now.'

'You can't change a culture overnight.'

'No, but apparently you can help them skip a thousand years of technological evolution. I guess it depends on what your priorities are.'

Bran stopped and stared at him. 'What's your point, Mr Brookes? Other than trying to piss off the people who want to help you, that is?'

'My point, Brandon, is that I'm not a resource. If you invite me to help you with your whole *Connecticut Yankee in King Arthur's Court* act, don't be surprised if I change things that you don't like. Besides, I've got a better idea.

Why don't you help me find a way to get back instead? Then we can both go.'

Bran threw his hands up in exasperation. 'That's exactly what Scattie kept saying! There *is* no back, that's why! You can *never* go back! Do you not think that if there was a way back she would have found it by now? Tell me, did she make it? Because you only mentioned Liv earlier. She didn't, did she? And even if we did manage to find another crossing point somehow, what's waiting for me there? What kind of life? I have no qualifications, no way of getting a job. Do you think I'm going to return home only to scrounge a living on benefits? If there even are benefits any more – when I was a kid I saw the way things were going. We're all in it together?' He snorted with contempt. 'I was on the school's Oxbridge fast-track programme, remember? I'm never getting that back now. And assume I *can* get a job – what good can I do there except fill another desk and pay tax until they let me collect a pension and finally die, just another old grey man in an old grey country? I think not, teacher.'

'I'll tell you what's waiting for you there: your loved ones.'

Bran's face twisted. 'Yes, I know. But I have loved ones here now. I have three wives, and they've all got their own husbands, and between us I've got five sun-children and twelve moon-children. They're my responsibility now. How can I abandon all of this' – he gestured around at the half-constructed watermill – 'when it's my job to make their lives better? Are you married? Do you have children?'

Nathan squirmed away from the questions. 'That's not the point.'

'You don't? Then how can you claim to understand anything of what ties me to this place? Still, that surprises me. Tell me, Nathan,' and despite how changed Brandon was it was still a shock to be addressed by his first name, 'what have you ever built? I mean actually. What have you physically brought into this world that will stand as a testament to you when you're gone?'

'*This* world?'

'Don't try to be clever, please. I'm offering you a place here. A purpose. A chance to build something. It's the least I can do, after all.'

'But this place isn't real!'

'And who are you to say that? Maybe this has all sprung out of my subconscious and it will all just disappear when I die. Maybe I'm already dead – maybe we both are – and this is all just my own personal afterlife. Maybe it's an echo of the past and there is no future and these people will never advance past the late Bronze Age no matter what I do. I've spent years trying to work out what this place is and the best conclusion I can come to is that *it just doesn't fucking matter*. All I can do is try to leave it better than when I found it. That's my reality.'

'Look, I see where you're going with this, and under different circumstances I'd be very tempted. But Sue is in danger, *now*, and I've got to do something about that. That's *my* reality. End of.'

'I know.' Bran laid a hand on his shoulder. The volatile mixture of passion, bitterness, love and anger had left him, leaving only a terrible sympathy that Nathan could barely look at because of what it implied. 'And I'm truly sorry, but there is nothing you can do for her, not from here. By all means, go back to the Pale Wood and try to find the timber track. Maybe with Bark Foot's death the way will be open again.' Bran pointed towards the mill, the farmstead with Arkan and the unnamed *shal* listening nervously to the impassioned exchange that they couldn't understand, and the wider Oendir valley, which stretched for leagues around them until the Wild Wood began. 'Just keep in mind that there's a place for you here, that's all.'

'I'll do that,' Nathan replied, and to his immense surprise found that he actually did.

25

PATHLESS

NATHAN WENT BACK TO THE PALE WOOD ON HIS OWN. None of Bran's people would accompany him to that haunted place, though he was given food, a fire-flint, water, and a weapon: a simple bronze dirk, which was all he could handle without training. Bark Foot might be dead, and the *afaugh* might have escaped, but there was no telling what else might have been attracted to such a place.

He found Bark Foot's wrecked camp easily enough, and was able to cobble together a rough shelter. While he worked his mind went back to Bran's cry of triumph when he'd discovered Bark Foot's broken spear, and he thought, *No, you weren't just looking to see if the timber track was open – you were looking for that, specifically. Why? And why weren't you surprised to find me here too?* It took him quite a while to get a fire going with such primitive tools and such damp material, but he managed it, banked it up, and went off to explore.

It was the utter silence that unnerved him most. With no birds, no breeze to move the trees, and the moss muffling his footsteps, all he could hear was the faint drip of the all-pervading damp and the distant roar of the river. Easy to believe how something like the *afaugh* could haunt these woods without detection. He felt like a ghost himself, slipping between the margins of the world, unnoticed and unmourned.

Locating the river, he found the remains of the timber track. It was rotten and crumbling, and didn't lead to the sunny uplands of Sutton Park, but to the sere and desolate landscape that Liv had described. He examined the river bank up and down, and found nothing. He crossed a narrow part of the stream over a fallen birch tree – awkwardly because of his injured hand – and crossed to the bogland on the other side. There was life here, of a sort, but little more than midges and a few frightened curlews. This close to the *afaugh*'s old hunting ground, he fancied he could smell its foulness behind every tree and under every stone, as if something had crept into hiding to die surrounded by its own excrement. Worse, he thought he detected the same taint on his own skin, so he stripped off and washed himself, pale and shivering, in the icy torrent.

In desperation he wandered back through the Pale Wood, calling for Bark Foot, Sue, Scattie, *anybody*, but the echoes of his voice fell dead in the damp air and he stopped, scared at how much his own voice sounded like the calls of the famished spirit. Bran was right, of course. If there had been a way home here, it was closed for ever.

It was too dark to return safely to the Oendir, so he went back to the embers of his fire, blew them into life, ate a little food, and slept.

* * *

NATHAN RETURNED TO THE OENDIR VILLAGE THE following afternoon, by which time the weather had become cooler. He huddled against the rain as he trudged through the maze of farm tracks towards the broad rise of the hill fort, and by so doing missed exactly how much had changed until he heard the peculiar heavy creaking rumble of wooden wheels. He looked up.

The watermill had been completed – overnight, it seemed. It was a clumsy, lumbering affair, as a machine fashioned with Bronze Age tools and no iron to fasten its joints was bound to be, but it was turning nonetheless, powered by a fast-flowing mill race, which was complete and lined in stone, with its axle disappearing into the wall of the steep-thatched millhouse. Two storeys high, it could have passed for medieval, and stood in stark contrast to the neighbouring roundhouses. It was completely impossible.

While he stood gawping, a door opened and a figure emerged. Arkan, now presumably the miller, saw who was standing outside in the pissing rain and bundled him in, shouting to those inside. Too astonished to resist, even if he'd wanted to, Nathan let himself be led to a fireside where he was given dry clothes, beer and freshly baked bread.

26

KINLESS

'This is all Un,' explained Bran. 'But not all its parts work the same.' He and Nathan sat in Bran's chamber in the great wheelhouse. It was busy and warm with the bustle of humanity, and the sounds of the thriving community outside – a welcome contrast to the inhuman stasis of the Pale Wood. 'I told you, time doesn't obey normal rules there. There are, very roughly, zones. The Pale Wood is one. This valley is one. The Wild Wood that surrounds it is yet another. Beyond here there are others, all different. Some of them are homes to tribes similar to the Oendir with whom we trade, but they are rare. I think they form themselves, or in some cases are deliberately created, around the presence of strong psyches, souls, whatever you want to call them. But each obeys different rules, and they don't mesh together neatly – the borders between them are fuzzy. It's not surprising that you experienced a slippage of time – it happens sometimes, although not always. I've been back there a few times myself, and I know how disorientating it can be.'

'You knew that might happen.'

'I suspected it probably would.'

'Why didn't you warn me?'

'Oh please. You weren't listening to *anything* I said. Don't try to lay your mistakes at my feet.'

Nathan couldn't argue with that.

Bran sat across from him, sipping something hot and fragrant from a pewter cup. Now that Nathan had the time and inclination to observe him closely, he saw that Bran's clothes were of finely spun and richly patterned wool; house-shoes of well-tooled leather were on his feet; gold gleamed on his fingers, wrists, and about his throat; even the chair upon which he sat was carved as elaborately as anything Nathan had seen in a museum. These were the trappings of a civilised culture, and there was something in the easy complacency of it that irked him. Bran's attitude reminded him of the way DI Hodges had sat when he'd visited Nathan on the hospital ward, after he'd been stabbed by Liv. Bark Foot's spear was mounted on the wall behind Bran's head, its shaft replaced, looking like a hunting trophy. Still, if Liv's account was true, Nathan supposed he couldn't blame Bran for celebrating the death of the creature that had tormented them.

'Bran,' he said, 'what exactly did happen to Scattie?'

Bran shrugged. 'I told you, she left,' he said simply. He set down his cup and began fidgeting with the empty cigarette lighter hanging around his neck.

'Yes I know, that's what you said before. Left why? Left for where?'

'We had much the same argument you and I had when

you arrived here. She was determined to find a way home and I was determined to make *this* place home. Eventually we stopped trying to persuade each other and she left, with my blessing.'

Your blessing. As if Scattie would ever have asked for it, or needed it. 'But where did she think she was going? She must have had some sort of plan.'

'If she did, she never said what it was,' replied Bran, still fidgeting, and Nathan knew with the absolute certainty born from a career of working with young people that Bran was lying. Still, there was a limit to how far he was prepared to antagonise the only person who could understand him around here, so he let it go for the moment. 'Look, I don't want to get into a pointless argument over things that are finished and done with. We need to be thinking about the future.'

'You're determined to make me part of your pet project, aren't you?'

'You saw for yourself that you can't get back. Where else is there for you but here?' There was something smug about the way Bran spread his hands, as if he'd just proved something obvious to a particularly dim-witted child. Nathan wondered which of his old teaching colleagues Bran had picked that up from.

'I met your dad last week,' he said casually, and something cruel in him enjoyed seeing the smirk wiped off Bran's face.

'You met…'

'Yeah. His exact words were, "We just want to know what happened."' Nathan sat very still and watched a storm front of conflicting emotions play across Bran's face as he got up and moved restlessly amongst his plans and models, tidying them into nice straight lines.

'Why would you tell me that?' he asked, without making eye contact. 'I don't understand why you'd say such a thing. Are you just trying to cause me pain for the sake of it?'

'No, Bran, I'm not. But your family is still there, desperate to know what happened to you. And Ryan's, and Scattie's. Okay, so I might not be able to help Sue, but I could find Scattie, or what she was looking for, or even some way of letting her parents know what happened to her. I owe them that at the very least. I owe them a duty to try.' He waited while Bran continued to fidget. 'We could go together.'

Bran was holding a model windmill and idly turning its tiny vanes as if winding up a propeller. He returned it carefully to its place, and when he turned back to Nathan his smiling politician's face had been restored. 'Well we can certainly thrash out the possibilities,' he said. 'Possibly under more convivial circumstances. Come on.'

Nathan followed Bran to one of the neighbouring wheelhouses. It seemed that all the larger or more elaborate structures within the hill fort's walls were public buildings, including a council chamber, grain store and smithy.

What hit Nathan first was the humidity, and his heart lurched as he recognised the building's function. It was much larger than the sweat-hut at the Moonbridge Institute, but just as hot and airless. The dressed stone walls were slick with condensation, and against them were stone benches where men and women sat, red-faced and perspiring, either chatting or sponging themselves down with thick mats of moss. More people wallowed in a pool, which ran concentrically around a central island where a cairn of stones glowed cherry red. Two young men who Nathan took to be *shals* were replacing them using a large stone crucible carried between them with a wooden yoke; it was obviously back-breaking work. Someone tossed a handful of herbs onto the stones to perfume the air, and suddenly Phoelix was there, in the water, glaring at him, covered in blood, and the water around him began to turn pink...

Nathan swallowed hard and blinked Phoelix away.

Bran looked at him in concern. 'Everything okay?'

The water was clear. There were no dead people to accuse him with their stares. 'I'm good,' he said, even though he was anything but good. The last thing he wanted to do was relax; every nerve screamed that despite the fuzziness of time here it was nevertheless slipping away from him and that he had to get moving, get doing something, anything other than give up and accept this. Nevertheless, he forced himself to calm down and be attended to by the *shals* – they smeared his body from hairline to feet with fine, silty clay which dried before being scraped off, and it genuinely did leave him feeling properly clean for the first time in days.

Afterwards he was given new clothes – a simple shift tunic belted at the waist and a loincloth, which felt uncomfortably like wearing a nappy – and a place to sleep in the ground-floor grain store of Arkan's mill.

* * *

IT DIDN'T TAKE NATHAN LONG TO SEE A SIDE OF BRAN which confirmed his suspicions that anywhere was better than the valley of the Oendir.

Erem and Arkan's *shal* – who Nathan had learned was called Ysil – was caught stealing flour. The punishment was a flogging. This would have been bad enough, except that it seemed that every member of the household was expected to participate – including Nathan. Ysil was tied to a post before the great wheelhouse, his back thin and pale in the sun, and Nathan watched as the eight members of Erem's immediate household – three adults and five children – each beat him once with a leather strap. Some were more enthusiastic than others. The two youngest children did little more than tap him gently and then run off. Erem herself struck Ysil so hard that blood flew, and grinned as she did it. When it came to Nathan's turn, he refused absolutely.

'But you have to,' Bran insisted. 'A crime against the family demands punishment *by* the family.'

'I can't. I won't. It's barbaric.'

'You don't have to actually hurt him – just a symbolic tap will do. It's the principle of the thing.'

'I won't be part of this, and I can't believe you agree with it.'

Bran took him by the arm and drew him aside roughly. 'Listen,' he said. 'If that *shal* escapes the law, it is a crime against the law, which is a crime against the whole community, which means *everyone* gets to beat him. You think he'll survive that?'

Nathan didn't answer. The few strokes that Ysil had

already received had made his back red-raw. No, he wouldn't survive.

'Then take some fucking responsibility for where you are and the people around you,' Bran growled, and shoved him forward.

Nathan took the strap and approached Ysil. Up close he could smell blood and sweat, and feel heat baking off the young man's quivering flesh. 'Sorry about this,' he murmured, and tapped Ysil lightly on the shoulder. Ysil flinched all the same, as if he'd been hit with an iron bar. Nathan flung the strap in the dirt and stalked away.

'Good man,' said Bran as he passed.

'Fuck off,' Nathan shot back.

THEY CAUGHT UP WITH NATHAN WHERE THE DARK TANGLE of the Wild Wood swelled in slopes and ridges at the valley's edge, amongst the fallen trunks of trees that had been cut to clear the land for more fields. He hadn't taken much: a knife and food for a few days. Nothing that should have been missed. He hadn't tried to run either, when he'd seen figures chasing after him, knowing that they could easily outpace him and track him even if he did make it into the forest. He simply sat on a tree trunk and waited.

Bran was accompanied by four spearmen from the fort. Nathan nodded at them. 'You're not even going to try to persuade me any more, are you?'

Bran looked him up and down, assessing, dismissing. 'No.'

'Why not just let me go? Why make this awkward?'

'Because you're an asset I can use, and I hate seeing useful things go to waste.' Bran planted his foot on the trunk next to where Nathan was sitting. Possessive. *Mine*. 'See this tree? It's useless the way it is. Heavy. Out of place. *Awkward*. But stripped, sawn, cured, planed and shaped, it becomes a useful building material. All it takes is craftsmanship and patience, both of which I have a ton of.'

'Believe it or not,' said Nathan, 'I have been thinking about what you said – your offer.'

'You have?'

'I was thinking about when you said it was the least you could do. Why did you say that?'

Bran shrugged. 'Just a figure of speech.'

'Possibly. Or the kind of thing said by someone trying to make amends. I've also been thinking about when you found me at Bark Foot's camp. Someone you haven't seen for a decade suddenly appears and you never once asked me how I got there, or what happened to me. Why is that?'

'None of this makes any difference now...' Bran reached down to pull him up by one arm, but Nathan shook him off. The spearmen bristled.

'You didn't even seem particularly surprised to see me there. You were more excited about finding that spear than seeing me. Is that because you already knew I was going to be there?'

Bran laughed, but the attempt was forced and mirthless. 'Now you're just being paranoid. Mr Brookes, listen to me. When we found you, you were half-drowned and unconscious. Of course I was surprised to see you; you just weren't in any state to notice.'

Nathan stood and faced him squarely. 'I'll tell you what I notice: the *afaugh*. The stink of it. It's all over you. I thought it was me, because it was *in* me, you know? And I've been trying to wash it off but it won't go. Did you think that I wouldn't smell it on you too? What happened, Brandon? Did it attack you? Did it kill Scattie? I don't think so, or you'd have said. So, what? Did you make some kind of deal with it? Is that why she fell out with you? Is that how you went from being a *shal* to Sir Boss?'

Bran leaned in close, and now Nathan could smell it clearly: the sweet-rotten stench of cannibalised flesh that clung to him like smoke. Bran looked him up and down with contempt, but there was something that stopped the younger man from looking him squarely in the eye – Nathan fancied that it might have been shame.

'Teachers,' Bran sneered. 'You never stop asking questions, do you?' He snapped the *rhon* from around Nathan's neck. 'Take him away.'

27

SHAL

ARKAN AND EREM'S *SHAL* WERE PENNED IN A ROUGH LEAN-to, which abutted the main roundhouse. It was roughly constructed, with large gaps between the stones of its walls and the tattered thatch of its roof through which drafts gusted, but the wall it shared with the house leeched some warmth, and so it was against this that Nathan and Ysil huddled when they weren't labouring. The first thing Ysil had done when Nathan had been flung in here was to take Nathan's hand in both of his and shake it, with great solemnity. 'Likewise,' he'd replied. 'So what are you in for?'

But Ysil just frowned and returned to his own corner.

'I know, never ask. You and me both, then.'

Bran came to see him only twice; the first time was to lay down the terms of Nathan's incarceration.

'This isn't necessarily a life sentence,' he said. There was a coolness in his manner, and Nathan realised he was seeing the Bran that everybody else saw – the politician. 'Many people become temporary *shal* as punishment for petty crimes, or to pay off debts – they do nothing more menial than clean up around the place. At the end of the day we're all neighbours and nobody wants people holding grudges. You, however, are nobody's neighbour. This could be a very long and very unpleasant experience for you.'

'What's my crime then?' Nathan sneered. '"Failure to follow proper risk-assessment procedures"? I don't think there's a tick box for "student becoming megalomaniac dickhead".'

Bran ignored him. 'While you're here, keep an eye on the milling mechanism. See if there are any ways it can be improved – made more efficient or productive – for when we build the next one. Come up with something decent, and you can be *shal* at my own hearth. After that, well, we'll take it from there. I remain hopeful that you can make a constructive contribution to this culture, Mr Brookes; I just think you haven't really had the time and opportunity to consider the incentives for doing so.'

There was no need for locks or chains, as Nathan quickly discovered; where was there to run? Bran had made it quite clear that everybody knew everybody else's business, including whose *shal* he was now, and that if he was discovered straying from Arkan's farmstead and into someone else's property, they would most likely flog him as a lesson to all the other Oendir's indentured servants: know your place.

It turned out that Ysil was a gifted mimic, and delighted in provoking Nathan into fits of reluctant laughter with his impersonations of Erem's family. On the first day of his incarceration Erem had made a great show of inspecting him, pointing out his obvious physical deficiencies and laughing.

After the second day, with no food in the meantime (and Ysil violently protective of his own scraps in those early days before they learned to be friends), she came to him after sunrise and forced Nathan to fuck her. When he'd refused she had shown him the burn scars on Ysil's buttocks, made with what looked like the red-hot tip of a knife, and he got the idea. After she'd gone, Ysil – who had been watching silently – performed a comical burlesque of her grunts and bounces, and offered him half a heel of stale bread. 'You'd get on a storm with Robbie,' Nathan said, and the sudden torrent of homesickness that this unleashed left him sobbing unashamedly.

His wounds scabbed and healed. During the nights he fought with the temptation to admit that Sue was far beyond his help now, aided only by the faint hope that the time discrepancies between the Pale Wood and the Oendir's region of Un might somehow be made to work in his favour.

He and Ysil taught each other a little of their own words and so were able to communicate through a weird pidgin language. Through a series of long, halting and frustrating conversations, he learned that Ysil was not one of the Oendir but came from a distant nomadic tribe of hunter-herdsfolk called the Eshetri. As a child he'd become separated from his family during one of their migrations and stumbled into the Oendir's valley where he'd been *shal* ever since.

Ysil was just old enough to remember the day that Brandon and Scattie had arrived. He said that after being taken in as *shal* they were treated with relative kindness at first. Both had been eager for tales of how to journey to the Bright Lands, which Nathan took to mean home – often sneaking out in the dark of night to quiz other *shal* like himself about such things, and earning many a beating (and worse besides) for doing so. Ysil had told them that his people, who had journeyed far and spoken with many others who had journeyed even further, believed that the Bright Lands lay past a barrier called the White Wall at the sunset end of the world.

Bran and Scattie eventually fled and were pursued into the Pale Wood, but their hunters never came home. Three days later Bran returned, invested with a great and terrible power. He slew those who had beaten him and all their sun-kin, took their *rhon* for himself and his companion, and spoke to those who sat on the hill, saying that he would bring them peace and plenty, or else war and famine. The Oendir had little choice but to accept him, and since that day Bran had been true to his word: peace and full harvests had blessed this valley. But Scattie would not stay. According to Ysil, she departed on her own quest for the White Wall, and had not been heard of since that day.

And then the strangest thing happened.

During the night Nathan awoke to find Ysil's fingers curled around his cock, and himself growing hard in response. He felt Ysil tense up, ready to be rebuked, and his hand began to draw away. After an eternity of indecision, Nathan reached out and replaced it, and as he did so he felt the weight of the loss of Sue shift. There was no blinding moment of self-revelation; he'd never thought of himself as gay and still didn't now, but here was comfort and affection – and perhaps in time, a kind of love – and knowing how rare those things were in any world he allowed himself to relax into Ysil's strange-yet-familiar embrace.

BRAN'S SECOND VISIT FOLLOWED TWO WEEKS DURING which even Nathan and Ysil became aware that unusual things were happening in the valley of the Oendir. For a start, there had not been one day of decent weather since Nathan's return from the Pale Wood. The best it had been able to muster had been a light drizzle, which for the season getting on towards harvest time was a source of increasing anxiety for the farmers, and made Erem cruel in turn. They heard of a neighbouring farmstead where an entire field of wheat was completely blighted overnight, and one on the other side where a sow gave birth to a late litter, every piglet of which was born without eyes.

The final straw came one morning when Arkan the miller led a grim-faced mob of farmers across the field to where Nathan and Ysil were clearing debris from an irrigation ditch. In one hand he held a half-empty flour sack, while the other dipped inside, scooped a fistful of its contents and then flung it at Nathan along with a mouthful of abuse. What hit Nathan in the face wasn't flour – it was harder, and it stung. He didn't need Ysil to translate: a hopper of grain had turned to gravel even as it had been milled.

The mob dragged Nathan up to the hill fort to the open space before the great wheelhouse. He was flung down into the mud, bruised and bloody, in front of Bran, who leaned on Bark Foot's spear, looked down at him and frowned.

'What do you think you're doing?' he asked, tossing the bag of gravel between Nathan's knees. 'You're just being childish now.'

'What do I think *I'm* doing?' Nathan responded, incredulous. 'I'm not responsible for this! You think I sabotaged the mill deliberately?'

'It's definitely preferable to what the farmers think you've been doing. And not just that, either.'

Nathan wiped filth from his face, and spat a mouthful of blood at Bran's feet. 'What the fuck are you on about?'

'The ruined crops, the mutant births. A woman had a miscarriage the other day – the child had no *spine*. Are we expected to believe that these are all just coincidences? The Oendir think you're cursed—'

Nathan uttered a hollow laugh and shook his head. 'You've finally lost it.'

'—that you're a demon from the Pale Wood, using magic to blight their homes, and they're demanding that I do something about it. Frankly, I'm considering it.'

'Don't call me Frankly,' Nathan muttered.

'*This is not a joke!*' Bran snapped, and the sudden violence of it shocked the hilltop into silence. 'Make. It. Stop.' Nathan could smell Bran's breath as it hissed from between his clenched teeth.

Nathan dragged himself to his feet and made an exaggerated show of brushing the mud and shit off a pair of invisible lapels, before squaring his shoulders and squinting sidelong at Bran. 'Let's say I am responsible for it. Why might that be? Face facts, Bran, this isn't the late Bronze Age, and you haven't travelled back in time. You aren't reshaping the future of human civilisation. This is Un. This is the place where echoes come from, the land of shadows – you've shaped it with your imagination into something you need, just like the people who created Bark Foot did when they needed somewhere to trap the *afaugh*. Ysil told me about what happened when you and Scattie arrived, and the things you did with its help. What I think seems to be happening is that Un is shaping itself in response to me now, too, and what I need, and the problem you've got, Brandon, is that I am very, *very* pissed off. I'm not sure I could stop it even if I wanted to – and I don't.'

'Innocent people are suffering.'

'You should have thought of that before you made me *shal*.'

Bran levelled the spear at his throat, and the light on its bronze blade ran like fire. 'You're right, I should have. I suppose this serves me right for giving in to nostalgia – for thinking that anything could change. I should have saved myself a lot of trouble right at the start and killed you like I was supposed to.'

'Wait – what do you mean, "supposed to"?'

'Oh please,' Bran sneered. 'Can you possibly be that naïve? You think any of this is coincidence? Yes, I made a deal with the *afaugh*. Of course I did. You would have too.' Bran tore the neck of his shirt open and exposed the scar across his throat. 'Remember this? You should have seen what those fuckers did to Scattie. So yes, I went into the Pale Wood and I offered it whatever price it wanted in return for the power to protect me and mine. And that price turned out to be you. Dead. With your head on a fucking pole. It knew you were coming. For all I know, it was the one who sent you those visions in the first place, to lure you here. You've been played all along.'

'That's impossible. How could it know I would be here *nine years* in advance?'

'How should I fucking know? I wasn't exactly in a position to ask questions. And besides, at the time I was more than happy to do it. To kill you.'

'Jesus, Bran, why? Why do you hate me so much?'

'*Because you left us!*' Bran screamed. 'You *left* us! You should have been there and you *weren't*! You should have walked with us, and then Bark Foot wouldn't have taken us, and Ryan wouldn't have died, and I wouldn't have become *this*!' There it was, then. Bran was red-faced and trembling, weeping, no longer a tribal chieftain but the lost sixteen-year-old that he'd always been underneath. The spear-point hovered inches away from Nathan's throat. He almost felt sorry for the boy. If it hadn't been for the *afaugh*'s taint seeping from his tears, he would have.

'Yes,' Nathan sighed. 'Yes, I left you. It was a shitty, selfish thing to do and I'm more sorry than you can possibly imagine for how things turned out, but what you are now is on you. The thing is, though, you didn't kill me, did you? You helped me. That's got to count for something.'

The spear-point dropped and Bran slumped, as if bone-weary. 'Kill you. Don't think it isn't still very appealing, but I'm afraid you simply don't get out of it that easily. You're right about this place, of course; what it really is. The *afaugh* was bad enough – imagine how much harm your murdered spirit would cause to my people. No, I can't kill you, and you won't be held, so you really only leave me with one choice.'

THEY BANISHED HIM WITH DRUMS AND FIRE. HE WAS stripped, beaten, his hands were bound, and they placed a necklace of birds' heads around his throat so that he would be cursed to the air, and smeared him with animal excrement so that he would be cursed to the earth. He was chased out of the Oendir valley by an even larger mob than the one that had first dragged him to Bran – beating drums, crashing sticks together, singing, screaming abuse, dogs snapping at him and old women spitting in his face, waving brands of fire with which they scorched him back to his feet every time he stumbled, until he reached the comparative safety of the Wild Wood at the edge of their land. Tara's words came back to him as he fled: 'The sacrifice takes on the sins of the community and by their death those sins are expiated.' In this way they cleansed their land of an evil spirit and returned to their homes in high spirits.

Nathan managed to stagger on for a few hundred metres past the forest's edge before collapsing. He didn't know how long he had been lying there before he heard movement in the bushes nearby, and could only look up numbly as Bran appeared from hiding.

'Hah,' he croaked. 'Knew you couldn't resist it.' With a tremendous effort he struggled to his knees, exposing his throat. 'Come on then, finish it. I know how this ends.'

Bran sighed. 'Once again you completely misunderstand me.'

From behind him stepped Ysil, carrying a large bundle of clothes and gear. He cut Nathan's hands free and got him into a more comfortable sitting position, gave him water, fretted over his wounds, cleaned his body and helped him to dress.

'Just exactly what is going on here, Bran?' Nathan said, when his voice was working properly again.

The spear shifted in Bran's hands and Nathan flinched, fearing that it had all been a lie, that Bran had simply decided to toy with him a bit longer before killing him after all. He waited for a blow that never fell. When he opened his eyes, he saw that the haft of the weapon was being offered to him instead.

'I don't understand.'

Bran looked exhausted. 'I know. You couldn't begin to. This wasn't made for me, and it wasn't made to hang on a wall. If you're going to find the *afaugh* you're going to need something to fight it. You're not the only one who's unimaginably sorry for how things turned out.' He moved to leave.

'How are you going to explain losing it?'

Bran turned back and offered him a last rueful smile. 'I'm sure I'll think of something.' And then he was gone, back to his tribe.

When Nathan had recovered sufficient strength – and with Ysil propping him up on one side and the spear propping up the other – they left.

28

THE FAR PASTURES

NATHAN AND YSIL TRAVELLED WEST INTO A WATERCOLOUR landscape of fog and mist, where vistas shifted like overlapping veils of gauze and bled into each other so that it quickly became impossible to gauge any meaningful progress other than by the rise and fall of the sun. Landmarks would shift between one vantage point and another, sometimes appearing in the opposite direction or disappearing altogether. Rivers and streams were capricious, changing course and direction apparently at random, and laughing with the voice of water chuckling over stones at their attempts to navigate. Nathan quickly found that the landscape reacted to his mood: when he became impatient or frustrated it would hamper him with boggy ground or coils of brambles, but that in contrast, when he calmed down and simply let the land be, it opened up with green swards and sunlit skies. At night, when he and Ysil made love, the sky blazed with constellations so ancient that he might have been transported to an alien world.

He healed, grew strong, and tried to reconcile himself to the bitter truth that Sue was by now long beyond his rescue, but each time he told himself this his memory replayed the image of her crouched at the top of the staircase, protectively cradling her children and begging him to tell her what was happening, as the *afaugh* grinned at him. It was a hook, snagged in his mind, which he was unable to pull free, so in those moments he took Bark Foot's spear and went in search of something to kill.

There were, besides the sun, only two points of consistency in the landscape of Un. The first was the presence of stone circles, monoliths, barrows and other monumental relics of humanity's infancy. These remained in the same positions relative to each other when all the land between them changed from one glance to the next. It was as if they were islands, or else places where human imagination and endeavour had pinned the world into a fixed reality with needles of stone or mounds of earth. Nathan and Ysil soon learned to make camp in these places, and by them were able to make some sense of their progress. Nathan wished he'd learned more about such sites, because he was convinced that their journey must be analogous in some way to the 'real' world, but suspected that so much had been lost to civilisation that this would have been impossible anyway. His ill-informed impression was that there were an awful lot more of them here than still existed in reality; the memory of stone, it seemed, was longer-lasting than stone itself.

The second point of consistency was the existence of human habitation – though in many cases the definition of 'human' seemed as blurred and indeterminate as the land. Many times they heard half-human voices calling to them from deep woods or black caves, trying to trap them or warn them away. They saw footprints in the mud around drinking pools, made by beings whose feet looked mostly human, apart from the thumbs, claws or partial hooves. They passed copses of ancient trees where faces formed out of twigs and leaves to watch them warily. They encountered family groups of hominins too primitive even for the concept of 'tribe' to apply. They met nomadic communities of ice-age hunter-gatherers who stalked game with weapons of bone and flint. And, occasionally, they came across familiar-looking settlements of roundhouses, farms, and walled hill forts like the Oendir. Here they were able to barter for food, lodging and news. Invariably, this included rumours of Scattie – but like the landscape itself, these stories were widely variable. In some she was a figure of legend generations old, with magical powers and feats ascribed to her name, of which she had many: Scathach, Kalmuneiu, Flidais, and a dozen more. In others she had passed by merely a matter of days or even hours before, prompting Nathan to chase after her only to discover that at the next settlement it had been months since her appearance. Frustration made him a grumpy travelling companion, which only delayed them further.

THEY HAD BEEN RUNNING THROUGH THICK UNDERGROWTH from a pack of lopers – half-human hunters with the hind legs of wolves and the voices of carrion birds – and losing, when Nathan blundered into a collection of sticks and feathers hanging at head height. He recoiled, slipped, and fell. Ysil skidded past him in the leaves and turned back, one hand outstretched to haul him to his feet, the other with his spear cocked to fling at the nearest loper, but they had stopped.

They were milling around and jabbering at each other, confused, angered and terrified of something that had blocked their progress. They made grasping lunges at Nathan and Ysil and shrieked their frustration as Nathan scrambled further out of reach.

'Why aren't they attacking?' Nathan panted.

'I think…' Ysil examined the crude mobile. It was a triangle of hazel sticks bound with twine and decorated with black feathers, and at its centre hung a stone daubed with blood. Looking left and right, he saw others hanging at intervals. 'Yes, wards. Crow's feathers and wolf's blood, probably. Well maintained. Someone of power lives here.' He looked at Nathan. 'You have mud on you, clumsy git.' *Git* was one of his favourite new words. Where Nathan had fallen to the earth there was a smear of it on his cheek. He wiped it off.

'Let's go pay our respects, in that case,' he said. They moved off quickly, not entirely trusting to the wards' protection, and when they were at a safe distance Nathan shoved Ysil into a bush. 'Clumsy git,' he grinned.

The village they came to was much the same as the many others they'd visited – a handful of roundhouses surrounded by small fields carved out of the forest close to a stream, the stink of animals, the ringing of a forge. Nothing on the scale of the Oendir, though; these buildings were wattle and daub, their roofs of turf rather than thatch. Field workers stopped to gawp as Nathan and Ysil passed, word ran ahead and before long a group of muttering villagers armed with rakes, shovels and pitchforks had formed to meet them. One or two had bronze hunting spears.

Then a female voice shouted and the group parted as an elderly woman – perhaps even in her fifties – pushed her way through. Nathan stared at her in shock. Ysil was speaking his usual words of welcome, but Nathan couldn't hear them, or anything, or see anything, because the focus of his attention had collapsed down to the woman's throat and what was hanging around it.

Grimy and much faded with time: a pink bandanna covered in little black skulls and crossbones.

'Where did you get that?' he demanded.

For her part, she seemed just as astonished. 'English?'

Hearing his own language was even more of a jolt. 'Yes – wait, what?' Nathan peered closer. 'Scattie?'

'No!' the woman laughed, and pointed to herself, saying, 'Sarah. My mother...' She waved her hand airily about as if to say *who knows?* Plainly what English she did speak was very rusty.

'*Mother?* But...' At the last settlement they had been told that a huntress from the other world had passed through only a few weeks ago. If this old woman was claiming to be her daughter, what had happened to the intervening time? What hope was there that she was even still alive?

With his head spinning, and Ysil doing all the talking,

Nathan let himself be led into Sarah's house and sat in a position of honour by the central fire, where food and water for washing was brought. Through a combination of her own broken English and Ysil's translation, they were able to understand each other, though Nathan didn't find what he heard particularly reassuring.

Sarah's father had been a hunter, on a journey many days from home when he had found a young woman, injured and near death. He brought her back to the village, saw that she was nursed and made well, and in time came to love her – and she him. When asked who her people were, she would only say that they were very far away and that she feared she would never see them again. So she stayed, and bore him a daughter, and for many years lived as one of the villagers, but she had never been one of them and was never content. She took to making her own journeys further and further away from the village, and the more she did so the more angry her husband became with her absence, until one day he confronted her with a simple choice: be with us or be gone. She chose to be gone, and went west, towards the mountains.

'You make it sound very simple,' said Nathan. 'You must have been very upset to see her go.'

Sarah shrugged. 'It was all a very long time ago,' she replied. 'My father took two more wives in his life, and both of them were good mothers to me, and now I am surrounded by my own children, so. But if you are looking for *her*, I very much doubt that she will still be alive.'

'Well then, hopefully I can still find what she was looking for,' Nathan replied. 'Do your people have any stories about the White Wall? Or the Far Pastures?'

Sarah's people could tell him little more than he had heard a dozen times already, but they were generous in their hospitality, giving Nathan and Ysil time to rest and re-equip, before waving them off with songs and wards against the creatures of the wilderness.

Scattie's path, like theirs, led inexorably west, in search of what was variously called the White Wall, the First Valley, the Hither Home, and a dozen other names besides, but all of which boiled down to the same thing: the edge of the world. It also led them higher, despite the day-to-day fickleness of stream and valley, into terrain that was becoming inescapably mountainous.

AT FIRST IT SMELLED LIKE ROASTING MEAT.

They thought that there was a hunter's camp nearby, and debated the wisdom of bartering some of their gear for food; pickings had been thin for the last few days and the aroma was making Nathan's mouth water. The smoke that rose from over the next ridge was what warned them: there was simply too much of it.

The village had been attacked recently enough that what remained of the roundhouses still smouldered fiercely, but enough time had passed for it to have rained, as a result of which everything steamed and hissed, and the ground gleamed with ash-black puddles. Only one building remained intact. The worst of the burned-meat smell came from where the steep conical roundhouse roofs had collapsed into craters, leaving scorched timbers to scratch at the air, and Nathan's stomach roiled when he realised what had made it rumble just moments before. There were few bodies lying in the open – all male, all armed with farm tools. No warriors or women.

'Slavers,' said Ysil, his voice thick with disgust. 'These were killed because they were stupid enough to try to defend their homes.'

Nathan was beginning to think that there were no survivors at all until he saw a few small, furtive faces peep out of the tree line.

Children.

There were only half a dozen of them, wide-eyed and dishevelled. A few were entirely naked, but all were shivering. The oldest – a girl of no more than six – was carrying an infant whose silence and stillness was even more disturbing than if it had been bawling. One child had a clubfoot. They stood just in the shadows of the trees, no doubt ready to bolt if the two men turned out to be dangerous.

'Too small or weak to work,' said Ysil. 'Or too unappealing to fuck. Maybe just too fast. The raiders will not have wasted energy chasing them down – they'll let the runts grow and breed, and come back in ten years or so to cull the strongest again. That's why they left that one house standing. It wasn't mercy or generosity. They were just managing their livestock.'

'Christ,' whispered Nathan. Then he shook himself. 'Come on.' He shouldered his pack and set off again through the smoking ruins.

'Wait – what?' Ysil stared after him, then pointed back at

the kids, who hadn't moved, and were watching with dull eyes. 'What about them?'

Nathan turned. 'We can't help them. I'm sorry.'

'Of course we can help them!'

'How? We have barely enough food for ourselves. They're too weak to walk far or keep up – will you carry them? And for how long? We have no idea where we're going or if there will be anyone to look after them when we get there. The most likely thing is that we'll have to avoid those same raiders ourselves, in which case all we'll have accomplished will be to deliver them straight into—'

'I know!' Ysil shouted. There were tears on his cheeks. 'I understand! There is nothing we can do! But we must do *something*!'

The kids had fled at the sound of raised voices – all except for the boy with the clubfoot. He stared at Nathan as if in some sort of challenge, and Nathan was suddenly terrified that the boy would say something, because he knew what it would be: *Piña coladas by the pool, sir?*

Ysil came back and laid a hand on his shoulder. 'Nathan,' he pleaded. 'I know why you feel you must press on at all costs, but—'

'*You don't know a fucking thing about me!*' he exploded, throwing off Ysil's hand. He cocked a fist and drew it back, breathing hard, then saw how Ysil was looking at him: with alarm, and the kind of fear felt upon encountering a wild predator by surprise.

'It seems not,' said Ysil carefully.

Nathan forced himself away, stumbled to the broken wall

of a house and braced himself against it with both palms, staring at the black puddle between his feet as he tried to calm his breathing.

The *afaugh* leered back at him from his own reflection.

He shoved away from the wall with a cry, tripped, and sprawled in the mud. The kid with the clubfoot fled.

Ysil trudged away through to the far side of the village and waited where the trail resumed its way into the wood, leaving Nathan to clean himself up as best he could. Nathan couldn't blame him. All the same, Ysil dismissed his inane apologies before they were halfway out of his mouth. 'You say that my world – Un, you call it – changes itself in response to your soul,' he said. 'But what if it is the other way around? There is an anger in you that was not there before. If we succeed in finding the end of the world, who will you be when we get there?'

'I don't know. I just hope he's not such a dick.'

They resumed their journey, but there was an unspoken weight that hung between them, making their feet drag just a little more than before.

'I KNOW THIS VALLEY!' YSIL PRESSED ON EXCITEDLY AT A pace Nathan found hard to match.

They came out of dense pine woods into a wide, tall-grassed valley between snow-streaked ridges, and saw the threads of smoke from a collection of dwellings by a stream. Herdsmen tending flocks of shaggy, long-horned goats found them first; they wore shirts and kilts of brightly patterned wool with many tassels and intricate knotwork, and they spoke in Ysil's own sing-song dialect. The Eshetri. Ysil's people.

His homecoming was enthusiastic, to say the least.

Their homes were large yurt-like structures, much like the Moonbridge sweat-hut, lighter and airier than the Oendir's stone roundhouses. Each was home to an extended clan group and Ysil was reunited with his amongst tears and ululations of joy on all sides. Though the small children he'd known were now adults, and the elders had for the most part journeyed to the Far Pastures of their ancestors, he was home.

There was of course much feasting, singing and telling of tales, and consumption of vast quantities of *shuf*, a drink made from fermented goat milk, which left Nathan with surprisingly little by way of a hangover but morning-after breath that smelled like he'd been brushing his teeth with rancid butter. The Eshetri also told him that yes, a woman of Nathan's people had stayed with them recently – barely a month ago – and that she had gone on, up into the snow seeking the Far Pastures on the other side. They would lend him all the help they possibly could, as thanks for returning their son.

'A *month*,' said Nathan, as he and Ysil lay together that night, surrounded by the warm murmur and rustle of his clan. 'But she left her daughter decades ago. Even if I do catch up with her, what am I going to find? A sixteen-year-old or a geriatric?'

'Why keep trying to catch up?' replied Ysil. 'You could stay. You could have a good life here. We would take wives, and our children would marry, and we'd lead long peaceful lives until we died as revered old men.'

'Yes,' Nathan laughed softly. 'I could be the founder of a new bloodline: the Brokeback Clan.'

'What?'

'Nothing. *You* could come with *me*. It's been good so far, hasn't it?'

'And when you find who you're searching for, what then? Will there be a place for me in your world?'

'I honestly don't know.'

'But you do know that if I did come with you, you would never find her.'

'What's that supposed to mean?'

Ysil turned to him, and in the darkness his head was in silhouette, his face unreadable and ultimately unknowable. But his fingers were warm where they touched Nathan's cheek. 'Did you never wonder why she has always eluded us, no matter how fast we followed? It is you. Un responds to you, just as it responds to Bran with his farms and machines, and you have set barriers before yourself without knowing, because as much as you need to find her, you know that it will mean leaving me, and you cannot bring yourself to do that either.'

Nathan snorted. 'There you go again. Always thinking the bloody earth revolves around you.'

Ysil prodded him in the ribs. 'It's true. You know it.'

Nathan sighed. 'I know. You are very wise, my friend. Despite your big head.'

'So what will it be? Will you continue with your search or

will you lay your burdens aside and rest?'

It sounded too much like something Phoelix had said. *You seem to be rushing towards some sort of confrontation.* 'There are deaths on my hands,' Nathan said. 'Old ones. New ones. I don't think I should be allowed to set those aside even if I wanted to – not until I've accounted for them first. I'm a stupid, stubborn asshole and I don't lay claim to any kind of wisdom, but here's what I think: nobody has an automatic right to a happy-ever-after. It has to be earned every day that you're alive.'

He felt Ysil nodding. 'That is good, then.'

'Good?'

'More wives for me.'

They both laughed, and kissed, and Nathan said, 'You know, of all the things I thought might happen to me, this is by far the weirdest.'

Nathan slept easily for the first time in weeks. He only awoke once in the night, and found the place next to him empty. Ysil was sitting by the hut doorway, staring out into the night. He almost went over to ask what was on his mind, but found himself oddly reluctant to know the answer. He went back to bed, leaving Ysil with his thoughts.

THE NEXT MORNING, A GOAT WAS FOUND DEAD IN THE upper pastures. The manner of its death provoked much debate and discussion amongst the Eshetri's elders. The animal had been torn apart and scattered across a wide area, and bore many bite and claw marks, which some said pointed to wolves or lopers, yet very little of it had actually been eaten, which led others to suggest that it was the work of something even worse – something that relished mutilation for its own sake. Nathan and Ysil had a much clearer idea of what it was.

'I'd been hoping to be able to stay for a bit longer, but there it is,' said Nathan. He was filling his pack in Ysil's clanhouse, eager to be gone. 'I don't see how it can have followed me, though. How could it have come back? *Why* would it come back? It's got everything it wants.'

'Maybe more than anything else it wants you to suffer,' Ysil replied. 'Or maybe it's a different one.'

'Jesus, don't raise the possibility of there being more of the fuckers.' Nathan looked across at Ysil. 'What are you doing?'

Ysil was packing his own bag. 'What does it look like? I'm coming with you.'

'Oh no, you're fucking not.'

'Nathan...'

'No!' He strode across the yurt and snatched the bag out of Ysil's hands. 'We agreed last night: you stay here with your people. You get all the wives, remember? This thing, whatever it is, it's getting worse the closer I get to the end.'

'All the more reason to have someone protecting you.'

'You said that if you were with me I would never find her, remember *that*?'

Of course Ysil remembered; it was clear from his expression.

'Oh no,' Nathan said, suddenly realising. 'No you don't. You don't care whether I find her or not, do you? You think we can just wander off into the wild chasing something that isn't there for the rest of our lives!'

'Would that be so bad? We'd be together, at least.'

'Ysil, you've just been reunited with your *people*! You've just come *home*! And if you dare say anything soppy about being at home wherever I am then I swear I will fucking hit you. After everything you suffered with the Oendir, you can't just throw that away! I will not be the reason for that. I refuse to let you.'

Ysil's voice was low, and angrier than Nathan had heard from him in a long time. 'I am not *shal* to you. You do not command me.'

'The fuck I don't.' Nathan upended Ysil's pack on the floor, spilling its contents, then snatched up his own gear. He stopped by Ysil and kissed him where he stood rigid, murmuring into his lips, 'If you follow me and fuck this up for me, I will kill you.'

While the Eshetri were distracted by their debate over what kind of monster had eviscerated a blameless goat, he crept out of their camp like a thief.

He went on alone, up into the mountains, following the rumours of Scattie's passing, through pine woods where snow crusted the ground and rimed the tree trunks.

Ysil's theory must have been correct, because within a matter of a few days he found her.

His ever-ascending route had led him far above the tree line to a seemingly impassable rampart of frowning granite cliffs, and he was wondering how he was going to get over them to the high plateau beyond – and wishing, not for the first time, that he had a set of crampons or at least a single decent ten-mil nylon rope – when he saw the thin trickle of smoke coming from a cave opening.

He approached cautiously, mindful of the occasions when he and Ysil had entered caves like this and found their inhabitants hostile, and often not wholly human. But Ysil wasn't here to guard his back any more.

The cave was a dozen metres up the cliff face with no obvious path; it wasn't a difficult scramble but stealth was impossible so he came at it from around and slightly above. An approach from below was too much of an invitation to have rocks thrown at his head. The stone underfoot was treacherous, snow-melt having refrozen into glass-smooth ice on every foot and finger hold. Crampons be damned – this was ice-axe territory. His fingers were numb by the time he had got to within a few feet, braced himself securely against the rock and levelled Bark Foot's spear at the cave opening.

'Scattie?' he called.

Nothing.

'Catharine Louise Powell, are you in there?'

He crept closer and peered in. Other than the fire, still smouldering close to the edge of the entrance, there was no sign of life. Mindful that there might be someone crouched at the back of the cave with a weapon, Nathan climbed down into it as slowly and unthreateningly as possible.

Still nothing.

The cave was empty of life, but its inhabitant's gear was all still here: a leather water bucket, animal skins drying on crude frames next to flint knives and scrapers, a pile of pine branches for a mattress, and against the wall next to it—

Her rucksack.

It was battered and almost unrecognisable, covered with animal hide, its belt and shoulder straps long since replaced with leather, but enough of the blue nylon was visible under the grime of years for him to identify it as hers. Nathan's heart sank; he'd missed her by mere minutes this time, and he tried not to think of what might have happened to make her abandon her belongings so abruptly.

The rucksack's contents were not especially different from his own – cordage, jerky, some flints and fire-fungus – except at the bottom. He found an old plastic poly-wallet, yellow and brittle with age, which she'd used to waterproof the bag, and in it a single piece of paper. He didn't know why this one had survived when paper was ideal fire-lighting material. Then he looked closer and understood; maybe she'd kept it out of a sense of irony. It was the risk assessment for the Sutton Park trip. School management paranoia over health and safety and the risk of being sued by parents had made them insist on every group carrying a copy.

Risk of getting lost:	Medium.
Control measure:	Groups to be accompanied by qualified staff at all times.

A shadow fell across the cave mouth and a voice yelled at him, '*Vaijo! Pel u tenyar! Upelya vayonin!*' A woman's voice, low and full of unmistakable threat.

'Scattie, is that you?'

In the shocked silence she came forward, still crouched, still wary, the point of a hunting spear cocked at him. With the light behind her it was difficult to say for sure, and yet he was sure all the same.

The spear-point dropped. '*Mr Brookes?* You scared the shit out of me, you fucking knob-end!'

29

SCATTIE IN UN

SCATTIE JUMPS DOWN INTO THE DITCH WHERE BRAN IS squatting, scaring the shit out of him. It's dark, his head is raging with fever, and she has been forced to learn stealth the hard way. She drops a handful of scraps in his lap. There are a couple of rotten apple cores, a burnt crust of bread, and an unidentifiable knuckle of some animal, which is all gristle and sinew. 'Grub's up,' she says.

In response, he coughs – a hacking, wet sound from deep in his lungs. 'Thanks,' he manages, sniffing.

They eat, if it can be called that.

'They're getting twitchy,' she says. 'We're going to have to move soon.'

He groans.

Their ditch is actually a hollow where a tree stump has been pulled from the ground, right on the edge of the Oendir's grazing pastures, under the branches of the Wild Wood which has been retreating further with each generation. It is as far as they can get from the farmsteads, yet as close as they dare get to the Pale Wood and the *afaugh*. The roaming pack of young men who have been hunting them for the past week fear this edge of their lands for that very reason, which makes it the safest of several bad compromises for Bran and Scattie; but there are also very few farmsteads in this area and so thefts are more readily noticed. This is why she has taken to stealing from pig troughs.

The Oendir's welcome was short-lived, once it was discovered that neither of them had a *rhon*, couldn't speak any kind of understandable language, and weren't about to cast any curses such as blackening the sun or turning the cows' milk to blood. Accordingly, they were made *shal*.

They'd thought it might even be bearable at first – an opportunity to regain their strength and learn something of where they were, so that ultimately they could escape and make their own way. After all, it wasn't as if they were chained up twenty-four hours a day, and at least they weren't being starved by Bark Foot on the one hand and threatened with being eaten by the *afaugh* on the other.

Escape had brought its own dilemma: they could flee into the wild and risk starvation, or scavenge on the periphery of civilisation and take their chances with the brutality of people. To make things worse, it was all taking its toll on Bran's health; the mild cold that his dunk in the river had given him quickly developed into something which Scattie suspected might be bronchitis, or worse.

As she slips into a thin doze, curled up on the ground, she

thinks that if his cough doesn't kill him the sound of it will attract their pursuers, and once they find him he will wish it had.

She cries, but it doesn't do any good so she stops.

When she wakes to the sound of shouting voices and barking dogs, she sees in the grey light of dawn that Bran has gone.

THEY CATCH HER, BECAUSE OF COURSE THEY WERE ALWAYS going to. She runs into the Wild Wood, and further, heading towards where she knows the land slopes down to the mist-shrouded valley of the Pale Wood. She knows that they've always been too scared to follow her this far, but this time something's different. Maybe it's because there are more of them. Maybe because they've got their dogs with them. Maybe the blood-thrill of hunting another human being is just too good to ignore.

Because this time they don't stop.

They bring her to bay right at the very edge of the Pale Wood itself; she trips on hidden rocks trying to run through the ankle-deep moss and there are dogs all over her, tearing at her clothes, but they're whistled away and she looks up into the grinning faces of a pack of two-legged animals who are infinitely crueller.

The last time she froze, almost unable to believe that was happening. Now, a kind of clarity washes over her, and she gets up into a crouch, pulling Ryan's lock-knife from where she has kept it hidden in her bra (which the Oendir, utterly confused by it, have never interfered with, bizarrely). Between Bark Foot, the *afaugh*, and now this, she thinks, *Because fuck you, that's why. Fuck every last one of you.* She knows that putting up a fight is going to make it worse for her, but she honestly cannot imagine things getting much worse than this. There are seven of them, and while they are smirking at her – no doubt looking forward to their sport – she unfolds the six-inch tungsten steel blade, and it gleams, oh how it gleams, like nothing these backwoods pigfuckers have ever seen. She knows it's harder and sharper than anything in their whole world and that she will be able to fuck up at least one of them very badly – this is not the first time she's been in a fight, and a crazy insane part of her is almost looking forward to being able to use something proper hardcore for once instead of just fists and hair-pulling – and by their sudden looks of uncertainty a few of them might be thinking that too, and for a moment she's seized with a terrible hope that it will be enough to make them back off.

But of course it isn't. They come for her.

Exactly what happens is something of an adrenalin-fuelled blur. She's aware that she's screaming and slashing wildly at them and the knife snags three, maybe four times in clothing and flesh. Then the world spins dizzyingly and smacks her in the back of the head and she knows that she's been knocked down, and she can't breathe because the wind's been punched out of her and she can't see because her view is blocked by one of the pigfuckers and she can't move because his weight is bearing down on her and in spite of her rage she begins to cry, *Don't do this, please oh please don't do this...*

Then the weight is gone and there is an *awful* lot of screaming. Human voices mingle with something she recognises only too well, and she thinks how wrong she was to imagine that things couldn't get worse.

For a long time after the screaming stops she lies there, but nothing else happens. She doesn't realise she has passed out until she awakens. Maybe it thinks she's dead.

Cautiously, she looks.

Her first impression is that someone has come along and repainted all the nearby trees a bright gloss red. The second is to wonder at how much stuff can come from inside a human body. The third is—

'Bran?' she whispers.

He straightens up from where he has been removing the *rhon* from around the neck of a corpse and smiles at her, and she realises that this isn't Bran – or at least it is, but he seems to be sharing his shape with something else, something that capers behind his face and leers at her with bloodstained teeth. 'I was wondering when you'd wake up,' he – or it – says. The hacking cough is gone. So is the red wound across his throat made by the Oendir harness, replaced by a clean white scar. His arms are red to the elbow.

She slowly backs into a sitting position against the tree, trying not to look too closely at the abattoir mess around her. She can't escape the smell, though – blood and shit and guts – but even underneath that she can detect the stink of the *afaugh*.

'I know how it looks,' he continues, 'but trust me, this is best for all of us.'

'Not for them,' she points out. Her hand is trembling and her mouth is dry. She feels like she has a hangover.

He looks around, surprised. 'Wait – you don't feel *sorry* for them...'

'Fuck, no. Just... oh, Bran, what have you done?'

'I've made a deal. The only kind of deal where we don't both wind up dead.' He smiles at her again, and the sight of it breaks her heart. 'I've found my tribe.'

Her knife is only a few feet away. She starts to inch towards it.

The *afaugh* stops what it's doing and comes to stand over her, and its mere proximity is enough to make her flinch. It tilts its head, looking down at her, considering. Then it squats, knees either side of her chest, and takes her chin in its hand. This close, the smell of death gags her.

'Don't you recognise me?' it murmurs. 'I haven't always worn this face, you know. He wants you, of course, but he'll never allow himself to admit it.' It lets her go. 'Still, the deal is struck. He's mine now. You are free to go and do whatever it is you think will make a difference.' Then its expression changes to something more human and confused. Bran whispers, 'Scattie?' then doubles over in agony. She scrambles out from underneath him as he screams and jack-knifes, and something pale and bloated pushes itself out of his throat – far, *far* too much of it for Bran's body to have contained in the first place – and vanishes between the trees.

* * *

THE OENDIR ACCEPT BRAN'S STORY THAT THE *AFAUGH* attacked and killed their sons, which is technically the truth, and are grateful for the return of their *rhons*, which have a much greater significance than simply being the equivalent of birth certificates. In some manner, according to a belief system that Scattie can't be bothered to learn because as far as she's concerned they're all fucking barbarian pigfuckers, some aspect of an individual's soul is in their *rhon*, and by returning them Scattie and Bran have done the families a great honour.

Not that they are trusted in the slightest. Far from it; the Oendir are deeply suspicious, and rightly so, but the one thing which cannot be denied is this: if Scattie and Bran were in league with the demon of the Pale Wood, why did they allow themselves to be treated as *shal* in the first place? This is the crack of uncertainty that she watches Bran widen over the days and weeks into a gap where he and she can make a place for themselves.

It is the last thing she wants.

Of course she knows why he is so keen to stay and make a go of things. How can he go home now, having sacrificed Ryan's soul to one entity and his own to its enemy? Throughout all of it, she can barely bring herself to be around him any longer than absolutely necessary.

She makes her own arrangements to leave without telling him, not that she is keeping it a secret. They haven't had more than a dozen conversations since their return from the Pale Wood but he finds out anyway, and meets her at the door of her tiny farmstead's roundhouse with a spearman hovering behind. The first of his many thugs, she thinks, unsurprised.

'Well here's a first,' she comments, eyeing them up and down. 'You, making new friends.'

His smile is thin. 'I'm afraid I can't let you go.'

Without taking her eyes off him, she unclips the waist-buckle of her rucksack and shrugs it to the floor. This is not because she intends to do a damn thing he says – it is because she is going to need room and flexibility to use the hunting spear that remains gripped in her left hand. Having intended to leave for some weeks, she has been taking lessons from a neighbouring farmer's son (all kinds of lessons, actually: hunting, fighting, fucking). It is a clear pre-dawn, sweet with dew, and busy with bird life. She inhales deeply, loving this time of day. 'I'm afraid you're the last person to "let" me do anything,' she replies. 'But assume for the moment that I give a shit. Why?'

'The bargain I struck with the *afaugh*. It doesn't want us at all – we were just bait, but with Ryan dead and Liv gone it's just you and me, and if you go too the lure won't be as strong, so I need you to stay.'

'Bait? Lure? For what? Bark Foot?'

'No. For Mr Brookes.'

This is so random that for a moment she is too surprised to speak. 'Mr Brookes? Why?'

'It didn't say. There wasn't really time to read the Terms and Conditions. We're alive, and its price is that it wants the bastard responsible for us being here in the first place.' Bran shrugs. 'I'm good with that.'

'Wait, it wasn't his fault...'

'Do you think if he'd been with us Bark Foot would still have snatched us out of the world?'

'I don't know, and neither do you, so don't go pointing the finger.'

'Look, I know you won't believe me and it's all irrelevant anyway. What's done is done, and the situation is what it is. I've been over it a million times and I really can't see any other explanation. I've actually come to make you an offer.'

'Not interested.'

'You haven't heard what it is yet.'

'Go on then, surprise me.'

'I want you to marry me.'

It is definitely a surprise. He lets her laugh until she cries and she has to lean against the door frame to catch her breath. The thug, who doesn't understand a word of this, grins and relaxes.

'It's only sensible,' Bran continues. 'Power amongst the Oendir is conferred by the number and status of one's marriages. As singletons we are little better than *shal*, but if we wed then I can protect you and—'

Her attack is unexpected, swift, and effective. She sweeps the haft of her spear up between the thug's legs, mashing his balls, and as he begins to bend forward in sudden agony she pulls it back and hammers him between the eyes, the end of its ash pole making a hard *pock!* noise, and he goes down in a heap. An eyeblink later she has reversed the weapon and has the razor tip of its bronze blade against Bran's belly.

'You were saying something about protecting me,' she says. As he opens his mouth to reply she pushes with the spear-point, silencing him. 'You and me are done. I'm going home. Anybody you send after me won't be coming back with all their bits. You get me?'

He nods. He gets her, loud and clear.

She picks up her pack, shoulders it, and sets off at a measured trot into the glorious haze of an untried dawn.

She travels amongst the peoples of Un – those that *are* people – collecting what wisdom she can about the crossing places back into the world. It is complicated by the fact that the tribes she visits believe that they *are* the world, and that what she is looking for is a way into the underworld, and so everything they tell her has to be teased out from the fog of myth and legend. In some places she stays no more than a matter of hours; in others, years. She takes their stories into her soul and their marks into her skin. She takes lovers – usually, but not always, they are people who can teach her about the land and how to survive in it; usually, but not always, they are men.

In time, she comes to realise that she is being followed. Rumours of pursuit reach her through the forest, the air, the streams. Sometimes she even sees the smoke of a campfire close behind. The fear that Bran – or the demon that rides him – has changed his mind and sent hunters to recapture her spurs her forward, but eventually she finds herself trapped in a cave in an impassable cliff.

And then it is now.

30

THE WHITE WALL

'So,' Scattie said, poking the embers of her fire with a stick and observing Nathan through the flames. 'You?'

The cave was narrow but deep with a high ceiling, which tapered to a crack and so drew the smoke cleanly away. It was a good choice, he thought, and she'd obviously been there for some time, judging by the number of animal pelts stretched out and drying on wooden frames. There was a bed of pine needles and a rawhide bucket of melt-water. Pieces of small animal meat were propped against the fire on skewers, roasting over the embers.

So Nathan told his tale, and by the time he was done they had picked the bones clean and tossed them out into the night.

Scattie didn't interrupt, just regarded him with a long, measuring gaze under which he started to feel uncomfortable. She was lean and weather-beaten, with a physique like a greyhound and eyes that watched the world with an ice-chipped squint of perpetual wariness. Her hair was neatly braided and he saw that half her left ear was missing, with a scar which ran down her neck and into the collar of her woollen shirt. Around her neck hung charms, beads, amulets and torcs made of everything from gold to mouse skulls, while the skin of her arms and face was busy with tattoos and the raised ridges of ritual scarification.

'Wow,' she said, eventually.

'Yep,' he agreed.

'No, "wow" as in "you really fucked up, didn't you?" So what happens now? Do you open a magic doorway home where I transform back into a child as if nothing happened, or do you atone for your sins and wake up from a coma and it was all a dream?' Her accent was strange, almost Scandinavian-sounding, as if it had been years since she'd spoken English, which it probably had been.

'To be honest, I was hoping you'd know. You've been here a lot longer.'

She gave a dry, rueful laugh. 'Sorry to disappoint you. I've followed up a dozen different stories about the end of the world from a dozen tribes, and none of them have come to anything. Sacred pools, sacred groves, sacred bloody standing bloody stones everywhere – nothing. Frankly, if I don't find anything at the top of this mountain – these "Far Pastures" – I'm tempted to just throw myself off the top and have done with it. Although it's academic at the moment since I can't actually get up the damn thing. I've been here two weeks trying to find a path, and I've explored for days in either direction, and this is the only bit that looks remotely climbable. I think the season changes as you get higher – it's more winter at the top than the bottom, if that makes sense.'

'It strikes me that what you could do with is someone with a background in mountaineering.'

She looked at him sideways. 'Know somebody like that, do you?'

'As it happens.'

NATHAN SPENT A GOOD COUPLE OF HOURS JUST SITTING ON a log, chewing a twig and staring at the cliff face, working it out in his head. There was a kind of shallow chimney formed by one face angling up against a vertical buttress which rose the full height – hard to say what was shadow in there and what was ice, but it would be slightly less exposed to the wind and probably their best bet. That said, there was no way they were getting up that thing without at least a rope to keep between them and plummety death.

Scattie showed him how to extract the roots of pine trees – incredibly tough and extending for many metres just under the earth – which pulled free like rope out of wet sand. She taught him how to split and re-braid the filaments into a thick, if not particularly flexible, cordage. There wouldn't be enough to reach all the way to the top of the cliff, but he could certainly make a safety line to link the pair of them together. He gathered a dozen pebbles of various shapes and sizes – chockstones to wedge the safety line into cracks and crevices as they went along – and for good measure he also made half a dozen 'blocks' out of the leftover cordage; big knots which could be wedged into wider crevices for added grip, each with a long loop for a handle.

While he was busy with the cordage, Scattie disappeared for two days, coming back with a big grin on her face, a rack of deer antlers over one shoulder and a pile of raw meat over the other. They fashioned the main branches of the antlers into two ice-axes, one for each of them, and the remainder of the prongs they wrapped with cordage so they could be gripped in the other hand and used on the rock like daggers. They lashed deer ribs to the underside of their footwear as crampons.

Nathan spent many days fashioning two yew branches into crude carabiners, boiling water in the rawhide bucket using hot rocks and then bending the wood in the resulting steam. It was awkward, sweaty work, even when they moved the fire outside the cave, and on one particularly sunny afternoon the itchiness of his woollen shirt became unbearable and he stripped to the waist.

So did Scattie.

It was impossible for him not to stare. She'd been breaking lengths of firewood into chunks by bracing them between two rocks and stamping on them. The tattoos and ritual scars on her face and shoulders continued over her stomach, back and breasts. She caught him looking away hurriedly, tossed the hair out of her eyes and frowned at him. 'And?' she said.

'Uh...'

She cocked her head and raised an eyebrow.

'Nice tatts,' he blurted out.

'Nice what?'

'Tatts! I said tatts!'

'Hmph.' She returned to stamping logs apart, but she was smiling while she did it.

In the end he managed to bend the yew branches into almost-complete circles a few centimetres in diameter.

'They're the closest we're going to get to carabiners,' he explained. 'They live on the safety rope. Whenever you jam one of those anchor blocks in a crack, you thread its handle into the ring through the gap in the wood there, and it links the rope to the block. We'll have to be careful they don't slip off because there's no way of locking them closed. Yew is dense and flexible – they used to make longbows out of it – but they'll probably break if they have to take the weight of either of us. Fuck it, the rope will probably break, come to that, or the antlers. We're screwed, basically, is what I'm trying to say.'

'No we're not,' she said. 'We're alive.'

Finally, they foraged in the woods for trees whose injured trunks wept big scabs of sticky resin, and Nathan melted them over as much of the gear as he could – especially the antler axes and crampons. 'It's waterproof and sticky as hell,' he said.

'I know,' she replied, and showed him where she'd used resin to glue the bindings of her flint arrowheads.

As they worked, she quizzed him on what had happened in the world during the years of her disappearance, but his answers just made her twitchy and frustrated. She wanted to know about her favourite bands and movie stars – which he hadn't heard of even when they'd been current – and in turn she couldn't care less about the recession, global austerity, or the Olympics. Oddly, the death of Prince affected her most deeply of all. 'My dad really loved him,' she said, and brooded for the rest of the day. It was the one and only time she ever said anything about her parents.

THE NIGHT BEFORE THEY CLIMBED WAS BITTERLY COLD. The wind gusted in at the cave's opening, repeatedly threatening to extinguish their fire. They were huddled close to it, keeping it alive, when she surprised him by pulling open his blanket and snuggling up against him, wrapping it around them both. He shrank back, but didn't get very far.

'Wait, what are you doing?' he asked.

'Shut up,' she answered. 'Body warmth.'

'Oh. Okay.' She was warm and solid and real against him, her head in the crook of his neck; her hair was pungent and oily and yet smelled of pine.

'Plus,' she added, 'I haven't had a man for a very, very long time.' Her hand slid up inside his shirt.

Despite himself, the warmth of her hand on his chest was getting him hard. He remembered how she had looked, bare-breasted in the sun, breaking firewood, utterly aware and unashamed of the effect she was having on him. His hands opened her shirt and sought out her breasts, then his mouth did too; she tasted of salt and smoke, and he nipped at her.

'Hey! Whoa!' she laughed. 'Steady on there, Mr Bitey!'

Like a man waking up, he blinked at her, then pulled back, clutching the blanket closed around himself. 'What do you think you're doing?' he demanded, shuffling to the other side of the fire.

'What am *I* doing? I should have thought that was pretty obvious,' Scattie replied coolly. Her gaze was frank, unoffended, and unapologetic. 'What's wrong?'

'What do you mean what's wrong? You're my student!'

Now she looked surprised. She pulled her clothes together. 'Seriously? I mean, fucking *seriously*? I thought it might have been because of your little shepherd boy – that at least would make sense. But *student*? After all this time? *Still?*'

'What did you expect? That's what you were the last time I saw you. That's all you've ever been.'

'Bullshit. I've seen the way you've been looking at me these last few days.'

'Look, I—'

'And it's okay!' she added hurriedly. 'I'm an adult woman, Nathan. What do you think I've been doing for the past nearly ten years – living in a convent? I've had lovers. Good ones, bad ones, quick shags, slow burns. I had a daughter, did you know that?'

'Yes, I met her.'

She glared at him. 'If that's supposed to be a joke it's not very fucking funny.'

'No, I met her. Sarah. She was wearing that pink bandanna you used to have.'

'Jesus! Why didn't you *tell* me? How is she?'

'Bit of a hard subject to bring up out of the blue, seeing as how she was middle-aged when I saw her – older than you are now. But she's as fine as can be expected in a place like this. She has a big family. Respected.'

'Did she – you know – talk about me?'

'She said that it was all a very long time ago and besides, her father took more wives after you left.'

Scattie laughed. 'That doesn't surprise me in the least. He always had an eye.' She prodded at the fire. 'I suppose you think I'm a terrible person for abandoning her.'

'I'm the last person to judge you for that, aren't I?'

'Face it, Nathan, I'm not the girl you left.' She looked across at him again, searching for something in his face, more curious than annoyed. 'Can't you see past her?'

The weight of her question hung with the smoke between them, threatening to crush him. He went to the mouth of the cave and stared into the night, feeling the weight of it out there too; under a clear sky of cold, insistent stars, hiding in the bristling mass of forest, which roared in the wind like an ocean. It was the same weight he'd felt in Bark Foot's stare – the measureless regard of a vast and impersonal Purpose, which cared nothing for such petty concerns as desire or grief or love or pain.

'No,' he said to her. 'I can't. I'm sorry, I wish I could, but I'm afraid that if I slept with you I wouldn't know what I was supposed to be any more.'

'O-kay,' she said. 'There's a possibility that you're overthinking this just a bit.'

'There's something else.'

'What,' she muttered darkly. 'You're gay? Oh, wait.'

'When I was with Ysil, and we were following you, you were always just ahead of us and we could never catch up. He said it was because while he and I were together, I didn't want to find you so I kept putting barriers in the way.'

'So you threw away a good thing to pursue an obsession with finding yours truly? I don't know whether to be flattered or to slap you for being such a fucking idiot.'

'What it boils down to is I'm afraid that if you and I get involved then we won't be able to find our way home.'

'Involved!' she laughed, and then stopped. 'Wait. This is about Miss Jones – Sue – isn't it? You still think you can help her, don't you? Shit, Nathan, even if you get back, do you honestly believe there's the remotest possible chance that there'll be anything left to save?'

He shrugged helplessly. 'I have to. I have no choice. It's who I am.'

She nodded towards the spear, which was propped against the cave wall. 'You going to kill the *afaugh* and be the new Bark Foot then? Guardian of the innocent and vulnerable?'

'If that's all there is left for me to do.'

She shook her head. 'So much macho bullshit. Well if you are, then you better get ready to kill the world, because that's what the *afaugh* is, it and Bark Foot both: the world. That's what the world does, it eats its children.'

'So much melodrama,' he returned.

'Pots and kettles, Mr Brookes. All that stuff about Sue and her kids, and her taking the morning-after pill all those years ago.'

'What about it?'

The flames of the fire made her shadow jump and loom on the wall behind her, like a separate living thing. 'The man who enslaved me and Bran and used us like animals was a farmer – just a farmer, ordinary guy with wives and kids, and they knew about it, by the way, no doubt about that, but it obviously wasn't a big thing to them because we were *shal*. It was more like the way you'd brand a piece of livestock, which kind of made it worse. I mean at school there were always girls who you knew had let a guy fuck them even though they didn't really want to, but is that the same thing? If you do it because you're afraid of being called a frigid whore by all his mates, is that different from doing it because someone has a knife to your throat?

'I don't think I'm particularly fucked up by it, but I don't really have any normal people for comparison, you know? I'm not entirely sure that anybody I've met since I got here is really human. Bark Foot was no better. For all his bullshit about being "Guardian of the Four Valleys" and "it has to be a sacrifice or it's meaningless", he still ate us out of the world and then tried to make us complicit in what he did to Ryan. He tried to make us say it was *okay*. What is that if not a kind of rape? Because then the *afaugh* rescued me, and Bran expected me to be grateful, as if that would somehow make it better. As if I could ever live in that community and work alongside those people and look that man in the eye every single day and not feel sick and dirty and at the same time want to stick my fist down his throat and rip his fucking heart out. I'm amazed I stayed there as long as I did without killing someone. That's why I had to leave Sarah, in the end. She deserved better than growing up with that for a mother.

'To stay here – to give up trying to get home and *make a go of it...*' She shook her head. 'I've tried, believe me.

I've stopped and settled and tried to put it all behind me several times, but it only lasts so long before I start getting angry and violent at good people for no reason, so I leave. Because to stay would be accepting that man's terms for my existence in this world. It would mean saying thank you to the monster, and I will *never* do that.'

She showed him her triskelion tattoo – or at least the burn scar where it had been. 'This was the first one I got, back when I thought the only way to survive was by joining the Big Boys' Club. Got a lot more since then, because there are a lot more ways to survive. So, you know, boohoo. Get in line.' Scattie wrapped her blanket tightly about herself. 'If at any point you decide to stop being a self-obsessed knob-end, you know where to find me.'

THEY STARTED CLIMBING AT DAWN.

They began by rubbing pine resin all over their hands and the toes of their boots. 'It's not quite climbing chalk but it'll have to do,' Nathan said.

There was less ice than he'd feared, which was a good thing because where he did have to use his antler axe it was so blunt compared to a modern steel one that he had to slam it in hard, every time afraid that it would snap. The granite was smooth, offering few handholds, and progress was slow, but the reindeer ribs strapped to their soles were springier than metal crampons and helped them find footholds where their primitive hide boots would have just slipped. He soon settled into a rhythm – left toe in *chunk!*, right toe in *chunk!*, left hand fingers solid, right hand axe in *chunk!* and pull yourself up – the familiarity of which was calming. Scattie caught on fast, watching him and following his route closely.

The system of chock-pebbles worked surprisingly well. As he climbed, he collected in the slack of the rope and tucked a loop of it into a crack, wedging it solid with one of the many stones of different shapes and sizes that he'd collected. As Scattie came past, she worked the pebble free and pocketed it, while he took in the slack again and placed the next one higher up. They progressed via a series of broad stone ledges where they could stop, rest, and check their gear.

Scattie's earlier observation that the seasons seemed to be changing the higher they climbed turned out to be true; they left something that felt like late summer – and could still see it below them, bright sunshine on the rocks and meadow flowers – but fifty metres further up they were striking away chips of black ice with numb fingers and watching their breath plume. That gave way to tiny yellow flowers springing out of the cliff face, and then the cycle repeated itself.

About a quarter of the way up Nathan became aware that Scattie was singing – just snatches of a tune more muttered than sung as she caught her breath between pulls and shoves.

'...when the sun shines we'll shine together... told you I'd be here for ever...' There was a pause while she hauled herself over a tricky outcrop. '...said I'll always be a friend... took an oath I'm a stick it out 'til the end...'

'Scattie,' he called back. 'Are you singing Rihanna?'

'Only,' she panted, 'ironically.'

'Ironically or not, I will cut this rope if I have to.'

'Fuck off, old man,' she laughed. 'It's from *Good Girl Gone Bad*. Thought you'd appreciate it. This climbing's a piece of piss.'

But it wasn't, and the inevitable, when it happened, unfolded in hideous slow-motion clarity.

Almost three-quarters of the way up Nathan became aware that her muttering and scrabbling had taken on a new and worrying urgency.

'Scattie?' he called down. 'You okay?'

'Fucking foot thing,' she grunted. 'Coming loose...'

The rawhide bindings on her left reindeer rib crampon were falling slack under the repetition of being strained and relaxed, and every time she got any purchase it slithered or twisted out of the way.

'Can you transfer your weight to the other foot?'

'What I'm *trying* to do...'

He saw that she was raking her right foot repeatedly down the stone, trying to score the foothold she'd been aiming for and only falling short by a fraction of an inch, but didn't trust that her left had enough stability to push hard on it for a long reach.

'Left hand's cramped to shit,' she grunted. 'Only decent hold I've got is with the axe. Could do... with a little... hand here.'

He took one of the emergency blocks and rammed the knotted end into a crevice as hard as he could, poking it in with his antler dagger, then hooked both its loop handle and the safety line onto the yew ring. The line was also attached to the cliff by a chockstone halfway along. Those, along with his own hands and feet, gave her six anchor points. He dug in and hung on. 'Listen!' he called. 'If I let go to come get you we'll both fall. Right now I'm your anchor. Work it out. You can do it.'

'Work it out,' she grumbled. 'Work *you* out, you knob—'

And she slipped.

The safety line sprang tight. The chock-pebble held for a second and then sprang free like a stone from a slingshot, and she dropped another foot before the line was caught by the yew ring. It snapped. Her full weight transferred to the line around his waist and would have pulled both of them off if he hadn't that very moment grabbed for the block's loop handle. Mercifully, the knot held fast in its crevice, but all the same it felt like he was being sawn through the middle. He could hear her cursing and scrabbling frantically. His axe began to slip, and he could feel the bone crampons on his feet bending like wooden rulers about to snap.

'Lose your pack!' Nathan yelled. 'Lose your fucking pack! Cut it off!'

Her ancient lock-knife made short work of the rucksack's straps and the bag tumbled away, taking with it her tools, food, and no doubt what few precious treasures of her old life she'd managed to hang on to. The relief in the strain around his waist was immediate. The drop had taken her down to a point where the granite was more broken and she was able to grab hand and foot holds.

They clung to the rock, gasping, hearts hammering.

When he helped her up onto the next ledge she flopped beside him. 'My life was in that bag,' she groaned.

'You're still breathing,' he pointed out.

'And your wooden ring thingy sucked.'

'It did its job. It soaked up enough of the kinetic energy from your falling fat arse.'

She swatted him weakly. 'Now is that any kind of language to use around your students? I notice you've still got yours.'

'Of course I have. What do you take me for?'

From that point on the rock began to slope ever so gently outwards and the climbing became easier. Towards the top, freezing blasts of wind from above tore through a rampart of boulders and down past them, carrying tatters of fog like dry ice curling over the lip of a laboratory beaker. An hour later they pushed and pulled each other through the broken cliff edge and into the land beyond.

31

TUONEN THE BOATMAN

THEY WERE ON THE EDGE OF A VAST TABLETOP PLATEAU OF sedge grass and wind-writhen heather. It was featureless in all directions except directly behind, without rise or hollow to provide variation and the only movement came from sheets of hill fog scudding past and around them at ground level to disappear over the edge. The horizon – if it even existed – was lost in a meaningless white haze. Nathan and Scattie looked at each other, equally at a loss.

'The White Wall?' he guessed.

She shrugged. 'The Far Pastures?'

'Let's see how far we can get.'

'Why not?'

They ate a little of the deer jerky that was left in his bag, and went on.

Without a clear sun in the sky and no shadows cast by the flat, directionless light, it was impossible to tell which direction they were travelling or how long they had walked. Unless they concentrated on their plodding steps, the endless streamers of cloud that raced past them created the illusion that they were flying at great speed; paradoxically, the lack of landmarks made them feel that they were making no progress at all. It was fundamentally disorientating.

'Hey,' she said. 'I think the ground is getting squelchier.'

It was true. There was a new dampness to the spongy ground, which sucked at their boots and filled their footprints as they passed. The sedge grew taller, replacing the heather altogether, and they found themselves sloshing ankle-deep and having to step carefully from one tussock to the next. Nathan was about to suggest that this wasn't getting them anywhere, when he saw the lake and the boatman.

At first there was a post: a tall, lime-whitened pole driven into the bog to act as a marker. A heron, roosting on top of it, flew off at their approach with leisurely strokes. Moored at the base of the post was a boat – not much more than a dug-out tree trunk large enough to seat maybe three or four people. Standing by the boat, as if he had been waiting for them, was a man wearing a cloak of woven reed-grass and feathers and carrying a long punting pole, but also wearing the trappings of a king: a gold torc around his throat, and a bronze sword at his side. Beyond him, the marsh became islets between deeper channels and then open water without a clearly defined shoreline, and eventually lost itself in the haze.

'I am Tuonen,' said the boatman. 'Where would you go?' And if nothing else had convinced Nathan that these were Ysil's Far Pastures, the fact that he could understand this figure's speech did so right then.

'We're here,' he breathed. 'Scattie, we made it. Sir,' he

said, approaching the boatman, 'is this the way out of Un?'

'That which you call Un is simply an echo of the mortal world, a land of mists and fogs which you shape with your own desires. You left it when you passed over the escarpment. You are beyond even such echoes here – beyond time, beyond life, beyond death, beyond any of the crude walls with which you divide up your understanding. From here, all of existence is open to you. All times. All lives. Where would you go?'

Scattie was unable to answer; she had collapsed to her knees, sobbing.

Tuonen bent to lift her face and thumbed away her tears. 'Where would you go, child?' he repeated gently.

'Home,' she whispered. 'Please, I want to go back home.'

'Surely you know by now that "home" and "back" are not the same place?'

'I don't understand. Please. I'm so tired.'

His fingertips left her chin and he paused, considering. 'Then I will send you home,' he decided. 'What will you pay me?'

She untied one of her many necklaces – her *rhon* from the Oendir – and offered it to him, but he shook his head. 'You will have need of it,' he said. 'You will have need of them all, for you have made yourself One From Many, and many will come to you for guidance and protection. I will take this.' He pointed to the lock-knife at her belt. It was the very last of her possessions from before Un, and she was clearly reluctant to part with it, but in the end had no choice. She climbed into the boat.

'Tuonen,' said Nathan. 'Are you saying that from here we can go back and change things we've done?'

'If your spirit is light enough to make the journey, yes.'

'Then I wish to go back. I have to put things right.'

The boatman took a long time to consider, looking him up and down, assessing, judging. Slowly he shook his head and said, 'No.'

The baldness of the refusal left Nathan speechless for a moment. 'I'm sorry, sir – please, but what do you mean, "no"?'

'You are too heavily burdened. You would sink my boat.'

'Oh. Right. Not a problem.' Nathan ditched his pack – everything except Bark Foot's spear – and made for the boat, but found his way was blocked by Tuonen's pole.

'You misunderstand me. You could leave all your belongings, your clothes, even your very flesh behind, and you would still be too heavy. The burden lies in your spirit.'

Scattie offered Nathan a rueful smile. 'I guess you should have let me fuck you when you had the chance,' she said.

A hollow terror began to open inside him. 'But… I don't… you have to let me on!' He brandished Bark Foot's spear at Tuonen. 'You don't understand – I let a terrible evil into the world and I have to get back so that I can fix things. I left Ysil! I have this! Bran gave it to me! What am I supposed to do with it now? Where am I supposed to go?'

The boatman was implacable. He might as well have been a statue carved of stone for all the sympathy he showed, and Nathan knew – at the bottom of the great black spiralling pit of horror and rage that was widening inside him – that this was a stone on which he would break.

'I'll do it,' said Scattie, holding out her hand. She had to repeat herself several times to be heard through the roaring disbelief that was deafening him.

Slowly his eyes wandered over to focus on her. 'You'll what?'

'I'll do it. I'll find the *afaugh* and I'll take care of it.'

'But it's not your responsibility.'

'No, but it's in my power.'

'NO!' He swung back to Tuonen with one final plea. 'It's the triple killing of kings!' he begged. 'I was stabbed, look!' He pulled up his shirt to show the scar from Liv's knife. 'For neglecting my students – the sin against wisdom. I was choked by a man whose family I thought should be mine; the sin of the hearth, right? I was nearly drowned by the warriors of my world for lying and defying the law. You saved me then! You opened the timber track when Bark Foot was dead and let me into Un!'

Tuonen shook his head. 'That was not me.'

'Well who was it, then?'

'It was one who is yet to be. One who is not you. You were not chosen for some great and terrible glory, for there is nobody to make that choice except yourself, and you have chosen to remain as you are. It is not I who bars your journey onward – you refused it long ago.'

'*What?* Where am I supposed to go, then? What else am I supposed to do? It should be me! I should be the one to take Bark Foot's place! Please! I beg you! You can't take that away from me, you bastard!'

Tuonen remained unmoved, for, having delivered his

judgement, no more needed to be said. Faced with that damning refusal on the one hand, and Scattie's terrible sympathy on the other, a stinking, peat-black flood rose up in Nathan's mind from the hollow place where his soul had been, and drowned his reason. 'Well then it won't be her either!' he screamed, and with a howl of rage and loss he hurled the spear at Scattie.

She threw herself backwards in the boat. The spearhead thudded into the gunwale inches above her head, then the haft snapped and fell away.

'Brookes, what the *fuck*?' she yelled at him, more astonished than angry, but Tuonen was already driving Nathan away. The boatman's sword was in his hand, burning with gold-green light.

'Get you gone!' he ordered. 'Back to where you began! Live among the beasts, ever shunned from people's hearths, and be what you have fated yourself to be!'

SCATTIE HID AT THE BOTTOM OF THE BOAT AND WATCHED as the figure that had once been a man she knew reeled away cursing and wailing, ripping great handfuls of grass from the earth and tearing them with his teeth, before dwindling to a pale phantom in the shifting fog and disappearing from her sight.

The boatman returned, took up his pole and steered them away into the still waters of the nameless lake. She didn't need to ask him what Nathan had meant when he'd said 'it won't be her either', or why Tuonen had refused her first choice of payment. She knew it in her flesh – in the tattoos and scars that crowded her skin, and the amulets that hung from her neck. In the lines that spread from the corners of her eyes and curved down either side of her mouth. In the scar down her neck given by one man and the stretch marks on her belly from a child given by another. Everywhere she'd been and everyone she'd known – loved or hated – was a part of her. That was what Tuonen had meant when he'd called her One From Many. It was what the people who had created Bark Foot had been trying to do: to create a god who would protect them by being the best and strongest of them. But she saw now how that had corrupted itself into an overweening arrogance in the righteousness of its own existence, untempered by weakness of fear or doubt. Like bronze, it was brittle, and could endure only so long before it broke.

Tuonen picked up the spear and examined where the head had snapped, then plucked the broken tip from the side of his boat. 'This will need reforging,' he said.

32

HYWELAN'S FORGE

Tuonen poled his boat away into the lake. Scattie had long since lost track of time and distance, and couldn't tell whether it was many days or mere hours before the sound of metal striking on metal rang out in the distance. The lake narrowed, or else became a wide, slow-moving river, because the banks were visible far off to either side, thickly crowded with dense woods.

A mass loomed out of the water and became an island; it was small, yet with enough space to accommodate a roundhouse from where the sound of smith-work came even more clearly. Tuonen steered to its shore and held his boat steady for her to climb out. Together they approached the house, and now she could hear the thump of bellows and the roar of a furnace.

Through the wide doorway she saw a man bent over a forge of glowing coals, surrounded by a hoard of weapons and treasure that made her gasp. The red forge-light gleamed on helms, shields and suits of mailed armour, which hung like curtains of metal rain from beams, while swords and spears were stacked against the walls like sheaves of corn. On shelves and in chests were heaped goblets, armlets, torcs, rings and crowns of every conceivable metal encrusted with a glittering blaze of precious stones.

'Hywelan,' said Tuonen.

The smith looked up. For all that his work was beautiful, he seemed to take no joy in it; the lines of his face were as set and rough-hewn as beaten lead. He put his tools aside and came forward, wiping his hands on a leather apron, and she saw that he dragged one leg behind him in a hinged brace.

'What happened to him?' she whispered.

'A king's greed,' replied Tuonen, but would elaborate no further.

'Boatman,' nodded Hywelan. 'Have you finally come to free me from this place?' His gaze took in Scattie. 'Or else bring me company, perhaps?'

'You're talking to the wrong person,' said Scattie, and tossed him the broken spear. 'I need a weapon to kill a monster.'

Hywelan examined the stump of blade with his thick fingers. 'This is ancient even for me,' he commented. 'Crude. Brittle.' He looked at her. 'But it can be done. What will you pay me?'

'That depends. What is your price?'

His eyes examined her body in much the same way as his fingers had done the spear. 'A night between your legs, perhaps.'

'Only if you fancy losing the use of your other one,' she retorted.

'Ha!' His face split open in a surprised grin and he clapped his huge hands together delightedly. 'A laugh! My price is a laugh. And you have paid handsomely!'

She shrugged. 'Whatever.'

He hobbled back to his forge. 'And you will also help me,' he added.

'Me? But I don't know a thing about blacksmithing!'

'Can you open a door and pick up a lump of metal?'

'Yes,' she replied acidly. 'I think I can just about manage that.'

'Good. Then go into the storeroom at the back and bring me what you find.'

She went into the roundhouse, having to dodge around and between the piles of Hywelan's hoard, and to the back, where there was a curtained-off room. Pushing through and into the dark, it was the smell that caught her – not a reek, more a sort of incense: oil and wood shavings and something with an underlying tang, something old and familiar, from another life.

Why can I smell WD40?

Then she bumped against something hard-edged, like a table, and some kind of tool rolled off and clattered to the floor, and the smell grew stronger and her outstretched hands met a wooden surface with a strange metallic bar at waist-height which it took her ages to recognise as a proper door handle, and even though it was impossible she knew where she was.

Her father's shed.

She fumbled at the handle with trembling fingers and opened the door into blinding sunlight. The impossible threw itself at her in the shapes and colours of her back garden at home on Laurel Road. She fell to her knees in short, trimmed grass, and simply stared around in shock. It was all there: the clothes line, the gravel path, the back gate that always stuck in the damp, her mother's kitchen garden of carefully tended herbs.

'Tuonen? Hywelan?' she called. 'What is this?' There was no reply except the sound of squabbling blackbirds and the background roar of traffic like an unseen ocean. 'If this is a trick it isn't funny.'

She'd been caught out by visions before; illusions spun by enemies out of shadow and memory to delude and confuse. But if it was a fantasy stolen from her mind, why was there a fishpond in the garden and solar panels on the roof where there had been none before? Where had the big old sycamore gone? As terrifying an idea as it was, there was the very real possibility that she was really, actually home.

But Tuonen had said...

But she'd been in Hywelan's house.

'What am I supposed to do now?' she asked the empty garden, but the blackbirds kept their own counsel.

The back-door key was in its usual place in the old hanging basket, and she opened the door as gingerly as setting a snare. Then the smell of the kitchen broke open a door in her mind which she thought she'd sealed up years before, and she was baking cakes doing homework finger-painting feeding the cat washing up cutting a finger unwrapping fish and chips polishing school shoes having a blazing stand-up row with Mum, and Mum was there, turning around at the sound of the back door opening.

'Mum?' she whispered.

Her hands flew to her mouth and she screamed, backing into a corner of the cupboards.

'Mum, it's me! It's Scattie!'

The hands dropped, the eyes widened even further and after a frozen moment Scattie's mother burst into tears. Footsteps came thumping downstairs with her father's shout of, 'Carol? Is everything...?' and then he was there too – greyer than she remembered and a bit thicker around the waist. But still Dad.

'Hi, Dad,' she said.

'Well fuck me sideways,' said her father.

THERE WAS TEA, OF COURSE – SHE WATCHED HER MOTHER make it as if she was performing some kind of miracle. She'd forgotten how quick and easy everything was – kettles, teabags, mugs and dishwashers. And biscuits. Custard creams, specifically. She'd scoffed half the pack sitting at the dining table and was swigging it down with great slurps of tea before she realised how strangely they were staring at her.

'But where have you *been*?" asked her father. His first reaction had been to call the police, but she'd begged him not to. He'd acquiesced, but made it clear that this was only for the moment, and on the condition that she tell them everything. The authorities would have to be notified at some point.

She gave his question some thought, not wanting to lie, unable to tell the truth. 'Travelling,' she settled on.

'Travelling *where*?'

'Oh all kinds of places!' she laughed.

'You've been hurt,' said her mother, stroking her half an ear.

'I was… careless.'

'You said you'd give us answers,' he reminded her. 'We need to get you to a doctor. Get you checked out. And you look like you're starving.'

'Dad…'

'Liam.' Her mother laid a hand on her husband's arm. 'Let her settle back in first. There'll be time for all that. Look at her – she's as shocked as we are. Let's just take some time to breathe. Catharine, do you want to see your room?'

Of course she did, and yet as she followed her mother upstairs, she found dread mounting with every step. Family photographs covered the wall beside the staircase, everything from her grandparents' weddings to the last summer holiday they'd taken in Portugal, her own face grinning out at her, shiny and spotty and sunburned. It struck her that there would never be a photograph of Sarah to join them.

No way was she telling her parents that she'd had a kid. It would have been easier to tell them about Un.

'You should know,' her mother said, pausing on the landing, 'that we didn't keep it the same. Sorry, love, we just couldn't. It was killing your father. He'll never say so. You know what he's like.' She gave Scattie a hug as she opened the door to her room. 'It's good to have you back, love.' At the threshold she looked back with a strange, sad smile.

For however long, Scattie thought, as her mother left.

It wasn't her room. It occupied the same physical space

as her room once had, but anything that might have made it hers had disappeared. Even the walls were a different colour. What was left was a clean, comfortable, minimally furnished spare bedroom, which a visiting stranger or distant relative could use without too much fuss. She sat on the edge of the bed, wondering how she'd ever managed to sleep on anything so soft and insubstantial, then experimented with lying down. The duvet closed in on her from all sides, as if trying to swallow her.

'No,' she grunted, struggling up. 'Just no.'

Her mother had the loft space open and was up a stepladder looking for 'Catharine's' old things – it seemed her parents had moved on, but only so far – when Scattie found her father out in his shed, tidying up the mess she'd made blundering in. There was no sign of any way back to Hywelan's forge, but she knew it was there all the same, like a thin place in the surface of the world back amongst the boxes of jam jars and bottles of home brew. Maybe every father's shed harboured a way into Un.

He was horrified when she told him how soon she was going to have to leave. 'What?' he demanded. 'But you've only been back – what – an hour? Why did you even come back at all, if you weren't going to stay?'

'I just...' She shrugged, at a loss. How could she tell him that home was the last place she'd intended to be? 'I found myself with a chance to pop by and let you know that I'm okay, that's all. I'm sorry it can't be for longer, but it can't be helped.'

'Your mother will be devastated again!'

'She'll get over it again.'

'What makes you think she got over it in the first place?' he shot back, with a harshness she knew she deserved. 'You think either of us did?'

'In a week's time this will seem like a weird dream. It's better that way, trust me.'

'No. Absolutely not. I'm not letting you go again. Whatever trouble you're in, we can fix it—'

'Dad, listen to me.' There was steel in her voice that she knew he'd never heard before, and it shut him up in surprise. 'I am going. I'm sorry that it hurts you both, but that can't be helped either. What you can do is choose *how* I go – either with an argument or not.'

He softened, as he always had – not because he was weak, but because at the bottom of it all he understood. *You look old,* she thought. *That wasn't part of the deal.* 'What do you need?' he asked. 'Money?'

'It's not going to make any sense, I warn you.'

'Nothing has so far. Why start now?'

'Okay then, I need something that can be forged into a spearhead.'

'See? Compared to the time you were sick out of your bedroom window and all down the back of the house, that wasn't so hard, was it?' He rummaged amongst the garden tools hanging on one wall and took down an old hand trowel. It was dented, and its wooden handle was split and weather-worn. 'This was your grandmother's,' he said. 'She was a stubborn cow too. A spear, you say? I think she'd have liked that.'

He dusted off his hands and squared his shoulders. 'Right, I'm off to break the news to your mother. I suggest you hide out here; it's always worked for me. Bring you a cuppa?'

She hugged him tightly.

'I know,' he whispered. He disengaged, wiped his eyes, and wagged a finger at her. 'No more custard creams, though. You think we're made of biscuits?'

When he brought the tea out and found her gone, he wasn't entirely surprised. Then he cried in a way that he could never let Carol see.

No time appeared to have passed in Hywelan's forge. The smith and the boatman were exactly where they had been, and the familiar smells of wood smoke, sweat and river mud surrounded her, letting her know she was home. She passed the trowel to Hywelan, who inspected it critically, nodded, and turned towards his forge. She caught him by the shoulder and turned him back. 'Just what the fuck was all that about?' she demanded.

'Most believe that the strength of a weapon lies in the way the iron is forged,' he replied. 'They are wrong. It begins with the way that the iron is obtained. Are you finished detaining me from my business?'

She let him go, and he set to work without another word.

'Did you know that was going to happen?' she said to Tuonen as they waited.

'Hywelan is his own law,' the boatman replied, and would be drawn no further.

Less than an hour later the smith presented her with the spear that had once been Bark Foot's and was now hers, but reforged for the same purpose. Unlike most of the other weapons in his hoard, its iron blade was undecorated but it gleamed just as brightly as any of them.

THEY JOURNEYED THROUGH THE DAY AND LONG INTO THE night, and Tuonen taught Scattie the secrets of Un – what it was, and how it might be navigated. Then in the darkness around her she heard the water take on a new music: that of a swift-running stream. The boatman poled his craft to the bank with expert strokes, finding a calm bend out of the current for her to alight. Trees crowded one bank, but not the other, and she recognised the smell of the place immediately: damp bark, moss and a lingering trace of decay.

'No,' she warned, gripping the haft of her spear. 'Not again. I won't live through that again. I'll die first.'

'As we agreed,' said Tuonen. 'I have brought you home, not back. This is your home. Guard it well.' And with a few strokes he was gone, his dugout canoe lost in the gap between a prehistoric river and a narrow stream trickling through Sutton Park.

She gaped: the sky on the other side was glowing, the clouds underlit in a way she thought she'd never see again, by thousands upon thousands of streetlights and headlights and the windows of countless houses filled with human souls in every direction as far as she could see, and she wept at the unseen beauty of her city. She found that she was standing at the top of the timber track, which zigzagged from her feet down to the stream's bank and became the footbridge for which she and the others had so desperately searched. It did not span the water entirely, however – one plank lay to the side, ready to make the bridge complete. Hers now, at her feet, to open or close as she wished.

Then the thudding of helicopter blades split the air, and the spell was broken. Electric torches bounced over the brow of the hill (*Fireflies!* she thought. *They look just like fireflies!*), accompanied by shouts and the crackling of police radios. She drank in every detail, almost overwhelmed, and nearly didn't see the man running ahead of them. His shape was a momentary silhouette against the sky as he panted and stumbled in the dark, and she backed a little way into the shelter of the trees on her side of the stream as the figure reeled to a halt at the water's edge.

'No!' it moaned. 'Not like this. Please, not like this.'

Brookes.

An amplified voice from the sky ordered him to put down the knife. She watched him paw and scrabble at the water's edge, apparently unable to see the timbers right in front of him, and remembered what he'd told her about how he'd fled from the police, and she knew that this wasn't just a vision – this was happening right now, right in front of her. If Bark Foot was dead, he'd asked her, who or what opened the track for him?

Now she knew.

She froze, dizzied with questions and implications. Why had Tuonen brought her to this place at this moment? Was it because she had offered to kill the *afaugh* in Brookes' place? What if she did something different instead? What if she kept the track closed and let him get caught and saved him the trauma of his time in Un?

'*What do you want from me?*' she yelled at the boatman's absence. Brookes gave no sign that he'd heard. '*I don't know how to do this sort of thing!*' Looking at Brookes, though, she knew one thing: letting the police catch him wouldn't save him from any kind of trauma – it would just replace the one she knew about with another, because the sickness of it was something that Brookes carried inside him. At least in Un he'd have some happiness with Ysil, for what that was worth.

The cops were yelling at him to *drop the fucking knife*, and a Taser was making its dry-twig-cracking sound, and Brookes collapsed to roll face-down in the water. All other arguments aside, she simply couldn't stand there and watch a human being drown. Knowing that the police wouldn't be able to see her unless she opened the track, she muttered, 'Ah, fuck it,' to herself and stepped down the bank to drag him from the stream. It wasn't very far to Bark Foot's camp.

Her camp.

She dumped Brookes in the wreckage of a lean-to shelter and looked around at the camp she had inherited. It would need a lot of work, she decided, but for the time being there was a young woman and her children who were not beyond her help, so she took her iron spear and set off into the world to do something about that.

33

THE *AFAUGH* IN UN

THIS IS HAPPENING NOW.

It is always happening, in the tepid twilight of a present without a past.

He is driven away from the timelessness of the Far Pastures by its guardian and into the icy mountain wastes of a past thousands of years before his own birth – bereft, finally, of everything except the gnawing, raging fixations that brought him here in the first place.

He stops, pulls out the piece of paper that he stole from her bag – the risk assessment, as if there has ever been a more ridiculous idea – and he tears it into strips, cramming them into his mouth, chewing, eating, swallowing them until he chokes himself. He weeps and laughs as he does this.

He rages at his abandonment across leagues of empty snow and rock. Soon he is starving and beaten raw by exposure, stumbling naked on emaciated legs across the high back of a glacier older than dreaming, and to a saw-toothed ridge of granite outcrops. Between two of them he finds tracks: human footprints. He follows them eagerly, desperate to not be alone. Maybe Ysil has forgiven him, and followed after all.

The tracks end at a body, half-covered by the drifting snow. It is little more than skin stretched over bones, but the cold has done its job well, and the corpse is not so decomposed that he fails to recognise his own face staring up at him in death. He looks behind and sees that there only ever was one set of tracks, and that his own feet make no prints in the snow. His gaze travels up from the broken, claw-like nails on his feet, his knock-kneed legs and wizened genitals, and the bloated swag-belly that hangs over them. Then his hands go up to feel the thin pipe of his own throat – too narrow, surely, to support the throbbing mass of his head – and then, finally, he explores inside his own mouth, his touch recoiling from the sharpened cannibal teeth he finds.

And the *afaugh*, finally knowing itself, looses a cry of such desolate, world-consuming rage that its echoes are carried in the blizzard-winds' howls for a thousand years.

The people of the Four Valleys hear its hunger in the depths of their ten-year winter and make sacrifices to their ancestors to save them, but the *afaugh* comes out of the mountains and begins taking their children because it remembers being told a long time ago by a person long forgotten that this is the way of the world, so they create a guardian who is One From Many and give him a great spear and set him to guard the crossing place of Un, and so the *afaugh* is trapped.

But over time the memories of men fail, and the guardian

grows weak, and in its own desperation it reaches into the world and takes sacrifices for itself; becoming, by so doing, like its enemy, and sealing its own fate. The *afaugh* knows these children, though all they see is its monstrous hunger. Ryan is taken and Liv escapes, but Bran and Scattie go deeper into Un and the *afaugh* follows. It strikes a deal with Bran: power in return for the death of its human husk, who it hates even more than Bark Foot. Now that it is beyond life and death and time itself, the *afaugh* does not fear meddling with its own past. Bark Foot is unearthed, and while it is distracted the *afaugh* lures Brookes with visions of the children, because it is linked to him; it *is* him. Oh, how it loathes and covets its long-dead humanity. It despises his weakness and his childish delusions of morality and longs to see him crushed, beaten, weeping, dead. At the same time it desires above all things that which he has – or nearly has – and so when the idiot finally dreams himself into Un, the *afaugh* takes him with a savage and unbridled joy at the notion that in the end he had only ever been possessed by himself. The bloodletting which follows is almost as sweet as his expression when the *afaugh* moves on and grins at him from behind another man's face, and he understands that it finally has what it has craved for three thousand years: the woman and her children.

And then it is now, as it has always been, a world without end.

34

THE ERINYES

TARA AWOKE FROM A DREAM THAT SHE WAS BEING SMOTHERED and found that it was true. Panicking, her hands went to her throat to claw away whatever was choking her, and found bandages swathing her thickly from chin to collarbone.

Hands laid themselves gently over her own and a voice murmured, 'Hey now, none of that. You'll spring a leak.'

With the voice came vision, and a face swam out of the blur.

'Mark?' Her lips formed the shape of his name, but her throat wouldn't give it life.

Pryce smiled. Looking at him closely, she saw that his cheeks were heavily dimpled with the fallout of what must have been terrible teenage acne. To others the scarring probably looked ugly, but when he smiled it seemed to her that the effect was like seeing something rumpled and strangely comfortable that a girl could curl up in on a cold night. She reached up and stroked his cheek, noting that there was a tube going into the back of her hand.

Ah, she thought, *that'll be the drugs talking.*

And yet.

'Thank you,' she mouthed.

He actually blushed. 'For my next trick,' he said, to cover his embarrassment, 'I will read your mind and answer all of the questions you currently can't ask.' He placed his fingers to his temple and frowned as if concentrating. 'You are in hospital in Bangor. You have been unconscious for nearly fourteen hours. I am single, available, straight and reasonably well house-trained.'

She laughed – a little snort through her nose.

He took a seat beside her and his smile disappeared. 'We don't know where Brookes is. He dumped your car and switched it with another, which we didn't pick up until he'd got to Birmingham, where he attacked Susannah Vickers' family last night.' He paused, obviously holding back extra bad news. 'He also broke into your lab and set fire to it. Everything was destroyed. I'm sorry.'

Everything. She recognised the words he was saying, but couldn't connect them to anything real. Rowton Man couldn't have been destroyed. Three thousand years of lying preserved in the earth, surviving wars and farming and industrialisation couldn't just be gone. It was inconceivable.

'No,' she whispered.

'There's more, I'm afraid. The hospital staff who saw Sue Vickers and her kids were pretty sure that she said it was her husband who attacked them, despite the fact that Brookes actually phoned and told us he was going to do it – it's like he wanted to be caught, but then changed his mind and legged it.

We trailed him to Sutton Park, but he disappeared in exactly the same spot where Olivia Crawford was heading when she kidnapped you. Crawford committed suicide in her cell last night – hanged herself from a light fixture. Everything's connected, but none of the connections make sense.'

'Why,' Tara whispered, and pointed to herself.

'Why am I telling you all this? Because I interviewed Steven Vickers a few hours ago, and he said that what attacked his family was a demon – from his description the same demon that Crawford described in *her* interview. But he didn't know Crawford, he never met her, so how could they be having the same delusion or hallucination or whatever? And he said that this thing jumped from Brookes to him, and then from him to Hodges, though he was in such a state I'm not sure he even knew what he was saying. I've driven back and forth between here and bloody Birmingham three times in the past twenty-four hours and I'm absolutely knackered. I want this all to be a load of bullshit but that's a luxury I don't have any more.' He laughed shortly and rubbed his eyes. She suspected that his lack of sleep was only partly down to all the driving. 'I can't believe I'm going to ask you this,' he went on. 'But is it true? Is that what attacked you? Is this *afaugh* thing real?'

Tara saw the cannibal teeth again, stained with her blood, and suddenly her heart was hammering. Something seemed to have sucked all the air out of the room. Seeing her struggle for breath, Mark stood, concerned, and moved to call a nurse, but she grabbed his hand and shook her head. The face of the demon leered at her in her imagination, daring her to name it, to summon it, so that it could finish what it had started.

Fuck you, she thought, and nodded. 'True. All of it.'

MARK WAS ASLEEP IN A CHAIR BESIDE HER BED. WHEN THE nurses had tried to move him he'd waved his warrant card and pulled rank, so they let him be. The nurse who brought him a pillow stopped by again after he'd dozed off and gave Tara a wink. 'That one's a keeper, love,' she said. 'When I was in for my biopsy, mine, well he brought me a magazine and a packet of biscuits and buggered off down the pub to watch the football, didn't he?'

The surgeon who'd operated on her throat told her that there'd be no lasting damage but she wouldn't be able to speak for a week or two. There'd be a scar, obviously, to which she whispered some quip about a whole new world of scarf-shopping opening for her. She hadn't even lost that much blood, really. She was lucky.

She thought of Liv Crawford hanging from a light fitting in a police cell. For some people, luck – good or bad – simply wasn't part of the equation.

She tried to sleep, but visions of Phoelix clutching the red ruin of his stomach screamed at her whenever she closed her eyes, so she asked for something from the nurses and they brought her some little white pills, which did the trick nicely.

* * *

When she woke up again, it was because Mark was shaking her gently. 'You've got a visitor.'

The woman who entered the room did so warily, like a wild animal checking out a cage, peering into the corners before approaching. She was dressed in a simple T-shirt, jeans and boots, but dozens of charms and bracelets clustered at her neck and wrists, and every visible inch of her skin was either tattooed, scarred or pierced. Her smell prowled the room with her, thick and dry, like incense.

'This,' said Mark, still obviously processing the information himself, 'is Catharine Powell.'

'Scattie, please,' said the woman. 'You are Dr Tara Doumani?'

Tara nodded, and raised questioning eyebrows at Mark, who merely shrugged.

'Good,' said Scattie. She climbed onto Tara's bed and sat cross-legged at its foot. 'We have a lot to talk about.' She nodded at Tara's bandages and frowned. 'You're going to need something to write on.'

'It wasn't that hard to find you, actually. Brookes told me everything that happened, and there are only so many hospitals in this part of the world.'

'Wait,' said Pryce. 'You spoke to Brookes? Where is he?'

'He's gone where none of us can reach,' said Scattie. 'Forget him.'

'That's not very helpful.'

She dismissed his indignation. 'He's irrelevant. He sealed his own fate years ago. What we have to focus on now is saving Sue Vickers and her children from the *afaugh*.'

Tara picked up the small portable whiteboard Pryce had begged from a nurse and wrote: *Don't know where any of them are.*

'I can't believe I'm saying this, but I'm pretty sure that the thing is in Hodges,' said Pryce. 'That's what Steven Vickers said, at least. It shouldn't be too hard to track Hodges down.'

'No,' said Scattie. 'We don't go anywhere near him. It's obviously using his police connections and resources to find her—'

'And he will,' put in Pryce. 'Nobody stays off-grid permanently, especially not with kids. She'll pop up in a week, max.'

'—but we are not strong enough to take it on, not until the three of us are together.'

3? wrote Tara.

'Yeah,' said Pryce. 'What do you mean? There are three of us already.'

Scattie shook her head. 'Sorry, Officer Sidekick, but you don't count. There are only two of us in this room with the authority to punish this crime.' She pointed to herself. 'Guardian, lawgiver.' She pointed to Tara. 'Teacher, shaman. But two aren't strong enough. We need to be three. We need Sue Vickers.'

Tara scribbled. *Sue: mother, hearth-maker?*

'That's it.'

Fates/Norns/Furies?

'You're the expert.' Scattie gave a small, grim smile. 'I like the sound of "furies", though.'

'What in God's name are you on about?' demanded Pryce. 'This isn't some fairy story we're talking about here!'

Scattie turned a withering look on him. 'Oh that's exactly what this is, Officer Sidekick. It's a fairy story – the real kind, where people get eaten. This thing that we are hunting is a creature of legend – not *from* legend, but *of* legend, as in *made* of. It operates at the level of myth, and that is what we need to be if it is to be killed.'

It has sinned against the human world: hearth & law & wisdom. Needs holy trinity of mad crazy women to bring it down ☺ Tara erased and wrote again. *But I'm not much good to anyone, current state.*

'Plus we still don't know how to find Sue Vickers, and we're not going to get to her before Hodges, that's for sure,' Pryce pointed out. 'He'll have her place watched twenty-four seven, and he has access to the police resources of the whole bloody country.' He was clearly still smarting from being called Officer Sidekick.

'I wouldn't be too sure of that,' said Scattie. 'I found you, I can find her.' She held up a handful of the amulets that hung about her neck. 'You don't imagine that these are just decorative, do you? I spent a long time in Un, and I've learned that there are lots of ways to track a person, not all of them physical. I'm going to need something of hers in order to do it – something that she has a strong emotional connection to. Most likely something at her home.'

Pryce was clearly sceptical. 'You know that it'll be

watched, don't you?'

She shrugged. 'It's not like we have much choice. Let me worry about that. What we also need is an arena, somewhere to trap it. Ideally somewhere old, where Un is close. I figure an archaeologist might be the sort of person who'd know of such a place.'

Tara thought for a moment, then she grinned. She drew for several minutes, then turned the whiteboard around and showed Scattie and Pryce what she'd produced. It looked like a cartoon desert island with three stick women, lollipop trees growing out of the sea and a stick figure with a saw-toothed mouth lying underneath them. The sun had a smiley face.

'Excuse my French, but what exactly the fuck are you on about?' asked Pryce.

Tara began to explain.

35

BLACK COUNTRY BOY

IT WAS A SUBDUED GROUP THAT PRYCE DROVE BACK TO Birmingham the following morning. Tara was still groggy from the painkillers and dozing on the back seat while the strange, feral woman Scattie sat in the passenger seat, watching the mountains give way to farmland. She seemed to be brooding on something – or looking for something – but he didn't dare ask what. That lethal-looking spear was propped between her knees, its blade angling back over one shoulder. Despite what he'd heard from Vickers' own mouth, he didn't trust her and found it almost impossible to believe the story she'd told, and the fact that Tara did wasn't much comfort.

They had reached the outer edges of the Midlands urban sprawl when she finally spoke. 'Where were you born, Officer Sidekick?'

'Why?'

'Just where were you born? Are you local?'

There couldn't be any harm in telling her, he figured,

though he didn't know why she was bothering with the small talk now. He checked the rear-view mirror. Tara was still asleep. 'Tipton,' he replied. 'Not too far away from here, actually. I'm Black Country born and bred.'

'We did a thing on the Black Country in school. I didn't pay any attention, obviously. Something to do with the Industrial Revolution, wasn't it?'

He nodded. 'All the suburbs we've been driving through just now – Wolverhampton, Walsall, West Bromwich – they were all coalfields in the nineteenth century. Heart of the Industrial Revolution.'

'Good. Pull over.'

He stared at her. 'What? Why? We're nowhere near Tara's place yet.'

'Just pull over. There's something you need to see – something that I think will help us.'

'I'm really not sure that's a good idea...'

She sighed. 'Well, I can wake Tara up and tell her, and she'll tell you to do it, and then you'll do it, or we can just cut out the middle-woman and let her get some rest. What do you say, Mark?'

He couldn't argue with that. At least she was using his proper name now. He left the motorway and followed her directions down minor roads and into a labyrinth of side streets in an area of factories, warehouses and industrial units. 'How do you know where to go?' he asked. 'And what are we looking for anyway?'

She had the window down and her eyes closed, as if sniffing the air. 'It's like following a sound,' she murmured. 'Or a smell.

Or the direction of the wind. Once you know what you're trying to find, it's unmistakable. Tuonen showed me.'

'Right. That's it—'

'A thin place. A way into Un.'

Pryce hit the brakes and pulled the car to a stop in a narrow, deserted street between rows of warehouses, then turned to her. 'Exactly what—'

He was staring right at the business end of a long and very sharp-looking knife, the kind he imagined was used for gutting and skinning animals. 'Get out of the car,' she said. She was absolutely calm.

'You bitch,' he growled.

'Sticks and stones, Mark, now get out of the fucking car.'

He glanced back at Tara. Impossibly, she still seemed to be asleep. Her head was lolling and a thin line of drool had made a damp patch on her front. She was snoring slightly. 'What have you done to her?' he demanded.

'Extra dose of meds in her breakfast tea. Don't worry, she'll be perfectly fine. But you and me need to have a little talk without any complications or interruptions. Car. Out. Now.'

He did as he was told. She was a lot faster than he'd given her credit for because when he straightened up he found her around his side of the car with her spear pointed at him. Its tip advanced, she pricked him under the chin and backed him up against the vehicle.

'On your knees,' she ordered.

'Now look—'

'*Get on your fucking knees!*' she roared, and the sudden vehemence of it caught him as much off guard as the touch of razor-sharp steel against his throat. He knelt, glancing up and down the street for anyone who might have heard. Hopefully someone was peering out of a window and calling the police right now. 'You're taking us straight to him, aren't you?' she spat. 'Straight to Hodges. *Aren't you?*'

'No of course not—'

'Don't you fucking lie to me! I can smell it! You haven't believed a single thing either of us has said since the beginning, admit it!'

'That's not true—'

'Demons and spirit worlds and bog mummies and all that? Bullshit! You can't possibly believe any of it. It's insane, isn't it? *Isn't it?*' She pressed closer and the tip of her spear pricked a small bead of blood from his skin.

'You're not insane,' he said very carefully, though in truth he'd never seen a human being look more unhinged than the woman looming over him right now. All he could do was play for time. 'But you're right, I can't believe it. There has to be some rational explanation.'

The spear-point was removed, though it hovered close by. 'Good,' she said. 'Finally the truth. I don't blame you. I mean, how could you believe any of it? I wouldn't, in your position. Do you remember what Tara told us Liv said to her? "If you won't be told, you'll have to be shown"?'

'What about it?'

'We're not done yet. Get up, and start walking.'

Scattie directed him to an alleyway between two of the industrial units – it was so narrow that his shoulders touched both sides as he walked, and so choked with weeds and garbage that each step was a battle to avoid tripping over. He despaired of there being any witnesses now, and wondered if she had simply taken him somewhere dark and isolated to kill him at her leisure. It was indeed getting darker – much darker than simply the shadows between buildings. Almost like twilight. There was a strange smell, which became stronger the further he walked – sulphurous and cloying – and it took a while for him to recognise it as coal smoke. Then the ground wasn't weed-choked concrete any more but cobblestones, and the alley widened into a sudden vista. Pryce gasped, falling to his knees.

He was in hell.

That was his first impression, at any rate.

Monumental brick chimneys reared into the sky, belching fumes that were lost in a roiling cloudscape, itself lit a poisonous orange by the fires and furnaces below. The walls of factories and foundries rose like soot-stained cliffs of brick punctuated with innumerable slitted windows, above a landscape of ash and slag heaps across which coal trains crawled painfully. Nothing lived here except the pale, emaciated spectres of workers, trudging in ant-lines to and from their endless toil with dead eyes. The air was thunderous with the thumping of hammers, the roaring of flames, and the clashing of steel, and it was acrid, burning Pryce's throat.

'What…?' he choked. His eyes were streaming from the toxic atmosphere.

'Un,' said Scattie. 'The Un of this place, of these people. Of *you*, Black Country boy. It changes. When me and the others were there, it took the form of a Bronze Age landscape because the timber track was a Bronze Age gateway, and because Bark Foot was a Bronze Age being, so that's what we experienced. Here, it's... well.' She gestured at the industrial hellscape. 'You can see for yourself. All told, I think me and Bran might have gotten off lightly.' She turned back to him. 'Now, describe it for me.'

'I don't understand...'

'In words. What you're seeing. Right now.'

He did, to the best of his ability, though his brain was reeling.

'Now pick up a stone and feel it. Keep it in your pocket.'

'Which one?'

'Any one. Doesn't matter.'

He looked at the ground, and decided on a cinder – a black, sharp-edged relic of burnt coal.

'Why not take a photo with your phone, since we're here?' she suggested. 'One of those panorama things might be nice.'

He did that too.

She moved closer to him, and the threat of her proximity made him flinch. 'Now. Tell me this is a dream. Tell me this is a hallucination. Tell me that a famine demon didn't come from this place and nearly bite out Tara's throat, and that it doesn't currently threaten a helpless woman and her children, as well as God knows how many other people besides. That none of this is real. Can you do that?'

He found that he couldn't.

'Are we cool, you and me?'

'We're cool,' he managed.

'Good. Then let's get back.'

They returned to the car, where Tara was still unconscious, but it took a while for Pryce to regain his equilibrium enough to start driving again. When he did, he got Scattie to tell him her story again, and this time he made sure he listened to every last word.

By the time they were close to Tara's house, Mark could see that she was starting to rouse. Scattie leaned back over her seat and grinned. 'Hey there, Sleeping Beauty.'

Tara yawned, grimaced and reached for her whiteboard.

R we there yet?

'Pretty much.'

Everything ok with journey?

'All fine. Me and Detective Pryce here have been having some quality bonding time, haven't we, Mark?'

'Quality,' he agreed. 'Absolutely out of this world.'

Good. Head hurts. Tongue feels like piece of burnt toast.

When Scattie read this out to Mark, he laughed shortly. 'Oh that'll just be the Mickey Finn she slipped you before we set off.'

Ha ha.

Scattie punched him on the arm a little too hard to be playful. 'Yes, ha ha, Mark, that's so very funny.'

He dropped Tara off at her house and walked with her to the front door while Scattie waited in the car. 'I'd still feel safer if she stayed here to look after you,' he said.

Tara shook her head, and mouthed, *We talked about this.* She was right, of course. There was no reason for the *afaugh* to come after Tara – with any luck it believed that it had killed her. Scattie was more use riding shotgun for him, and even that had been the cause of a long argument. Scattie had maintained that he wouldn't know what he was looking for in the Vickers' house, but he'd argued that at least as a policeman he had a right to be there, and if Hodges – or the *afaugh* inside him – had set someone to watch the place he could talk his way out of it. Whereas she wasn't exactly subtle, he'd pointed out, which she'd had to concede.

'Right then,' he said. 'Get your things together and we'll be back soon.' He turned to go, but Tara pulled him back and surprised them both by reaching up and planting a quick kiss on his mouth.

'Also, er, yes, there's that,' he mumbled, then winced. 'Jesus, I sound like fucking Hugh Grant.' He cupped her face and kissed her back. 'I will see you soon.'

She nodded and closed her front door. He waited until he heard the bolts being secured and then went back to the car, where he found Scattie grinning.

'What?' He scowled.

'Nothing,' she replied. 'I just think it's sweet, that's all.'

'Christ,' Pryce muttered as he started the car. Nightmarish spirit worlds and cannibalistic demons were the least of it.

A QUICK CIRCUIT OF THE BLOCK CONFIRMED FOR PRYCE THAT the Vickers' house was being watched by a female plainclothes officer in an unmarked car – someone he didn't recognise, but then this wasn't really his patch so it wasn't surprising. It seemed that the *afaugh* was being thorough. After leaving Scattie two streets away in the car, he walked around, approached with his warrant card and tapped on the driver's window.

'I'm just popping in to check something for DI Hodges, Sutton Coldfield,' he said.

She barely glanced at his identification. 'No problem,' she replied. 'The scene-of-crime lads finished with it yesterday, and apparently someone is supposed to come by later to secure the door, but in the meantime it's all yours.'

'Has the husband turned up?'

She gave a hollow laugh. 'I've been here since seven and *nobody's* turned up.'

'Cheers.'

In Pryce's job there were few things quite so disconcerting as walking around a deserted home. It wasn't the silence so much as the little things left unfinished or undone – the junk mail uncollected from the mat, the dirty plate unwashed in the sink, the shirts unironed in the laundry basket. They were like the echo after a scream. The sense that their owners might be just around the corner or in the next room created a prickly sensation on the back of his neck, as if he were being watched by invisible eyes. The bloodstains on the hall carpet and around the door didn't help, either. He shuddered, and resolved to make this as quick as possible.

Something that she has a strong emotional connection to, Scattie had said. They had bounced ideas back and forth about what that might be on the drive over here, and he thought he knew where to find it. He headed for the stairs and the master bedroom.

The bedclothes were still in disarray, and his imagination filled the scene with Steven Vickers throwing them back in a panic as he heard something attacking his wife. Pryce found himself staring at the bed as if mesmerised, and shook himself.

'Concentrate, dickhead,' he growled, and resumed his search. He drew blanks in the wardrobe and the dresser drawers before he thought to look under the bed. In a large storage box were two shoeboxes, one labelled 'Matthew' and the other 'Jacob' in black marker. In the latter he found a plastic wristband from a maternity ward, plaster casts of baby footprints and handprints, a bundle of 'Congratulations! It's a Boy!' cards, and, right at the bottom, a square of tissue paper carefully folded around a lock of wispy blond hair.

'Bingo.' He pocketed the tiny parcel and turned to go.

'Something I can help you with, Detective?' said a familiar voice behind him.

Pryce spun round.

Hodges was standing in the doorway, grinning. He had never been a slender man at the best of times, but now he seemed to actively bulge; his suit was stretched at the seams and his skin was shiny, like an overstuffed sausage casing, or as if something else was sharing his body. Something eager to come out and feed. Scattie had been right, and if she hadn't already forced Pryce to acknowledge the reality of Un he'd still be trying to convince himself that the thing standing in front of him was his boss, probably even as it was coming to bite his throat out. Pryce knew there would be no bluffing his way past.

'Nothing that getting the fuck out of my way wouldn't fix,' he replied.

'Interesting that it should be you,' said the *afaugh*. 'I thought she'd send a friend or a relative, but you're neither, and you haven't come for money or passports.' It cocked its head to one side and regarded him with narrowed eyes. 'What are you up to, Mark?'

He didn't bother to reply, but began edging his way towards the window.

'No matter,' it decided. 'I'll take the answers straight from your brain when I take your body. This one isn't in terribly good shape anyway.'

It changed as it leapt for him, hands becoming claws as they grabbed for his throat. Pryce's self-defence reflexes kicked in and he ducked under its reach, driving a fist into its midriff. It expelled a surprised *oof!* into his face, and he gagged on its stench. Moving past it, he kicked at the back of one of its knees and it collapsed to the side with a grunt of pain, giving him space to dodge around the foot of the bed and towards the door. How it got up and behind him again so quickly he couldn't imagine, but he was within a yard of reaching the upstairs hallway when the *afaugh* crashed into his back and bore him to floor with its weight.

'Fight or not, it's all the same to me,' it drooled into his ear. Pryce thrashed, but its arms were winding around his neck and shoulders like pale ivy, immobilising him. 'You're still just meat.' He felt the points of its teeth on his skin at the back of his neck and prepared himself for one last doomed heave.

Then there was a heavy sound like two large rocks hitting each other and the teeth were gone. The *afaugh* tumbled backwards off him, screeching.

He looked up. Scattie was in the doorway with the ceramic lid of the toilet cistern in both hands, having just backhanded the creature across the room with it. She dropped it and hauled Pryce to his feet. 'Did you find something?' she asked.

He nodded, dazed.

'Good. Come on.'

'We should finish it off,' he protested, then saw that the *afaugh's* skull, where it had been smashed flat on one side, was already reshaping itself as the creature began to crawl towards them, snarling. 'Okay, no,' he conceded. Together they fled the house by the back door while the *afaugh* screamed in pain and fury.

'Why didn't you use your spear?' he panted, as they ran along the alley behind the house.

'Seeing me will have been enough of a shock to it,' she explained. 'Don't want it to know what I can do.'

'Jesus, is there anything you *can't* do?'

'Well I can't bloody drive, for one thing!' she said, as they reached his car.

'Point taken,' he said, and took out his keys.

36

SYMPATHETIC MAGIC

'Like calls to like,' said Scattie to Tara. 'It's how the *afaugh* was able to send visions to itself as Brookes, and it's how we'll find Susannah Vickers.'

She had removed one of her bracelets – little more than a wizened loop of what looked like rawhide embellished with a few small bones – and was dripping molten wax from a candle onto it, sticking down and sealing all around its circumference the baby hairs which Pryce had retrieved. Tara watched, fascinated despite the scepticism, which refused to die even now. Pryce had gone to see what kind of second-hand vehicle he could get for cash, since the police resources at the *afaugh*'s disposal would have flagged both his car and credit card.

'I learned this from an old shaman in Un,' Scattie continued. 'It may work in the world too, or it may not, but there's no stronger bond than that between a mother and her child, so it's the best chance we've got. Susannah's love for her boy, and my love for my daughter. You know how water dowsing works?'

Something 2 do with forked stick? wrote Tara.

'Mm-hm. The dowser holds the branching ends of a forked stick in each hand and walks along where he thinks there's water flowing underground, and the end of the stick dips down when he walks over it. It's not the stick that's magic, more that it's a sort of antenna for magnifying the dowser's own senses.'

Is that what the bracelet is: your forked stick?

Scattie made a strange, rueful smile as she continued to drip the wax. 'You're going to think this is sick and strange.'

As opposed to?

Scattie laughed. 'The bracelet is my Sarah's *iho*,' she said. 'Her umbilical cord. It's a tradition in her father's tribe to wear them, probably related to the *rhons* that the Oendir wear. I've never taken it off since the day I left her.'

Seen infants with pierced ears and tattoos. That's sweet in comparison. Just don't tell me you ate the placenta.

'Ate it? Gross! Of course I didn't eat it!' Scattie continued working on the bracelet for a moment, then looked up. 'No, just burned it and painted Sarah's face with the ashes.'

That's a joke, right?

Scattie just winked at Tara, who remained none the wiser.

Some time later, Mark returned with the keys to a barely roadworthy Ford Transit van. 'Right,' he said. 'Shall we get this show on the road?'

* * *

'EXCUSE ME, SIR? DI HODGES?'

The *afaugh* turned around from where it had been glaring out of Hodges' office window into the darkening sky. A young uniformed police officer was hovering in the doorway, gripping a piece of paper nervously.

'What is it, Constable?' it snapped.

'It's, uh, the Vickers case, sir,' replied the constable. He advanced, deposited the piece of paper on Hodges' desk and then retreated to the doorway. 'We've just had a call from Humberside police. The owner of a caravan park in Grimsby phoned to tell them that a young woman with an injured hand and two small boys rented one of his statics just today. Paid with cash, no car registration, no phone number. Shall I get them to send a patrol round?'

'No, that won't be necessary. I'll go up there myself.'

'Yourself, sir? But that's a three-hour drive.'

The *afaugh* smiled in what was supposed to have been a reassuring way, but the constable retreated a step. 'We wouldn't want the young lady to become spooked, now would we?' it said, reaching for Hodges' coat. 'After all, I'm a familiar face.'

SUE WOKE UP, BECAUSE MATTY WAS CRYING AGAIN.

She dragged herself out of bed and changed his nappy on autopilot, her head still clogged with half-remembered nightmares. She picked Matty up and jigged him in her arms as he grizzled, wandered past the small bed where Jake was twitching and whimpering in his sleep, paused to stroke his hair and shush him, and peered out between the static caravan's tattered net curtains.

The streetlights of an unfamiliar town were scattered across the darkness like the embers of a fire kicked over in haste. In the fuzziness of another broken night's sleep she couldn't remember exactly where she was. Somewhere north. She'd taken as much money as she could from the first ATM she'd found, ridden National Express buses at random for twenty-four hours and stopped at the furthest trailer park she could find, paying cash all the way. No cards. Nothing traceable. She hadn't even taken her phone with her, but left it in the hospital. She didn't know how long the money would last, but was aware that she wasn't really thinking at all – just running.

Then headlights speared the night and she knew that she hadn't run fast or far enough. There was no hope of escape now. Oddly, she felt quite calm, as if she'd always known that it could only ever end this way.

'Shh, baby,' she murmured to Matty. 'I won't let the bad man hurt you or your big brother. Mummy's here.'

Her injured hand throbbed as she jigged him, heading for the small galley kitchen and the extremely sharp knife she'd found in one of the drawers earlier today. She'd also kept back a lot of the codeine that the doctors had given her, but hadn't reckoned on how little time she would have when it came down to it. She'd envisaged something peaceful, the three of them going to sleep together, but it seemed like even that was going to be denied her. Tyres crunched on the gravel outside.

'Fuck you,' she whispered to the thing out there in the dark. 'Not me, and not my babies.' She picked up the knife as she heard car doors thump open and footsteps approach the caravan. Matty was a good boy; he would be quick and quiet, but Jake would need hugging tightly.

Sue had the blade against his skin when she was suddenly overwhelmed by a huge wave of love surging into her from somewhere which felt like it was at once the edge of the universe and as close as her own skin, a love which also carried with it a hollow weight of regret and aching loneliness. She realised she was crying, but couldn't remember when that had started. Then a woman's voice spoke to her, as clearly as if the invisible stranger was standing right next to her.

'You don't want to do that, really you don't. It will be okay. Trust me.'

The door burst open and three people she'd never seen before in her life piled in, shouting. A man grabbed the knife out of her hand. The other two were women. One – young and otherwise conventionally pretty – had the kind of facial tattoos she'd only ever seen in pictures of Maori people.

'Hi, miss,' said the tattooed woman, and it was the same voice she'd heard in her head just now. Beneath the body art she even looked vaguely familiar. 'It's me, Scattie Powell. We've come to rescue you!'

That was when Sue collapsed.

37

THE LOST COUNTRY

TARA SAT IN HER BEACH CHAIR ON TOP OF A HIGH, GRASSED dune and looked out over a drowned land. For the moment the tide was in, and on this bright July day in high season the fringes of the Norfolk shoreline were busy with holidaymakers: potato-shaped people in deckchairs; kids playing ball games; dogs tearing around in small tornadoes of sand; teenagers in the surf; fathers too big for their kids' inflatable boats; and kite-surfers whose rigs hung in the sky like airborne jellyfish. Tara looked past them all to where the Wash – a huge, square-shaped bay cutting deep into the east coast from the North Sea – glittered over sandbanks until in the haze there were the white bristles of an offshore wind-farm and the blurred coast of Lincolnshire.

The particular stretch of the Norfolk shoreline where Tara was sitting – just east of the town of Old Hunstanton – boasted the peculiarity that it was one of the few beaches on this side of the country where a person could watch the sun set over the sea. She had watched one sunset so far since she arrived, and wondered how many more she would see before the end.

Sue's children, at least, were safe. They had been left with Pryce who – judging from the expression on his face when a two-year-old and a five-year-old were handed over to him – would probably rather have gone toe-to-toe with the *afaugh*. Then she and Tara had made a series of easily traceable credit-card transactions at pubs and service stations as the three of them, Scattie included, had journeyed south to get here. It was a gamble; there was a chance that the *afaugh* would go straight for the boys first and use them to draw Sue out, but Scattie thought not; wounded as it was, it couldn't afford the luxury of time to bait her.

Tara watched the tourists playing and remembered when she and Nathan had traded their stories in Sutton Park, and he had told her about looking down on the land from Rowton Bank, about imagining the land layered upon itself age by age, and the lives of the people on it. The Wash, she knew, was once a key point of entry for Viking invasions; King John had lost his jewels here. And thousands of years before that it had been part of a fertile green landscape that stretched all the way to what was now mainland Europe. Somewhere in that playground of sand were the remnants of flint tools and the mussel shells they opened, and further off to her left, in the chalk cliffs below the town, were the fossils of corals and ammonites. Doggerland, it was called. An ugly name, she thought, for a drowned world.

But perfect for what needed to be done.

It was Britain's island status that had made her father move his family here from Lebanon. 'An island is easier to defend,' he had been fond of saying. During their rare but impassioned arguments about European politics she had been fond of pointing out that eight thousand years ago Britain had been attached to Europe and probably would be again one day, to which he would habitually grump that he should never have taken her fossil hunting as a child. But she saw, behind his anger, the pride at how smart his daughter had become.

Behind her, sheltered from the North Sea's easterly winds between two rows of high dunes, beach huts marched away along the shoreline in pastel shades of blue, pink and yellow. The one directly below her, where Sue was currently making tea, belonged to Tara's family.

It was one of the few luxuries that her mother's careful scrimping and saving had afforded them. The kitchen cupboards of their flat in Yardley had been covered in old picture postcards of the British seaside, many of which had come with Mrs Doumani from Beirut; as if owning a beach hut would make her children properly English. This was not to say that Tara's mother was a reckless romantic. A fabric trader's daughter, she had a shrewd eye for an investment, and prices had skyrocketed in the years since the Doumanis had bought the hut; today it was worth more than they'd paid for their flat.

Sue put her head out of the hut door and called, 'Tea bag in or out?'

Tara held up her whiteboard: *Out!*

'On the way!' Sue withdrew.

The hut was basically a large and luxurious garden shed on stilts, painted in sun-weathered hues of sea and sand: a single room full of beach furniture and toys, a simple gas hob and sink, and a cheap but sturdy IKEA futon. It backed onto one row of dunes so that the rear was at ground level but the front was elevated, reached by a set of wooden steps. It could be locked only from the outside, with shutters on the windows and large padlocks on the door. Local bylaws prohibited people sleeping in the huts overnight, so Tara's father had made one modification which was almost certainly against planning regulations: under the futon a trap door led to the stilted space underneath, so that the hut could be locked but still enjoyed when the beach warden did his rounds in the evening. Now, it meant that the three women could sleep here instead of in the town, and thereby keep harm out of everybody else's way.

Tara raised a pair of binoculars to her eyes. She scanned the tourists, looking for a solitary individual. He – or perhaps she; the *afaugh* could have taken another host – wouldn't be bare-chested or in a swimsuit. It would be wearing something to hide the bandage covering a wound that wouldn't heal.

She could have saved herself the trouble; when it came, she saw that its arrogance was so great that it wasn't even making a pretence of camouflage.

The shape of Detective Inspector Chris Hodges lurched its way along the ridge of dunes overlooking the beach, making straight towards the hut. His suit was threadbare and torn at one shoulder, his shoes waterlogged, trousers drenched to the knee and covered in sand and seaweed, and a large dark stain on his breast testified to the wound that was slowly killing him. His face was pallid and waxy through blood loss, with great dark circles around the eyes. Calmly, she got up, folded her chair, and went back to the hut.

Sue looked up, questioning, and Tara nodded.

THE *AFAUGH* KNEW IT SHOULD HAVE ABANDONED THIS DYING body by now. The bleeding couldn't be stopped entirely and the wound absolutely refused to heal, plus some sort of infection had set in and it stank. But a policeman was so *useful* in tracking people down, and the shrivelled scrap of humanity that was all that remained of Nathan Brookes relished torturing Hodges for everything he had done to him.

It found the right hut – it could smell the woman's fear from yards away – and climbed the steps. It was almost disappointed that she hadn't chosen to run, but then maybe she'd given up and finally seen the inevitability, the *rightness*, of all this. She was standing on the threshold brandishing a toy cricket bat, as if that could possibly do her any good.

'Get out of that man,' Sue demanded. 'He's done nothing to you. This is between you and me.'

The thing wearing a human shape prodded at the wound in its chest and glared at her. 'Oh that I definitely will do,' it snarled. 'He's not good for much more than a day anyway. I'll move on, don't you worry. Who knows? I might move on to you. I've never had a cunt before.' It started to climb the stairs towards her. She retreated into the hut, right to the back. She was trapped.

'Where are the children?' it asked.

'Safe from you, you bastard,' she spat. 'What do you want? Why me?'

It stood at the threshold, examining the interior suspiciously: the beach toys, the futon, the little gas stove.

The three mugs of tea.

SUE FOLLOWED THE *AFAUGH*'S GAZE. NOW IT KNEW SHE WAS not as alone and vulnerable as she appeared. She felt her heart actually lurch with shock. *Oh you stupid, stupid cow,* she moaned silently, because now she had no choice. If she didn't have its full attention they might all die. Loosing a scream of rage and terror, she leapt forward and smacked the *afaugh* around the side of his head with the cricket bat.

It was too weak to dodge, and took the blow square, but not so weak that it couldn't rip the bat out of her hands and fling it out of the window. It leered at her, and she saw that one of its eyes had gone bright red. 'You remember how when you were fucking that useless prick Brookes you used to keep your eyes open when you came so that he could see how good it felt for you?'

'You can't know that,' she whispered, appalled despite all that she thought she had prepared for this. The fact that it could know something so intimate about her was viler than anything so far. Still, she definitely had its full attention now.

'Why do you never do that for Steven?' it continued.

'Why is that?' It took a step closer. Not enough. 'I'll tell you what I want, what I really, really want,' it sang, and giggled. 'I want you to be looking at me when I kill you so that I can see you finally understand how terrifying and lonely it is going into Un, knowing that everything you love is still in the world and not being able to do a single fucking thing about it.'

'Never,' she said, and slowly, deliberately, turned her back on him.

The *afaugh* roared its outrage at this final rejection, this dismissal, and she hunched her shoulders for its violence – but it never came. The trap door in the floor slammed open and Scattie pulled herself through in a single clean movement. The *afaugh* wheeled in surprise, but seeing the bright gleam of her spear and the clear rage on her face, hesitated. Her enemy uttered a low, guttural sound, which might have been a growl or a purr. 'Girrrlll...'

'*Afaugh!*' Scattie cried. 'You have no right to claim the shape of a man! Cast it off now and stand naked before me – or are you so ashamed by what you've become?'

'Oh but I like it in this man!' it laughed. 'You more than anyone must know how long it's taken me to get here.' It nodded at her spear. 'Besides, you won't use that, not on this body.' It stroked its blood-stained torso and slid a hand inside the front of its trousers, where something jutted. It leered at her. 'You won't kill an innocent person.'

'The first time we met,' she said, 'you told me that he wanted me but that he'd never allow himself to admit it. At the time I thought you meant Bran, but you didn't – you meant Brookes. That's why he wouldn't sleep with me in the mountains. You meant Nathan – you meant yourself.'

It flinched from being recognised.

'Well, okay then.' Scattie tossed the spear to the floor and stood with her arms open. 'Come on. Take me.'

Its eyes narrowed, sensing a trap.

'Seriously.' She beckoned it forward. 'I heard you say that you wanted to know what it felt like to have a cunt – well, come on then. Have mine. Come on, big boy!' she taunted. 'Or aren't you man enough?'

With a howl it was on her, and she had just enough time to wonder if she hadn't just made a terrible miscalculation of its strength, and then it was vomiting itself into her and

WAIT. WHAT IS THIS?

This is me, you fucking knob-end.

Why can't I... Why can't I...

Now stop struggling. You're only going to hurt yourself, and I wouldn't want that. That's *my* job.

LET ME GO!

What, so soon? But we've only just gotten to know each other. Don't tell me you need your space already.

Fuckyoukillyourapeyoucutyourtitsoff...

Squeeze.

...eatyourchildrenscreamingfromyourbelly—

SQUEEZE.

Aieeegodnopleasemakeitstopmakeitstopmakeitstop!

Silence. Stillness.

Good. Behave. What did you think would happen, you pathetic piece of shit? You're very good at insulting and hurting and violating, but did you seriously, for one second, imagine that you could ever control me?

The wordless, inarticulate raging of a thing with its leg in a trap, gnawing and tearing at itself but unable to get loose.

Don't fret, honey. I'll let you go, just as soon as we're home.

SUE AND TARA WATCHED SCATTIE CONVULSE ON THE FLOOR. Sue had snatched up the spear when the *afaugh* had attacked, and had the blade poised over the wild woman's throat just in case the demon proved to be too strong. Tara held Scattie's hands, comforting, lending strength.

'And if it *is* too strong for you?' she'd asked, when they'd been making their plan.

'Then at least one innocent life will have been spared,' Scattie had replied. 'I should have been dead long ago.'

Scattie grew calmer, but Sue kept the spear pointed at her all the same. Hodges had collapsed on the floor, no doubt through shock and blood loss. There'd be time enough to tend to him, Tara thought, but only if Scattie won.

Finally Scattie lay still, and opened her eyes. 'Hard...' she rasped. Her voice was the rasp of wind over sand. 'Fighting me. Do it quick.'

Sue and Tara helped her to her feet, bracing her on either side. She was unsteady, her body a mass of tics and twitches as she fought to maintain control. Her hands gripped theirs painfully tight. The wound the *afaugh* carried had appeared below her collarbone, blood spreading down her chest.

38

THE SEA HENGE

THE JOURNEY ALONG THE SHORELINE WAS DIFFICULT WITH the *afaugh* fighting Scattie for every single step. To anyone watching they must have looked like two friends leading their drunk companion home after too many mojitos, but there was no danger of interference. For one thing, Sue was still carrying a great iron-tipped spear, using it as a walking stick.

The demon's struggles became more intense the closer they got to the passing place into Un, as if it sensed its proximity – and probably it did. Here, in the world, it could hide, wounded though it was, potentially for ever. There, it could be forced to take its own form, and be killed.

At the end of the last century, during a particularly low tide, a ring of ancient wooden stumps had been uncovered in the shifting offshore sands, and was quickly named Seahenge even though it had no connection to the more famous and much larger Stonehenge hundreds of miles away in Wiltshire. Nobody could tell for certain who had built it or why, but it had been dated to over a thousand years before even Bark Foot's time, when the sea here had been land. Seahenge had since been dismantled, preserved and reconstructed in a museum, but Scattie knew that the land remembers what people do not, and that Un is the place of lost things. When Scattie had said that they needed an arena for battling the *afaugh*, Tara had known that this would be the perfect place.

All the same, it was a good hour's walk. Hand in hand, lending strength to each other, they carried their struggling enemy.

By the time they reached the sprawling emptiness of mud flats and sandbars, the tide was almost out. There were no boundaries to the world here; it was impossible to tell whether they were walking through water or sand, or whether the water was estuary or sea, or where the sea ended and the sky began. They inhabited a glittering haze without form or measure, and knew that this too was Un, and that from it could be reached all the shores of life and time.

The *afaugh* gave one final, despairing lunge and almost mastered Scattie; she floundered and fell in the thigh-deep water, dragging the three of them under with her. They struggled, coughing, back to the surface, to find themselves…

…in a salt-marsh of scrub grass and crying birds, close to a ring of tall, upright wooden posts.

Tara stared around, open-mouthed. 'My God!' she croaked. 'This is—'

'Note-taking later,' grunted Scattie. 'Demon-slaying first, okay?' She crawled into the henge and expelled the *afaugh* from her body with all the relief and revulsion of a food-poisoning victim evacuating their bowels.

The creature immediately tried to flee, but the traps Scattie had set between the trunks the day before caught it in short order.

The three women studied it where it lay, writhing and choking in a snare, which bit deep into its already thin neck. The spear wound in its chest was its own now, and its blood was black, like tar. It spat at them as they approached.

Scattie bent close. 'You remember when we met Tuonen the Boatman, and you said it should have been you who suffered the threefold death? Well you're going to get exactly what you wanted, my dear. I told you at the time, you really should have let me fuck you.'

Scattie took the iron spear from Sue, and pronounced her judgement in a voice of thunder.

'You have set yourself against hearth, law and temple. You have violated those for whom you should provide; you have defied those to whom you should owe fealty; you have closed your ears against those whose wisdom you should heed. You are an abomination and a sickness in the world, and for this your death shall be threefold.'

The last thing the *afaugh* saw was not human women standing over it but three towering figures with blazing, terrible eyes, which saw every scrap of its soul and judged without mercy.

And it screamed as the Furies took their vengeance.

EPILOGUE

SEVEN-YEAR-OLD JAKE VICKERS WAS PART OF A TRIBE NOW, and he loved it. Sue watched as he and the other kids were lined up at the edge of a grassy downhill slope by their instructor – who herself couldn't have been much out of high school – with their wooden weapons from the gift shop. Jake had chosen a spear; its plastic head was blunt and completely harmless, but all the same, seeing it gave her a chill. His face, like those of the other boys and girls, was daubed with lines and spirals of blue woad. It too reminded her uncomfortably of Scattie and her tattoos. But then Jake caught her eye, waved and grinned a grin of unadulterated childish delight. She waved back. If anything of last year's nightmare lingered with him, there was no sign of it. Still, she watched him carefully.

'Now then,' said the instructor. She was dressed in the coarse tunic and leggings of an Iron Age warrior, but her accent was Australian. 'Coming up that hill is a legion of Roman soldiers who want to steal all your sheep. What I want you to do is wave your swords and spears to scare them off and shout as loudly as you can, "Go home, you stinky Romans!" Ready?'

Her warband gripped their weapons and stared grimly down the hill at the advancing and entirely imaginary invaders.

'Go!'

The hilltop erupted in a cacophony of shrill screams, jeers and farting noises. Sue smiled and turned to Tara, who was watching her staff with the same kind of pride that Sue watched her son. 'This place is great,' Sue said.

'Thanks.'

Castell Henllys was a reconstructed Iron Age village atop a hill, consisting of a cluster of thatched roundhouses and, on the lower slopes, farmsteads with crops and pens of sheep and pigs. As well as being a tourist attraction it had a serious archaeological purpose in experimenting with putting the theories of how Iron Age culture worked into practice. All around them visitors were wandering in and out of roundhouses where costumed staff were working looms, baking bread, forging metal and staging mock duels with blunted blades.

'I didn't think you were into this side of things,' said Sue.

'After what happened I didn't really have much choice. That was about as "hands-on" as archaeology gets – a bit hard to be happy with old bones any more.'

'Speaking of happy...' Sue glanced pointedly at Tara's left hand, where a ring glittered on her third finger.

Tara blushed. 'And you and Steve...?'

Sue sighed. 'No. Too much for him to process, apparently.

He still sees the boys, so it's not that much of a thing, and maybe one day.' She shrugged. 'But then again maybe not.' She was pleased to see that Tara was wearing a plain T-shirt that left her neck bare; she wore the W-shaped scar on her throat openly, like a challenge. 'What do you tell people when they ask about that?' she said.

Tara's hand went to her throat reflexively, but then she shrugged. 'This? I tell them I cut myself shaving.'

They laughed together, and it was good.

'I've heard from Scattie,' Sue said, and its baldness clearly took Tara by surprise. 'Well, not heard *from* exactly. Heard *about*. Sort of.'

'Sort of?'

'I keep an ear open for stories about, you know, strange things. Just in case.' Despite having seen the *afaugh* die – despite both of them having wielded the blade that killed it – Sue thought that they would probably always be watching for it, or something like it, to return.

'So there was a story in the news about an attempted child abduction in Sutton Park a few months ago. Apparently some pervert had been following a mother and her two kids, and when she stopped to buy ice creams he snatched the older one.'

'Jesus,' breathed Tara. 'Did they get him?'

'Yes and no. They found the little boy about an hour later, sitting on the edge of that well – Rowton's Well, I think it's called?'

'That's the one. Where Liv Crawford took me...'

'That was the first funny thing – you know how open that

area is, and they'd already searched it once. The other thing was the boy's story. He said that the bad man had taken him into the trees on the other side of the stream…'

'…except we know that there are no trees on the other side – not in this world, anyway.'

'Exactly. And that the man was talking funny and touching himself when this strange woman appeared – a woman with drawings all over her face. She told the boy not to be afraid and carried the man off screaming into the trees, and when she came back she showed the boy how to get to the well where his mummy would find him. Obviously this was dismissed as the kind of story a little kid who had read too many fairy tales would make up.'

'Obviously.'

'But it does make you wonder.'

'She's still out there isn't she? Guarding the timber track?'

Sue watched her son running around in the sun with his new friends, waving his toy spear and yelling at imaginary enemies, much as three thousand years ago another boy would have done exactly the same thing in exactly the same place, and smiled. 'Yes, I rather think she is.'

'I'M GOING OUT TO THE SHED!' LIAM POWELL CALLED TO his wife.

A vague *mmhmm* came back to him from where Carol was sitting in the kitchen. He sighed, took the mug of tea – the second one that he always put out for Scattie, because it was the last thing he'd promised her and he always kept his promises to his little girl – a packet of biscuits and the bit of skirting board which needed planing, and closed the back door behind him. It was unlikely Carol was even aware that he'd left the house. Since Scattie's second disappearing act his wife hadn't seemed to be aware of very much at all.

It was an evening towards the end of October, and a chill was very much in the air. He walked down the garden path, past the leaves that needed raking and the roses that needed pruning back for the winter, and the thousand and one other jobs that weren't going to get done, just like the one he carried. He was kidding himself; that bit of skirting board was never going to be planed. He was going to shut himself in his shed and do what he always did: sit in his wicker chair and stare at the old photographs of Scattie he had pinned up on the inside of the door. Amongst the many boxes and tins and jars of odds and ends he had an old cigar box full of the letters she had written to the flower fairies when she was very little. She'd write notes asking them how the garden was doing at certain times of year, and asking them for help to find lost things, or for advice when she was sad. He and Carol had been more than happy to indulge her for as long as they could, knowing how quickly she would become too old to believe in such things, and when she folded up her notes and placed them under the special blue stone beneath the apple tree at the end of the garden he would wait until she was asleep before collecting them, writing replies in tiny, quivery handwriting, and placing them under the same blue stone for her to find in the morning. Scattie was always delighted when the flower fairies replied, and even when she was old enough to know that it was really just her father, the joy that it had brought never turned that knowledge into disillusionment. It was a single, simple act of uncomplicated love and silliness, which he clung onto as she entered the turbulent waters of adolescence… and then she was just gone.

So he was going to sit and read through the letters again, and when he was sure that Carol had gone to sleep he would creep upstairs and slip quietly into bed without disturbing her and wonder how much longer he could possibly keep doing this.

The first thing he did when he got in the shed was reach for the mug of tea that he had set out for her last night, which would be cold and needing to be thrown away, because of course she wasn't actually going to drink it, was she?

Except that tonight the mug was empty.

He stood looking at it for a long while. Then he replaced it with a hot one and added two custard creams as an afterthought. He picked up the box of fairy letters to take back into the house, hoping that Carol hadn't already gone to bed.

At the threshold he stopped, looked back, whispered, 'Night, night, Scattie-girl,' and locked the shed door behind him.

ACKNOWLEDGEMENTS

My agent Ian Drury at Sheil Land for finding this story a home, and my editor Miranda Jewess at Titan Books for finding all the bits that didn't make sense.

Every mountain leader and Duke of Edinburgh Award assessor whom I've been privileged to walk with over the years and unknowingly contributed ideas, anecdotes, and bad jokes, quite a few of which made it into the book; especially Guy, Wayne, Tony, Chris, Ritchie 'Chief Badger' Evans, and Phil Ascough, who was taken from us much too soon.

Daves Tamplin and Palfreyman for tips on prehistoric rock climbing.

Rachel Moore and Becks Gilbert for general medical advice but particularly on what happens when someone gets their finger bitten off.

Every young person who's ever been on an expedition with me; thanks for not disappearing mysteriously or getting yourselves killed.

I've taken a few small liberties with some of the locations

(most especially that of the Titanic Café), for which I hope my Brummie friends will forgive me. Any mistakes with the archaeology are entirely my own, due to research consisting largely of watching old episodes of *Time Team*, although two books proved invaluable: *Birmingham: the Hidden History* and *The Archaeology of Sutton Park*, both by Michael Hodder.

Last, as ever, to TC, Hopey and Eden. I love you, but the shed is mine now.

ABOUT THE AUTHOR

JAMES BROGDEN IS A PART-TIME AUSTRALIAN WHO GREW UP in Tasmania and now lives with his wife and two daughters in Bromsgrove, Worcestershire, where he teaches English. He spends as much time in the mountains as he is able, and more time playing with Lego than he should. He is the author of the novels *The Narrows*, *Tourmaline*, *The Realt* and *Evocations*, and his horror and fantasy stories have appeared in various periodicals and anthologies ranging from *The Big Issue* to the British Fantasy Society Award-Winning Alchemy Press. Blogging occurs infrequently at jamesbrogden.blogspot.co.uk, and tweeting at @skippybe.